SPIRIT FIRE

Also by Glen R Stott

Heart of the Bison
Neandertals Book One

Search for the Heart of the Bison
Neandertals Book Two

Dead Angels

Timpanogos

Robyn

SPIRIT FIRE

Neandertals
Book Two

Glen R Stott

Spirit Fire
Neandertals Book One

Copyright © 2014 Glen R. Stott

ISBN (sc)

Library of Congress Control Number: 2014902115

Printed in the United States of America

Glen R. Stott rev. date: 2/14/2014

Dedicated to Chi*Ki

Contents

Prologue
Ref: *Heart of the Bison*, Neandertals Book One
Beginning of the Alliance—23,454 BCE

The old Cro-Magnon man leaned back against the altar rock and looked up at the giant painting of the aurochs on the wall of the Ceremony Room. The last of his torches would soon die, and he would be left alone in the dark. The Ceremony Room was a large cavern located deep in a mountain. It was a place where the hunters of the tribe went to paint their daring deeds on the smooth walls and perform the ceremonies that helped make their hunts successful. His people called themselves "the People." The old man was called White Cloud. He was the Guardian of the Ceremony Room.

The lands of the People were also occupied by the elusive, ugly Neandertals. His people called them Cave Dwellers, and many of the People argued the Cave Dwellers were not human but evil imitations that would one day rise from the caves to kill the People.

In his youth, White Cloud forced a Cave Dweller he encountered on a hunting trip to mate with him. When he was finished, she ran away. Many years later, White Cloud would discover the Cave Dweller was called Kectu and she had a child called Tuk. Too late, on the day she was killed by the People, he discovered Tuk was his child. He saved Kectu and Tuk's son, his grandson, and ran away with them to live with a clan of Cave Dwellers. His grandson's name was Sun Fire, but in the language of the Cave Dwellers he was Shekek.

Shekek grew up to be the leader of the Cave Dweller clan. Three years of drought had weakened the clan and threatened its destruction. White Cloud and Shekek traveled to White Cloud's village hoping time had mellowed the People and that by joining the People and the Cave Dwellers together, they could blend their different talents to save each other during hard times. The People had better hunting tools and skills than the Cave Dwellers, but the Cave Dwellers had highly developed senses of sight, smell, and hearing. Combining those abilities and skills on a hunt would produce far better results. After spending the winter hunting with the Cave Dwellers, many of the People wanted to start an alliance.

Then, with their deep connection to the earth, the Cave Dwellers predicted a strong earthquake. The People moved their belongings from their village located at the base of a high rock cliff. White Cloud, as Guardian of the Ceremony Room, went deep into the mountain to the Ceremony Room, hoping the Great Spirit would spare the Ceremony Room if he were there.

When the earthquake was over, White Cloud rejoiced that the Ceremony Room had been spared. When he tried to leave, he discovered the front of the cliff had fallen and blocked the entrance to the tunnel that led to the Ceremony Room. He was trapped. He returned to the sacred cavern to die. When the last torch burned out, he sat against the altar rock and dreamed of a dark-haired woman who would find the Ceremony Room far in the future and open it again.

Outside, the village of the People had been buried by the falling rocks. Their lives had been saved by heeding the advice of the Cave Dwellers. The tribe split, part to find a new location for a new village while the rest joined with the Cave Dwellers to form the Alliance. The Alliance was destined to last thousands of years.

CHAPTER 1

Rayloc—The Shaman

Summer 3304 BCE

Rayloc stopped at the entrance to Seccolog's dwelling. It was constructed of a log frame covered with animal skins. It was the largest dwelling in the village because Seccolog was the chief. For three years, Rayloc had been the shaman of Seccolog's village. He took a breath and hit the entrance post with the piece of deer antler tied to the post. Seccolog's watery voice called out, "Enter a dwelling where Zendolot, praise to him, rules."

As Rayloc pushed the cowhide cover and entered, he saw Seccolog sitting on his leadership robes. He wore a sheepskin loin cloth looped over a cowhide waistband in front and back. Around his shoulders hung a light cape made of swamp grass. His long hair and beard were tangled and unwashed. His fat jowls hung from his face and rested on his chest. He had always been a fat man, but in his later years, he had become so big he could hardly walk. He and his dwelling were ragged and unkempt. The dwelling was uncomfortably hot and smelled of burnt wood, old food, and body odor.

Bolanlik, Seccolog's heritage mate, was serving him goat's milk with bread and honey. She was the same age as Seccolog, but she was as boney as a starving goat. Her leather dress hung from her shoulders and fell loosely below her knees. It was made simply from deer and goat hides.

Sincolad, Seccolog's oldest son, sat near his father with his back to the entrance. He did not turn to greet Rayloc. Sincolad was dressed in only a loin cloth. His leadership tattoos of parallel lines were displayed on his back and legs, showing he would be the next chief. Sincolad had not struggled for anything his entire life. He appeared thin and strong, but Rayloc knew his body and mind were soft. From his early years, he had used his position as the oldest heritage son of the chief to avoid the challenges of physical exercise. He never took his hunting lessons seriously. He was not fit to lead goats, let alone a village. Just looking at the two men was an insult.

"Rayloc, come, sit." Seccolog pointed to the bearskin robe of honor on the ground near him.

"Why have you called for me?" Rayloc was short and stocky, much stronger than he looked. He was proud of his clothes, which were made by the best seamstress in the village. Each of his legs was covered with a cowhide legging that went from his midcalf to upper thigh. Each had a cowhide strap that stretched over his hip and tied to a cowhide waistband and a leather drawstring to tie them around his thighs. His crotch was covered with a sheepskin loin cloth looped front and back over the waistband. He wore a deerskin vest that was open in the front. All his clothes fit right, and the stitching was uniform and straight.

"I have received a messenger from Romelog's village south of the Ice Mountains," Seccolog answered.

Rayloc sat in silence, avoiding the temptation to ask what the messenger had said and trying to ignore the rancid smell of Seccolog's body. After waiting a short time, Seccolog continued, "Romelog offers his daughter to become heritage mate to Sincolad."

"That's impossible!" Bolanlik exclaimed. "Why didn't you tell *me* this? You *know* how I feel about the southern villages. They killed my brother! They are animals!"

Seccolog turned to his son. "You are nearly forty summers old. You have six pleasure mates, and yet you will not choose a heritage mate. After I die, you will be chief. You must have a heritage son to take your place as chief of the village when you die."

"But I do not like any of the females of this village. I've been told the daughter of Romelog is a beauty."

Rayloc winced at the whiny tone of Sincolad's voice.

"I will not have it!" Bolanlik screamed. "No son of mine will take a southern woman as a heritage mate … not even a pleasure mate," she added in disgust. "I hope all the southern villages are sent to the dark caverns to serve Dracolut."

Dracolot was the brother of the great god, Zendolot. Dracolot raped Afrodiluk, the female god Zendolot loved. Zendolot changed the suffix of

Dracolot's name from "lot," meaning male god, to "lut," signifying fallen god, and banished him to the dark caverns below the earth. There, Dracolut led evil, manlike creatures called droglits that came from the caverns on dark nights to capture and torture the people.

"Sincolad must take a heritage mate. It would be an advantage to create a bond with Romelog's village," Seccolog said weakly. "It's the closest of the southern villages. Romelog is a powerful and respected chief. He can control the salt and shell trade from the southern villages. You know how you like the pretty shells from the southern villages."

"Sincolad, you will take Conchelik as your heritage mate. You will do it *before* the next full moon." Bolanlik turned to Seccolog. "That is the way it will be, and I will hear no more about it. Salt and shells," she added in disgust.

Conchelik was one of Sincolad's pleasure mates. Leaders in the villages had many pleasure mates but only one heritage mate. Only sons of the heritage mate could become chief when their father died, unless the heritage mate did not produce a male heir, in which case a son of a pleasure mate could be chosen. Conchelik was a favorite with Bolanlik, though she had not given Sincolad a son.

"The village needs more salt," Seccolog said apologetically. "I must send a trading party through the Ice Mountains to trade. Chief Romelog will be angry if I deny him Sincolad."

"Send Rayloc to explain to Romelog that Sincolad already has a heritage mate. Romelog will just have to accept that."

"Romelog will be angry," Seccolog whined. "He will not trade fairly with my village if I do not give him a heritage son."

"Your village is larger than Romelog's village," Rayloc said. "Send fighters and demand a fair trade."

Fighters were trained in physical contests. Disputes between villages were settled by contests between the fighters of the villages.

"Force? My father tried force once. You remember. He lost. The village lost honor and had to pay tribute. Must you always talk of force and fighters? We have traded with the southern villages for salt and shells from before you were born. We always trade fairly.

"You will take Sincolad to help smooth things over. Sincolad will offer another of my sons to take Romelog's daughter, Pothialik, as heritage mate."

"Sincolad must not offer any of *my* sons!" Bolanlik exclaimed.

"Romelog has offered a daughter of his heritage mate. Both Aduclad and Podeclad need heritage mates. I should respond to Romelog with a son of my heritage mate."

"Impossible! You will *not* honor a southern village with one of *my* sons!"

"But—"

"Wait! There is a pleasure mate son you could send. Send the son of the camp whore. Send Sadolad."

"But Romelog will expect a heritage son. Sadolad will not do."

"His mother was from that village. Send him back. They will take him because he is one of them."

"We cannot tell them he is of the southern villages. Rundolik is the only female that has come from the southern villages. We told them she died without children."

"I don't care. Don't tell them. They will still *have* to accept him because he's a gift from Seccolog."

"You see what a chief must put up with? Zendolot, praise to him, help me," Seccolog said to Rayloc in an appeasing voice. "You will take extra flint to smooth things with Romelog. I will order Sadolad to take Pothialik as his mate and join Romelog's village. Sincolad will take a copper ceremony hatchet to appease Romelog."

"Tell Romelog that Sadolad will become a fighter or a hunter for his village. He will be good for Romelog's village," Bolanlik added.

Rayloc knew Bolanlik had always hated Rundolik because she was young and pretty but mostly because she was from the southern villages. Seccolog tried to move Rundolik into his dwelling as a pleasure mate when she was pregnant with Sadolad. At Bolanlik's insistence, Rundolik was sent to be a servant of the fighters before Sadolad was born. Even though everyone knew he was Seccolog's son, he was never accepted by the family. He was raised by the fighters, almost as a mascot.

Sincolad held a gourd of goat's milk, which he casually sloshed and spilled on his hand. "He belongs to the southern villages. He's not worthy of Seccolog's village." He absently rubbed his left thumb along one edge of the wheel of life as he spoke. It was a small marble disk with a hole in the center. Each of the chief's heritage sons was given one as a token of honor.

"A son of the chief should stay with his own village." Rayloc was not against the plan, but he liked to aggravate Bolanlik whenever he could. Seccolog would be stupid to send Sadolad to the southern villages. The truth about Rundolik would get out, and there would be trouble. But trouble would suit Rayloc. He might find a way to use it to his advantage.

"Sadolad is twenty-three summers old now." Rayloc felt the burn of Bolanlik's voice as she talked down to him. "He's not a child. It's time for him to find his way. He has never belonged with this village. His mother was a camp whore, and he is a disgrace to this village."

"Rundolik was sent to the camp of the fighters *after* she came to this village. Before that, she was the daughter of one of the favored goatherds of the southern villages." Rayloc expected this to upset Bolanlik—he was not disappointed.

"Watch what you say!" There was fire in Bolanlik's eyes.

"It will be as Bolanlik … as *I* have said." Seccolog stood as he spoke to Rayloc. "You will go with Sincolad to the southern villages. You will take Sadolad and offer him to Romelog to take Pothialik as his heritage mate. He will stay and become a member of Romelog's village. May Zendolot, praise to him, bless them."

"I will do as you say." Rayloc left with his jaw clenched to hold back his words of contempt. Seccolog should not have let Bolanlik get away with speaking to him in such a disrespectful manner. Seccolog was worse than a woman. Sincolad was just like him.

Even as a child, Rayloc dreamed of organizing and leading the villages. Unfortunately, he was not a son of the chief.

Before Rayloc was made shaman of the village and changed his name to Rayloc, he was called Raylad. Raylad was too small to ever be a leader of hunters. The hunters were the choice men of the village. The only place of leadership left to Raylad was a spiritual calling. He had followed that path until he became the assistant shaman. He could not advance until the shaman, Nacoloc, died.

After two years as assistant shaman, Raylad became impatient. No one ever discovered who had slipped into Nacoloc's dwelling and slit his throat. Raylad seemed as surprised and saddened as everyone in the village. Raylad was given the role of shaman. His name was officially changed from Raylad to the shaman form of Rayloc.

Rayloc had vivid nightmares that Zendolot would allow Dracolut to bring the droglits to destroy him and everything he wanted. The droglits were short, manlike creatures with powerful muscles. When brave and honorable men died, they were sent to the skies to join the stars and the great god, Zendolot. Cowards and those who dishonored the People were sent to the deep caverns where they were ruled by Dracolut. All who were sent to the deep caverns were guarded and tortured by the droglits. Eventually, they would turn into droglits. Since the murder of Nacoloc, fear of Dracolut and his droglits haunted Rayloc's nights.

Seccolog's village was one of the strongest villages, but Seccolog was weak and afraid of confrontation. He let chiefs of smaller villages take the lead in intertribal affairs related to hunting areas, trading rituals, and scheduling rendezvous. It seemed Seccolog only wanted to preserve his life of privilege, even at the expense of the rest of the village.

Rayloc's life goal was to unite all the villages into a large union with one powerful ruler. Rayloc would be that ruler's shaman. As Rayloc walked through the village, thinking about the possible outcomes if Romelog discovered what really happened to Rundolik, an idea began to grow in his mind. Slowly a smile spread across his face.

Rayloc was anxious to get to Romelog's village to begin his plan. Most of the summer had been wasted because shortly after his meeting with Seccolog, Sincolad became sick with a stomach problem that made travel impossible. It was past midsummer before he was well enough to leave. They crossed the Ice Mountains just before winter snows closed the passes. Romelog welcomed them to his village and set up camp to pass the winter.

The first step of Rayloc's plan would come in late winter when Sincolad planned to inform Romelog that Seccolog was giving him Sadolad.

Sincolad became sick again after setting up camp. Rayloc's plan seemed doomed when Sincolad lost his mind because of a fever and ran off in the snow. By the time his hunters found him, he had suffered a case of frostbite on his little toe. Fortunately, he recovered in time to prepare for the day Sincolad would make his proposal to Romelog.

Winter 3304/3303 BCE

On a warm morning, when nearly all the winter snow was gone, Rayloc watched as Sadolad participated in a practice contest with bows and arrows. Romelog's fighters tied a goat stomach from the morning's slaughter to a tree. Each of the fighters shot an arrow at the target from thirty paces. One hit the stomach at the top. Two others hit the tree. The rest missed everything.

"It looks like everyone managed to hit the forest," Sadolad laughed, "but I thought the goat's stomach was the target."

"The wind is wrong," Bedoclad said.

"You have to allow for the wind."

"I did, but it's still tricky."

"I bet my hatchet I can hit the small part at the bottom." Sadolad referred to a piece of the small intestine that was still attached.

"You may be good, but nobody's that good."

"What do you bet?"

"My hatchet against yours."

Sadolad picked up a fist full of dust and held it above his head. As he let the dust filter from his fingers, the gentle breeze blew it lightly to his right. Sadolad put an arrow to the string of his bow. He flipped his head to clear his long, blond hair from his face. It blew to the side as he pulled string of his bow until it rested on his cheek. He wore only loose-fitting leggings pieced together with animal skins, a leather tie around his waist, and a loincloth that looped over the leather tie in front and back. Rayloc admired the strength of the muscles in Sadolad's arms and across his chest as he stretched the powerful bow to its limit. Sadolad was tall and lean. Even after winter, his skin was colored a golden brown. His clear blue eyes stood out from the color of his face. The string snapped with a loud pop.

"Wow!" Kendolad exclaimed.

"Lucky shot," Bedoclad said.

"I bet my hatchet and my belt I can do it again."

Bedoclad hesitated.

"Never mind. Bring me my arrow."

Kendolad retrieved the arrow. Sadolad calmly took aim and hit the same spot.

"Okay, okay." Bedoclad handed Sadolad his stone hatchet. "By Zendolot, praise to him, it was worth a hatchet to see that."

Everyone laughed with Bedoclad as he handed Sadolad the hatchet. "If we ever do have a serious contest with your village, I hope Seccolog doesn't make you a fighter first."

Sadolad's face clouded over. Rayloc saw his opportunity. He approached the young man. "Sadolad, you are very good at the fighter games. It's too bad Chief Seccolog has not let you become a fighter."

"I have reason to believe someday I will be given the opportunity. My brother, Podeclad, has promised to speak for me. He has influence with Chief Seccolog."

"You may be a fighter sooner than you think. Podeclad will have nothing to do with it. He has no influence with Bolanlik. She will never allow you to be a fighter in Seccolog's village."

"What do you mean? First you say I will be a fighter, and then you say Bolanlik will never allow it."

Rayloc led Sadolad from the group. "Sincolad will never accept Pothialik as a mate of any kind. This is because Bolanlik hates all the southern villages."

"What does that have to do with me?"

"I will explain everything to you, but you must promise not to say anything of this to Sincolad until I say the time is right."

"Sincolad has always hated me. I have nothing to say to him. You may take that as my promise."

Rayloc told Sadolad that when Bolanlik was a child, her brother was killed in a fighter's contest with a southern village. The contests were not aimed at killing, but they were dangerous, and fighters were occasionally killed accidentally. Bolanlik would never believe her brother's death was an accident, and she had hated the southern villages since.

When Bolanlik became heritage mate to Seccolog, she put up with Seccolog's pleasure mates because it was the custom. Then one summer, he came back from the southern villages with a pleasure mate from Romelog's tribe. Bolanlik was upset that he would bring a woman from a southern village.

The woman was the daughter of a highly honored goatherd. In order for Seccolog to get her, he had promised, under oath to Zendolot, that if Bolanlik's sons died and Rundolik had sons, they would have the rights of heritage sons.

When Bolanlik found out about the oath, she was angry. Then when it was discovered that the woman was already pregnant, Bolanlik went crazy. Seccolog had made it possible for a son from a southern village to be chief of Seccolog's village. She wanted the woman killed before the baby was born, but that was not possible. She forced Seccolog to send the woman to the fighters to be a camp whore.

When the baby was born, it was a beautiful boy. Bolanlik's screaming and yelling lasted for days. The only way she could be calmed down was for Seccolog to promise he would never recognize the boy as his son. Even though the boy was never allowed any of the privileges of his birth, everyone in the village knew he was the son of the chief.

As Rayloc concluded the story, he watched Sadolad's eyes widen. "The woman was my mother!"

"It's true. Rundolik was sent to be a servant to the fighters, to cook, clean, and satisfy their sexual needs. It broke her heart. She lived a miserable life under the nose of Bolanlik. Bolanlik hates you because you are Rundolik's son. You would be chief if something should happen to her three sons. Too many in the village know about the oath."

Sadolad stood up and started pacing. "I was told my mother was always a camp whore, and I was a mistake my father made. I was told I could not be part of my father's family because of what my mother was. Why has no one told me the truth?"

"It was forbidden. I risk everything to tell you this. That's why you must not mention this to anyone else until I tell you the time is right."

"My mother lived a miserable life and died young, and now you tell me this all happened because of Bolanlik?"

"What I tell you is known by the older members of the village."

"What has any of this got to do with me becoming a fighter?"

"You have not been told the true reason you were sent on this trading trip."

"What reason?" Sadolad's anger and impatience were obvious in the tone of his question. Rayloc had counted on this reaction.

"Bolanlik has found the only way to get rid of you. You have been sent as a gift from Seccolog to Romelog. Sincolad will reveal Seccolog's plans to you and Romelog soon. Seccolog hopes to appease Romelog before the summer trading by offering you to Romelog's village to take Pothialik as your mate. The day you become a fighter or a hunter in Romelog's village, you will lose all your rights in Seccolog's village."

"All I know is Bolanlik and Seccolog killed my mother by destroying her life!"

"Shush. You must remain quiet and calm."

"I don't know what to feel. I don't know what to do. How can I go back to Seccolog's village when all I want to do is kill him and Bolanlik? But how can I stay here when my friends and my life are north of the Ice Mountains?" Sadolad sat down and put his head in his hands. "My life is ruined." Then he looked at Rayloc. "Why did you tell me this now?"

Rayloc looked into Sadolad's eyes. He was clearly angry, but Rayloc could see pain in his eyes also. These were the tools of his plan. "It's no secret I often disagree with Seccolog. He's a weak leader. He allows his village to be cheated in trading by all the other villages. Sincolad is just like his father. The village will never become a strong village while it is led by Seccolog or any of his heritage sons."

"I see this is so. Many of the fighters feel the real chief of the village is Bolanlik. Perhaps it's better for me to become a fighter in Romelog's village."

"The fighters are right about Bolanlik. Seccolog's village is a village of women. You have a chance now to get away from those who hate you and are jealous of you. Pothialik is a beautiful young woman. If you take her as a mate, you will be highly honored in Romelog's village. Romelog will make you a fighter. You are skilled. He might even make you a hunter."

"You think I should do as Seccolog and Bolanlik want? Sacrifice my birthright to make things better for them?"

Rayloc was pleased to hear the sarcasm in Sadolad's question. What he had proposed was a chance for a new life with honor and happiness. A weak man would be tempted to accept it.

"I have merely tried to show you how things are. If you disobey Seccolog in this, it will be his right to disown you. Seccolog will make you a field man … lower. You would lose your birthright. Bolanlik has made all your choices bad ones."

"I will kill them first!"

"Then you will be killed, and Sincolad will change his name to Sincolog and become chief, and everything will be the same. Bolanlik will have won. You will have lived and died for nothing."

"I will not have died for nothing."

"If you're sure you do not want to stay with the southern villages to benefit Seccolog and Bolanlik, there may be a way for you to have your revenge and live to make changes to the village."

"What way?"

"Be patient a few days, Sadolad. Give me some time to work out a plan."

"Find a plan, Rayloc. I don't know if I can hold my anger. I cannot answer for my actions if Sincolad tells me to stay and take Pothialik for a mate."

"Just a few days, and then everything will work out for you." Rayloc left Sadolad by the fire to think about the many things he had told him.

The next day, Rayloc went to talk to Romelog. He didn't know Romelog well, but he had to recruit him for his plan to work. Rayloc took a deep breath to calm his nerves and then knocked on the post of Romelog's dwelling. "Come, enter a dwelling where Zendolot, praise to him, rules." Romelog indicated a robe of honor for Rayloc. Romelog was tall and well built. The muscles of his chest and stomach were visible through the open front of his sheepskin vest. His clear blue eyes were accented by his long, gray hair and beard. He looked, moved, dressed, and talked like a chief.

"Thank you for allowing me to talk to you. It is an honor for me to visit Romelog." Rayloc sat on the robe of honor.

"It has been five summers since Seccolog visited from the northern villages. Seccolog was getting too old to travel even then."

"Seccolog enjoys the leisure of old age. He has become too old and heavy to cross the Ice Mountains."

"I also have become too old to travel. It is good that my old friend Seccolog has sent his son, Sincolad. It will be good for Seccolog to unite our villages by having Sincolad accept Pothialik as his heritage mate."

"Seccolog desires to maintain friendship between his village and your village for the sake of fair trading." It was an affront to maintain friendship to make sure trading was done fairly. Rayloc was happy to see the confusion his statement brought to Romelog's eyes.

"Does Seccolog think Romelog's village would cheat his friend?"

"How is Seccolog your friend?" Rayloc began to work his plan slowly.

"I do not understand your words. You do not speak for Seccolog. I will speak with his son." A scowl covered Romelog's face.

"You are right. I don't speak for Seccolog. He sent Sincolad to speak for him. Sincolad will tell you he will never take Pothialik for a heritage mate. He will tell you Seccolog offers another of his sons to take Pothialik for a mate."

"Aduclad?"

"Not a son of his heritage mate."

"A pleasure mate son?"

Rayloc was pleased at the incredulous tone of his question. "A strong, handsome, young man, who will be offered to become a member of Romelog's village. He will make a strong hunter or fighter that Romelog's village can be proud of."

"This is not what I expected. I must think on this."

"There is a secret about this young man. A secret that even he did not know."

"What secret?"

"You must promise not to say anything about this to Sincolad until I tell you it is time."

"I say what I will say when I choose to say it."

Rayloc could see the emotions building in Romelog's face. "I must leave." Rayloc stood up. "I thank you, and I hope you will accept Sadolad as an honored member of your village. It is Seccolog's plan that his son stay with the southern villages as a gift to ensure friendship and fair trading." Rayloc spoke in a light, friendly tone, but he stressed "fair trading" as he bowed and began to back out of the dwelling.

"Wait! Is this secret important?" Romelog demanded as much as asked.

"Only Romelog can judge this." Rayloc struggled to maintain a calm appearance though he churned inside.

"I will hold my tongue until the time is right." Romelog pointed to the robe of honor. "Now, what is this important secret?"

Rayloc returned and sat on the robe. "Sadolad is already a member of your village."

"How can that be?"

"Sadolad's mother was a member of your village."

"That cannot be so. Only Rundolik has gone to Seccolog's village."

"The boy's mother is Rundolik."

"That is not true. Rundolik died of sickness before she had any children."

Rayloc sensed a flicker of doubt in Romelog's voice. Now was the time to press his point. "That is what you were told so you would forget about her and there would be no more questions about her. Sadolad was never told his mother came from the southern villages. Bolanlik hated Rundolik and Sadolad. She made Seccolog send Rundolik to serve the fighters."

Romelog's face turned red, and his eyes widened. This was the reaction Rayloc had hoped to see. He would have to direct Romelog's anger to fit his plans.

"Why does Seccolog send Rundolik's son to me now?"

"Seccolog does whatever Bolanlik tells him to. Bolanlik can only see this is a way to get Sadolad out of the village. You are not supposed to be told who Sadolad is. Sadolad never talks of his mother because she is an embarrassment to him. It is forbidden for anyone in the village to talk of her. It is a secret Seccolog thinks will never be known."

"Why did Bolanlik hate the mother and child?" Romelog's voice had turned cold.

"Bolanlik hates the southern villages because her brother was killed by a southern village."

"But that was an accident many summers ago."

"Bolanlik never forgets or forgives. Seccolog promised Rundolik's father if she bore him sons they would fall in line behind the heritage sons. By this promise, Sadolad would become chief if Bolanlik's sons die. If Sadolad becomes a fighter or a hunter for your village, he will lose his rights in Seccolog's village. This is the reason Bolanlik sends him to you."

"Sadolad is not a fighter or a hunter in Seccolog's village?"

"A pleasure mate son and one in line to be chief should have been a hunter, but Bolanlik would never allow Sadolad to hold any honor. He has great skills that will make him a great fighter or hunter.

"Bolanlik will never allow any of Seccolog's sons to take a mate from the southern villages. She sends Sadolad because it is the only way to be rid of him."

"I do not deal with women!" Romelog stood up and began to pace. "By the justice of Zendolot, praise to him, this is an insult I will punish."

"Bolanlik knows this is an insult. She glories in this kind of hidden insult."

Romelog turned to face Rayloc, standing with his arms folded and his feet apart. His eyes narrowed. "Why are you telling me this?"

Rayloc knew his answer to that question would be vitally important, but he was not ready to divulge everything yet, so he attempted to lead Romelog from the subject. "I cannot be ruled by a woman anymore. I look for a way out."

"You would like to join my village? I have a shaman. I have no use for another."

"My life is in the North. I do not want to join any other village because I want to live where my family and friends are, but I do not do the bidding of a woman. Is this wrong?"

"No. It is a hard thing to leave a life behind. It is hard to leave a calling behind." Romelog turned his back and took a step. "I must send you all back. There will be no trading. Seccolog must answer for his lies." He turned to face Rayloc. "I cannot accept Sadolad until Seccolog restores him to his rightful place. He must be made a hunter in Seccolog's village. Then, I would allow Pothialik to be his heritage mate, and then he would not lose his birthright. That was Rundolik's right, and it must not be stolen from her son."

"I will think on the wisdom of Romelog." Rayloc stood. "Sincolad is just like his father. He comes to you carrying the secret. He will try to trick you into making Sadolad a hunter or fighter in your village to steal from him his birthright. Even after Seccolog dies, Sincolad is not a man you can deal with in openness and honesty. We must all think on this problem. We must not tell Sincolad we know about his lies until we have the right solution."

"We will talk of these things again. I will meet Sadolad and talk to him. I will not speak of this to Sincolad until I have talked to Sadolad."

Rayloc bowed and left. The plan was now proceeding, but there were still dangerous steps to take.

Two days later, Romelog invited Sincolad and his men to participate in the arrow ceremony. Rayloc knew the time to push his plan was coming, but he didn't want to do anything before this important ceremony. All winter, Romelog's craftsmen had prepared shafts, points, and feathers to make arrows for the summer hunts.

The spring feast and arrow ceremony was celebrated at the end of winter. Before the food was served, the leader of the arrow makers always put together the first ten arrows from the shafts, points, and feathers that were prepared during the winter.

Romelog sat at his appointed spot near the large ceremony fire in the center of the village. Sincolad sat near Romelog on the side where the chief and the hunters sat. The hunters held the honored places. They would be given the best arrows to hunt food for the village. Fighters would get the low-quality arrows to use in games and demonstrations.

Descolad, chief arrow maker, stepped to the place of honor in front of Romelog. "I have come from a winter of preparation for the summer hunts." Descolad wore a vest of reeds. On his head was a woven hat with a point that looked like an arrowhead. Leather stockings went from his ankles to his knees. Feathers were attached to the sides and backs of the stockings. He wore a cowhide waistband and a sheepskin loincloth. "I bring the luck of the great god, Zendolot, praise to him, in the parts of the arrows we make for the hunters."

"Present your arrows," Romelog commanded.

Descolad signaled for the pitch, the sinew, and the feathers. They were placed on the ground before him. "This pitch and sinew will hold the arrows together. These feathers will guide the arrow true when the hunter shoots. Hodeclad, bring the ceremonial shafts."

An old man came to the fire circle. "I bring the ten best shafts to honor the great god, Zendolot, praise to him." Hodeclad handed ten wooden shafts to Descolad. They were straight and true. One end was notched to receive the flint arrowhead, and the other end was notched to hold the arrow to the string of the bow when it was shot.

Hodeclad extended his right hand. Descolad took a flint dagger from the tools in front of him and cut the old man's thumb. Descolad smeared the blood from his thumb on the arrow shafts near the end where the arrowheads would be attached. "The lifeblood of Hodeclad calls the blessings of Zendolot, praise to him, to these arrow shafts."

When Descolad was done, Hodeclad backed away.

"Godelad, bring the ceremonial arrowheads," Descolad ordered.

Another old man came to the fire circle. "I bring the ten best arrowheads to honor the great god, Zendolot, praise to him."

Godelad handed ten flint arrowheads to Descolad. Godelad extended his right hand, and Descolad cut his thumb with the ceremony dagger. Descolad smeared the blood from his thumb on each of the arrowheads. "The lifeblood of Godelad calls the blessings of Zendolot, praise to him, to these arrowheads."

When that was done, Godelad backed away.

"Descolad will make arrows for the village to bring good luck to the hunters on the summer hunts," Romelog said.

Descolad carefully attached feathers and arrowheads to each of the ten shafts. When he was done, he presented the finished arrows to Romelog.

"We have prepared shafts and arrowheads for many arrows," Descolad said. "Tomorrow we will begin to put them together to make arrows for the summer hunts. The great god, Zendolot, praise to him, will bless the new arrows."

"This is good. Let the women cook the food," Romelog ordered.

As the food was being prepared, Romelog passed among the hunters and gave the ceremony arrows to those who had shown valor and skill in the most recent hunts. It was a great honor to receive a ceremony arrow marked with the blood of the craftsmen who had made them. Only hunters, chiefs, and the heritage sons of chiefs were given these special arrows. Everyone expected Sincolad, an honored guest and heritage son of a chief, would be given an arrow. When Romelog gave Sincolad an arrow, Sadolad left the camp. Rayloc could see it was hard for him to control his anger.

Romelog handed the arrow to Sincolad. "Now is the time to talk of your visit and the joining of our two villages."

"I am honored you have offered your daughter, Pothialik, to me as heritage mate. I am saddened to tell you I already have a heritage mate."

"I was told you had not accepted a heritage mate."

"I took my heritage mate just last summer. Her name is Conchelik."

"One of your heritage brothers will be acceptable."

"I have brought my father's favorite pleasure mate son, Sadolad, to Romelog. I know this is not the heritage son you expected, but my father makes him a gift to Romelog's village. Sadolad is the strongest and most skilled of my father's sons. He will join your village, and your daughter will not have to live across the Ice Mountains."

Romelog looked past Sincolad at Rayloc. Rayloc nodded. "Is this Sadolad a hunter?" Romelog asked.

"No."

"Is he a fighter?"

"No."

Romelog leaned forward. "He is a young man, but he is more than old enough to be made a hunter or a fighter."

"My father has waited because he was not sure whether to make him a hunter or a fighter. My father would prefer to make him a hunter, but you see how he chooses to associate with the fighters."

"I will think on this gift."

As soon as Rayloc was sure Romelog was not going to reveal what he knew, Rayloc left to find Sadolad. He saw him not far from the village. Rayloc marveled at the skill and strength Sadolad had, though he was still a young man. His face was strong, framed by a square jaw. He nose was straight and narrow, like his mother and the people of the southern villages. It was obvious why Bolanlik did not want to see his face. "Your anger shows," Rayloc said.

"I can't stand to see Sincolad honored."

"You're right to feel this way. You are also right to walk away from the camp. Romelog knows of Seccolog's treachery."

"Then why does he honor Seccolog's son?"

"Romelog follows the proper customs while he decides what he will do."

"It's a disgrace to honor Sincolad with a ceremony arrow. It gives him honor, and it gives him luck. It's wrong to give him luck at this time."

"Think what would happen if Romelog refused the arrow. Sincolad would know something is wrong. In his anger, he might leave. Romelog must make Sincolad feel nothing is wrong until he decides what must be done."

"When will Romelog decide?" Sadolad's tone was filled with sarcasm. "I also have been betrayed. I have something to say about what must be done."

"You're right. Romelog understands this. He plans to decide what must be done tonight. He asked me to invite you to come to his dwelling after the people of the village have settled for the night. He is anxious to hear what Rundolik's son has to say."

"For the first time in my life, I feel pride at being referred to as Rundolik's son. I will meet with Romelog and my mother's people. We will decide how Seccolog's betrayal will be avenged."

"Romelog has also asked me to come to his meeting. I will be proud to go to the meeting with Sadolad."

"Good."

Sadolad and Rayloc paused before entering Romelog's council dwelling. Rayloc knew what he wanted from this meeting, but he didn't want to be the one to suggest it. He took a deep breath, exhaled, and then tapped on the entry post.

"Come, council with Romelog in a dwelling where Zendolot, praise to him, rules," Romelog said. Sadolad and Rayloc entered Romelog's dwelling.

"I am honored," Rayloc said.

"Seccolog has offered Sadolad to take Pothialik as his mate," Romelog said to Sadolad.

"It is true my father offers me to the village of Romelog in order to ensure friendship and fair trading between his village and your village." Sadolad spoke in a formal manner, using words Rayloc had suggested.

"Is this Sadolad's wish?"

"Pothialik is a very beautiful woman. I would be pleased to take her as my mate, but not by a lie."

"What lie?"

"I am sent to your village to make Romelog think Seccolog makes a sacrifice for friendship. But in his eyes, I am the least of his sons. I am sent to Romelog to trick me into giving up the birthright Seccolog has kept secret from me."

"I have been told you are the son of Rundolik, daughter of Dencolad of my village."

"Rundolik was my mother. I was not told of the honored place she held in your village until now."

"I have spoken to Dencolad. He is pleased to find he has a grandson but upset at the treachery to his daughter."

"Rundolik died miserable and unloved," Rayloc said. "She was robbed of her life because of hatred and jealousy. Seccolog and Bolanlik robbed her of her son's love and respect. Now they try to rob her son of his birthright."

"I would be honored to take Pothialik as my mate. But I am not a hunter or even a fighter. It would not honor her to become the mate of a man who has no calling. It is my birthright to be chief of Seccolog's village if all Bolanlik's sons die. I would lose that birthright if I become a hunter or a fighter in Romelog's village. I cannot honorably take Pothialik as my mate unless I am made a hunter in Seccolog's village first."

"How would Sadolad become a hunter in Seccolog's village? Should I insist he make you a hunter before you take Pothialik?"

"Bolanlik will not accept this under any condition," Rayloc insisted. "It must be remembered, all decisions have to be accepted by her."

"I will not deal with a woman!" Clearly, Romelog was angry at the suggestion he make a plan to appease a woman. "I will break trading with Seccolog. I will make Sadolad an honored hunter in this village."

"I am honored by your offer. It would be a good thing, but I will not be a traitor to my mother. I will not give up the birthright that was promised to her."

"Seccolog has three healthy sons, and he is an old man," Romelog stated. "It is unlikely all three will die before Seccolog. If any one of them becomes chief, the birthright will then go to him and his sons. It is not possible for Sadolad to become chief."

"What you say is true. I do not hold the birthright with a hope of being chief. I hold this birthright because it is the only honorable thing I have from my mother."

"You would go back to face the anger of Seccolog?"

"I do not fear Seccolog's anger. It would dishonor Romelog if I take Pothialik before I regain honor in Seccolog's village."

"You speak wisely. Dencolad will be proud of his grandson."

"And what of the treachery to Romelog's village?" Rayloc asked Romelog.

"There will be no trading between our villages."

"You would withhold the benefits of trade between the two villages from your own people?" Rayloc asked. "You punish your village as much as you punish Seccolog." There was a long period of silence. Rayloc dropped a hint. "It is too bad Sadolad is not chief. Then, Sadolad could take Pothialik as heritage mate, and friendship and trading between the villages would be assured." Again there was a long silence.

"Many problems would be solved if Seccolog and his heritage sons were dead," Romelog said.

"Seccolog deserves to die for his treachery," Rayloc added. Again the three men sat in silence.

"Sadolad would make a good chief. Most of the fighters are loyal to him." Rayloc tried to keep the conversation going without suggesting his own plan.

"Is this true?" Romelog asked Sadolad.

"This is true."

"Of the hunters and fighters that came with you, how many are loyal to you?"

"The two fighters Seccolog sent are my friends. All the hunters are loyal to Seccolog."

"That is true," Rayloc said. "Seccolog sent his most loyal hunters with Sincolad."

"The wrongs Seccolog has committed cannot be left without justice," Sadolad said.

"You speak of the death of Seccolog?" Rayloc prodded to bring the decision he wanted.

"I speak of the death of my mother, Rundolik! This death belongs to Seccolog. This death cries to Seccolog for justice."

"I speak of insults to Dencolad and to me," Romelog said.

"There will be much anger," Rayloc said. "There are many who follow Seccolog. He is the chief."

"I do not care. Let them kill me."

"No one would attack Sadolad if he were chief," Rayloc said.

"This is so," Romelog said to Sadolad. "It is your birthright to be chief. The only way to have justice for the shame and death of Rundolik is for you to receive the birthright she died to get."

"All the old members of the village know Rundolik was deceived and betrayed," Rayloc said. "It is a new thing to judge and kill a chief. Many would resent it. Many would fight against it. But if he is killed quickly, most in the village would see the wisdom and benefit to the village. Seccolog is a bad leader. Sincolad would be no better."

"You talk of killing Podeclad?" Sadolad asked.

"There must be no man who can claim the heritage."

"Podeclad has always been my friend. He is the only person of my father's family that ever supported me. He has done that despite the anger it brought from Bolanlik. He must be spared."

"If any of Seccolog's sons are left alive, it will provide a starting point for your enemies to gather. No matter what you think about Podeclad's feelings for you, they will disappear when his father, mother, and brothers have been killed. There is no safe way to save him."

Sadolad sat silently.

"If you are not ready to remove Seccolog and all his sons, it is better for you to remain in Romelog's village," Rayloc said.

"This is true," Romelog agreed. "If any of Seccolog's sons remain, all the killing will have been for nothing. It will not lead to the justice you seek, but will lead to more killing."

"This justice is hard," Sadolad said.

"If the killing is done quickly, and Sadolad is made chief, few would resist," Rayloc said.

"They would not resist on their own, but they could be led to resist," Sadolad reluctantly agreed. "It is true; the only way is to kill Seccolog and all his sons and grandsons ... even those who are of the pleasure mates. Once there can be no other chief but me, there will be no one to lead a rebellion."

"This is much killing," Romelog said. "It would set a bad example."

"To kill only Seccolog and his heritage sons would bring discontent among the villages with no result. If we do as Sadolad suggests, there will be an outcry, but when the other villages understand, and when they see Sadolad's strong leadership, they will accept what has happened."

"All Seccolog's sons, daughters, and pleasure mates must die. We must not take a chance anyone would make a claim. Only I will be the true chief."

"This is much killing," Romelog said again. "I have never heard of such a thing. I do not want to start this new thing. It would be very hard if other villages see this as the way to get rid of a chief who is not liked."

Rayloc's plan was slipping. "This is not just a chief who is not liked. This is a chief who has insulted other villages. You see what he did to Rundolik of your own village. Now, after hiding what he did, he tries to trick Sadolad out of his birthright. Sadolad is a grandson of your village. Seccolog tries to cheat your village. He lied to you about Rundolik. A leader such as this is no leader at all. All the other villages will realize this is true."

"How many fighters would follow you?" Romelog asked Sadolad.

"All the fighters would follow me. Many hunters would also follow me. The hunters who came with us are the most loyal to Seccolog. If they are all killed, most of his support will be gone. Romelog must help in this."

"What must be done must be done quickly," Rayloc said.

"My fighters are trained for contests. They have not learned this kind of killing."

"This is not a time for weakness," Sadolad said. "All fighters learn to kill animals when they help on the hunts. They must now be shown it is right to kill other men when the chief and Zendolot, praise to him, call for it. What we do is right. It is the only right way to undo the wrongs that have been done by Seccolog and those who support him. Romelog and his fighters must be strong."

"For all the generations of the people, fighters have honored their calling to be fighters for the villages through contests and games," Rayloc said. "This has been right because there has never been such treachery as Seccolog has created. With this kind of treachery, a new response is needed. Now, fighters must be stronger. Seccolog did not worry about killing when he sent Rundolik to serve the fighters. He killed her spirit, and then her body died. This is killing the innocent. Fighters must be willing to kill those who kill the innocent."

"A new time has come," Sadolad said. "This new time was brought by Seccolog. All the consequences of this new time belong to Seccolog. Romelog must now give me fighters to take back the birthright that belongs to me."

"How would this be done?" Romelog asked.

"I will kill Sincolad," Sadolad responded. "I will need help to kill the hunters. After Sincolad and his hunters are dead, Rayloc and I will return to Seccolog's village. We will sneak into the village at night and gather my fighters. We will kill those who need to be killed before morning. When the sun rises, Rayloc will change my name from Sadolad to Sadolog. I will be chief, and my fighters will stand beside me. When it is known I am the only one with the birthright to be chief, I will be accepted. Then I will announce that Pothialik will be my heritage mate and Romelog's village supports me. Everyone will know a new, strong friendship is made with the southern villages that will benefit all the People. A time of friendship without betrayal will begin. All people will celebrate the brave actions of those who have supported Romelog and Sadolog."

"When Seccolog and all his heirs except Sadolad are dead, there will be nothing for the village to do but support Sadolad to become Chief Sadolog," Rayloc said.

"Any who resist must die," Sadolad said.

"It is not possible to kill everyone. The killing must be tempered," Romelog cautioned.

"Romelog gives wise counsel," Rayloc said. "There will be strong support for Sadolad if you send some of your fighters with him. When the fighters see that the southern villages support Sadolad, they will be convinced it is right for Sadolad to lead. There will be less rebellion and less need to kill."

Romelog sat pensively. Rayloc needed something to overcome the final hesitation. "There is one more thing that will ensure success. I propose Sadolad take Pothialik to be his heritage mate before he goes back, so the friendship between the villages will be sealed. All the People of both villages will support the new relationship between the villages."

Romelog sat in thought. "I will send fighters. Sadolad will take Pothialik as heritage mate. Our two villages will be as one across the mountains."

Romelog stepped outside the dwelling. A hunter was stationed there. "Cortalad, Locolod's fighters are camped together in preparation for games and contests tomorrow. Go tell them to come to my dwelling. Have them come one by one from different parts of the village. Tell them to avoid Sincolad's tent and the tent where his hunters sleep."

The fighters gathered rapidly. Romelog explained what was happening and what was expected. After he explained everything, Sadolad stepped to the center. He spoke softly, but his words were strong. He explained again the treachery of Seccolog and his family. He stressed the treachery against Rundolik, and as her son, he was their brother. "Tonight, we start a new road of honor. Tonight, we show that killing of the innocent will not be allowed. A new friendship will begin between the northern villages and the southern villages. I will take Pothialik as my heritage mate to seal the friendship between the two villages. I will become Sadolog. Then, a new time of friendship between north and south will start." Sadolad had a compelling way of speaking, and he made the men's spirits burn. All the men in the dwelling wanted to follow him.

Romelog named the fighters who would go to Sincolad's hunters' tent. After they left, Romelog called upon two fighters to go with Sadolad and his two fighters to Sincolad's tent.

"When we get there, we will enter his tent with our daggers ready," Sadolad said. "I want him tied and gagged so he knows what is happening when I kill him. Before he dies, I want him to know Rundolik's son will kill all his family. I want him to know I will take my birthright."

The joining of the villages was just the beginning for Rayloc. He would find his way to power through Sadolog.

Shortly after leaving for Sincolad's tent, Sadolad returned. "Sincolad is dead?" Rayloc asked.

"We could not find him. I left two fighters to bring him here when he returns."

As the night progressed and there was still no sign of Sincolad, Rayloc organized a search. During the search, it was discovered that one of Sincolad's hunters, Kodelad, was also missing.

The sun came over the horizon, and still no one had found Sincolad or Kodelad. Rayloc was getting anxious.

"Somehow, Kodelad must have escaped from the hunter tent and warned Sincolad," Sadolad said. "They must be running back to Seccolog to warn him. We must send fighters through all the passes to catch them."

"I don't think they will try to cross the mountains. We have all their bows and arrows and their traveling clothes," Romelog said.

Just then, two fighters brought Kodelad to Romelog. "What is the meaning of this?" Kodelad shouted. "Sincolad will hear of this when he returns."

"Where did Sincolad go?" Romelog asked.

"He has gone to meet with the leaders of the other southern villages."

"He went in the middle of the night without taking any of his hunters?" Sadolad asked.

"He doesn't explain his actions to you."

"Maybe he should learn to."

"I don't believe he has gone south," Romelog said.

"What he does or does not do does not depend on what you believe," Kodelad said. One of Romelog's fighters slapped him on the side of the face so hard he fell to the ground.

"He would not speak to a chief like that if he did not already know he is going to die," Sadolad said. "I do not know how he and Sincolad found out, but Sincolad knows our plans, and he has run to warn his father."

"Without a bow and arrows and travel clothes, he will die in the mountains," Romelog said.

"The only way to be sure is to send fighters to find him," Sadolad said. "There are only four passes through the mountains from here. We must send fighters to follow each trail."

"I will send fighters as you say, but we will question Kodelad more. He will tell us the truth before he dies."

Rayloc knew there would be much pain for Kodelad. "Kodelad, tell me now which pass Sincolad took. If you tell me true, I will see to it that your death is quick."

"I will tell you and that son of a camp whore nothing!"

Looking into Kodelad's eyes, Sadolad said, "Romelog, when you are done with this worthless animal, cut his manhood from him and shove it down his throat so he chokes to death on it." He stepped back and began to laugh at Kodelad. Kodelad tried to spit, but clearly, his mouth was dry. Sadolad laughed louder.

"The easiest trail back goes through the Ibex Pass," Rayloc said.

"My brother is weak. He has always looked for the easy path, but this time, I think he will take the shortest path. That would be the Bear Pass. I will take four fighters and follow the trail through the Bear Pass."

As they spoke, one of Romelog's hunters brought a woman forward. "This is Sudolik," the hunter said. "She has important information."

Sudolik stepped boldly forward. "This man came to me last night asking for supplies to go on a hunt." She pointed at Kodelad. "He said he wanted to go on a hunt alone to prove to the hunters he could hunt as well as them. He did not want them to know what he was doing, so he left his hunting gear in his tent. I thought he was a friend, so I helped."

"You helped him to go on a hunt in the night?" Romelog asked.

"He told me he was leaving just before daybreak so he could return before midday. I got him a bow and twelve arrows from the curing tent. The bow was finished except for smoothing and decorating it. The arrows only needed to have feathers and points attached. I got some points and antler pieces to finish them and some feathers. I got three finished arrows. I got a quiver, but the rod was broken, so I got some sinew to fix it. I got a pack to tie to his waist and another one to tie on his back. I also provided two birch bark carriers. There were some other tools, hot fire coals and twigs, and some birch fungus because he said he had some stomach problems."

"Sincolad has had stomach problems all winter," Rayloc said.

"Anything else?" Romelog asked.

"I packed food for two meals, some einkorn bread, dried goat, and dried deer. I think that was all."

"Where are your shoes?" Sadolog asked Kodelad.

Kodelad looked back at Sadolog but said nothing. Rayloc could see Kodelad's shoulders shaking. "Bring me a torch from the fire," he commanded one of Romelog's hunters.

When he returned with the torch, Rayloc took the torch and pushed the fire into Kodelad's midsection. Kodelad screamed and tried to pull back, but the hunters held him.

Rayloc pulled the torch back and asked, "Where are your shoes?"

"I gave them to Sincolad. They aren't traveling shoes."

"Besides what Sudolik told us, what else does he have?"

Kodelad hesitated, and Rayloc thrust the fire toward him. Before the flames reached the raw, blackened skin of his stomach, Kodelad answered, "He had his ceremony ax, a coat made from strips of fur, a bearskin hat, the ceremony arrow, and his dagger."

"What else?"

"I think that was all. I can't remember anything else."

"Where was he going?"

"He was going to warn his father."

"Warn him about what?" Rayloc demanded.

"I was outside the tent when you were planning to kill Sincolad and all the hunters." He turned to Sadolad. "I heard your plans to kill all Seccolad's family."

"What pass did he take?" Sadolad asked.

"He didn't say, but he was in a hurry. I think he would take the Bear Pass."

"Why didn't you run with him?"

"There were only supplies for one man. He had to hurry to warn his father."

"No. He wasn't worried about warning his father," Sadolad said. "If that was his worry, he would have sent you. You are a strong hunter. If he had sent you, we could not catch you. Sincolad only worries about himself. Because of that, he and his father will die … and so will you."

"I will send fighters to all the passes," Romelog said.

"I want to be the one to kill him. I want him to know the son of Rundolik is taking revenge for what he and his family did to her. I want him to know Seccolog's heritage mate and all his sons and daughters will be sent from this earth for what he did."

"I will instruct my fighters to bring him back alive, if they can," Romelog said. "But the most important thing is to make sure he does not escape."

"Agreed," Rayloc said.

"According to the girl, he couldn't have started before the middle of the night. He's not as far ahead as I feared," Romelog said.

"Don't worry. My brother is a weakling. We'll catch him before the day is over."

"There will be a great deal of trouble with Seccolog if Sincolad tells him what happened to the hunters," Romelog said.

"Sincolad will not get away. I will take care of my brother and my father."

"I'll go with you," Rayloc said to Sadolad. "We must take your best tracker," he said to Romelog.

"Take Modolad; he can track anything. Go, and may the great god, Zendolot, praise to him, guide you."

Sadolad turned and began jogging out of the village. Four fighters followed him. When he turned to follow, Rayloc said to Romelog, "Throw that suckling pig into the fire."

"No!" Kodelad screamed, but there was no mercy for him.

Modolad found fresh tracks headed north toward the Bear Pass. When they reached a small stream where the terrain started to get steep, Modolad found signs that Sincolad had stopped to rest and eat. He left a small leather strip that Modolad determined by the smell had been wrapped around dried goat's meat. "He probably ate some of the einkorn and drank his fill of water from the stream before moving on. You can see where he sat down to rest."

"A strong man would not have stopped to eat. This shows he's already tired," Sadolad observed.

As they followed the trail through the forest, dark clouds began to form. Rayloc was concerned Sincolad might get away if he reached the summit ahead of them and a storm came.

Light snowflakes started to flutter in the breeze when they reached the tree line. Again, Modolad found evidence that Sincolad had stopped to eat before pushing on to the top.

"There!" Modolad shouted. Rayloc could just make out the form of a man struggling up the mountain.

"The storm is almost here!" Sadolad shouted. "We can't let him get over the summit."

Sadolad started jogging. The others followed.

The path in front of them was uneven and rocky. In many places there were patches of old snow that slipped below their feet, making the climb difficult. The light flurries were already starting to thicken. In spite of the difficulty, or perhaps because it slowed Sincolad, they were gaining.

Rayloc could see Sincolad had reached a point just a short run from the top. For some reason, Sincolad stood on an exposed area where the sun and wind had cleared the old snow. A skiff of new snow lay on the barren ground. Sadolad broke into a run, leaving Rayloc and the others behind.

Rayloc saw Sincolad duck behind a rock. Sadolad was focused on the ground as he struggled through drifts of old snow. Sincolad jumped from the rocks with an arrow in his bow. Rayloc and the others shouted a warning, but it was too late. Fortunately for Sadolad, the arrow went wild.

Sincolad put another arrow in his bow and shot it. This time it came closer. Sadolad dove behind a rock and pulled an arrow from his quiver.

Sincolad started running up the mountain. He had gone only a few steps when an arrow hit him in the back just below his left shoulder. He stumbled and fell, breaking the arrow as he rolled.

He staggered to his feet, dropping his pack, his bow, and his ax. He stumbled about eight paces downhill. When he stopped, he looked down the hill.

Sadolad was putting another arrow in his bow when Rayloc caught up to him. Sadolad put the arrow back in his quiver. "He's not going to make it. Come on. I want him to see my face and hear my voice as he dies."

Sincolad fell and rolled into a depression in the ground. He crawled to a large rock at the end of the depression. He pushed his back against the rock. His left arm stretched across the rock motionless. His right hand was inside his vest on the left side as if he were clutching his heart. When Rayloc and Sadolad reached him, Sincolad blinked his eyes. He was breathing heavily.

"Well, Sincolad, imagine finding you running up a mountain. My weak, old brother trying to run away from me! What a joke. Even funnier, trying to shoot me with an arrow. Too bad you thought practice was a waste of time."

"You are a rude son of a whore."

"You may call me a rude whatever-you-want, you will die anyway."

"We have the same father. You cannot kill your own brother."

"I will kill you, and your spirit will go to the dark caverns to be ruled by Dracolut. It was Dracolut's brother, Zendolot, praise to him, who sent Dracolut to the dark caverns. I do no more evil to you than Zendolot, praise to him, did to his brother. Your destiny is to become a droglit in the caverns of Dracolut. It is my destiny to be one of the brightest stars that light the nighttime sky. You and your whole family must die."

"You leave … my family alone."

"Your whole family is weak, just like you. I am the only son of my father who is strong enough to lead the village." Sadolad looked around. He walked up the hill and picked up Sincolad's bow. He removed the string and threw it aside. He cut the groves from the bow and laid it against the rock Sincolad had hid behind. Sadolad picked up Sincolad's ax and waved it at Sincolad. "See how the ceremony ax is made by forcing a branch to grow through the middle of another branch?" The angle between the point where the head of the ax was attached and the handle was made by splitting a live branch and forcing another live branch through the middle, and then allowing the two branches to grow together before harvesting the wood for the handle. It made a decorative, symbolic handle, but the joint was not strong. "This ax is useless," Sadolad continued. "Useless because it's weak. Weak just like you and your family. There will be no such useless axes in my village." Sadolad laid the ax near the bow.

"My ... fa ... ther ... will," Sincolad coughed several times, "kill ... you."

Sadolad walked back down to Sincolad. "If you had been strong, you could have escaped. If you could shoot an arrow, you could have killed me. If Seccolog was strong, he could kill me. You and your family are weak. You will all die because you're weak." Sadolad had picked up Sincolad's quiver. "Broken ... as it should be."

"Please leave ...my family out ... of this. It's ... like you ... say. I am ... weak."

Sadolad pulled the two remaining finished arrows from the quiver. He broke one across his knee and then carefully put it back in the quiver. He looked closely at the second arrow. He turned to Rayloc. "This is the ceremony arrow Romelog gave you. It should have been mine." Sadolad broke the arrow and put it back. "Here, I will leave these for your spirit," he said to Sincolad. "Broken and unfinished arrows are just right for you." He threw the quiver to the side.

"Do ... what ... you ... want ... with ... me. Leave ... my ... fam ... ly ... a ... lone."

"Your blood is pouring out on the ground."

Sincolad looked down at the growing pool of blood. Sadolad moved close and leaned his face next to Sincolad. "After all Seccolog's children and grandchildren are dead, I will be chie—"

Sincolad swung his dagger around, raising his whole body to give power to his thrust. As he shot his right arm out with his dagger, Sadolad jumped back, but not fast enough. The dagger drove deep into his left shoulder. Sadolad screamed in pain. He felt a sharp snap in his shoulder. He reached out with his right hand, grabbed Sincolad by his right shoulder, and threw him against the rock. The dagger fell to the ground. Sadolad pulled out his own dagger. "Go ahead ... finish the job ... murderer!" Sincolad screamed and collapsed against the rock.

Sadolad lashed out at Sincolad's arm with his dagger. "So it is with anyone who raises a weapon against me. Soon I will be Sadolog, but you and all your family will be dead." Sadolad pulled up Sincolad and threw him face first across the rock. His left arm was still lying on the rock, but now it was across the front of his chest. It had partially cushioned him as his body twisted and smashed into the rock. His right arm hung at his side. Sadolad smashed him on his left side with his elbow several times. "You die now." Sadolad jerked at the bearskin hat Sincolad was wearing so hard he broke the strap that held it. He threw it to the ground and grabbed Sincolad's hair and pulled his head back. He put his dagger against Sincolad's throat. Sincolad made a gasp. Blood foamed from his mouth. Sadolad let his hair go, and Sincolad's face fell once again onto the rock. "Almost you drive me to kill you fast. You are a dead man, Sincolad. You will die slowly, knowing all your family will follow as soon as I and my fighters reach the village."

The other men from Romelog's tribe finally caught up. "Is he dead?" one asked.

"If he's not dead, he soon will be," Rayloc answered

"Let's collect this stuff and get back to the village before the storm gets worse," another of the men said.

"No," Sadolad said. "His things are useless. They are unfinished or broken. We will leave this broken, useless man with his broken, useless things."

"You are bleeding," Rayloc said.

"Yes, the little weakling managed to sneak a stab at me, but it will heal."

"Let me wrap it to stop the bleeding. Look … when you stop the blood, it looks like there is something inside."

"I think the dagger broke. I felt something snap. The tip of his dagger must still be in my arm. We will have the healer get it out. I will wear it around my neck to remember the fate of those who are weak."

Sadolad and his men left Sincolad against the rock. The snow fell harder, and Sincolad's body and the depression he was in were covered with snow. The summer would be cooler than normal. His body would freeze-dry and be protected beneath the snow and ice for more than five thousand years before being discovered by hikers. Then forensic scientists would try in vain to solve the mystery of his murder. He would have many names: L'Uomo del Ghiàcio, Der Mann im Eis, Ötzi, or just plain Iceman. His mystery would outlive Sadolad.

Summer 3303 BCE

Rayloc stood on the foothills overlooking Seccolog's village. The full moon was high in the sky. The village consisted of forty-two dwellings and three large structures for meetings and ceremonies. His plan was intricate. Seccolog's dwelling was closest, located on the south end of the village. Sincolad's dwelling was on the north end. Seccolog's pleasure mates were located in two dwellings near his. Some of his son's pleasure mates and their children were also in those dwellings. The rest of the pleasure mates and their children were located in three other dwellings near Sincolad's dwelling. First, Sadolad, his fighters, and the hunters from Romelog would silently overpower Seccolog's dwelling and kill all the occupants except Seccolog. Sadolad wanted Seccolog to witness the complete destruction of his family and all his descendants. From there, the hunters and fighters would spread out to capture all of Seccolog's family and descendants and bring them to Seccolog's tent. Sadolad's men would bring Podeclad and Aduclad and kill them before Seccolog's eyes. They would get Conchelik, Sincolad's heritage mate. Rayloc knew Sincolad's child should have been born by now. After making sure Conchelik and her child were dead, they would begin killing all the pleasure mates and their children. All that had to be done silently, so the village would not be alarmed. Rayloc's chin was quivering and not just because of the chilly night air.

Sadolad gave the signal to begin. Rayloc walked beside him, with twenty-six hunters and fighters following. As far as Rayloc knew, nothing like this had ever happened in the history of his people. Tonight's actions would turn Sadolad into Sadolog and make Rayloc one of the most powerful shamans in the land.

Rayloc, Sadolad, and eight fighters burst into Seccolog's dwelling without knocking, while the remaining men stood guard around the outside. Several people were sitting on robes around a large evening meal. Seccolog struggled to his feet. Podeclad and Aduclad were both there and jumped to their feet also.

"What is the meaning of this? What are you doing in my village? Where is Sincolad?"

Sadolad rushed Seccolog, stepped behind him, and put a dagger to his neck. Seccolog struggled, and Sadolad pushed the dagger into his neck. Blood started to flow. "Everyone be quiet, or you will all die." Sadolad's voice was cold and threatening. "Bind and gag everyone." There were three women there besides Seccolog, his sons, and Bolanlik.

Rayloc pushed Seccolog aside and stood in his place. Several of those who were tied tried to call out, but only muddled sounds came through their gags. "Seccolog is a poor leader—a weak leader. His sons are all weak and are not worthy of leading a village such as this."

Sadolad drug Seccolog in front of those who were now tied and lying on the ground. "Seccolog, you took my mother as a pleasure mate from Romelog's tribe. You broke all the promises that were made to her and her father."

Sadolad turned to Bolanlik. "You forced my mother to be a camp whore. You caused her pain, and you caused her death. Now, death comes to your dwelling."

Sadolad raised his left hand. At that signal, the fighters cut the women's throats. At the last second, Sadolad held the arm of the fighter who was to kill Bolanlik. Podeclad and Aduclad struggled to get to their feet, but the fighters knocked them down. Seccolog stared blankly at Sadolad.

Sadolad spoke to Bolanlik. "Sincolad ran from me like a woman. He died as a coward running for his worthless life."

Bolanlik shook her head as tears ran from her eyes.

Sadolad walked to Aduclad and stuck a dagger into his heart as two warriors stood him up. Then he turned to Podeclad. "Podeclad, you were my friend, but our friendship can no longer be. You must pay for the evil of your father and mother."

Podeclad bumped one of the fighters holding him with his shoulder and spun away from Sadolad. Sadolad grabbed him by the chin from behind and cut his throat. Blood spurted from the wound as Podeclad spun around to face Sadolad, covering Sadolad with his blood before he fell dead.

"My men will find and kill all the pleasure mates in your family, along with all their children," Sadolad said to Seccolog. "They will be brought here before the sun rises, and you will see them all die before you die. You will see the end of your seed." Turning to Bolanlik, he added, "Know this: I will be chief of this village. My heritage mate is Pothialik, daughter of Romelog. Our children will rule over this village forever. Seccolog and his sons will be forgotten."

As the women and children were brought and slaughtered, the tent filled with the smell of blood and body wastes. The sun was rising. Rayloc had not seen Conchelik. "Where are Conchelik and her child?"

One of the fighters came forward. "She ran from the tent holding the baby. One of the fighters shot her with a bow and arrow. She fell but was not dead. The fighters stabbed her and her baby before they could cry out and wake the village."

"Where are the bodies?" Rayloc asked.

"We left them hidden behind the dwelling because we didn't want to take a chance of being seen with the bodies. I was sure she was dead, but I stabbed her and the baby several times more, and then I cut her throat."

Sadolad turned to Seccolog and Bolanlik. "The end of you and your family comes now," he said to Seccolog as he pulled his head back and cut his throat. Rayloc watched with fascination because Sadolad had to cut into Seccolog's throat several times in order to cut through the fat and get to the arteries.

Sadolad turned to Bolanlik, who crouched on the floor still tied and gagged. "I watched my mother die a slow, miserable death because you sent her to the fighters. I didn't care, because, on your orders, everyone told me Rundolik was nothing but a worthless camp whore. My mother was all the family I had. You have watched your family die. One last thing is required of you—prepare yourself."

The fighters lifted Bolanlik to her feet and held her while Sadolad plunged his dagger into her heart.

After the killing was done, Rayloc gathered the leaders of the village. He clenched his teeth to stop his jaw from shaking as he waited with the rest for Sadolad to appear. Everything depended on how the village responded to what Sadolad would say. Rayloc's future was in Sadolad's hands. The bodies of Seccolog and his two sons were laid out in front of the tent. The leaders began to question what had happened. Sadolad strutted into the meeting, taking the place of the chief at the meeting table. He wore Seccolog's finest leather clothing. One of the best seamstresses had worked on it most of the night to make it fit. The questioning stopped, and everything went silent. "You know me. I am Sadolad, son of Seccolog and Rundolik. You know of Seccolog's oath that Rundolik's son would become heritage son if Seccolog's sons all died. Sincolad died in the mountains, and you see Seccolog and his other sons before you. I come to the leaders of the village to present my claim. I am chief of this village by heritage bloodline."

An old man stood. "I am Beladad. We all know of the oath. Seccolog and his sons Aduclad and Podeclad have been killed. We are told Sincolad is also dead. Can Sadolad become chief through murder?"

Rayloc stood. "It is well known Seccolog broke his agreement with Rundolik's father. Seccolog did not honor and esteem Rundolik as he promised. Seccolog tried to steal Sadolad's birthright by sending him to another village. Seccolog dishonored his promises. Seccolog dishonored this village. For these things, he deserved to die."

"Many were killed who did not help Seccolog do these things," Beladad said.

"All members of Seccolog's family knew of the promises. All agreed with him," Rayloc answered.

"I am the only bloodline chief of the village," Sadolad said.

Beladad spoke up. "Sincolad has a son who is Seccolog's heritage bloodline. The agreement with Rundolik is invalid as long as a bloodline heritage son lives."

"What do you mean, Beladad?" Rayloc said.

"Upon the death of Seccolog, Sincolad's son became chief."

"No!" Sadolad shouted. "Conchelik is dead, and so is her child!"

"I don't see the body of Conchelik and her son."

"Where are the bodies?" Sadolad demanded of the fighters that had just returned from Sincolad's dwelling.

"There was a mistake," one of the fighters answered. "The body was Fredalik. She was carrying a travel bundle, not a baby. She must have been following Conchelik."

"Who is responsible for this treason?" Sadolad shouted.

"Wait!" Rayloc stood with his hand in the air. "We will check this story, but all this is not important. Seccolog promised if Bolanlik's sons died, Rundolik's children would become the heritage children of Seccolog. Sincolad's son was not born when the agreement was made, and his son is not Bolanlik's son."

"The agreement does not limit the heritage sons to those who were alive at that time. Sincolad's son was born before Seccolog died. He is heritage son by law," Beladad argued.

Sadolad walked to Beladad and looked coldly into his eyes. "The agreement made by Seccolog does not say anything about other heritage sons. Whether Sincolad's son is alive or not makes no difference."

Beladad quietly sat down.

"We will do the ceremony to change Sadolad's name to Sadolog. This village will have a new chief," Rayloc said.

Rayloc preformed the ceremony with the proper formality. Sadolad received the robes of chief from Rayloc and became Sadolog.

When Rayloc and Sadolog were alone, Sadolog said, "We must find out if Conchelik has escaped."

"I will find the truth," Rayloc said. "But even if she did get away, the ceremony is complete. You are chief now. The leadership of the village will always rest in your hands and your heritage sons."

"Find out if Conchelik is alive. If she and her son live, we must find them. Many will share Beladad's argument. It is dangerous to have anyone who might make a claim to my authority."

"You are right, Sadolog. We will find their bodies. If they are not here, we will search the earth to find and kill them."

Summer was nearly over, and though there were some signs of dissatisfaction in the village, most everyone accepted Sadolog as chief. Rayloc knocked on Sadolog's dwelling post.

"Enter a dwelling where Zendolot, praise to him, rules," Sadolog ordered.

Rayloc stepped into the tent. Pothialik moved the robe of honor for Rayloc and returned to her place behind Sadolog. She was pregnant with Sadolog's first child. "Several chiefs have joined together to say they will not trade with this village unless I pay them tribute," Sadolog complained as Rayloc sat on the robe.

"What will we do?"

"I will challenge them."

"I have heard that many villages have joined to fight Sadolog. We must ask Romelog to loan some of his fighters to help."

"No. I have already heard from Romelog. He is now threatened by the southern villages. They say he must pay them tribute for helping me. Romelog is asking me to send fighters to him. If I do not, he says he must join with the other southern villages. We were the strongest village, but the other villages join together to hold me down with tributes."

Rayloc listened to these words in anger and frustration. He had planned to be the strongest and most powerful shaman in the land by being shaman of the strongest and most powerful village. "All the villages resent the way you became chief. All the other chiefs want to make an example of Sadolog. They do not understand the promise Seccolog made to Rundolik. They do not know about the treachery Seccolog's family did to you and your mother."

"We should call for a rendezvous to explain these things."

"I tell you these things to show your power is not stolen. This is not a time to bend to the other chiefs." Rayloc watched Sadolog's eyes turn cold. It was as if Rayloc had accused him of being like his father. "You would never do such a thing," Rayloc added with emphasis.

"No, I would not. I spoke only in sarcasm. I would kill them all first!"

"I know you would. They think they can give orders to Sadolog, but they do not know Sadolog." Rayloc was encouraged by Sadolog's anger and willingness to fight.

"I will take fighters at night and kill all the chiefs."

"This is a good way, but it will enrage the villages all around. They will think of Sadolog as one who sneaks in the night."

"I will not pay tribute to other villages."

"Yes. Much better that they pay tribute to you."

"But how will I get enough fighters to force them to pay tribute?"

"I have ideas, but they need the wisdom of a powerful leader. These are ideas that should not be discussed in the presence of women."

Sadolog told Pothialik to find something to do outside of the dwelling.

"Sadolog, you took me for a heritage mate to make a strong bond with Romelog's village. I carry your child. If it's a boy, he will be your heritage son. Everything you do now will form the life he will lead. I have left my home because I see that an alliance between your village and my father's village will create strength."

"This is a council of men, Pothialik. Say what you must and then leave." Sadolog was firm. Rayloc thought of Seccolog and Bolanlik. What a difference!

"My brother is heritage son in Romelog's village. He is weak. I have thought many summers that the village will be weak when Romelog dies. I have seen the strength of Sadolog. I see a man who will change old ways to strengthen his people. My father begins to show weakness. Sadolog is not a man to depend upon such men. Sadolog will take bold new steps to change the old ways."

"Pothialik speaks the thoughts of Rayloc," Rayloc said.

"My words are to support Sadolog in times of change. I have seen how the other villages mock Sadolog. I know he is not a weak chief. The old ways say this village must remain weak. I see that Sadolog is a strong leader, much too strong to be a servant of old ways that hold him down. He will make new laws and new ways. Many will try to fight against the change Sadolog will bring. I will make any sacrifice for Sadolog and this child I carry. They are my family, my only family." Pothialik walked from the dwelling.

"Sometimes I do not understand that woman," Sadolog said.

"She sees much for a woman. She understands the need for change and the trouble change will cause."

"And that's what your plan is about?"

"Yes."

"Tell me your plan."

"Fighters make contests to show strength, skill, and courage. If a village with a few good fighters challenges a village with many fighters, even when the good fighters win, they have to fight on against the extra fighters. While they fight with the extra fighters, the first fighters rest. Then, the rested fighters challenge the good fighters again, while the last defeated fighters get to rest. In this way, the good fighters are finally worn down and defeated. This is not a fair way to decide a winner. Fighters are injured and sometimes killed in this process. You have strong fighters, but the other villages have more fighters."

"This is the way it has always been. In this way the village with the most fighters must win."

"Sadolog has the best fighters. Sadolog's village should be the strongest, but now they band together."

"This is true."

"The other villages join together to hold you down. In the old way, you will lose."

"This is unfair."

"This is a new thing. Pothialik has said Sadolog must make a new way. I say you must make a new kind of fighting to win against these villages that join together against you. You must make a kind of fighting where the village with the best fighters would defeat villages with many fighters."

"A new kind of fighting is needed. One where the fighters who win can also rest."

"This would be fair, but it would not be accepted by the other villages. We must make a new way of fighting that does not require other villages to agree."

"How can I make the other villages fight the way I choose?"

"Sadolog must surprise the other villages with a new kind of fighting. Sadolog's fighters must fight to kill those who fight against them. In this way, they will only have to defeat a fighter one time. Fighters who have not learned to fight this way will be surprised. Many will give up rather than die."

"Word will spread. Soon, all fighters will fight to kill. Contests will become bloody, and both sides will lose."

"Sadolog must surprise the villages to fight them one at a time. The first fights will happen before the villages hear of this fighting. Sadolog will force the fighters of the village he defeats to join with Sadolog's fighters. Fighters will be honored. They will share in the wealth they take from the villages. Women from the defeated villages will be given to strong fighters. Tribute will be given to the fighters, and their families will be treated better than all others. Then, all fighters will be loyal to Sadolog. Each village will pay tribute to support the fighters. Soon, all young men will want to be fighters. They will be higher than hunters. Only the best will be allowed to join. In this way, the fighters of Sadolog's village will grow stronger. Then, let that news travel. Many villages will give up to Sadolog without a fight, as soon as they know they must die if they fight."

Sadolog sat in thought momentarily. "Zendolot, praise to him, stands for peace and harmony. But he creates peace by strength and power. Zendolot, praise to him, banned Dracolut to the dark caverns. He organized the spirits of the brave men to be stars and guard the night. Through this power, Zendolot, praise to him, keeps evil trapped in the dark caverns. When I was a young man, I dreamed of the kind of fighting you talk about. I planned it all out just as you have described it. This is power. This new fighting needs new words."

Both men sat in silence. Rayloc was excited in a way he had never experienced. On the night he killed Nacoloc, he felt something similar, but now he was on the verge of something greater than he had ever imagined. With this new fighting, he and Sadolog could command all the villages. There had never been anyone as powerful as they would be.

"We will call this new fighting, *war*," Sadolog said, "a short word that will carry strong meaning. It will create fear in all who hear it. Fighters will be called warriors. Warriors will be the only favored group of the village. There will be no more hunters. Our best hunters and fighters will become warriors. There will be no hunter ceremonies. Rayloc will create a new ceremony … a warrior ceremony. The warriors will be called Sadolog's army. The warriors will be on earth just like Zendolot's stars are in the sky. They will become stars when they die. The night sky will become so bright when storms come that Dracolut will not leave the dark caverns."

Rayloc strained to remember all the new words Sadolog made up. Sadolog sat straighter. Rayloc could see a new pride, a new purpose in Sadolog. "It will be done as Sadolog says."

"In the villages we conquer, there will be no chiefs to lead rebellions against me. In all villages, it must be as it was with Seccolog. Each village must be cleansed of all who could make a claim to leadership."

Rayloc had not thought of this. "Such killing will create rebellion."

"Such killing will create shock and fear. There will be no one to make a rebellion against me. The best fighters and hunters will die or become my warriors. I will be called Warlog. They will be taught to honor Warlog. Any who make rebellion will be killed. Each village will be ruled, temporarily, by one of my most trusted warriors. My warriors who are left to lead the villages will be called warlents. In time, we will pick a strong man from the village to rule. He will be called Warlog's governor. There will be no more chiefs in the villages. By picking a governor from the village, the people will feel my trust, but the governor must be loyal to me. The People will see I am a strong, fearless leader who will give support and trust to those who are my friends. My armies will protect all the villages. All the villages will be joined into one great village. I will call this the Empire. It will be Zendolot's Empire. I will govern Zendolot's Empire for the good of all, and the only tribute that will be paid will be paid to me. Any villages that do not honor me and my rules will be punished by my armies."

"This is a good plan," Rayloc said, not hiding the admiration in his voice.

"When there are no chiefs but Warlog, there will be no other names with log at the end. There will be no other leader in the land. I will be chief of all the villages, chief of all the warriors, chief of all the People. I have been sent by Zendolot, praise to him, to rule over this people. I will watch over them and bring unity and cooperation to all my empire. My warriors will be called Warlog's army. I will rule all the land through my army. Rayloc will create ceremonies for the warriors to pledge obedience to Warlog and none else.

"As the army travels across the land, it will grow. No defeated village will be allowed to have its own warriors. Each village will give new warriors to my army. They will give hunters, workers, cooks, and camp whores to support the warriors. The warriors will practice the skills of war and fight wars when I tell them. The rest of the time will be free time to play, eat, and pleasure themselves with the camp whores.

"I will govern all trading. There will be no more fights over hunting areas or trading. I will bring order and peace to all the People."

Rayloc had thought about having power and even about how to get it. But Warlog had thought much deeper about it. He had a clear idea about the problems of getting power and a plan to keep and use it.

As Rayloc returned to his dwelling, he thought about the new ceremonies. He would be the one to create new spiritual foundations of a new world order that would be governed by Warlog, with Rayloc as his first assistant.

Warlog spent the first part of the summer picking and training his best fighters and hunters to be warriors.

In midsummer, Warlog led his new army south. It was hard for Rayloc to make another trip to Romelog's village so soon, but it was clear Warlog needed Romelog's help to ensure early success in his new war. Rayloc was confident

Warlog could convince Romelog to join with him. On the trip across the Ice Mountains, Warlog taught his new warriors the importance of fighting to kill.

If Romelog accepted Warlog's concept of war, they would choose his strongest hunters and fighters to become warriors. If Romelog did not support Warlog, his village would be the first to experience modern war. By the time they arrived, Warlog had made a plan to defeat Romelog if it became necessary. He set up his camps around Romelog's village according to his war plan.

Romelog welcomed Warlog and his men. After a feast to celebrate the alliance between the villages, Rayloc and Warlog were invited to Romelog's dwelling to discuss plans to deal with the southern villages.

"I am grateful my friend Sadolog has come to honor the friendship between our two villages. In honor of this great day, I give this puppy to Sadolog. It is the strongest of a litter from the best goat dogs of this village. The goat dogs watch and protect the goats. They are patient and caring to the goats, but they are strong with wolves that threaten the herd. So it is with a great chief and his people. So it is with Sadolog, my friend."

"I accept this gift from my friend Romelog. This dog will symbolize my leadership of the People. I will call him Kozid." Warlog took the puppy and smiled.

"Now we have enough fighters to defeat any village. The coastal villages have cut off salt and shell trade with my village. At first they demanded tribute to trade, but now they refuse to trade at all. This is an insult. We must completely crush them."

"I agree. Your problems are similar to my own."

"As soon as we defeat the southern villages, I will send my fighters north with Sadolog."

"My village is unprotected and under great pressure because I have come to help Romelog. When you send your fighters north, what will the southern villages do to your village? Won't they come to take tribute and teach you a lesson?"

"If they do, you will send your fighters back to punish them."

"And if I do, what will happen to my village while I am gone?"

"I do not understand. What are we to do?"

"We must fight so that other villages will never dare challenge us."

Warlog explained the new kind of fighting and the new words. "I have changed my name to Warlog," Warlog concluded.

"Many will reject Warlog's new fighting," Romelog said.

"There is no organization among the People," Rayloc said. "Trading is governed by the strength of the individual villages. If the southern villages choose to force Romelog's village out of the salt and shell trade, what can you do? Nothing! This is not fairness. Treachery, such as Seccolog was responsible for, is ignored. There is no way to correct such things. The People need a strong leader who can stand for small villages and ensure fairness among all villages."

"This is so, but you talk of starting killing that will spread to all the villages."

"No. I will create an army of the strongest warriors. At first there will be fighting and killing, but soon my army will be so strong no village will challenge me. By the time I have conquered three or four villages, my army will have grown, and its reputation will become known throughout the land. Villages will learn no one can stand against me. When that time comes, there will be no more fighting and no more war. My men will be the strongest and best-trained warriors in all the land."

The puppy, Kozid, struggled and whined in Warlog's arms. "I will train this dog to be a war dog. He will fight side by side with the warriors, and from him, we will breed a new kind of dog ... war dogs that will fight my enemies.

"When the villages are under my leadership, trading disputes will be decided fairly, without fighting. The People will be ruled by justice. There will be peace, and all villages will prosper. I do not bring killing and conflict. I bring peace and well-being."

"You argue well. I see this future of peace and fairness among the villages of the People. I worry about what must be done to make it happen. I worry about rebellious villages and the killing that will grow from such rebellion."

"There will be no rebellion. What single village could create an army on its own to challenge the army Warlog will create from all the villages? When I have created a new order among the villages, all villages will prosper. There will be no need to rebel. It will be unnecessary and useless. This is the natural result of war."

During the winter, new warriors were selected from Romelog's village. Warlog taught them the new kind of fighting—he taught them war.

Summer 3302 BCE

As summer was beginning, Warlog led his army to the first village he would challenge. When the challenge was issued, Rayloc watched the village's fighters assemble to answer. The chief, Kedolog, stepped in front of his assembled fighters and walked from the village with his arms up and his palms forward, making the sign to talk. The village was located at the top of a small hill. Their crops were on the other side of the hill where a small spring flowed.

Warlog's army consisted of twenty-seven warriors from his and Romelog's villages. Rayloc counted only sixteen fighters behind Kedolog. Fourteen hunters stood where they had a good view of the contests.

Warlog's warriors would have to fight their way up the hill. Rayloc began to doubt Warlog could win. What if the warriors lost their courage? What if Kedolog's hunters joined to help the fighters when they saw them being killed? Rayloc realized his whole future depended upon what happened on this morning. If Warlog lost today, Rayloc's dreams would be over.

As Kedolog came down the hill, Rayloc thought of the years Warlog had spent growing up as a mascot for Seccolog's fighters. He hadn't been a leader. Warlog could die on this hill, along with Rayloc's dreams. A wave of nausea come over him, and his knees were weak.

"I am Kedolog, chief to this village. Who are you, and what is the meaning of this challenge?" Kedolog spoke loud enough for all to hear. He was taller than Warlog. He wore only shoes, loin cloth, and leggings. The muscles of his chest and arms glistened in the sun. His shoulder-length hair blew in the breeze. There was anger in his eyes.

"I am Warlog. I come for payment for the wrongs you put upon Romelog and upon me."

"I do not know you. I have not wronged you or your people. Romelog is a traitor to the southern villages. He assisted Sadolad, the son of a camp whore, in the murder of Seccolog and all his family."

"That woman was called Rundolik. I am told Rundolik was a daughter of the southern villages. I am told Seccolog made her a camp whore."

"What a chief does with one of his women is not important, and a camp whore is a camp whore. You come with many fighters, but my fighters are strong and skillful. Leave now!"

As Kedolog continued to mock Rundolik, Warlog shouted, "You have insulted Rundolik. For that you must die."

Kedolog took a step back. Warlog pulled the hunting hatchet tucked in his belt.

"What are you doing with that?"

Warlog swung the copper-headed hatchet with deadly accuracy at Kedolog's neck. The hatchet sliced through his neck neatly. It severed all the blood vessels, though it missed the bones. Kedolog's head flopped back, and blood spurted out in a fountain visible to everyone. His body wavered as if it would stand in defiance, and then it crumpled to the earth. Something had changed forever.

The whole field hung in silence. Warlog seemed to sense the question that grew in the minds of his men. "Attack! Attack!" he shouted. His men stood in shock, on the verge of running from this new war. Warlog put an arrow in his bow and took quick aim at Kedolog's strongest fighter. The fighter tried to dodge. The arrow just missed his heart, lodging in his shoulder.

Kedolog's fighters screamed in unison and started running down the hill. The attack of the fighters was slowed as a storm of arrows flew at them. Six fell dead, and two more were wounded. Warlog's men responded the way they were taught.

There was another pause, and then Kedolog's hunters sent arrows on Warlog's new army with deadly accuracy. Seven of Warlog's men fell. Kedolog's fighters renewed their charge, and the hunters ran down the hill to join them.

The men on the right side of Warlog's line held their ground against Kedolog's fighters. Kedolog's hunters hit hardest on the left side. The men on that side were falling. Warlog had brought men who were prepared and trained to kill, but in the face of an actual enemy, they were as frightened and uncertain as Kedolog's men. In fact, Kedolog's hunters were the most aggressive in the fight. Rayloc could see that if the left side of Warlog's line failed, Kedolog's hunters would come up on the right side. Everything would be lost.

Rayloc saw Warlog drop his bow and pick up a spear in each hand. He charged toward the left side of his line screaming. He threw his first spear at close range. It hit one of the hunters in the heart. Warlog raced forward and joined his men. He drove his remaining spear into another hunter's chest.

Rayloc could see through the dust and confusion that Warlog was running past his retreating men. Then he was alone among Kedolog's hunters. He had struck so fast that none of the hunters had been ready to retaliate. Warlog pulled a dagger from his belt in each hand. Kedolog's hunters had now turned to him.

Warlog dodged the thrust of the first spear. Rayloc screamed at the warriors. Warlog quickly spun around from a crouch and moved under the spear to strike at the hunter's thigh with the dagger in his left hand. Rayloc knew the warriors couldn't hear his screams. He started running toward the retreating warriors, screaming and waving his arms in the direction where Warlog was battling. Rayloc could see some of Kedolog's men on the ground.

Somehow Warlog had gotten one of their spears, which he was waving around to keep Kedolog's men back.

As Kedolog's men began to tighten the circle around Warlog, his warriors rallied and raced back up the hill.

Warlog's men burst into the circle with such furry that three of the hunters were killed, and the rest retreated up the hill. The battle progressed up the hill for only a short time. Once Warlog's men were advancing all across the line, Kedolog's fighters and hunters dropped their weapons and ran.

The battle had not lasted long enough for the shadows of the sun to move. Nine of Warlog's warriors were dead. Two more were seriously wounded, and several had minor cuts and bruises. Fourteen of Kedolog's hunters and fighters were dead.

Warlog was wounded, but his wounds were not serious. His war plan had worked, but the price was high.

After Warlog and his warriors had quieted the village, Rayloc explained to the villagers how Warlog would bring fairness, justice, and prosperity to all the People. He told them what a warrior was and the many benefits of being a warrior, and he offered the opportunity to become a warrior to the strongest survivors of Kedolog's men.

Rayloc had barely finished creating the warrior ceremony by changing the old hunter ceremony. All the men of Kedolog's village who accepted the call to be a warrior and all Warlog's men participated in the new Warrior Ceremony of the Hand swearing to obey and honor Warlog.

Warlog rested a day, and then he addressed the village. "I am Warlog the Great Eagle of Zendolot. Zendolot, praise to him, has sent me to bring order and prosperity to all the villages of the People. There will be no more fighting between villages over trading. Villages will no longer have fighters. All people will work to produce food and clothing. All villages will be more prosperous. I will govern all trading. Today, I will appoint one of my warriors to govern this village. He will be called warlent. There will be no more chiefs in the villages of the People. When you are ready, I will appoint a wise member of your village to govern for me. He will be called Warlog's governor.

"As you live in peace according to my law, you will prosper. You will pay a small tribute to me to maintain an army. In the past, strong villages have taken advantage of the weak ones. This will never happen again. From this day on, the villages of the People will devote all their energy for the welfare of the People in the Empire of Zendolot. There will be no rich or poor. Everyone will share equally in the bounty of the earth."

There was much unrest among the members of Kedolog's village. His oldest son, Fradolad, was sent to Warlog with questions. After listening to Fradolad's complaints and questions, Warlog asked all Kedolog's family be brought to him. "Fradolad has come with questions for me regarding the new laws that I bring. As son of Kedolog, it is his right and duty to come to me this way. If he should die, then it would be his brother's duty, or his son, or nephew. This is so for all Kedolog's descendants. This questioning brings unrest and threatens to destroy the peace I bring. This cannot be allowed now, tomorrow, next summer, or ten summers from now. It is not their fault, but all who carry the seeds of Kedolog bear fruit of unrest and rebellion. Like weeds in a garden, they must be plucked out."

At Warlog's signal, his warriors killed all Kedolog's family. It was necessary to use force to quiet the village.

Warlog and his warriors remained in the village for two more days to make sure Warlog's government was strong and all signs of rebellion were suppressed.

"I am anxious to get started with my army," Warlog said to Rayloc.

"We must make certain what we have gained is not lost when we leave."

"What you say is true, but I'm sure some people of this village have run away to warn the others of our new way of fighting. You saw how many of my warriors were lost even though we surprised Kedolog's men. The army is supposed to grow, but even with the new warriors we gained, we have two less warriors than when we started. We must fight villages that have been warned. They will be prepared to kill."

"This is more difficult than we thought. But I watched these men fighting, and I noticed that at first the men on both sides approached the battle with hesitation. As much as we tried to prepare our warriors to kill, when they were faced with killing, they held back."

"The first arrows were deadly."

"They were, but until the first men fell, the idea of killing was only an idea. When our warriors faced the reality of what they had done with those first arrows, that's when there was hesitation. That's when Kedolog's men attacked. Because of our hesitation, they chased our men back. At first the fighting was uncertain on both sides, but the anger increased when they realized they had to kill or be killed. Then the men on both sides were trying to kill without hesitation until the moment Kedolog's men broke and ran."

"This is true. There was a great deal of killing ... more than I expected. That's why it's so hard to increase the size of my army. By the time the killing is over, there are not enough men left to rebuild the army. If we lose more men at the next village, the army will be even weaker. In two or three villages, we will not have enough men to continue. I expected my army to grow, not shrink."

"To talk about killing and to actually kill are not the same. You saw it with your warriors. The losses we suffered resulted from those moments of hesitation after the first arrows."

"How can we impress upon the warriors that they have to fight without hesitation?"

"I don't think that's necessary. These warriors have proven themselves. They broke through the old ways of contests. They all fought with ferocity at the end of the battle. These men will not hesitate again. Even though the other villages are warned. Even though they talk of killing in a fight, their hunters and fighters will hesitate, just as your warriors did this time, but your warriors will not hesitate. They have passed through something none of their opponents have. When the other village's men hesitate, that's when your warriors will crush them. Each time they fight, they will become stronger in their minds. Everything depends on the first moments of the fight. That's when the man who has fought to kill will have the advantage."

"I hope what you say is true. I will take my warriors forward tomorrow. I don't want to give them time to think about what we do."

"You're right. You must move while their blood is still hot."

"I will leave you two warriors to make sure this village has a strong government."

"A few days will be enough. I will make one of the warriors the warlent, and I will follow as soon as possible so I can set up your government at the next village."

Near the end of summer, Warlog's army returned to Romelog's village. "I have heard of your great successes," Romelog said in greeting.

"We have beaten all the southern villages, and they are now part of the Zendolot's Empire."

"I have heard there was much killing."

"It is as I said it would be. At first, the villages fought. They could not resist my army. After each victory, my army grew. Soon, it was known throughout the land that no one could stand against me. Then people welcomed my army with flowers. Rayloc has organized all the villages and set warlents to govern them according to my law. All the southern villages will be controlled from this village."

"I have prepared a great feast for your return."

It was a great celebration. The morning after the celebration, Warlog ordered his army to kill Romelog and all his family. All except Pothialik, who was still north of the Ice Mountains. It would not be necessary to kill her because her children would be Warlog's children.

The next day, Warlog left with his army to cross the Ice Mountains before the first winter storm. When Rayloc entered the valley, he was dumbfounded by what he saw. The fields were trampled, the orchards burned, and the dwellings destroyed. Only a few old members of the village were left. They were barely able to find enough scraps of food to live.

An old man came from the remains of a burned dwelling. "Warlog, I am Nodelad."

"I know, Nodelad. Tell me what has happened to my village."

"Many people have come from the southern villages this summer. They brought stories of a new kind of fighting with much killing. The northern villages came to destroy Warlog's village with more fighters than I have ever seen. They give a warning to Warlog."

"What do they say?"

"The fighters have taken all the people of Warlog's village to their own villages. They say Warlog must return to the southern villages. They say they have heard of Warlog's new fighting. They say they will kill Warlog and his army if he does not return to the southern villages. They say there is no place for Warlog among the northern villages."

"What of Pothialik?"

"Pothialik had a healthy heritage son for Warlog. When the fighters came, they talked of killing Warlog's heritage son. Pothialik sneaked out of the village with him. The fighters chased after her and the baby. They killed them, so there would be nothing for Warlog on this side of the Ice Mountains."

Warlog said nothing. He walked to the remains of his dwelling. Rayloc followed him. "What shall I do now? I have lost all I fought for. My village is lost, my people are scattered, and I have lost Pothialik and my son."

"Warlog can have more villages and more heritage sons. The northern villages do not know the strength of Warlog's army. They laugh at Warlog now, but before next summer is over, you will destroy those who did this. You will take revenge, and then all the villages in the North and South will pay tribute to Warlog. You will make a new village and take a new heritage mate and have many heritage sons."

"You have known me, Rayloc, but you have not known me. I do not want another heritage mate. Pothialik was given to me to make a political gain. She was a convenience then, but she has become my reason to conquer. Without her, my spirit has no force. An empty man is not a conqueror. Leave me now."

Once again, Rayloc's plans were threatened. "All these plans started before Pothialik. The force that drives these plans is deeper than Pothialik."

"Rayloc, my old friend, before Pothialik, I was driven by hatred for Seccolog and his family. I was driven to get even for what they did to Rundolik. I have done that. After they were dead, the fire in my heart began to die. It was then that Pothialik kindled a desire in my spirit to create an empire for my children."

"But you will still have children. You are a young man."

"Maybe," Warlog answered without conviction.

Nothing Rayloc said could move Warlog from his desolation.

As the sun set, a woman walked into the village. Her clothes were ragged, and her face was dirty. She carried a small baby sleeping in her arms. Her face was gaunt. At first no one recognized her, but then Rayloc did. He told her about Warlog's despair and followed her to Warlog's dwelling.

"Who is this man sitting in the ruins of Warlog's dwelling and talking of defeat?"

Warlog lifted his head. He turned slowly. "I know this voice, but who are you?"

"I have stayed in the mountains and foothills near the village, waiting for Warlog. Waiting for the greatest warrior the world has ever seen. I hear he is not a man. I hear he quakes in fear of Cadelog, leader of the northern armies. I hear this from Rayloc. But Rayloc doesn't know the man who held me in his arms. He doesn't know the man who told me of his great dreams to bring peace and happiness to all the People. Rayloc doesn't know the dreams I've known."

"Pothialik? Is it truly you? They said you were dead." Warlog stood up. He looked intently at the thin woman before him. "When I left, you were fat with child. Now, you are only the bones of the woman I left."

"I have lived in the mountains eating bugs in order to make milk for your son. He is heritage son of Warlog the Great Eagle of Zendolot. Your enemies would kill him. See what they have done to your village. See what they have done to your family. They tell you to leave the land of your fathers. Who are these men to order Warlog the Great Eagle of Zendolot? Who tells him to leave as a yelping dog? They do not understand the wisdom and power of Warlog."

"Pothialik brings the hope of all the people with her." Warlog took his son from her arms. "It's true, these men of the northern villages do not understand the danger they have made. They have heard of war, now they will learn of war. By the power of Zendolot, praise to him, and the promise of this heritage son, I will punish those who attacked this village and tried to kill Pothialik. I will establish my law and my peace in all the land. My son will be called Pothelad until he is a man, and I am too old to govern the People. Then he will become Warlog the Great Eagle of Zendolot. No army can prevent that. Rayloc, make preparations. We leave in two days."

CHAPTER 2

Sotif—The History Man

Summer 3292 BCE

Sotif sat on the thinking rock in front of the Heart of the Bison cave located about halfway up the low mountain southeast of the Winding River village. He thought of the great priestess, Kectu, who had sat upon this stone hundreds of generations ago at the beginning of the Alliance between Earth People and Sun People. Kectu was a great shorec of the Earth People. She gave the Spirit Fire to the Earth People. The fire she started still burned in the cave behind Sotif. He thought of Kectu's grandson, Shekek, who had started the Alliance between the Earth People and the Sun People. The Earth People were short and muscular. Their faces had small chins and low foreheads. Their mouths and teeth were large. Their eyes were set deep below protruding brow ridges. They had light skin, blue eyes, and light brown hair. Sun People were tall and agile. They had long chins and high foreheads. They had brown skin and black or brown hair. Their eyes were brown. Like Shekek, Sotif was a half-breed, part Sun People and part Earth People. Sotif's mother was the daughter of one of the ancients of the Earth People. His father was one of the tradition men of the Sun People. When he was weaned, he was taken from his mother. He had never known his mother or father. He was not sad because of this. He was bred and born to be the History Man of the Alliance. He belonged to the Alliance, and the Alliance was his family.

Sotif looked out over the valley. According to the stories, in Kectu's time it was filled with trees of a dense forest. Now, the village occupied a large portion of the land on the east side of the river. Much of the land was cleared, and fields of einkorn waved in the midsummer breeze. Scattered around the fields were fruit trees. On the grassy hillsides, goats and sheep foraged.

An old man approached Sotif. "The Supreme Council will meet soon. Sotif must help Senlo with the ceremony robe," Senlo said in the simple language of the Earth People.

Sotif stood. "Sotif will help Senlo." Sotif also spoke in Earth People language when he talked to Senlo. Senlo was the History Man of the Alliance.

"Senlo has become old. Senlo must give the ceremony robe to Sotif," Senlo said.

Sotif had studied under Senlo's guidance since he was eight summers old, in preparation to become the History Man when Senlo became too old. "Is Sotif ready to become History Man?" Though Sotif felt he was ready, he wanted Senlo's assurance.

"Sotif is ready. Sotif has been ready many seasons. Senlo is ready to rest. It is time for Sotif to take the ceremony robe Sotif was born to bear."

"Sotif has confusion. Sotif cannot name the cause of this confusion."

"So it always is with the History Man." As they walked, Senlo explained that each History Man must search for the meaning of his time. "Today Sotif must go to the Supreme Council with Senlo. Today Sotif must begin the search for the meaning of Sotif's time."

Sotif walked with Senlo to the meeting tent in the Winding River village below the cave called the Heart of the Bison. Sotif's brown, scraggly hair hung past his shoulders and swirled around his face in the breeze. His breath whistled through the space where the first canine on the right side had been pulled out two seasons ago because it had rotted. There was a scar across the side of his stomach from an accident during a hunting game when he was a child.

The Winding River colony of the Alliance, like all the other colonies, consisted of a village of Sun People and a clan of Earth People. The Earth People of each colony lived in a cave near the Sun People village. Usually the name of the colony and the name of the village were the same. In the Winding River colony, the Earth People cave was named the Heart of the Bison. That was the name Kectu had given the cave when she discovered it.

The ceremony structure was located near the southern end of the Winding River village. It was fifteen paces long and eight paces wide. The walls and roof were constructed of split logs. Inside, several log poles helped support the roof. At the northern end, there was a long, low table made of chiseled wood. The members of the Supreme Council sat around the table on robes placed on the ground.

Sotif followed Senlo to the table and helped him sit down. Senlo sat next to the head of the table. He placed a short, hardwood stick with one end burned black on the table in front of him. This was the symbol of the History Man. The members of the Supreme Council were already seated, except Tall Tree, the supreme leader of the council. Red Deer, chief of the Winding River tribe, sat at the end of the table opposite Tall Tree's space. Lewtud, shomot of all the Earth People, sat across the table from Senlo. Jeklot, leader of the Heart of the Bison clan of Earth People, sat next to Senlo. Long Shadow, shaman of the Winding River village of Sun People, sat across from Jeklot. Lotend, shomot of the Heart of the Bison clan, sat next to Long Shadow. In the rest of the structure were other secular and spiritual leaders of the colonies of the Alliance. Although not all colonies were represented, the structure was nearly full. After seating Senlo at the table, Sotif sat with the onlookers.

Tall Tree strutted in, accentuating his strong, tall body. He stood poised at the head of the table until all was quiet and everyone's attention was on him. He was Sun People. He picked up the speaking stick and pounded it three times on the table.

"There is much to discuss," Tall Tree began. He spoke the language of the Sun People. Sotif was impressed by Tall Tree's sense of place and position. Tall Tree was only three summers older than Sotif, but he commanded respect. "Hard times have come to the land. All across the Alliance there has been drought for many summers. Food is scarce, and the Alliance becomes weaker each summer. Generations ago, there were many colonies spread all across the world. There was much trading among the colonies. This made the Alliance strong. Now, the colonies are few and far apart. It's difficult to trade. It's difficult to help each other. The Alliance must change or our children's children will not know the Alliance."

A middle-aged Sun People man stood in the crowd. "I am Clear Stream, chief of the Sun People of the Deer Mountain colony. I ask to speak to the Supreme Council."

"The Supreme Council will listen to the words of Clear Stream." Tall Tree passed the talking stick to Clear Stream.

"The Deer Mountain colony is in the center of the eighteen colonies north of the Snow Mountains. There are many tribes of Sun People around our colony that are not part of the Alliance. Many of those tribes are closer to the Deer Mountain colony than the colonies of the Alliance. The chiefs of the eighteen villages believe the law forbidding trade with tribes of Sun People who are not part of the Alliance must be abolished. This will strengthen all people."

Lewtud requested the talking stick. He had a low forehead and almost no chin. His skull stuck out in the back like a bun. He was Earth People. "Lewtud speaks the mind of all the Earth People. The Memories and Traditions say the Sun People who are not of the Alliance killed the Earth People in the West. The Memories and Traditions say the Alliance must not trust the Sun People who are not of the Alliance."

"Who saw the Sun People kill the Earth People?" Clear Stream challenged.

Senlo requested the talking stick from Lewtud. Senlo spoke in the language of the Earth People. "Many people think the clans of the West are no more. Many people think the Sun People killed the clans of the West. These ideas are stories passed from parent to child. These ideas are not the Memories and Traditions. There are no Memories that say what happened. There are no Traditions that say what happened."

Sotif was surprised at Senlo's words. It was well known among all the People that the Sun People had killed the clans of the West. But thinking of Senlo's words, Sotif could not think of a Memory or a Tradition that said those things. He had believed it for so long he had never questioned its origin. The History Man must not only know what the Memories and Traditions say, but he must also know what they do not say. He had felt ready to be History Man, but now doubts entered his thoughts.

"That which Senlo says is true," Tall Tree agreed.

Clear Stream asked for and received the talking stick. "This fear of Sun People comes from the thinking of old men. Once, the Alliance was strong and covered the whole world. Then, it was wise to be separate from the other Sun People tribes. Now, things are different."

Red Deer took the talking stick. "There is much land on this side of the Snow Mountains. There are not many tribes of Sun People who do not belong to the Alliance here. If the eighteen colonies of the North move south of the Snow Mountains, there would be plenty of land, and the colonies would all be close together. Trading would be easy. It would be easier for the clans to bring ashes together for the Spirit Fire Ceremony. The Alliance would be stronger."

Clear Stream took the talking stick. "You would confine all our people to a small space. The clans of the Earth People don't like to move. They'd have to find new caves to be near the Sun People villages. Earth People are close to the earth. This lets them know weather and predict earthquakes. They see, hear, and smell better than any animal. These things are important to the Alliance. Earth People are tied to the earth, so change is slow with Earth People. Sun People find better ways to raise crops, better tools, and better ways of living. Sun People seek change and make change. This is also good for the Alliance. Moving is easy for Sun People, but it's difficult for Earth People. It pulls at their bonds to the earth. This is bad for the Alliance. The only way to strengthen the Alliance is to trade openly with all the tribes of Sun People."

Lewtud took the talking stick. "Earth People always hide from Sun People that are not part of the Alliance. The other Sun People do not know about Earth People. If trading begins, the other Sun People must find out about Earth People. If trading begins, the Sun People must want to kill the Earth People. The Sun People that are not of the Alliance cannot be trusted."

"This is an empty fear," Clear Stream sounded impatient as he took the talking stick again. He began to raise his voice. "Even Senlo says nobody knows what happened to the clans in the West. Sun People didn't kill them then, and they don't kill them now. There may be clans and tribes in the West. There may even be another alliance. We cannot let our life depend upon what old men think might have happened in the West many, many seasons ago. Trading with all people must begin or soon the people of the Alliance will be no more."

"What does Senlo say of the Sun People?" Tall Tree asked.

Senlo took the talking stick. "Senlo says … the Memories and Traditions do not answer this question. Senlo says … it is a longtime fear that the Sun People that are not of the Alliance killed the Earth People in the West. Senlo says … this may be a true thing. Senlo says … this may not be a true thing. If Sun People start killing Earth People, who could fix the mistake? Senlo says … such a mistake could not be fixed. Senlo says … it must be a big wrong to trade before the People find out if Sun People must kill Earth People."

"How are we going to know that, unless we start trading?" Clear Stream asked.

Lewtud took the talking stick. "Lewtud cannot answer this question. Clear Stream cannot answer this question. Even Senlo cannot answer this question. Trading can come only when the answer is found."

Tall Tree stood and raised both hands. "I've heard all the arguments. Now we should vote, but there is more to know. If we start trading with the others, it won't be possible to keep the Earth People hidden. Clear Stream believes this wouldn't be a problem. But if he's wrong, it would be too late to undo what would be started. If the Sun People do kill Earth People, the Alliance would be destroyed.

"We must find the answer before we vote. The Memories tell us at one time there were many tribes and clans in the West. The question of what happened to those people is important. It's possible that far to the other side of the Great Plains there are clans of Earth People living with tribes of Sun People. Before we decide to risk everything, we must know the truth about the clans and tribes west of the Great Plains."

"This is wise," Clear Stream agreed. "We should send men west to find the answer."

"We will send men across the Great Plains to see if there is a solution in the West," Tall Tree said.

"This is an unknown land," Senlo said. "This land may contain unknown dangers."

"If there are dangers in the West, it's better to see what they are than to wait in ignorance," Red Deer argued.

"The Memories say there is a good land in the West," Jeklot said. "The Memories say many clans lived there. The Memories say the Sun People came. The Memories say the Sun People killed too many of the food animals. The Memories say it became hard for the Earth People. Jeklot says ... the Supreme Council must wait to decide what to do until after the men return from the West with truth."

"We will choose two strong hunters to go west," Tall Tree said. "They will see what the land is like and if there are Sun People and Earth People there."

"Tall Tree must send a strong man of the Earth People to help find the Earth People," Lewtud said. "Tall Tree must send a strong man of the Earth People to talk to the Earth People of the West."

"Lewtud is right," Tall Tree agreed. "We will send a strong man of the Earth People with the hunters."

Sotif had a strong feeling of foreboding about the West, but he didn't know where it came from or what he should do about it.

Sotif began the long walk to the History Room. The day to take upon himself the ceremony robes of the History Man had finally come. It was the kind of day a man would want his mate, his parents, and his children to see. It was a time of pride and celebration for all family members. For the History Man, it was different. The child who was bred to become the History Man had no family. His father and mother mated only to give him a body. The History Man was a child of the Alliance. When he was small, that which would make it possible for him to have children was cut from him.

Sotif walked from the sunshine into the Heart of the Bison. The pungent aroma of the Heart of the Bison filled his nostrils. He had inherited a sensitive nose from his mother's people. It was easy for him to separate the many individual smells of the Heart of the Bison. He loved the fresh smell of wood burning in the Spirit Fire. He could pick out the odors of human habitation—stored food, body aromas, and wastes that accumulated but had not yet been removed from the cave. These were the smells of his home. Senlo said he would be a traveling History Man. Sotif could not imagine anything that could drive him from the cultural and spiritual center of the Alliance. He was sure Senlo was mistaken in this.

The light of his torch closed around him when Sotif entered the tunnel leading to the History Room. This was the spiritual center of his calling. He had come here when he was a trainee to contemplate the many paintings on the wall. Each time a significant event happened to the Alliance, the History Man of the time would design a painting to symbolize what had happened. The tradition man would then make a new story to explain the painting. Sotif wondered if he would be called upon to design a new painting. Would something so important happen during his time as History Man? It had been many generations since the last painting.

Sotif walked into the History Room. All the members of the Supreme Council were present to witness the passing of the ceremony robe of the History Man. A great pride wrapped in a sense of humility rushed over Sotif. He would soon take his place as an important member of this powerful group of men.

Senlo used a torch he had ignited at the Spirit Fire to light each of the eight torches of the History Room. In the flickering light of the torches, Sotif saw a small circle of rocks in the center. In the middle of the rocks there were dried wood and kindling. Senlo stood behind the circle of rocks facing the painting of the First Family. It was near the bottom of the wall. It depicted the story of how the shorec of the Earth People, Kectu, gave the Spirit Fire to the People. Kectu had mated with a Sun People man named White Cloud, and they had a daughter named Tuk. The painting showed that Tuk mated with Sky Runner, son of a great Sun People chief. Their son, Shekek, started the Alliance. All the other paintings of the History Room radiated out from this one.

"Sotif, come to the center of the History Room," Senlo commanded.

Senlo told the stories of the Memories the Earth People carried from birth in the hereditary part of their brains. The Memories told of the beginning of life on earth in the water and how that life came from the water and spread over the land. That life got very large and then was killed by fire from the sky. Mother Earth then put the first ancestors of people in a hot land where fire was spit out of the ground. Then the ancestors moved to a cold land, and the Earth People came into being. After many generations, the Sun People came to the land of the Earth People. "The Sun People did not honor Mother Earth. Mother Earth could not feed all the people. So say the Memories. The Memories are true."

Then Senlo explained the Traditions of the Earth People. The Traditions taught that Mother Earth sent a great shorec named Kectu to the Earth People. Kectu gave the Spirit Fire to the Earth People. The Alliance between Earth People and Sun People was begun by Kectu's grandson, Shekek. After many generations, the Alliance grew to cover the earth. Then a great flood came and destroyed the Alliance in the East. "The Alliance became. The Alliance is. The Alliance must always be. The Alliance honors Mother Earth. The Alliance honors the Great Spirit. So say the Traditions. The Traditions are true."

Then Senlo concluded, "These are the Traditions of the Alliance. These are the Memories of the Alliance. There are many more Memories. There are many more Traditions. Sotif has learned these things. Sotif is ready to become the History Man of the Alliance. Who would speak against this?"

No one spoke.

"Sotif must make a fire in the History Room hearth," Senlo said.

Sotif took the torch from Senlo. He had to focus on relaxing his arm to prevent the torch from shaking in his hands. He ignited the fire with the torch that had been ignited by the Spirit Fire. Senlo put his hand out, and Sotif handed the torch back to him.

Senlo began the ceremony. "This fire is a child of the Spirit Fire. The Spirit Fire has never ceased to burn since the day Kectu gave the Spirit Fire to the Earth People." Senlo explained that the Spirit Fire was a symbol of Mother Earth's promise to protect the Alliance. From the beginning of the Alliance, all Earth People, when they died, were burned in hot fires that reduced their bodies to ashes. Some of these ashes from each person were saved, and once a year all the saved ashes were taken from the clans to the Spirit Fire. There the ashes were sprinkled into the Spirit Fire in a special ceremony. The spirits of the dead were released in the smoke of the fire to join all the spirits of all the Earth People that had gone before. After the ceremony, the remaining ashes were collected so they could be taken back to the clans. There they were put in the ground where crops grew. In this way, the bodies of all Earth People who had died since the Days of the Beginning were joined with all the living Earth People. "And so the Spirit Fire burns with the circle that binds the living and the dead," Senlo concluded.

Senlo put a stick of hard wood so one end rested in the fire and the other end rested on the rocks of the hearth. "The flames of the Spirit Fire purify the stick of the History Man. This stick must be given to Sotif. Sotif must keep this stick of the History Man until the time to pass the ceremony robe of the History Man to the next generation. On that day, Sotif must make a new child of the Spirit Fire in the History Room. On that day, Sotif must put Sotif's stick into the child of the Spirit Fire." Senlo pulled his History Man stick from his robe. He carefully put his stick in the fire near the end of the stick that would become Sotif's History Man stick.

As Senlo's stick burned, Senlo reviewed the important events of his time as History Man.

When he was done, he took Sotif's stick from the fire. "All the history of the Alliance has been taken from Senlo's stick to Sotif's stick by the power of the Spirit Fire. Sotif will stand and remove Sotif's robes."

Sotif did as he was told.

"Sotif must carry the sign of the History Man." Senlo blew on the end of Sotif's stick until it glowed red. With the glowing stick, he drew a line across Sotif's chest below his breasts. The skin burned and blistered and bled. Sotif struggled to hold back the cry of pain that choked his throat. The smell of his burning flesh mingled with all the other odors of the History Room. "This sign comes through the Spirit Fire from all the History Men since the beginning. Sotif will not show this sign to the world. Sotif will remember the history of the Alliance is burned into Sotif's body. Sotif will remember the history of the Alliance is burned into Sotif's spirit."

Senlo cooled the stick in a bowl of water. "Sotif must drink this water."

Sotif drank the water. It was a little warm and tasted of the ashes from his stick. When he had finished the water, Senlo rubbed the ashes at the end of the stick into Sotif's wound, making sure it was tattooed. Sotif's knees shook, but he did not flinch.

Senlo took the History Man ceremony robe from his body and stood naked in front of Sotif. Sotif saw the dark scar beneath Senlo's breast. Senlo put the robe on Sotif. Sotif was surprised at how heavy it felt. Senlo took the robe Sotif had worn and put it on. He turned to the rest of the Supreme Council. "Senlo gives the new History Man to the Supreme Council."

It was done. The mantle of the important calling was now passed on to the next generation.

Three days later, Sotif's first official act was a meeting with Luko, shomot of the clan associated with the Finger Lake colony of the Alliance. The Finger Lake colony was located in the most remote part of the Alliance, far north and east of the Heart of the Bison. It took eighty days of hard travel to come from the Finger Lake colony.

Lewtud, shomot of all the clans of the Earth People, brought Luko and a young Earth People man to the meeting place located near the Spirit Fire. The young man had clear blue eyes. He was taller than most Earth People, but not as tall as Sotif. He was obviously nervous. He stayed behind Luko. "Many summers have passed since Luko has come to the Heart of the Bison," Sotif said in the language of the Earth People.

"This trip is hard for Luko. Luko has important business. Luko brings Rodlu to Sotif. Rodlu has a request to make of Sotif. Rodlu has a request to make of Lewtud."

"What request does Rodlu make?" Lewtud asked.

"This Rodlu asks that Rodlu be made one of the Ancients. This Rodlu was not born of the Ancients."

"A man must be born of the Ancients to be one of the Ancients. The Ancients carry the Memories of the Earth People. If Rodlu is not born of the Ancients, Rodlu must prove Rodlu has the Memories of the Ancients. This is not a thing a man can have for wanting." Sotif knew the ceremony to make one of the Ancients, but he had never seen it done.

"Rodlu asks a big thing," Lewtud said. "What makes Rodlu worthy of a big thing?"

"Rodlu is not like others. Rodlu never played with others as a child. Rodlu chooses to think on a thinking stone. Rodlu chooses to talk of the Memories. Rodlu has very strong Memories."

"All the Earth People have strong Memories," Lewtud said.

"This Rodlu prefers to think?" Sotif asked. This was a point in the boy's favor.

"This Rodlu is a thinker. This Rodlu is a dreamer. This Rodlu sees the past. This Rodlu sees the future."

"Lewtud must speak with this Rodlu," Lewtud said.

Luko gave a signal, and the young man spoke. "Rodlu comes to the History Man. Rodlu comes to ask for the honor of being one of the Ancients of the Earth People."

"The Ancients carry the clear Memories of the Earth People," Lewtud said. "The Ancients pass the Memories to their children through their life force. A man becomes one of the Ancients if the man's father is of one of the Ancients."

"Lewtud speaks a truth," Luko agreed. "But sometimes a man comes with deep Memories. Sometimes the father of such a man is not one of the Ancients. Sometimes the History Man makes such a man into one of the Ancients."

"This is true," Sotif said. "It is difficult for a man to prove worthiness to be one of the Ancients."

"Sotif speaks a truth," Luko said. "Rodlu has more than just Memories. Rodlu is a thinker. The Traditions say thinkers are close to the heart of Kectu. The Traditions say thinkers learn from Kectu."

"Luko says Rodlu has strong Memories," Lewtud said. "Rodlu must tell Sotif of these Memories. Rodlu must tell Lewtud of these Memories."

"Luko would speak of other things first," Luko interrupted.

"Speak," Lewtud responded.

"The Ancients say Rodlu has Memories of the eastern Spirit Fire that even the Ancients do not have."

"Rodlu must tell the council of the Memories of the eastern Spirit Fire," Lewtud said.

"Rodlu has Memories of the trading routes to the eastern villages of the Alliance," Rodlu said. "The Memories show the mountains and caves of the eastern clans of the Alliance."

"These are Memories the Ancients of Luko's clan do not have," Luko stressed.

"The eastern clans are no more," Sotif stated. "These Memories are useless."

"All Memories are valuable to the Earth People," Luko responded.

"Luko has said Rodlu sees the future. What future does Rodlu see?" Sotif asked.

Rodlu responded, "Rodlu has feelings of the future. Rodlu says … the Alliance must change. Rodlu says … a time of change for the Earth People comes. Rodlu says … there is an answer for the Earth People in the East."

"It is a high thing to be one of the Ancients," Lewtud said.

"There are very few stories of men who are not born of the Ancients being made one of the Ancients." Sotif did not like Rodlu's talk of change.

"Luko says … Rodlu is worthy to be one of the Ancients. The Ancients of Luko's clan say Rodlu should be one of the Ancients."

"A time of trial and questioning has come to the Earth People," Sotif said. "Many of the clans north of the Snow Mountains complain about the sacrifice to exchange ashes in the Spirit Fire. Luko's clan makes the trip only every other summer. Do the Ancients of Luko's clan think this is right?"

Luko sat silently.

"Would the History Man decide the fate of Rodlu based upon the actions of others?" Rodlu asked.

"Luko has asked the History Man to decide Rodlu's fate based upon Luko's words. Luko has asked the History Man to decide Rodlu's fate based upon the Ancients' words. Sotif says … Luko's words to come only every other summer make a wrong. Sotif says … the Ancients' words to come only every other summer make a wrong. Sotif hears many people say the Alliance must change. The Traditions are the strength of the Alliance. The people must not change from the Traditions. This is a big wrong."

"Sotif says a truth," Rodlu responded. "The Traditions must not change. Rodlu says … modern pressures push the Alliance. Rodlu says … the answer will be found in the East."

"Must Rodlu be this answer?" Sotif asked.

"Rodlu does not know the answer."

"Sotif knows the answer. The answer to all questions must be found in the Heart of the Bison. The answer to all questions must not be found in the East." Sotif was angry at this young man and all who wanted to make changes.

Rodlu started to say something, but instead he bowed his head and backed away from Sotif.

Sotif preformed several other official duties after Luko left. He was tired and hungry. As he walked toward the Spirit Fire, Luko intercepted him. "Luko has travelled a great distance to talk to Sotif about Rodlu. Rodlu is young. Rodlu has offended Sotif with talk of change. This is idle talk of a young man."

"The purpose of the Ancients is to keep the Memories. It is not the purpose of the Ancients to talk of change."

"Rodlu talks of change, but Rodlu does not ask for change. Rodlu has many Memories the Ancients of the Earth People do not have. As Rodlu grows, Rodlu will put his mind on those ancient Memories. The Earth People and the Sun People will be better for this."

"When Rodlu grows, Rodlu must come back. Then Sotif will see if Rodlu should be one of the Ancients."

"This is a long trip. Who knows if Rodlu will ever make such a trip again? Would Sotif talk to Rodlu one more time? Would Sotif tell Rodlu what Rodlu must do to be made one of the Ancients?"

Sotif looked at the Spirit Fire and sighed. "Where is this Rodlu?"

"Rodlu sits on the thinking stone in front of the Heart of the Bison."

Sotif followed Luko from the Heart of the Bison.

Luko touched Rodlu on the shoulder. "Luko has looked for Rodlu. Sotif, History Man of the Alliance, wants to ask Rodlu some questions."

Rodlu stood and looked at Sotif.

"Sotif would speak more of this change from the East," Sotif said

"Rodlu does not understand what this change is. Rodlu says … this is not the time for Rodlu to be made one of the Ancients."

"Rodlu has made a long trip for this. Does Rodlu change so easily?"

"Rodlu has thought of this on the thinking stone of the Heart of the Bison. Rodlu has heard the thoughts of Kectu through the thinking stone. Kectu has given Rodlu the wisdom of Mother Earth. Rodlu must return to the village. Rodlu must be strong and patient. Mother Earth has an important plan for Rodlu."

"Then Rodlu has made this big trip for nothing?" Sotif asked.

"Not. This trip has taught Rodlu to wait for Mother Earth. This trip has given Rodlu a message from Kectu. Rodlu has heard the message of Kectu. The message is the purpose of this trip."

The next day, Sotif watched Luko and Rodlu leave the Winding River village with the other leaders who had come from north of the Snow Mountains. *What a strange young man*, Sotif thought, but he had a feeling Mother Earth had a purpose for him.

Across the valley, Sotif could see the small group of men leaving to explore the lands west of the Great Plains. The group included Dark Cloud and Blue Sky of the Sun People and Jotek of the Earth People. They would travel to the Fish River colony at the western border of the Alliance to spend the deepest part of the winter. Then they would continue their journey next summer.

As Sotif watched them, a strong sense of change flooded his mind.

CHAPTER 3

Tincolad—The Warrior

Winter 3289 BCE

"Your mother has been very sick for a long time," Lendoclad said.

"But she will get better," Tincolad insisted.

"Testolik has been sick too long. I think she is too weak."

"Liar!" Tincolad shouted and hit his father in the chest.

Lendoclad grabbed Tincolad by the shoulders and pressed his fingers into the joints. "You are fourteen summers. You are a young man now. You must not act like a child."

Tincolad tried to hold back the tears. How could his father expect him to be a man now?

"Look at me, Tincolad." Tincolad looked into his father's eyes. His own eyes burned with tears, but they did not spill on his cheeks. "Your mother is weak. I've seen this sickness many times. No one lives when they get this sick."

"No!" Tincolad shook his head slowly.

"Listen to me, Tincolad." Lendoclad tightened his grip. "Your mother has something important to tell you. You must be strong for her."

Tincolad stopped struggling. He took a deep breath. "I will be a man."

"This is hard; everyone knows this is hard. I'm proud of you. Go to your mother." Lendoclad did not give compliments freely. Beneath his grief, Tincolad was proud his father trusted him to be a man.

Tincolad thought of his mother's round, full face. He had not seen her in many days. He looked at the woman on the sleep robe. She was not his mother. This woman's face was drawn and gray. She was not the color of a person. Her eyes were sunken, and her cheeks were hollow. The tent had the nauseating smell of sickness and death.

"Come sit beside me." It was not his mother's voice. Some evil spell must have exchanged his mother for this thing of death. He cautiously moved closer.

"My son," it said.

"It is Tincolad." Even as he said the words, they seemed wrong.

"Tincolad, my son. The image of your father."

Everyone always said he looked like his mother. He bore almost no resemblance to his father. Tincolad looked even more closely at the sick woman. He could not think of a response to this woman's strange words.

"Oh my Tiny Tin, you have grown into a man. You are Tincolad now."

At the mention of her pet name for him, a light shown in her eyes, and she smiled. Tincolad recognized his mother. He fell on his knees beside her. "Mother!"

"Tincolad, you must listen to me. I have important things to tell you."

"I will listen, Mother."

"A long time ago, when I was a young woman, I lived in a settled village. My family was a leading family in the village. My life was easy and pleasant. I was used to an easy life, and I thought it would always be that way. It's the kind of life I was made for."

"Why did you leave such a life?"

"One day, Warlog came. In all the villages where Warlog went, he killed the families of the leaders. He conquered my village. The people of my family were the leaders, and he killed them all. I escaped and ran into the wilderness. I was starving, and Warlog's warriors were close when Lendoclad and his tribe of wanderers found me. They hid me from Warlog's warriors and saved my life.

"Soon after that, Lendoclad took me for his mate. I have lived with Lendoclad and his people since then, but I have always longed for my life in the village where I was born.

"Warlog killed my family. My mother was your grandmother. My father was your grandfather. Warlog killed them and your aunts and uncles and many more."

"Why have you never told me of your family and your village?"

"I have had my reasons, Tincolad. I have thought of the past. I have longed for the past and for my family. This sickness that eats my life from me is not found in the villages. It is a sickness of the tribes that wander. So you see, my son, if Warlog had not chased me from my village, I would be healthy still. I am young, but Warlog has finally reached out to kill me.

"I will soon be out of Warlog's reach. You will be the last of my father's seed. If Warlog ever finds you, he will kill you because he hates and fears my family. As death comes to me, I see clearly. All the people of this tribe know I ran from Warlog. All the people of this tribe know Warlog searches for you."

"The people of this tribe are our friends. No one in the tribe would say anything about me." A shadow fell across his mother's face. Tincolad shivered. She was silent for a time, and then color came to her cheeks.

"You are wrong, my son. Most of the people would keep silent, but it only takes one to tell Warlog."

"Who would do such a thing? Name him, and I will kill him."

"I cannot say who would betray you. I trust only Lendoclad."

"It has been many summers since you ran from Warlog. Surely, he no longer has interest in you or your child."

"There is more that I cannot explain to you. When the time is right, Lendoclad will tell you everything. Then you will understand."

"What more? You can tell me."

The woman took several breaths that rattled in her chest. She seemed to be unable to speak. She squeezed Tincolad's hand with surprising strength. "There is only one thing you can do, only one way to save your life and repay my death and the death of my family. You must kill Warlog."

"How can I do—"

She squeezed his hand so hard it was painful. "Promise me. You must promise me on your life that you will kill Warlog and his son." Her face was red. She lifted her head from the robes. "Promise me! Promise me!" she demanded.

"I promise ... on my life."

His mother's head dropped to her robes, and she let out a long sigh. "I have talked of this with Lendoclad. He will take you from this tribe. He will help you. Trust only him." Her face quickly went pale, and she was once again the stranger. She breathed three more labored breaths, and all was quiet. Her face relaxed, and though it was pale and thin, it was the face of Tincolad's mother.

Tincolad wept bitterly when his mother's body was buried. "I do not understand why I must leave this tribe to kill someone as great as Warlog. I do not see how this can be done," Tincolad said to his father.

"Tincolad, you're still young. There is much you do not understand. This tribe is a wandering tribe. All wandering tribes are looked down upon by the villages. Even in this tribe, I was never considered great."

"But, Father, you are much respected by everyone."

"It is true, but this was not always true. When your mother came to the tribe, she was a high-born woman from an influential village. I could hardly believe she accepted me. She was always a great woman. Every day, I thanked Zendolot, praise to him, for my good luck. I'm respected in the tribe because my mate was Testolik. She honored me by being my mate. With each passing summer, my position in the tribe increased because of her influence.

"She asked me to protect you and lead you to Warlog. She asked me to help you kill Warlog. This isn't something I would choose for you or me. Some say I should not honor promises made, now that she's dead."

"Mother said I wouldn't be safe in the tribe."

"You've been safe for fourteen summers. I think you would be safe as long as this tribe avoids Warlog's armies. Testolik was always fearful for you. In our moments alone, she always talked of the day when you would be a man. Her dream has always been that you would one day repay Warlog for the death of her family and that you would assume your place of honor in her village."

"But I'm a wanderer. I wouldn't know how to live in her village."

"I think it would be foolish to try to kill Warlog. It would be safer to remain with this tribe. You are much honored here."

"I believe it would be safer. But I have promised my mother on my life that I will repay Warlog for her family. Warlog killed my mother by driving her into the wilderness. I will keep my promise. I will kill Warlog."

"Your mother knew your will. She told me to place the decision in your hands. She said you would choose your destiny to kill Warlog. I will help you."

"Mother told me there is something I must know."

"You mother and I thought much about how to kill Warlog. The only way to get close to him is to join his army. We must wait until you are old enough. When the time is right, I will tell you all, and we will make our plans. You must be patient until then."

Two days later, Tincolad and his father left the tribe on a mission to find a way to kill Warlog. Tincolad had no idea how it would be done, but he dreamed only of killing Warlog. He didn't care if he died so long as he could face Warlog, tell him he was Testolik's son, and then kill him.

Summer 3287 BCE

Rayloc was finally the most powerful shaman in the known world. He was Warlog's advisor in all matters. Rayloc knocked on Warlog's tent post.

"Rayloc, enter a dwelling that honors Zendolot, praise to him."

Rayloc sat on a robe of honor. "The warmth of summer comes at last."

"It's been many summers since the last time we led my army in conquest."

"Warlog, Zendolot's Great Eagle, has conquered all the world."

"I have ten armies, and my empire stretches over all the land. It includes all the villages and wandering tribes of the People, but there is more of this world than we see."

"What do you mean?"

"My empire goes to the seas north, south, and west. We have not gone to the sea in the East. I have heard there are fertile lands and other villages in the East."

In the beginning, Rayloc had pushed Warlog to conquer all the People. Warlog just wanted to subjugate the villages that bordered on his village's territory, but once Warlog had begun, he seemed to be caught up in the excitement of the wars and the power of his armies. When the wars were over, and it was time to govern his vast empire, Warlog showed no interest. He left the governing to Rayloc. These were very good times for Rayloc. He was the most powerful man in the world.

"I'm tired and bored with the Empire. I think I should organize an army to explore these new lands."

"Whom would you leave to be head of the Empire?"

"My son, Pothelad, is thirteen summers this year. He's becoming a man. Pothialik is a strong woman who can teach him to be a strong leader. You would stay to give support and advice as you do now. You can help teach him to lead. He's much more suited to this life of leisure. I need to be traveling and conquering the world. Sometimes, I think I would be happy to finally conquer every village in the whole world, from sea to sea to sea to sea. Other times, I hope there is no eastern sea. I hope the world goes on forever, so there will always be new lands and new people to conquer. I think I'm just a warrior and nothing else. You're made to govern, and I'm made to conquer."

Rayloc knew if Warlog left him in charge, he would have even more power over Pothelad than he had over Warlog. Pothelad was much more like Seccolog than Warlog. He was lazy and self-indulgent, but for some reason, Warlog couldn't see this. With Warlog gone, Rayloc would have complete control of the Empire. "If you go to this new land and find nothing, then what would you do?"

"Messengers from the eastern army arrived this morning. They will be here in two days. They bring strange people that came to them from lands far to the east."

"Ah, so this is why your desire to conquer has returned."

"Maybe so. I'm not happy sitting around with no battles ... no adventure. These new people do not speak like we do. Some of my leaders have learned to talk with these strange men. They say they are part of a great alliance. These strange people traveled two summers to reach our eastern villages. I think their great alliance is looking for people to conquer. Such a great alliance is a threat to us and our people. I will learn from these new people, and then I will take an army to make them part of the Empire."

"There are a lot of old stories. It would be a waste of time to follow all them." Rayloc could tell Warlog had already made his decision. Pretending to resist was good politics.

"True, but these people are real. My army is bringing them. I will see and learn from them before I take my army east."

Two days later, Rayloc heard that the scouts from the eastern army had arrived at a camp outside the village. News quickly spread through the village that the eastern army had captured a live droglit and was bringing it to the village. There were no stories of anyone ever capturing a droglit. Rayloc went directly to Warlog's tent. "I heard the scouts brought a droglit."

"Heldolad has just given me a report of the travels of the eastern army. He has a story to tell of people from the East. It is good you are here."

"The scouts say they bring a droglit prisoner," Rayloc repeated.

"I have seen this person and some of his magic," Heldolad said.

"Tell us about this droglit," Rayloc said.

"He comes with two of men from the East. They speak strange words, but some of our people have learned to speak as they do, and the men from the East have learned to speak as we do. They call themselves Sun People. They call the droglit Earth People. The Earth People man makes strange sounds we do not understand. The Sun People understand the sounds he makes.

"The People from the East and the strange man travel with us freely. We had not thought this strange man was a droglit. He's stronger than two of our strongest warriors. It would be very hard to hold him if he decided to leave."

"Why does he come?" Warlog asked.

"The People who came with him say they were sent by their leader to explore our lands. They come to see if there are villages here. They are interested in finding out about our people. They say they come to trade."

"How do these people have a droglit?" Rayloc asked.

"The men with him say they come from a strong alliance between Sun People and Earth People. They say the Earth People live in caves near the Sun People villages. The Earth People use their magic to help the Sun People."

"What magic?" Rayloc asked.

"They know when a storm will come many days before it comes. They can tell if the winter will be hard. They know when the last freeze of winter has come, so the Earth People know when it is the right time to plant corps. They can see better than the eagle. They smell better than the wolf. They hear better than the ibex."

"These are strange powers," Warlog said.

"I have seen some of these powers."

"We must not bring this evil to the village," Rayloc said.

"What do you mean?" Warlog asked Rayloc.

"Always in the past, the droglits have used deception and magic from deep in the earth to ensnare the spirits of the People. Now, they come from their caverns into the light to enslave all the People. They must have new magic."

"These Earth People seem to be helping the Sun People. How do you know they are droglits?"

"They are strange-looking things that live in caves to be close to the deep caverns. They bring magic to trick and enslave the People. This magic of knowing the weather comes from the deep caverns. The droglits have deceived the People of the East. Zendolot, praise to him, has seen this plot. Warlog has built an army powerful enough to destroy the droglits. I see Zendolot's plan when he planted the seeds of conquest in Warlog's heart.

"This droglit came to take information to the rest of the droglits to help them enslave our people. If they succeed, all the earth will become like the deep caverns. All the People will become slaves to the droglits forever. The sun will cease to shine on the earth, and everything will be as dark as the deep caverns. Only Warlog and his armies stand between the droglits and the end of our world. Who can question Warlog's authority now?"

"We will go to the camp of the eastern army to see these strange people from the East. We will see if they bring a droglit with them."

The next day, Rayloc went with Warlog. Heldolad took them to his tent, and one of his captains brought the three strangers. Two of the men looked like the People. They were a little shorter, and their faces were rounder. Their skin was darker, and their eyes were brown instead of blue. The differences were not great. But the third was completely different. Rayloc could see immediately it was not of the People. It seemed to be more animal than man. It was much shorter than the People, and its head was flat. Rayloc knew that was so it could live under the low ceilings in the deep caverns. Its mouth and teeth were large. It had almost no chin or forehead. Its mouth and nose protruded out almost like the muzzle of a dog. Its eyes looked out darkly from below a large brow ridge. Its skin and hair were light, and its eyes were blue. Rayloc could see great muscles on its short arms and legs that showed from the animal skin it wore. Rayloc shuddered at the sight of it.

Heldolad said something to the two people. They responded in a language Rayloc did not understand, but they sounded like the People. One of the two said something to the droglit, and it responded. The sound it made was a deep guttural rumble that sounded as ugly as the droglit looked.

"I have told them they are in the presence of Warlog. They say they are honored. They speak our language, but you have to listen closely to understand them," Heldolad said.

The taller of the two strangers said, "Dark Cloud am I. We are brought a long trip. We have been under you much time. We families worry. Where we are? We need go we home soon."

"What is this animal you bring?" Rayloc asked, pointing to the droglit.

"This Alliance brother. Bring he good magic of earth. This not animal."

"What do you call this animal?"

"This Alliance brother, not animal. He is Earth People. Call we him Jotek."

Rayloc sniffed dismissively. "This *is* a droglit. We will not meet with him here."

"What is droglit?" the short stranger asked.

Warlog stood up. "Take the droglit out and tie it with the goats."

"The Earth People man is Alliance brother," Dark Cloud insisted. "He is we friend. Keep we him here."

"I have been told Jotek has magic that is good for the People," Warlog said.

"Yes, much good magic."

"I will send Jotek to my magicians to learn of this magic."

"Go we must with him. The Alliance brother cannot speak words like you. Go we must to tell what speak he."

"Our magicians will know his words," Rayloc said.

"He is we friend. Ask we to go with he."

"No," Warlog insisted. "He will teach our magicians. You will teach me your language and your ways. Then we will all go to your land. We will meet your people. We will be friends. We will trade. Jotek must go with my warriors to teach my magicians. Then he will come to you."

The people of the East spoke with the droglit in their language, and he answered in his deep, ugly language. "Our Alliance brother says go he will."

"We will take him to our magicians. He will be an honored guest to teach and learn," Warlog said.

The droglit was led peacefully from the tent.

"I must learn all about your people, your language, and your customs so we can be friends and trade. You will go to my village."

"We friend will be where?"

"The droglit must go to our village of magicians to teach his magic," Rayloc said.

"One of we must go with we friend to tell you he words." Dark Cloud sounded firm.

"Our magicians have magic to understand strange words," Warlog said. "If they have trouble, we will send one of you to help. There is much we need to learn from you. And you need to learn much from us. It is better that both of you come to my village."

"Much hard is this. Go we with you now, but soon we must see we friend."

"Agreed. You go with my warriors to my village."

Warlog's warriors led the two men away.

"We must kill the droglit now," Rayloc said after they were gone.

"I thought that was your intention in separating him from the others, but shouldn't we learn what we can from him first?"

"The droglits have magic we don't understand. While we're trying to learn, the droglit might begin using its magic. How would we know? Somehow, they have tricked all the eastern people. It would be dangerous to let it live. We can find what we need to know from the other two."

"You're right. Take care of it."

Rayloc went to the tent where the droglit was being held. He walked up to it and looked closely at its face. It tried to smile, but Rayloc could tell it was nervous. "Kill it and burn the body."

The droglit ran for the opening of the tent, throwing Rayloc into the dust as he ran. Rayloc had not thought it could understand his language, but it was clear the droglit's magic was strong. "Kill it!" Rayloc roared from the ground.

It ran a few more steps, and then it fell with many arrows sticking from its body. Rayloc's nose, left arm, and several ribs on his left side were broken. Before being taken to the medicine man, Rayloc instructed the warriors to burn the body as quickly as possible. "Burn it in the hot fires of the copper-smelting hearth so there are only ashes left."

The medicine man bound Rayloc's right arm to his side. The break in his arm was so near the shoulder there was no way to realign and set the bone. The only thing he could do was keep it immobile and give Rayloc strong dream medicine to help with the pain. Even with the dream medicine, Rayloc was in great pain.

For the first nights after the attack, Rayloc slept only fitfully. He had nightmares of droglits led by Nacoloc pouring from the earth to destroy him. Guilt and fear over the killing of Nacoloc filled his mind and spirit. He became convinced all the droglits must be found and destroyed.

After three days, the doses of dream medicine were finally low enough for Rayloc to think. He called the head warrior to him. "What have you done with the body of the droglit?"

"We burned the body as you said. When the fire went down, we gathered the ashes and buried them away from the campsite."

"I don't know his magic. His spirit may come back to repair his body. Dig up the ashes and scatter them in the wind."

Rayloc dropped off into a fitful sleep filled with dreams of hordes of droglits swarming over the land, turning the eastern villages against the western villages. The droglits brought wars, sickness, and poison to the land. The only way to save the People was to destroy every droglit.

When Rayloc woke the next morning, he knew why Zendolot had sent him. The salvation of the People depended upon him and Warlog's armies. Rayloc would learn all he could from the two strangers. He would go with Warlog and his armies to make sure all the droglits were destroyed. Their ashes would darken the eastern skies.

Rayloc gathered charms of feathers, small polished stones, and colored cloths, which he blessed and added to his clothing to protect him from droglits.

Winter 3287/3286 BCE

After traveling almost two summers to catch Warlog's army, Tincolad was getting impatient. It was not easy to know where Warlog and his army were.

Last summer, they heard rumors that Warlog was gathering his armies in the eastern part of the Empire. They traveled the last part of the summer in that direction. Winter was nearly over, so they began traveling east again.

One morning, Tincolad and Lendoclad met a large group of men who were also traveling east. One man came to greet them. He was about the same size as Lendoclad. He wore a coat made of woven grass. His boots went high up his legs and were tied with leather straps crisscrossed up his calves. He carried a spear in his left hand and a bow slung over his shoulder. He had a large pack tied to his back with a quiver of arrows tied to it. His hair was cut straight across his forehead just above his eyebrow, and his beard was cut straight across below his chin. That was the hair of a warrior.

"What is this group?" Lendoclad asked.

"We are warriors from the northern army. Who are you?"

"I am Lendoclad, and this is my son, Tincolad. We search for Warlog's army. We wish to join his army and march with him."

The man looked first at Lendoclad and then at Tincolad. Tincolad did not like the way the man seemed to be sizing him up.

"The armies of Warlog are always looking for good men to join. Especially now that the great war is about to begin."

"What great war?" Lendoclad asked.

The man looked suspiciously at the two. "What village are you from?"

"Take us to Warlog, and we will answer all *his* questions," Tincolad answered defiantly.

The man looked at Tincolad, and his eyes narrowed.

"You must forgive the boy," Lendoclad said. "He is young, and sometimes he forgets to show respect."

The man studied Tincolad. Tincolad puffed his chest and stuck his chin out.

"Tincolad!" Lendoclad shouted.

The man started to laugh. "Don't worry about the young man. I am Rencolad, warrior in the army of Warlog. The boy shows more bravery than good sense, but bravery is hard to find. Good sense is easy to teach. So, you want to join Warlog's army?" He directed the question to Tincolad.

"Not just any of his armies. I look to join the army Warlog leads." Although he knew the man was a trained warrior, Tincolad did not fear him.

"Well, young man, your courage is strong, and your desire to follow Warlog is admirable. It's not easy to join any of Warlog's armies. You must have a sponsor who will teach you the difficult skills of war. You must have a teacher with patience to teach you good sense."

"Tell me where Warlog and his army are, and I will find someone there to teach me this good sense you talk of."

"I have taught other young men to be warriors. Perhaps I would teach you."

"Thanks," Lendoclad spoke up before Tincolad could say anything, "but we look for the army led by Warlog himself."

"We travel to the Olive village. Our guide says we are almost there. That's where Warlog is building his army to travel east to destroy the droglits."

"Droglits!" Tincolad had been told of the droglits since he was a young boy. "The droglits are deep in the caverns of the earth. Has Warlog found a way to invade such deep caverns?"

"Haven't you heard?"

"What?" Lendoclad asked.

"Last summer, the eastern army brought two people from the East. They brought a droglit with them."

"A real droglit?" Tincolad asked. "How did they get it out of the deep caverns?"

"It was real, and it was alive. It attacked Rayloc. It was killed with many arrows. The people of the East said there are many droglits in their land. They have used magic to fool the people of the East. Rayloc says the droglits are building an army to come and enslave all the People. If they succeed, the sun will no longer rise, and all the earth will be as dark as the deep caverns. All the People will serve droglits, and there will be no more happiness in the land.

"Warlog is building the largest army ever. Soon, he will leave the Olive village to fight the droglits and destroy them forever. We go to join the great army. Some say it will take four or five summers to travel so far and destroy the droglits. We must go to the edges of the earth."

"We will also volunteer to go with Warlog to kill droglits," Lendoclad said.

"The boy can study to be a warrior, but you're too old. An army on the move needs strong men to do the work of moving, setting up camps, and taking them down. I'm sure there will be work for you." Then he turned to Tincolad. "It's not easy to become a warrior. If you choose to become a warrior, I will train and sponsor you."

Tincolad could not believe his luck. He would be a warrior in Warlog's army. He was sure being a warrior would make it easier to kill him, but there was no doubt there would still be great risk.

Tincolad and his father joined with Rencolad's group. They found Warlog's army several days later, just as it was preparing to make the epic trip east.

Summer 3284 BCE

Tincolad and his father traveled two summers with Warlog's army. During that time, he studied and practiced the skills needed to become a warrior. Because of the rigors of travel, it took him extra time to complete the requirements to pass the tests. He used the time to learn all he could about war and how to plan it.

According to the custom, Rencolad gave Tincolad a puppy at the beginning of Tincolad's training. Tincolad named the puppy Razid. Razid was trained to be a war dog while Tincolad was trained in the skills and knowledge of the warriors.

Tincolad developed a great deal of respect for the men who could call themselves warriors. He spent most of his time with them, listening to stories of Warlog's conquests.

Tincolad began to avoid his father because his father constantly talked of plans to kill Warlog. Tincolad came to believe Zendolot sent Warlog to create an army to defeat the droglits. The future of the entire world depended upon Warlog and his army. Warlog was the only man who could lead the army against the droglits.

Today, Tincolad would go through the Warrior Ceremony. Only those who had proven themselves could be part of this secret ceremony. As Tincolad pondered all these things, Lendoclad approached him. "I've looked everywhere for you."

"I wanted time alone to think about becoming a warrior."

"I'm proud of you, Tincolad. It's a difficult thing to be a warrior."

"It's true." In Tincolad's mind, he was trying to think of a polite way to end the conversation before it went into subjects Lendoclad wouldn't understand.

"Once you are a warrior, you will get closer to Warlog. You should find a way to be assigned to be one of his guards."

"I don't want to be a guard. I want to be where I can fight the droglits."

"The best chance to kill Warlog will come if you're a guard."

This was the conversation Tincolad had dreaded. "This is not a good time, Father. The whole world is in danger. We must defeat the droglits first."

"Do you so easily forget the pain Warlog brought to your mother? Do you forget he killed all her family? Do you so easily forget your mother is dead because of Warlog?"

Tincolad knew his father would not understand. He was too old, and his mind was too narrow, but Tincolad tried anyway. "You do not understand warriors and armies, Father. An army needs a strong leader. Warlog is the only one who can lead this army. Without Warlog, the army will fail, and then the droglits will capture the world. They will drag all the spirits of men to the dark caverns."

"You so easily forget the evil of Warlog."

"I forget nothing, but I also know it's not an easy thing to make an army. Perhaps some hard things were done. You can't eat the venison unless you kill the deer. A strong army is needed. An army cannot be strong without a strong leader. Zendolot, praise to him, sent Warlog to create an army before the droglits could move west. Only a man close to the power of Zendolot, praise to him, could have created an army as strong as this one."

"You would be foolish to believe the things Warlog's warriors say to convince you to become one who defends Warlog. It's known he killed his own father."

"Times are difficult. We must all do difficult things. We must sacrifice our personal wants and feelings in order to defeat the droglits. There's more to think about than personal wrongs and misunderstandings."

"Misunderstandings? I've seen you with the others who train to be warriors. I've seen you take advantage of the privileges trainees are given. I thought you did it to fool Warlog and his warriors. Now, I see you have fallen into the temptation of a warrior."

"You do not hear the words I speak!"

"You are not my son, Tincolad. You are son to Warlog and all he stands for. It was my mistake to think you could be strong enough to stand against him!"

"You speak strong words, Father! I only wish I did belong to Warlog's family!" Tincolad shouted in a way he did not intend.

"Except he killed all his family, didn't he?" Lendoclad shouted back. "If you decide to join Warlog, you are no longer my son. You are more a son to Warlog than to me."

"I must join Warlog to save the world from the droglits. From this day, you are no longer my father. I warn you, do not try to harm Warlog. I will see you dead before I let you interfere with the destruction of the droglits."

Tincolad turned from the man who had been his father and walked away. Today, he would become a warrior and lose his father. It was a difficult time.

Rencolad led Tincolad to the ceremony tent. Tincolad had hoped his father would reconsider and give his support for the ceremony. There was no sign of him outside the tent. Several of the most important warriors were there, including Rayloc.

"Enter a ceremony tent of the great god, Zendolot, praise to him," Rayloc said.

Tincolad entered the tent of honor; only the select could enter. Inside, he stood in front of Rayloc.

"Today is a great day for all the People," Rayloc began. "Today, the forward scouts have returned. The first village of the eastern people has been found. The scouts say they saw droglits in the village."

Tincolad's heart jumped. Droglits had been a thought—a story—a fear. Now, they were real! They were close, and he would be fighting them soon.

"The armies of Warlog are on the eve of the greatest war in the history of all the People," Rayloc continued. "Zendolot, praise to him, chose Warlog to unite all the People and create an army strong enough to defeat the droglits. Warriors will be tested to the limits of their physical strength. They will be tried by the magic of the droglits. Some of our warriors may weaken in the face of the work Zendolot, praise to him, chose them to do."

Tincolad looked around him. In this tent were the greatest warrior leaders of the army. These men would not weaken. He knew he would not.

"In this tent are Warlog's leaders. It is good we have this time to come together in the Warrior Ceremony. It is good all of us who lead the armies of Warlog have this time to review the importance of what we do by seeing this ceremony.

"We are fortunate Tincolad comes to us now. He has prepared himself to become one of the strong, loyal warriors for Warlog. He has been ready to become a warrior for many moons, but we have waited until now, the eve of this great war, to perform this ceremony.

"Therefore, Tincolad is the best-trained warrior to have ever passed the Warrior Ceremony. He will fight with power in this greatest war."

Why can't Lendoclad see things as they are? If only he could be here in this tent to hear these words, Tincolad thought, but he realized only warriors and those who were about to become warriors were allowed to see the Warrior Ceremony.

"Who brings this man to the Warrior Ceremony?" Rayloc asked.

Rencolad stood. "Rencolad brings Tincolad to the ceremony tent." Then Rencolad reviewed the history of Tincolad's coming to the army. He talked of his training and some of the proud moments when he had accomplished the required feats. "Tincolad has studied longer than other warriors because of the added duties of a traveling army. No warrior has been better trained or achieved such high levels of skill before becoming a warrior. Tincolad also has great ability to understand how to plan war. He will be one of the greatest of Warlog's leaders. I am proud to present him to Rayloc."

"Is Rencolad prepared to give his blood to make Tincolad a warrior?" Rayloc asked.

"Yes." Rencolad put his left arm forward. Tincolad had noticed all the warriors had at least one scar on the inside of their left forearm. This scar was made of two sloping lines joined so they made a point like an arrow, pointing toward the wrist. Some warriors had several of these scars nested inside each other going up their arm. Rencolad had six scars.

Rayloc used a sharp flint blade to make a new cut on Rencolad's arm above the sixth scar. Blood ran down his arm into a small wooden cup Rayloc held. When the cup was full, Rayloc wrapped a soft skin bandage around Rencolad's arm.

"Come forward, Tincolad."

Tincolad stood in front of Rayloc. "Does Tincolad wish to be a warrior in Warlog's army?"

"Yes."

"Put your left arm forward."

Rayloc cut Tincolad's arm just as he had done to Rencolad. He collected a small wooden cup of blood and then bandaged the arm.

"The Warrior Ceremony is in two parts. Zendolot, praise to him, made the People to rule over all the animals. Zendolot, praise to him, made some men to be hunters. The hunters came to the shaman of the tribe to learn the secret promises of the hunter. For generations and generations, the hunters were the favored men of the People. Then, a new time came. Zendolot, praise to him, sent Warlog to unite the tribes of the People. Zendolot, praise to him, sent Warlog to create warriors to rule over the People. Now, the hunters are no more. The favored men of the People are the warriors.

"At first, no one knew why Zendolot, praise to him, sent Warlog to unite the People and build a strong army. The threat of droglits explains all. Because of the wisdom of Zendolot, praise to him, there is an army prepared to destroy all droglits. The army of the People follows Warlog to the greatest war the world has seen. When the droglits are destroyed, their leader, Dracolut, will have no more power. There will be peace in all the earth for all time.

"Tincolad has studied and prepared himself to be a warrior. He comes asking to become part of this greatest war."

Tincolad realized he was part of something that would save every village and change the world forever. He was lucky to have been born at this most important time.

"The first part of the ceremony comes from the ancient Hunter Ceremony of the Hand. It was the ceremony that all hunters participated in from the first creation of the People. This ancient ceremony has been changed to the new calling of the warrior. Tincolad, put your left hand forward with the palm down."

Tincolad put his hand forward. The movement made his wound burn, but he focused on Rayloc and did not flinch. Rayloc brought the handle of a dagger up to Tincolad's palm. "Hold the dagger. The hand cannot grip the dagger of the warrior strong enough to fight without the strength of the thumb. Of all parts of the hand, the thumb is most needed to provide the strength to hold the weapons of the warrior. The thumb of the hand represents Zendolot, praise to him. The strength of the People comes from Zendolot, praise to him.

"When the warrior points the direction to go, he uses the finger next to the thumb. It represents the shaman of the People. The shaman is closest to Zendolot, praise to him. The shaman points the right way for all the People. Point this finger."

Tincolad pointed the first finger at Rayloc.

"The next finger is the tallest and strongest finger. This finger represents Warlog. All decisions, all power, and all honor belong to Warlog. Zendolot, praise to him, chose Warlog to strengthen the People. Close your hand and point with the Warlog finger."

Tincolad did as he was told, pointing again at Rayloc.

"The next finger is the warrior finger. This finger gives its support to all fingers of the hand. The warrior pledges his strength and allegiance to Warlog and Zendolot, praise to him, through the shaman.

"The last finger is the smallest finger. This finger represents the traditions of the people. Make a fist and point the Traditions finger."

Tincolad pointed the smallest finger at Rayloc.

"Make a fist again. Now, Tincolad will learn a lesson. Point the warrior finger."

Tincolad tried to point the warrior finger, but it would only point straight down.

"This is the lesson of the warrior's hand. The power of the village comes from Zendolot, praise to him. The teachings that guide the tribe come from the shaman. The strength to lead the tribe comes from Warlog. The force that holds the village together comes from the traditions. The Zendolot thumb, the shaman finger, the Warlog finger, and the Traditions finger can all stand alone. The warriors are those who band together under Zendolot, the shaman, and Warlog to defend the village and the traditions of the village. The symbol of the hand reminds the warrior he does not stand alone. His strength comes from Warlog and the shaman. Only when they stand can the warrior stand with them. Tincolad will show what he has learned by explaining the meaning of each of the fingers."

Tincolad easily explained each finger. The concepts were easy, especially with the hand for a reminder. When Tincolad was done, Rencolad sat down.

"This part of the ceremony comes from the ancient Hunter Ceremony of the Hand. In the old ceremony, the warrior finger represented the hunter, and the Warlog finger represented the chief of the tribe. There are no longer hunters or chiefs. The old Ceremony of the Hand has been replaced by the Warrior Ceremony of the Hand.

"The second part of the ceremony teaches the spirit of the warrior." Rayloc handed Tincolad the container of Rencolad's blood. "Rencolad has brought Tincolad to Rayloc. Rencolad has vouched for Tincolad by his blood. This is the blood of the warrior. This blood carries the courage and strength of the warrior. Tincolad will now take upon himself the power and allegiance of the warrior by drinking this blood of a warrior."

There was a pause. Tincolad was not sure what came next. He slowly raised the container to his lips. Rayloc nodded. Tincolad drank Rencolad's blood. It was warm and salty, but there was sweetness to it.

"The power of the great warrior, Rencolad, flows through Tincolad's body."

Rayloc took a small sip from the container that held Tincolad's blood. "The blood of the new warrior, Tincolad, flows in the body of the great shaman of the People. The blood of all true warriors flows in the body of Rayloc."

Then Rayloc handed the container to Rencolad, and he drank the rest of Tincolad's blood.

"Tincolad and Rencolad are warrior brothers," Rencolad said. "In all battles, we will fight for each other. We will protect each other. If Tincolad should die, a part of Rencolad will die with him. If Rencolad should die, a part of Tincolad will die with him. So it is with the warriors of Warlog's army."

Rayloc took both containers and put them in the fire. Each of the men who had witnessed the ceremony passed by the fire and breathed in some of the smoke. Rencolad and Tincolad were the last. When they had passed, Rayloc took Tincolad by his shoulders and stood face to face with him.

"Now, Tincolad is a warrior. You are one with the army of Warlog in body by the blood you gave and the blood you drank. You are one with the army of Warlog in spirit by the smoke of the blood fire that you have breathed. All the parts of the ceremony are sacred to Zendolot, praise to him. You must never talk of these things, except in the ceremony tent and only with warriors who have passed through the ceremony.

"Tincolad must wear the hair of a true warrior." Using a bone comb, Rayloc combed Tincolad's hair from the top of his head straight down all around. Then, using a ceremony dagger of copper, he cut Tincolad's hair straight across his forehead, two finger widths above his eyebrow and from ear to ear, leaving his face exposed. Then he combed Tincolad's beard straight down and cut it straight across about three fingers below his chin. Last, he cut the rest of Tincolad's hair to a length that matched the length of the beard.

"There are two warrior signs you must make when you are in the world outside this tent. The first is the warrior greeting. It is made by bringing your left hand to a square with your left hand open and the palm facing forward. This sign is used to greet another warrior. The sign brings to mind the Warrior Ceremony. It is called the Warrior Sign of the Hand. This sign is made to show the warrior scar on your forearm to the other warriors when you make the sign. One scar shows you are a warrior, bound to Warlog by blood. Each additional scar shows you have brought an additional warrior for Warlog's army.

"The second sign is the Battle Sign of Warlog, Zendolot's Great Eagle. This sign is given as a challenge to opposing armies just before an attack. It is made by putting your left hand high in the air with the knuckles facing the enemy. With this sign, the sacred warrior scars are turned away from the enemy and toward the warriors with you. With your hand held high, you make a fist with only the Warlog finger standing. Warlog's enemies learn to fear this sign, while Warlog's warriors gather strength and unity from it.

"Welcome, Tincolad, warrior in the army of Warlog, Zendolot's Great Eagle."

All the great warrior leaders gave Tincolad the Warrior Sign of the Hand. Tincolad gave the sign back, and the ceremony was complete. Tincolad knew he was a true warrior of Warlog's army. It all fit together so simply but so powerfully. Tincolad understood the deepest meaning of being a warrior. It was a promise to Zendolot. It was even bigger than Warlog. If he could just explain all this to Lendoclad, then he would understand how important Warlog's army was, but Tincolad could not reveal the Warrior Ceremony to anyone. Even if his father never understood, Tincolad knew he would always be true to the body and spirit of the army of Warlog. For the first time in his life, he was truly a grown man. He was a warrior. He always would be. He knew a time was coming when he would have to risk his life for his people and Zendolot.

The time of war had finally come. Tincolad did not know if he wanted the eastern people to submit peacefully or if he wanted war. He was afraid of being killed, but he wanted a chance to show his bravery. One thing he did know—every droglit had to be killed and destroyed in the fires of Zendolot. Based upon the things that had been learned from Dark Cloud and Blue Sky, there was a range of very high mountains. On this side of the mountains, there were four colonies of eastern people. On the other side, there were eighteen more colonies. The cultural center of the Alliance was one of the colonies on this side of the mountains. Near that colony was a cave they called the Heart of the Bison. In that cave was the Spirit Fire of the droglits and a room with paintings about their history.

Warlog's army would have to conquer two villages on the way to the Heart of the Bison. The first, the Fish River colony, was near a big river called the Fish River. The next was a much smaller colony called Winter Rest.

The army began to set up camp on a low hill overlooking the Fish River village. Dark Cloud and Blue Sky were animated and excited. Warlog stood at the edge of the hill above the medium-sized village. A group of ten men from the village came to greet Warlog's armies. They made no effort to use the weapons they carried as they warily approached Warlog's camp.

Warlog picked Rayloc and eight other men to go with him to meet with the men from the village. Tincolad had been picked to be one of the eight. Three of the men from the village stepped forward to greet Warlog. Warlog walked to them with Rayloc beside him. Dark Cloud and Blue Sky introduced Warlog to Strong Bison, the chief of the village. "I am Warlog, Zendolot's Great Eagle, chief of all the tribes of the People," Warlog said in the language he had learned from Dark Cloud. Tincolad had learned a little of the language. He understood Warlog's greeting and could make out much of what was said.

One of the men said something about being a chief. It was harder to understand him. He spoke a little differently and very fast.

Warlog told the man he had come to learn about the people and begin trade between their peoples.

Tincolad understood the chief of the eastern people say their leader was named Tree, and he lived many days from this village.

"Everything is as the eastern people told us," Rayloc said to Warlog in their own language. "We must find the droglit caves and destroy them."

"I will see if these men will join us peacefully or if there will be war." Warlog told Strong Bison he wanted to talk to the village the next day.

Warlog had kept most of his army hidden from Dark Cloud and Blue Sky on the trip east. The next morning, Warlog's main army came to Warlog's camp. Warlog marched into the Fish River camp with sixty-two of his strongest warriors as a bodyguard. The rest of his army took positions around the village. Because he was still a new warrior, Tincolad remained on the hill.

Tincolad could see Warlog talking with Strong Bison. Both men were moving their hands and arms as they talked. Warlog stepped to the chief, pulled his dagger from his belt, and stabbed Strong Bison in the heart before anyone could save him. According to the plan, Warlog would offer the eastern tribe a chance to join the Empire in peace. If they refused, Warlog would kill the chief. That was the signal to attack. The men of the village were outnumbered and unprepared. The attack was vicious and skilled. The village was defeated so quickly many in the village did not know there had been a fight. Nearly half of the men in the village were killed. Those who remained quickly surrendered. By the time Tincolad got to the fight, it was over.

Warlog's terms were simple: either join the Empire and accept Zendolot or die. A few resisted. Warlog had them and their families executed immediately. Everyone else in the village took an oath to Warlog. Then Warlog had Strong Bison's family brought to him. After saying something about the danger to everyone of leaving the chief's family alive, he ordered his warriors to kill them.

When Tincolad saw the family of the chief killed, he became confused. Rencolad had taught him of the need to kill the family of the chief. It had seemed right then, but seeing the killing of the women and children of the chief's family was very different.

Rayloc organized the village as he had organized all the other villages Warlog defeated. He selected a warlent and five warriors to establish order. The strong men of Strong Bison's village who had sworn allegiance to Warlog were forced to join his army.

The next day, Rayloc led many of the warriors to the droglit cave. Some of the men from Strong Bison's village who had sworn allegiance to Warlog led the way.

Tincolad was one of those assigned to go with Rayloc. He was anxious to find the droglits and begin the process of destroying them. When they arrived, there were many droglits outside the cave. Tincolad was surprised to see females and immature droglits at the cave. In all the stories he had ever heard, the droglits were always described as adult males. Tincolad had never considered droglit families.

As the warriors approached the cave, the females and young ones ran into the cave. Several males came forward. They were short and stocky. To Tincolad, they looked much stronger than any man he had ever seen. They were uglier than Tincolad imagined, but they didn't look or act ferocious. In fact, Tincolad thought he could detect puzzlement and fear in the expressions on their faces.

When they got to the cave, Rayloc told the men from the village the warriors had to kill all the droglits. Rayloc did not speak the new language as well as Warlog, and it was difficult for Tincolad to understand. It seemed some of the Fish River men were arguing with Rayloc. Rayloc gave the order to kill the droglits. Warlog's warriors sent a storm of arrows. All the droglits outside the cave were killed. Rayloc ordered the warriors to go in the cave to kill all who hid there.

The killing of those outside the cave happened so fast Tincolad did not have a chance to kill a single one. Tincolad advanced to the cave. There was a lot of confusion at the cave entrance. Some of the Fish River men were arguing, while others were trying to keep the warriors from entering the cave. Some were even using weapons to fight the warriors. As he approached the cave, Tincolad was shaking with excitement and anticipation of the glory he would win. If he could tell his father he had killed a droglit, Lendoclad would be proud of him and finally realize why Warlog was important.

By the time he reached the cave entrance, the Fish River men who had fought the warriors were killed or captured. Tincolad rushed into the cave. There was a fire and several torches in the cave. Tincolad had a hard time seeing at first. There were shadows of droglits scurrying in all directions. They were large and small. There were screams, and even though Tincolad could not understand the words, he could hear the terror in the sounds they made. It was not what he had expected.

Tincolad's eyesight adjusted to the dim light. The warriors were using daggers and spears to kill the droglits at close range. One droglit came running toward Tincolad. He thrust his spear at it, but the droglit was too fast. It grabbed the end of the spear. For a short pause, Tincolad looked into the droglit's eyes. He did not see the anger and hatred he expected. The face was full of confusion and hurt.

Tincolad tried to pull his spear back, but the droglit used its strength to swing the spear around, smashing Tincolad against the side of the cave. The shaft of his spear broke, and he slumped against the wall.

The droglit quickly grabbed him and threw him to the floor of the cave so hard it knocked his breath out. Tincolad could not believe the strength of this droglit. Then he saw the droglit was a female! The droglit put the point of Tincolad's broken spear against his neck. The cold stone of the sharpened point pressed against his skin, and he knew he would die. He was calm and not afraid. Again he looked into the eyes of the droglit. The confusion in its eyes turned to sadness. It dropped the spear and turned away.

As Tincolad caught his breath, he saw the female looking for something. The female ran a couple of steps and picked up a small droglit. Tincolad was sure it was crying. The female stood with the small one in its arms, and three warriors thrust spears into her. It dropped the small one and took one look at Tincolad before falling. Another warrior smashed the head of the small droglit with a club. This was not the war Tincolad dreamed of.

Tincolad tried to stand. His head spun, and he swallowed the bitter vomit rising in his throat. He dropped to one knee to keep from falling. The female droglit pulled the body of the little one to it, tenderly cradling it in its arms. It looked at Tincolad. He tried to turn away, but there was something about the female's eyes that held him. It was almost as if it could talk with its eyes. Tincolad could almost grasp its meaning—almost. Tincolad watched the pool of blood around it growing, and then its eyes closed.

Finally, Tincolad stood up. He had faced death, but in a situation he had never imagined. Would he have run if he could? He did not know the answer. The battle was over. It was a battle with no glory—no honor. Tincolad stumbled from the cave with several other warriors. For a few moments, all was silent except for occasional moans of droglits that were dying. A few warriors began to shout and cheer. The celebration quickly spread through the warriors. Tincolad joined. They had completely wiped out the first cavern of droglits.

Rayloc climbed to the highest stone in front of the cave. "Warriors of Warlog … hear my words. Today for the first time in all the history of the People, we have fought the droglits face to face," Rayloc paused and then shouted, "and we have won!"

A great cheer rose from the warriors. Tincolad cheered as loudly as anyone. He saw the many strong droglit males that had been killed. He brushed the female from his mind. He regretted he had not killed a single strong male, but he would be better prepared next time. Rayloc held up both arms, and there was silence again.

"The eastern people who brought the first droglit to Warlog say the droglits have much magic. We have shown these droglits the power of Zendolot, praise to him, and the army of Warlog. We must not be foolish. We do not know all the magic of the droglits. To be certain nothing remains of this cave that will allow more droglits to find their way from the deep caverns, we must clean everything from the cave. There must be no trace of the droglits left inside. In order to make sure none of the dead droglits use these bodies to come back to life, we must build hearths like the copper smelters use. We must burn these bodies in the hot fires so that not even a small bone is left to let the droglits back. The ashes from the fires must be scattered in the wind. ,

"Warlog and his army will storm through this land." Rayloc's voice rose as he spoke until he was screaming at his loudest when he said, "Until the last droglit is turned to ashes." Tincolad was caught up in the celebration.

The men from the Fish River village stood silently watching the celebration. Rayloc spoke to them in their language, and they started moving the bodies of the droglits near the area where the warriors were making the hearths. Many of the eastern men had tears running down their cheeks.

Tincolad recognized the female when she was dragged from the cave. The small one with the smashed head was taken from her and put in a pile of small bodies.

There were droglit bodies everywhere. It had been a great victory. The thrill of the victory settled into the drudgery of the cleanup. The food was collected to be taken to the Fish River village for the people there. Warlog's warriors were forbidden to eat any of the droglit food. It was to be given to the eastern people to replace the food Warlog's army would take from them in tribute.

Soon the air was filled with smoke and the smell of burning flesh. It was late in the day when two warriors threw the body of the female into a fire. Tincolad had been drawn to look at it several times during the day. In spite of everything, he knew this female could have killed him, and it had chosen not to. More than once he wondered why.

As the body began to blacken in the fire, Tincolad walked to the pile of small droglits, picked up the one with the smashed head, and threw it into the fire with the female. He watched a short time and then went back to the work of cleaning up.

Later, when ashes were scraped from the hearth, Tincolad put some of them into a small leather bag he had found in the cave. He wanted to keep a part of the female with him for good luck.

It would take one or two days to finish the cleanup and destroy all the bodies. Rayloc selected several warriors, including Tincolad, to take him and the men of the Fish River village back to the village. Most of the warriors remained at the cave to finish the cleanup.

When those who returned to the village arrived, Rayloc went to report to Warlog. Tincolad got something to eat. There was much excitement among the warriors, but Tincolad found a place to be alone. After the confusion of the fighting, Tincolad learned that six of the Fish River village men who had tried to protect the droglits had been killed. None of Warlog's warriors had been killed by the droglits. Their strength must have been lost when they left the deep caverns.

It was dark when Rayloc and Warlog came from Warlog's tent. Rayloc called the village together.

"I am Warlog, Zendolot's Great Eagle," Warlog began in the language of the people of the East. He said something about men of the village who had tried to protect the droglits. Most of those men had been killed, but several were captured. Rayloc brought them back to the village. Warlog brought them out, and Rayloc brought their families. Warlog said something about treason, and then he ordered his warriors to kill the men and their families.

Tincolad and the other warriors had to use their spears to threaten the people in the village in order to control them. Soon everyone settled down.

"I am Warlog, Zendolot's Great Eagle." Warlog told the people that the village was part of the Empire and he would protect it. He said some other things about government, but Tincolad couldn't understand everything. One thing was certain; Warlog was in control.

Tincolad went to his sleep robes. He had seen much in the past days that disturbed him. Most of Warlog's army traveled several miles away from the group led by Warlog. Tincolad learned that the main army encountered several villages along the way. Warlog's warriors attacked the villages to obtain supplies. It was bloody, but Tincolad understood sacrifices had to be made to save the world from the droglits.

As Tincolad lay on his sleep robes thinking of the women and young children of the village who had been killed, the words of his mother came back to him. His family on his mother's side had fallen exactly as the people of this village. If Warlog found out who his mother was, Tincolad would meet the same fate.

He wanted to help kill the droglits. He was sure destroying the droglits and seeing the goal of ridding the earth of their threat somehow justified the required methods.

The droglits were uglier than he imagined. When he first saw them and the different way they moved and the awful sounds they made, he was convinced they were droglits sent to destroy the People. But when the killing started, things were different. Remembering the eyes of the female increased his confusion. Why had she spared him? The question and her eyes haunted his dreams.

CHAPTER 4

Broken Stick—The Protector

Summer 3286 BCE

For Broken Stick, time was unreal and immeasurable. He walked with a group of Warlog's warriors as they gathered Earth People in the village. The warriors came from a land far away. They had light skin and hair with blue eyes like the Earth People. When Warlog attacked, he and his warriors came fast and killed everyone who resisted them. Before Broken Stick could decide what to do, it was over. Some of the killers spoke the language of the Sun People. They told the people that in their language they were called warriors. The warriors killed Chief Strong Bison and all his family. They ordered Broken Stick to join with them or he and his family would be killed. He joined and went with them to the Earth People cave. He and his friends had no idea what would happen. The leader gave an order, and the warriors began killing the Earth People. Some of his friends near the cave tried to protect the Earth People. Broken Stick was at the back of the army. He had no weapons. All the Earth People were killed, and Broken Stick was still trying to figure out what to do. When they got back to the village, all his friends who had tried to help the Earth People were killed along with their families. Time crept, and he wondered why he was still alive. Perhaps it was because he lacked courage to fight.

The one called Rayloc spent the next morning separating the village into areas and assigning warriors to teach and lead the people. He called them warlents. He told each family how much of their food and possessions were to be given to Warlog as tribute. During the day, the warriors found seventeen

Earth People—males, females, and children in the village. Rayloc called them droglits. Warlog called the village together in the evening.

"I am Warlog, Zendolot's Great Eagle. I come to rid the land of droglits. Anyone who hides or protects a droglit will be killed along with all his family." Warlog spoke the language of the Sun People well. Broken Stick had no trouble understanding his words.

When Broken Stick realized Warlog was going to order his warriors to kill all the Earth People, something came over him he could not control. He stepped from the group of warriors he had been forced to join. He was tall and strong. At this moment, he did not fear Warlog or his warriors. Two of Warlog's warriors grabbed him by his upper arms. He did not resist their hold, but he stood immovable ten paces from Warlog. One of Warlog's warriors pulled his dagger and approached Broken Stick. The muscles across Broken Stick's chest rippled, but he looked steadfastly into Warlog's eyes without moving.

"Geylot!" Warlog shouted before the warrior plunged his dagger into Broken Stick's chest. The warrior stepped back. "Who are you, and what do you want?" Warlog demanded in Broken Stick's language.

Broken Stick spoke confidently. "I am Broken Stick, a new man in the army of Warlog, Zendolot's Great Eagle. I come to say something about droglits." At first Broken Stick had no idea what he would say or do—he just knew he had to do something. When he started to talk, he remembered he had heard Warlog planned to cross the Snow Mountains. An idea came to him.

"You are bold. Speak," Warlog ordered.

"I do not know all the new teachings Warlog, Zendolot's Great Eagle brings. These are things I must learn. I do know things of the Alliance between the Sun People and the droglits. I think some of the things I know would be useful to Warlog, Zendolot's Great Eagle."

"What do you ask for these things?"

"I ask only that you remember my loyalty if the information is useful. I ask that my family also be remembered. If my suggestions offend Warlog, Zendolot's Great Eagle, I don't intend to cause offense, but only to help. I ask only that you forgive my rudeness and help me to know the new teachings you bring."

"Broken Stick has my permission to speak. I will decide if the information has value and how you will be rewarded after I hear it. Speak!"

"The droglits are strong. They can be used to do much of the hard work in a warrior's camp. They can help the hunters find animals. They can tell the camp when to prepare for storms. This is important for a large group trying to move through this country."

Rayloc spoke to Warlog in their strange language.

When Rayloc was finished, Warlog said, "My shaman says the droglits are dangerous. They come from the deep caverns to destroy the world. What do you say to these words?"

"I don't know the deep caverns. I know the Snow Mountains. These are the highest mountains in the land. If Warlog, Zendolot's Great Eagle, wants to cross these mountains with his warriors, he will find the strength and skills of the droglits useful."

"How will we control the droglits?"

"The droglits put much value on the females and children. If you keep the females and children separate, the males will work hard to protect them. If you let the males know their females and young will only eat what is left over from the warriors, they will do their best to make sure your warriors find meat in abundance."

Rayloc and Warlog had a discussion in their language. Broken Stick thought Warlog might agree to save the Earth People, but Rayloc was arguing with him. Warlog finally whispered something, and Rayloc dipped his chin and stepped back.

Warlog turned to Broken Stick. "We will take these few droglits. We will guard them closely. We will see if they can be controlled and if they are useful to my army."

Warlog turned to the rest of the village. "I have talked with my shaman regarding the fate of these droglits. It is my desire to make peace with the Sun People. I make no peace with droglits. Broken Stick has said these droglits can help my army cross the Snow Mountains. They will live as long as they are useful. The females and young will be kept separate from the males. They will be protected and cared for by my warriors. This protection will be given only as long as the male droglits are useful. If one male droglit rebels or tries to escape, the protection will end. All the droglits ... males, females, and young will die. This is my promise.

"Broken Stick has offered this agreement. He will help guard the droglits. If the droglits rebel or try to escape, Broken Stick will die with them. If the droglits prove useful and cause no trouble, Broken Stick will be rewarded when the army crosses the Snow Mountains."

Broken Stick was relieved the Earth People would not die today, but he realized this was only a temporary solution. He didn't want the Earth People to help Warlog's army cross the Snow Mountains. He would have to find a way to escape with the Earth People before they got to the Snow Mountains.

****

Tincolad grew up hearing stories of the deep caverns and how evil and ferocious the droglits were. Before the attack on the droglit cave, the warriors in Warlog's army talked among themselves with great bravado about battling droglits, but Tincolad sensed it was surface bravado.

The fight at the cave was their first encounter with real droglits. After a bad night, Tincolad woke to find that the warriors who had stayed in the village were curious about the droglits and the details of the battle. What did they look like? Did they use magic? What kind of weapons did they have? How many were there? How did they fight?

The night had been difficult for Tincolad. But as the morning wore on, he joined with the warriors who had been at the cave in their enthusiastic description of the glorious defeat of the first droglits. Gradually, the picture of the female's eyes left his mind. He bathed in the glory of the attention he got from being in the first battle with droglits. When asked how many droglits he had killed, he answered that in the confusion of the battle and the darkness of the cave he could not be sure.

Tincolad was still glorying in his newfound status when Rayloc brought the droglits he had found in the village before Warlog. Seeing the fear and confusion on their faces threw Tincolad into confusion again.

"Rayloc will have these killed. Let's get close; maybe Warlog will choose us to help kill them," said one of the warriors who had been hanging on Tincolad's every word.

Tincolad hesitated. "Yeah … sure, let's go. I'll show you how it's done." He and several who had been hanging around him pushed closer to Rayloc. As Tincolad got closer, his resolve returned. He hoped he would be chosen to kill a droglit.

Before the killing of the droglits began, one of the men of the Fish River village stood before Warlog. Tincolad could not understand everything, but he could tell the man was arguing to save the droglits. From what Warlog and Rayloc said together in Tincolad's language, it was clear the strange man was arguing to spare the droglits so they could help Warlog's army. Warlog made his decision. The droglits would be spared! Tincolad could not believe what he heard.

All evening there was a great deal of upset among the warriors. The leaders explained that the droglits had been spared so they could be used to help the army travel in this new land. Many of the warriors agreed it was a wise decision. Droglits could help the army move through the Snow Mountains quickly so the villages on the other side could be defeated before they could organize and train an army of their own.

Tincolad sided with those who felt it was better to destroy all droglits as fast as possible. Warlog's army was strong enough to travel through this country and cross the Snow Mountains without the help of droglits. Warlog's army could easily defeat the Alliance whether it was organized or not. Tincolad had become a warrior so he could kill droglits. He had missed his first opportunity. Now, the second had passed.

Tincolad had another bad night. He woke several times from vivid dreams of the Warrior Ceremony. He dreamed of his face with Rencolad's blood dripping from his chin. Rencolad's blood boiled in his body. He was a warrior, but in his first fight, he had let the eyes of a female droglit prevent him from doing the duty of a warrior. When he woke, he knew that in the next battle with the droglits, he could not hold back. He had come to kill droglits. He had prepared himself to kill droglits. He was confident he would distinguish himself in the next conflict.

Tincolad went to get his first meal of the day feeling good about his future. Rencolad sat beside him. "Good morning, little brother."

"Good morning."

"What do you think of these droglits?"

Tincolad swallowed the piece of meat he was chewing. "I was worried about the rumors of their strength and magic. I'm happy to see they are much weakened by leaving their deep caverns. We will defeat them easily."

"We will see when we cross the Snow Mountains."

"What do you mean?"

"I have spent much of the night with Warlog, Rayloc, and the other leaders of the army. Warlog told us the stories of his first conquests. The first battles were easy because no one was prepared to fight his kind of war. He conquered all the southern tribes in one summer. The northern colonies were more difficult. There, the tribes organized large armies. It took three summers to defeat them.

"Things are like they were there. We will easily defeat the Alliance south of the Snow Mountains because we have surprised them. But we have to be wise about the Alliance north of the Snow Mountains.

"Warlog's goal is to settle everything on this side soon enough to cross the Snow Mountains this summer. The quicker we attack north of the Snow Mountains, the less time the Alliance will have to prepare.

"What I tell you now is important. Warlog has a plan, but only warriors who are to be part of the plan will be told about it. You have been chosen to be part of the plan. What I am about to explain, you must not repeat."

Tincolad's blood was rushing. He would be an important part of the secret plan to kill all the droglits. Surely, his father would be proud of him then. "What do you want me to do?"

"Many warriors question Warlog's decision to spare the droglits found in this village. This is an idea Warlog was thinking about before Broken Stick suggested the droglits could help cross the Snow Mountains. Warlog does not need droglits to move his army. He did not spare the droglits for that. Broken Stick gave Warlog a reason to keep the droglits without creating suspicions of what he is really doing."

"I don't understand."

Rencolad looked both ways and then spoke quietly. "The droglits we fought were different in many ways from what we know about droglits from our traditions. Light and sunshine change them. No one in Warlog's army knows what magic these droglits still have.

"Warlog wants to know more about them. He has kept these few alive for that purpose. Warlog picked me to be in charge of guarding the droglits, and I have picked several warriors to help me. You are one I have picked to help."

Tincolad could see the wisdom of Zendolot in Warlog. "What do you want me to do?"

"You will watch the droglits closely and learn their language. Droglits speak with a language using sounds people can't make. You won't be able to learn to speak their language, but you must learn to understand them like the eastern people do. You must also learn to understand and speak the language of the eastern people.

"Warlog believes the hardest part of the war will be next summer. He wants several warriors who understand the ways and language of the droglits and the eastern people. The only way this can be done is to keep some of them alive. Broken Stick gave Warlog an excuse to keep them.

"If Broken Stick and the captive droglits ever suspect what's going on, they won't cooperate. That's why you must not discuss this plan with anyone. The fewer who know about it, the less likely it will accidently slip out. You must pretend to be interested in the droglits and the eastern people. They must think you are learning their languages out of a personal interest."

"I came to kill droglits, not to learn about them."

"I know. That's the same reason I came. Warlog asks us to do something more important. Things went badly in this village. Several of the men from this village fought for the droglits at the cave. These people are too attached to the droglits. It causes too much anger among these people to know how the droglits must be disposed of.

"In the future, we will not take people from the village to the droglit caves. Only one person will show us the location of the caves. He will be sent back to the village before the killing begins.

"By the time people from the villages see a droglit cave, all evidence they were there will be gone. There will be no signs of droglits and no stories of how they died. They will be forgotten. That's why we need some or our men to understand the droglits. Even Rayloc agrees with this plan.

"As soon as we have learned all we need, we will kill them. You will have your chance then. The information you get will be used to make it easier for the army to find and kill the droglits."

Tincolad saw the clear reasoning in this plan. "I'm honored you think of me for this important job. My first desire is to kill droglits, but I will accept this new calling, and I will do my best to learn the languages and find out all I can about droglits and the eastern people."

"Good. Since it was Broken Stick's idea to save them, Warlog has asked him to help work with the droglits. You will work with him. He will teach you his language and help you understand the words of the droglits. You have already learned some of their language from the two who led us here. You must learn these things quickly. You must be a friend to Broken Stick."

Tincolad slept well for the first time in days. He and his father had been avoiding each other since their fight before Tincolad became a warrior. Tincolad would be one of the most important contributors to the complete destruction of the droglits. In the end, his father would understand and be proud of him again.

****

Sotif got up early. It was hot and humid, but it was more than weather that made sleep difficult. Messengers from the Fish River colony arrived ten days ago. They brought distressing news of hordes of men who came from the

West. At first the stories were sketchy, but more messengers kept arriving. Each brought unbelievable news. Sotif had moved his sleeping quarters from his normal place in the Heart of the Bison to the village so he could be close in case of an emergency.

As Sotif sat cross-legged on his sleep robes, there was a knock on the tent post. "Who is there?"

"Red Deer." There was stress in Red Deer's voice.

"Enter, Red Deer."

Red Deer pulled the cover back and stepped in.

"What causes Red Deer to wander through the village so early in the morning?"

"More messengers arrived late last night. The news they bring is important. Tall Tree is holding an emergency meeting this morning."

"What news do they bring?"

"Tall Tree waits for us. He will explain everything."

Sotif put a light summer robe over his shoulders and hurried to the meeting. Tall Tree was already seated in the place of leadership. Blue Lake, leader of the hunters who supplied meat for the Winding River colony, was seated beside Tall Tree. Hard Rock, shaman of the Sun People, was just taking a seat beside Blue Lake.

"Welcome," Tall Tree said to Sotif.

"Thank you. What is the purpose of this early meeting?"

"Everyone knows of the rumors of a large group of men who have come upon the Fish River colony. Last night, more messengers arrived, bringing terrible news." The sun came over the horizon, and the hot yellow light of a new day rolled over the village. "The men who come from the West are led by a man called Warlog. He comes to destroy the Alliance and force all Sun People to obey his commands, accept his beliefs, and pay tribute to him. He comes to destroy all Earth People. He teaches that Earth People come from the caves to destroy the Sun People. Warlog has conquered the Fish River colony. He has killed all the Earth People of that clan. Many Sun People were killed. Warlog's men fight by killing those who oppose them."

"I have never heard of such a thing!" Blue Lake said.

Sotif saw a deep shadow of doom settle on the faces of those in the meeting.

"How can our men fight men who kill?" Red Deer directed the question to Blue Lake. Blue Lake had no response.

"How many of the people of the Fish River colony were killed?" Sotif asked.

"The messengers say more than half of the men were killed," Tall Tree answered. "They say those who survived the fight were forced to join with Warlog's men. They will be trained to fight his way."

"We will have to learn this fighting," Blue Lake said. "We will have to fight men the way we hunt animals."

"Warlog and his men have started moving east," Tall Tree continued. "They will destroy the Winter Rest colony and then come to the Heart of the Bison. Most of the Sun People of the Winter Rest colony are running. The first should arrive in two days."

"What of the Earth People at the Winter Rest cave?" Lewtud asked.

"The messengers say most of the Earth People have chosen to stay," Tall Tree answered. "Some of our men will also stay to help them defend their cave. They will hide in their cave, but if Warlog finds them, they will fight. Their cave is on a steep hillside. It will be hard for Warlog to defeat them in their cave."

"What will we do when the people of the Winter Rest colony arrive? This village is not big enough to shelter so many," Red Deer asked.

"Our problem is not how to care for the Winter Rest colony," Tall Tree answered. "We cannot fight Warlog's army until we gather more men, and we must learn this new fighting where killing is the object."

"How will we do that?" Sotif asked.

"We must gather our people and escape to the other side of the Snow Mountains before winter."

"No!" Sotif let his gaze drift from man to man as they waited in silence for him to continue. "We cannot abandon the History Room or the Spirit Fire. They are the center of the Alliance."

"This is not a choice. If we stay, we will die, and Warlog will still have the Spirit Fire and the History Room. If we escape over the Snow Mountains, we can organize the men of the colonies to defeat Warlog. After Warlog is defeated, we can restore the History Room and the Spirit Fire."

"The messengers tell us of a kind of fighting our men do not understand," Blue Lake said. "We cannot stand against Warlog."

"We must cross the mountains," Hard Rock said. "We have been surprised by men who are too strong for us. We must escape now and prepare to fight later."

"Prepare for what?" Sotif asked. "What is the Alliance without the Spirit Fire and the History Wall?"

"What Hard Rock says is true," Tall Tree said. "If we stay to fight Warlog now, we will lose, and many will be killed. Warlog will still have the Heart of the Bison, and we will be destroyed."

"Our men are strong and skillful," Sotif argued. "They can kill. This is not much to change."

"Warlog comes with many men who have practiced this killing," Blue Lake said. "He brings more men than we have ever seen."

"We will have more men when the people of the Winter Rest colony arrive. We can also send messengers to the Flat Ridge colony to send all their men," Sotif said.

"The Flat Ridge colony is too far away," Tall Tree said. "The messengers say Warlog brings more men than all three of these villages. The only hope for the Alliance is to escape through the Snow Mountains. If Warlog can be held on this side of the Snow Mountains until snow closes the passes, we will have all winter to organize a large force of men from all the colonies. The men will have time to learn about this new way of fighting. Next summer, we will be able to defeat Warlog if he comes north."

"The Spirit Fire has burned constantly for hundreds of generations. This string will be broken if it is put out," Sotif said.

"The Spirit Fire must be moved north," Hard Rock said.

"No!" Sotif said. "In ancient times, the eastern colonies were covered by a flood for moving the Spirit Fire. It is the will of Mother Earth to keep the Spirit Fire in the Heart of the Bison. If we show strength to defend the Heart of the Bison, the Great Spirit and Mother Earth will turn everything in our favor."

"The Sun People will not sacrifice their lives in a useless attempt to fight Warlog," Long Shadow said. "If we had a chance to win, it would be different. The stories of Mother Earth and the Great Spirit are old Traditions. They are idle talk during idle times that have no meaning in modern times."

Sotif stood. He was shaking so that he had to take a short pause to get control of his voice. "This is the talk of new generations. It is the talk of the greedy ones who do not want to make sacrifices to Mother Earth and the Great Spirit. It is the talk of those who do not respect the Traditions of the Sun People or the Memories of the Ancients. This is the kind of talk that causes the Great Spirit and Mother Earth to withdraw from our land."

"The Memories of the Earth People are not empty," Lewtud insisted, speaking in the language of the Earth People. "The Memories of the Earth

People are the way out of these modern days. The problems of these days come because the Sun People do not honor the Memories. The problems of these days come because the Earth People do not honor the Traditions. The solution is to honor the Memories. The solution is to honor the Traditions."

"Lewtud and Sotif speak well and honorably," Tall Tree said. "Do the old stories tell Lewtud and Sotif to let everyone die to save a cave that cannot be saved? The Spirit Fire will not stop Warlog. The History Room will not slow Warlog. There are many colonies of the Alliance over the Snow Mountains. There the Alliance will stand together to defeat Warlog. I have seen the valleys over the Snow Mountains. It's a fertile land with room for all the Sun People and the Earth People. It's a land where the Sun People are strong. Warlog cannot come to the land across the Snow Mountains."

Sotif could hardly contain his anger. "Tall Tree would abandon the Heart of the Bison forever?"

"The Heart of the Bison was good for many generations, but it has become isolated. The Alliance lives across the Snow Mountains. It's time to move the center of the Alliance to where the people of the Alliance live."

"No!" Sotif shouted. "The Heart of the Bison is the center of everything sacred to the Sun People and the Earth People."

"Sotif is a respected History Man of the old ways," Tall Tree said. "He fights for the old ways, but the old ways no longer serve the Alliance. The only hope for this colony is to run through the Snow Mountains. We will split into groups. The first groups will run through the pass. The last group will be made of the colony's strongest men. This group will lead Warlog in circles and delay him so the rest can escape. This group will delay Warlog until the Earth People say the first big storm comes. Then they will escape through the Antelope Pass ahead of the storm. Warlog's army will be stuck south of the Snow Mountains until next summer. This will give us time to organize the colonies to defeat Warlog and his men. We will send messengers to the Flat Ridge colony to escape also."

"This is a good plan," Hard Rock agreed.

"You would abandon the Heart of the Bison forever?" Sotif asked again.

"We will begin a new history and a new kind of Spirit Fire for the Alliance."

"Tall Tree would abandon all the Memories and Traditions of the Alliance?"

"Old teachings do not help or serve the people in these modern days," Hard Rock argued. "History Rooms, Spirit Fires, and sacrifices are things of the past. It takes more than old Memories and dead beliefs to protect the people from men such as Warlog."

"When you call upon the colonies north of the Snow Mountains to unite, what will they unite around? The people need the uniting force of the ceremonies and sacrifices. You take away all they would fight for and then expect them to fight and die. For what?"

"They will fight for their lives and the lives of their children," Tall Tree answered. "They will fight for peace to live free. You would have them fight for dead stories and dusty icons."

"The Earth People clan of the Heart of the Bison will not run from Warlog," Lewtud stated. "The Earth People clan of the Heart of the Bison will fight to protect the Spirit Fire."

"The Alliance is as old as the hills," Blue Lake said. "There are many who say the time has come for the Alliance to end. I hear people saying Warlog has come to break the Alliance. They say we should not fight this because the time of the Alliance is over. I don't agree. The messengers say Warlog has come to kill all the Earth People. Who here is ready to see all the Earth People destroyed?"

There was a long silence, and then Tall Tree spoke. "This is why we must abandon the Heart of the Bison now. If we stand up to Warlog one colony at a time, he will run through the lands of our forefathers, destroying the Alliance colony by colony. He will kill all the Earth People, clan by clan. We must make it possible for the people to escape to the North. This is the only way to defeat Warlog."

"This valley cannot be defended," Hard Rock said, "but the Heart of the Bison can be defended with a few strong men. The entrance is long and narrow. Warlog's men would have to attack in small numbers that can be stopped in the entrance."

"If the Heart of the Bison is defended, it would help the rest to escape," Long Shadow added. "Warlog knows much about the Alliance. He must know the Heart of the Bison is important. If it's defended, he may delay following those who cross the Snow Mountains."

"If we leave twenty men with food and supplies," Hard Rock said, "they might even be able to hold the Heart of the Bison through the winter. That would be long enough for Tall Tree to organize men to return early next summer and drive Warlog from the land."

"If we make a stand here, the Great Spirit and Mother Earth will assist us," Blue Lake added.

"Mother Earth can protect the Heart of the Bison," Hard Rock said. "Mother Earth would not require a large number of men. Lewtud can stay and protect the Heart of the Bison. With Mother Earth's help, he will not need many men. The rest of the people can cross the Snow Mountains to safety."

"This idea is good," Tall Tree agreed. "We will prepare the tribe to leave. The first group should be ready to leave in a couple of days. If Mother Earth and the Great Spirit are with us, we will create an army of the Alliance to return next summer and drive Warlog from our ancient lands."

"Lotak says ... the Ancients were led to this place by Kectu. Kectu is sister to the Spirit Fire. The Spirit Fire cannot die. This is the first story of the History Room. The Ancients are close to the Great Shorec, Kectu. The Ancients cannot abandon the Heart of the Bison."

"Always some of the Earth People travel with the Sun People to tell the weather and guide the hunters," Tall Tree said.

"Lotak knows this," Lotak said. "Lotak must send Earth People with the Sun People. Most of the Earth People will stay. The Ancients must stay. The clan of the Earth People must defend the Heart of the Bison. The clan of the Earth People must defend the Spirit Fire of Kectu. So Lotak says, so it shall be."

The other representatives of the Earth People repeated, "So Lotak says, so it shall be."

"The Earth People will not be able to defend the Heart of the Bison against Warlog's men," Tall Tree said. "The Ancients of the clan are important to keep the Memories. They cannot fight. What Hard Rock says is wise. Warlog will not be able to leave an armed cave of strong men behind him. He will have to leave many men behind to guard the cave or he will have to attack it. We will leave forty Sun People men to protect the Heart of the Bison."

"This is a good plan," Sotif agreed. All the other members of the council agreed to the plan. Sotif was not happy the village would be abandoned, but he was happy the Heart of the Bison and the Traditions of the Alliance would be protected. He knew if they fought to protect the Heart of the Bison and the Spirit Fire, Mother Earth would not let Warlog win.

Sotif returned to the Heart of the Bison after the meeting. He was greeted by the familiar smells of the cave. The Spirit Fire blazed thirty paces in front of him at a point on the side of a hearth about six paces in diameter. The fire watchers continuously moved the fire around the hearth by adding fuel on the side in the direction they wanted it to move. The Spirit Fire made a complete circle around the hearth with each cycle of the moon. Cooled ashes were removed each day, directly across the hearth from the burning fire.

As Sotif watched the Spirit Fire, he thought of the Spirit Fire ceremonies. During the ceremonies, the Spirit Fire was fed until it filled the entire hearth. Flames leaped into the air, and the radiant heat could be felt throughout the main cavern. The ashes of the Earth People who had died were added to the Spirit Fire during the Ceremony of the Ashes.

Sotif walked to the fire watchers. It was their job to make certain the fire moved around the hearth in time with the phases of the moon. There were always three watchers on duty day and night.

"The fuel stock is getting low," Sotif said to one of the fire watchers.

"Kelso welcomes Sotif to the Spirit Fire. Kelso has requested more fuel for the Spirit Fire. The extra fuel must be brought before Earth's Fireball falls into Mother Earth."

"Good. Sotif goes to the History Room."

Kelso picked a ceremony torch from a rack and ignited it in the Spirit Fire. Sotif took the torch. "Sotif thanks Kelso." Sotif looked around the large cavern. Earth People had lived in the Heart of the Bison hundreds of generations. Surely, they would live there always.

As Sotif walked down the tunnel to the History Room, he thought of the many, many people who had walked down this tunnel to immerse themselves in the beauty of the paintings and the majesty of the history they showed.

Once in the room, Sotif ignited the eight ceremony torches. These torches could only be ignited by flames brought from the Spirit Fire. For all the generations since the First Painting was done, the only illumination to ever light this room had come from the Spirit Fire.

Sotif sat cross-legged in front of the First Painting and inhaled the smells of the History Room. He studied the First Painting. It showed the Guardian, a great Sun People Spirit Man representing the Great Spirit. Next to him was Kectu, shorec of the Earth People, representing Mother Earth. The Great Spirit and Mother Earth were the creators of the earth, sun, moon, and stars. The First Painting symbolically showed that Kectu of the Earth People and the Guardian of the Sun People mated and had a daughter. According to the Traditions, the daughter was named Tuk. Sky Runner, a great Hunter of the Sun People, mated with Tuk. They were depicted below Kectu and the Guardian. The painting showed that Tuk and Sky Runner had a son. Tuk and Sky Runner were killed in a fight between the Sun People and the Earth People. Shekek, their son, was raised by Kectu and the Guardian. It was

Shekek who created the Alliance and brought the tribes of the Sun People and the clans of the Earth People together in the Heart of the Bison. The Heart of the Bison was the symbol of the Alliance between the Sun People and the Earth People.

The symbolic power of the Alliance was the Spirit Fire. Kectu gave the Spirit Fire to Shekek. It was called the Spirit Fire because it contained the spirit sister of Kectu. The Spirit Fire had burned continuously since the beginning of the Alliance.

Sotif looked at the other paintings on the History Wall. They depicted the major events in the history of the Alliance from its beginning to the present time. The First Painting was the most important because it told of the beginning. The largest painting was the Great Alliance Painting. This showed the time when the Alliance covered the whole earth. It took two years of hard travel just to go from the Heart of the Bison to the Mammoth cave in the East. Because the distance was so great, sparks from the Spirit Fire were taken to the Mammoth cave. In those days, there were two Spirit Fires.

Above the Great Alliance Painting was the Flood Painting. It depicted the time of the great flood that had destroyed the eastern part of the Alliance when Mother Earth was angry because the Alliance split the Spirit Fire. After the loss of the Mammoth cave, Mother Earth took all mammoths from the earth to show that the Mammoth cave was no more. Now, the only mammoths were on the History Wall paintings.

After the great flood, the Alliance began to decline. It had shrunk to just twenty-two colonies.

After so many seasons of being the center of the spiritual and cultural ties of the Alliance, the History Room, and the Spirit Fire were threatened from two sources. First, there were people of the Alliance who wanted to change the laws of the Alliance. Second, Warlog was coming to destroy the Earth People and force the Sun People to forsake the Memories and Traditions. Sotif was sure Mother Earth and the Great Spirit would protect the Alliance if the people held strongly to the Memories and Traditions their ancestors had honored for many, many seasons.

Even before Warlog, the colonies of the Alliance were falling away from the Memories and Traditions. There was much murmuring, and many were proposing changes. The colonies of the North wanted to distribute sparks from the Spirit Fire so each clan would have its own Spirit Fire. Many shomots, especially from the farthest clans, said mixing of ashes in a central fire was not needed. All clans were joined together by Mother Earth, and therefore, journeys to the Spirit Fire were no longer needed. These people had lost the meaning of the flood and the end of the mammoths.

With so many other ideas and proposed changes, it was hard to maintain the purity of the Memories and Traditions. Warlog was being sent to punish the people and force them back to the strict observance of the original promises Mother Earth and the Great Spirit had made with the people of the Alliance.

Sotif looked at the many paintings of the History Room bathed in the light of his torch. After so many generations, Mother Earth would not allow the History Room to be desecrated or the Spirit Fire to be extinguished. Sotif shivered at the thought of what it would mean to lose these two symbols of the Great Spirit's agreement with the Sun People and the Earth People. Only by returning to the bosom of Mother Earth and the heart of the Great Spirit could the Alliance find the strength to resist the threat of Warlog and others like him.

Several weeks later, Sotif sat on the ceremony rock and watched the last of Tall Tree's tribe leave the village that had been inhabited by the Sun People since the beginning. This last group consisted of the strongest men and women.

The cave was stocked with food, and the underground river provided plenty of water. The long, narrow entrance to the cave would be easy to defend. Sotif was sure the forty strong men Tall Tree left would be enough to protect the cave.

The messengers who arrived yesterday said Warlog had passed the Winter Rest colony. He had destroyed the Earth People. There was nothing between Warlog and the Winding River village.

Tall Tree set the village and the fields of grain on fire. All the unripe fruit had been cleaned from the orchards. Tall Tree did not want to leave anything behind that Warlog could use. The fields south of the village were burning. Smoke began to curl up from the village itself. Fires in the north fields were blazing.

Sotif thought of Warlog and this new killing. What did Warlog want? Why had Mother Earth allowed so much killing?

By evening, most of the fires had burned out. The village and all the fields were destroyed. In the deepening dark of a moonless night, the remaining hot spots glowed as angry red eyes all across the valley. Occasionally, a breeze stirred a red spot into yellow flames that raged at the sky and then died back to red. The whole valley was alive with twinkling, flaring, and dying fires. The smell of smoke filled the air and filtered into the Heart of the Bison.

Sotif had sat on the thinking stone all day, watching the destruction of the valley he loved. He was sore and stiff when he stood up. He wondered why he was alive to see such a terrible sight. The Supreme Council of the Alliance would certainly want to have a painting in the History Room. All the villages south of the Snow Mountains would be destroyed. There would be much of this new fighting next summer. Sotif realized it would be many years before all the destruction could be repaired.

There were no stories of anything like this. Sotif walked into the cave trying to picture how the new painting would look. It would be the saddest painting since the big flood.

The next two days were an uneasy time for Sotif. On the morning of the third day, the lookouts reported Warlog would enter the valley before midday.

A large group of men came into the valley before the sun was at its highest. The warriors ran through the village whooping and yelling. They tore through the remains of the village looking for anything of value, creating a cloud of dust and ashes. Sotif walked slowly back into the Heart of the Bison. His feet shuffled, and his head hung down like an old man.

****

As Warlog's army approached the Winding River village, advance warriors brought back information that the Winding River village was being abandoned. Then the sky over the Winding River village was filled with smoke. Even after hearing all the stories and seeing the smoke, Broken Stick was shocked at the sight of the burned village and crops when they came over the hill overlooking the Winding River village. He had many happy memories of a time two summers ago when he had spent the summer with his uncle in the Winding River village. Foremost on his mind was Bright Moon. She was a neighbor to Broken Stick's uncle. They had spent many hours together that first summer.

Last summer, Broken Stick had spent a week with his uncle. Bright Moon had matured, and the two young lovers talked of a future together. He planned to return to the Winding River village this summer to ask Bright Moon's father to give her to him as his life mate.

Broken Stick found the ashes of Bright Moon's dwelling. He wondered if he would ever find her. A shadow fell across the ashes in front of him. "Is this where she lived?"

Broken Stick looked up. A young man wearing the leather belt, loin cloth, and vest of a warrior in training stood in front of him. "Yes, Bent Spear."

"Where do you think they are?"

"Warlog and his warriors will ask the same question. We must say we do not know. We must not make any guesses that will help Warlog."

"It's good they have run. Warlog's army is stronger than all the colonies on this side to the Snow Mountains. I hope they have run across the mountains."

"We must not say anything of this to Warlog's warriors."

"What do you two there?" It was Rencolad speaking in the strange manner and accent of these western people who were just learning the language of the Sun People.

"Just looking to see if anything useful survived the fires," Broken Stick replied.

"Come, you two. The droglits must you guard."

Broken Stick had discovered two of his friends from the Fish River colony. He got Rencolad to assign them to help guard and protect the Earth People. Bent Spear was one, and Rushing Water was the other. The three hoped to escape with the captive Earth People sometime before winter snows made travel impossible. So far, none of them had an idea how to do that.

Broken Stick noticed six men walking up toward the Heart of the Bison. Some men came from the cave, and there appeared to be a short conversation. Then the six men started back down the hill. Tincolad found Broken Stick at the droglit campsite. "Warlog sent warriors to Bison Heart. Bring back leader of you to talk, they will. Only six down come. Leader of you, not come. Why wonder I."

Broken Stick liked the young warrior. He didn't think Tincolad was a killer like the other warriors. "I don't think my people will come from the cave. I think they will not let Warlog in the cave."

"Big, is this cave?"

"I haven't been in the cave." Broken Stick had gone in to see the Spirit Fire two summers ago, but he would not tell Tincolad. He was always careful about how much he told this inquisitive young man.

"How many droglits inside, live there?"

"Who knows how many people are there now? Perhaps they have heard Warlog kills all the Earth People."

"Evil, droglits are. Magic use they to fool people of you."

"What is the reason to fool my people?"

"Droglits from deep in earth, come. All people of I, this know. Dracolut leader of they, is. Dracolut sends they to trick people of you. When all people tricked, are, then Dracolut, the sun take from earth, will he. Then all people in dark, live. All people Dracolut, serve must."

"The magic of the Earth People helps my people. Because of the magic of the Earth People, my people have better lives."

"This magic to fool you, Dracolut sends. When fooled are you, quickly comes he to take sun."

"We have lived with the Earth People for hundreds of generations. The Alliance is as old as the mountains. The sun always shines, and life is better with the Earth People."

The young man seemed puzzled by this response. He questioned Broken Stick about the meaning of hundreds of generations. Broken Sick could tell it made Tincolad uneasy to find out how long the Earth People had been helping the Sun People.

A larger group of men started up the hill. A warrior came and said something to Tincolad. He was very excited.

"Goes now Warlog, to talk. People of you refused to come. Warlog kill all, will. People of you will fight much?" Tincolad asked.

"I don't know," Broken Stick said.

Tincolad ran after the other warriors.

****

Soft Cloud had never been to the Winding River village, but she cried when she saw the devastation as she walked over the hill. This had been the center of her beliefs. She had often thought about making a trip to see the Heart of the Bison and the Spirit Fire.

Soft Cloud's family had delayed running from the Winter Rest village when they heard of the devastation of the Fish River colony. They barely got out in time. As they were travelling, her younger brother hurt his ankle. They were hiding across the ravine from the Earth People cave when the killers attacked the Earth People. They killed everyone, including women and children. Soft Cloud was seventeen summers old, and it was the saddest day of her life.

Soft Cloud and her family stayed hidden two days near the cave while her brother's foot healed. They watched the killers clear the cave out and burn all the bodies and their possessions. Soft Cloud and her father sneaked to the cave after the killers left. The ashes of their fires had been scattered, and there was nothing of the Earth People left in or around the cave; it was as if they had never existed.

Soft Cloud and her father collected traces of the ashes that were left. They would run to the Winding River village and the Heart of the Bison and give the ashes to Sotif so he could add them to the Spirit Fire.

Soft Cloud had finally reached the Winding River village, but her family was dead, and she was a captive of the killers. The killers were setting up a camp just north of the burned village. When she and the other camp women were brought to the camp, they were taken to a part that was set up for camp workers.

One of the killers untied her from the women she had been tied to for two days. The women in the camp were dirty, and their clothing was torn. In all their faces, Soft Cloud saw pain and shame. She knew she looked the same. She knew her own pain and shame. She noticed a woman who seemed familiar. As Soft Cloud approached, she recognized her from Winter Rest village. She wasn't a friend of hers, but it was someone she knew.

"Sparkling Water?" she said.

The woman jumped to her feet and started to back away.

"Don't you remember me? I'm Soft Cloud."

Tears came to the eyes of the other woman. "I thought all the Winter Rest women were in my camp. Where did you come from?"

"I was only caught two days ago. The killers found us and killed all my family but me. I have never known such pain."

Sparkling Water came to her and hugged her. "These are hard times. I don't understand. They say the people of the Winding River village have run away, but some are hiding in the Heart of the Bison."

"You're a camp woman?"

"Yes," Sparkling Water answered in a whisper of shame. "It's a hard life … worse than I could imagine. You must not call them killers."

"Why?"

"You must use the words of their language. Their word for killing is war. Killers are warriors. The leaders are warlents. The chief is Warlog. Their word for woman is whore. These are the important new words you must know. The men with the straight hair and beards are the warriors. You must do whatever they say. Those are the important things to know."

"What about running away?"

"They have trained dogs to chase whores. Some say the dogs eat whores when they catch them. It's a hard life. Only the Great Spirit and Mother Earth can stop Warlog."

"Do you have friends?"

"I know some people from Winter Rest. I have met others from Fish River. My best friend got hurt. She was killed because she couldn't work. The warriors brought whores with them, but it's hard to be friends with them. You can't understand what they say."

Soft Cloud sat on the ground near a tent. The ashes she and her father had gathered were back in the camp with the bodies of her family. After stacking her family like firewood, the warriors dragged her to their camp. She was dumped with a group of women who were tied together around their waists in groups of three.

She had befriended the two girls she was tied to. They were from the Fish River village where their families were killed. They were taken to work in the warrior camps. Their chores included cooking, cleaning, and making the warriors feel good.

"To mate?" Soft Cloud had asked.

One of her new friends answered in a cold voice filled with hate, "To mate … no this is not mating. I don't have the word for this. It's mating, but it's not mating. They join, they hurt, they do things I have never thought about, and then they toss you aside. If you are broken and bruised, and you don't do your work in the morning to fix their meal and clean their mess, they beat you."

That night, she had learned firsthand what the girl was talking about. Three different warriors had used her. All that night, she thought about dying. In the morning, she was bruised and sore. *Maybe they will kill me if I refuse to work*, she thought, but the women tied to her made her continue.

Soft Cloud shook her head. That was only two days ago. She could not go on like this. She knew she had to find a way to escape. There were six warriors spaced around the camp where the women were. Each one had a large dog.

Not far away, she saw two groups of Earth People. One group included women, children, and a few old Earth People. The other was all young Earth People men. If they could all join together, there might be a way to escape. It was something she needed to think about; otherwise she faced a life without hope, and she might as well die.

She wondered what her life would be even if she escaped. The warriors used her even when she was tied to the other women. She couldn't look at the other women, but she knew they had had their turns before and probably would again. It was so hard to lie beside a woman—tied to her—while she was being used that way. How could she ever mate with a man to have her own children? The thought of being with any man made her sick. It would be better to be killed and eaten by dogs than do that again.

****

Tincolad was surprised at the devastation of the Winding River village as he came over the last hill with the Earth People he was guarding. From this distance, the dwellings in the village looked like blackened stumps in a burned forest. The land around was also a blackened wasteland. The people of the Alliance had burned everything. He walked by orchards where the fruit lay rotting on the ground, too green to use.

Warlog's army had spread out in many groups looking for stragglers and food. Now, they were all being organized into one large camp. The Earth People women and children were being gathered northeast of the main camp, away from the river. Not far from the Earth People was an area set aside for the camp whores. Tincolad could see there were many of the brown-skinned women from the villages Warlog had defeated. They seemed to be in particularly bad condition.

When the camp was set up and the guards were placed, Tincolad walked to the main camp, which was located on the riverbank south of the destroyed village. From there he watched the messengers go up the hill toward a cave, which must have been the Heart of the Bison. They were sent to bring the leaders back to talk with Warlog. A few people came from the cave, but it was too far away for Tincolad to see what they looked like. In a short time, the messengers came down alone.

Tincolad noticed Broken Stick watching the messengers coming down. He talked with Broken Stick about why the people from the cave refused to talk with Warlog. Tincolad tried to get some useful information about the cave and the people in it, but Broken Stick seemed to know very little. He tried to explain to Broken Stick that the droglits were fooling his people to put them under their power, but Broken Stick didn't understand. Broken Stick told Tincolad his people had been joined with the droglits a long time, as long as the mountains had existed. Tincolad was confused by that. The droglits should have taken them to the dark caverns by now. He wondered why it took the droglits so long.

Broken Stick had been teaching Tincolad the language of the eastern people. They had a backward way of speaking that made learning difficult, but added to what he had already learned, in just a few days he could understand many simple ideas, and he could get some of his own ideas across. Now, Tincolad understood much of Broken Stick's language, and he was beginning to understand the droglits.

When the first warriors got back from the cave, Tincolad guessed they had refused to come to the camp to meet with Warlog. Tincolad was surprised to see the second group leave to go up to the cave. This time, Warlog was with them. He ran from Broken Stick to where Rencolad and his warriors were waiting.

Tincolad saw several people come from the cave to meet with Warlog. This time, they spent much more time talking before Warlog and the warriors started back down the mountain.

When they got down, Rencolad was called to meet with Warlog and his counselors.

"Do we kill the droglits now?" Tincolad asked Rencolad when he came from the meeting.

"The leaders of the Alliance will not leave the cave. Warlog will have to force them out."

"We should kill the droglits now and gather the army to attack."

"The army has to attack through the entrance to the cave. Warlog could see from the meeting point that the entrance is small, not like the caves of the other droglits. We cannot attack with the whole army at once."

"What does that mean?"

"This is not a problem of needing more men to make the attack, since only a few can go through the entrance at a time. Some of the Sun People say this opening is narrow for a long way. This is a new kind of problem. Warlog will try to attack it, but if that doesn't work, he will have to think of something else."

"We could starve them out."

"They have food stored for the winter. That's another reason why we must take the cave."

"When do we kill the droglits?"

"There is no need to kill them right now. We must take the cave, and then Warlog will decide what to do next."

Tincolad was disappointed. He had started to go to his father's tent several times, but he had nothing to offer. If only he could tell him he had killed droglits and helped save the People. He wanted to tell him he was secretly learning the language and the ways of the droglits so the army could kill them, but he had sworn to Rencolad he would tell no one about the plan.

The days went slowly for Tincolad. Twice Warlog attacked the cave, but both times he found the tunnel into the cave too difficult to get through. This was the first time Warlog had been stopped. Tincolad wanted to join the warriors in the fight. In his mind, he would not be a real warrior until he had fought and killed a droglit.

****

Sotif was frightened the first time Warlog attacked. Blue Lake and his men stopped the warriors in the entrance. Three days later, Warlog attacked again, and again Blue Lake stopped him. Blue Lake lost six men in those attacks. He changed how he placed his men to protect them from the arrows that came in. As Blue Lake made adjustments, Sotif gained confidence.

The defense of the cave would go well as long as they had arrows. Warlog's warriors had shot many arrows into the tunnel. Some were broken when they hit the walls of the cave. They were made to fit the bows Warlog's warriors used. Blue Lake's men and the Earth People gathered the enemy's arrows and rebuilt them to make suitable arrows for their bows. Blue Lake told Sotif he could defend many more attacks.

Ever since it was decided Tall Tree and the people of the village would leave, the Earth People had been working to seal off the tunnel into the History Room. There had been several dwellings and other structures constructed in the cave with rocks that were brought in from outside. These rocks were used to seal the tunnel. The work was completed when Warlog's army arrived. It could be opened again, but it would take much more time and effort for the Sun People to undo what the much stronger Earth People had done. If Warlog did succeed in taking the Heart of the Bison, Sotif hoped he would not want to expend the time and effort to destroy the History Room.

As Sotif was thinking, the light from the tunnel was blocked. Long Feather sounded the alarm. The Sun People took their places and began shooting arrows into the tunnel. But this time something was different. There were no arrows coming back, and there were no screams from wounded warriors in the tunnel. Something was coming down the tunnel at a steady rate that was not slowed by the arrows.

Blue Lake screamed, "Stop shooting!" In the dim light from the tunnel, Sotif could see a heavy wooden shield moving steadily through the tunnel. Several men followed Blue Lake into the tunnel to stop it. The men behind Blue Lake pushed him into the arrows that had been shot into the shield. Some broke off, and the shivers of the shafts pierced his body. He screamed in agony. By the time the men pulled him from the shield, several arrows were in his body. "Put boulders in front to stop it," he ordered. Several Earth People ran to take boulders from the tunnel to the History Room, but before they could bring them, the shield came into the cave, and Warlog's warriors spilled from both sides.

At first, Blue Lake's men contained Warlog's forces near the entrance to the cave, but they could not stop the continual flood of new warriors running in from behind the shield. Blue Lake's men were overpowered, and most were killed. Warlog's warriors drove all the survivors from the Heart of the Bison.

The sun hurt Sotif's eyes as he stumbled from the cave. Most of the Earth People were killed in the cave. Blue Lake and Long Feather were both dead. Only seven of the forty Sun People who had stayed to defend the Heart of the Bison were still alive. Three of them were wounded. They had to be carried from the cave.

Sotif recognized Warlog. Warlog looked at the captives. "You," he said, pointing to Sotif. "Come here."

Sotif walked to Warlog.

"You are of mixed blood. You were here when I made the offer for the Sun People to leave."

"It is true."

Warlog said something to one of his captains in a language Sotif did not understand. The captain had several warriors bring the seven remaining men of Blue Lake's forces. "I offered food and freedom to all of Blue Lake's men," Warlog said to the captives in their language. Warlog turned to Sotif. "I offered freedom or death to these men. I keep my word." He gave an order in his language, and four arrows were shot into those who were not wounded. Then seven warriors cut the throats of all seven. Sotif was horrified, not only with how fast it was done, but with the coolness and lack of emotion shown by those who killed and those who watched.

Sotif was ready to die. His personal loss had no meaning. The Heart of the Bison was now in the hands of Warlog. All the Memories and Traditions of the Alliance would be lost. The History Room might be destroyed, but the most terrible thing of all—the Spirit Fire would be extinguished after so many generations. Mother Earth and the Great Spirit were through with the Earth People. There would be nothing left now to hold them together. They would be scattered and lost.

"What is your position with this people?"

Sotif was sure Warlog already knew much about him. "I am Sotif, History Man of the Alliance between Sun People and Earth People."

"I am told by those I have conquered that this cave is called Heart of Bison."

"Yes." Sotif's voice sounded flat to him.

"I am told it has a room of paintings and a spirit fire."

"The Spirit Fire was given to the people by Mother Earth. It was not started by men. It has burned without stopping for hundreds of generations. It must not be allowed to die."

"I will think on this. Where is this room of paintings?"

"The room has been sealed."

Warlog spoke with a man who had come from the cave and then to Sotif. "My men have searched the cave. They found some food. Tell me where the rest is stored."

Sotif hoped if he cooperated with Warlog, the Spirit Fire would be spared. "I will show you."

Warlog took Sotif back into the cave. The familiar smell of the cave was mingled with the smell of blood and death. Sotif led Warlog to the main storage room. Warriors were already looking through the food and preparing to carry it out. "All the food is stored in this room. There is a river in one of the tunnels that provides water."

"Are you sure this is all the food? My warriors tell me this is not enough to feed all the people and droglits that were in the cave."

"This is the main storage room. Most of the food is here. The Earth People who lived here have some food in their dwellings. The Earth People eat much all summer so they get very fat. During the winter, they eat little. At the end of winter, they are all thin."

"The droglits who live in this cave—where do they hide?"

"There are no hiding places, but the cave is large, and there are several tunnels. I do not know all the places someone could find to hide in."

"Call to the droglits and tell them to come to the main cave."

"I have heard Warlog kills all Earth People. I do not want to call them to their death."

A flash of anger appeared in Warlog's eyes, but it disappeared. "No matter, my men will find everything. Show me where the painting room is."

Sotif showed him where the rocks were piled at the entrance to the History Room. "This tunnel is sixty-five paces long. It has been filled with rocks all the way from the paintings to this entrance."

Several warriors brought a man into the cave. He was dressed in a hairy horse-skin robe. His face was tattooed with symbols of red, yellow, dark blue, and black. His hair was long and tangled. He wore a band around his head with two eagle feathers pointed up above his eyes and one raven feather hanging down in the back of his head. His nose was crooked as though it had been broken. His left arm hung limply at his side. He had a strong sulfurous smell. Warlog spoke with this new man. At first they argued, but then they reached an agreement.

"This man is Rayloc," Warlog said. "He is my Spirit Man. Rayloc says it is good you have blocked the painting room. He says when we have removed everything we need from this cave, your people must block the cave. No one will ever see the bad work of the droglit painters. Soon, no one will remember where they are. I will allow the droglits to live to block this cave. They will help my men cross the Snow Mountains. Rayloc says that because you are the Spirit Man of your people, you shall live. He will take you as his assistant, and you will teach him the Traditions of the Sun People. When your people are conquered, they will join with my people and will obey my Traditions. You will learn my Traditions so you can teach your people to follow the laws of Warlog, Zendolot's Great Eagle. The Traditions of the Alliance will be gone from the earth. Rayloc wants to understand them before they are gone."

"I will teach Rayloc all the Traditions of my people, but I must do it from this cave. Rayloc must let me keep this Spirit Fire because it is the promise of the Traditions of my people."

Rayloc stood close to Sotif. Though Rayloc was shorter than Warlog, he was taller than Sotif, and he had to look down at him. His breath was sickening sweet.

"Understand words of this man ugly, do I." Rayloc's words were pronounced strangely, but they were words of Sun People language. Sotif could understand him, but he did not speak the language as well as Warlog. "Keep this man ugly, will I. Learn from this man ugly, will I. Know ugly people Traditions, will I. Close this cave, will droglits. Zendolot, to him praise, true god, is. These people, learn will. If droglits not block cave, will die they. Only on Zendolot, to him praise, receive honor. True people of

Warlog, not give honor to Great Spirit of you. Fake, is Great Spirit of you. Weak, is Great Spirit of you. Spirit Fire, die will. Traditions of Great Spirit know, will I. Show weakness of Traditions of you, will I. Help me, will this Sotif or die, will he."

Sotif struggled to understand. "Does Rayloc say he will destroy the Spirit Fire and those who believe in the Great Spirit?"

"True, this is. Strong, Zendolot, to him praise, is. People of you and droglits, fear and fast run. Only people believe in Zendolot, to him praise, live will. All others, die must."

Several warriors came out of the tunnel from the river carrying vases on their shoulders. Water sloshed as they walked. Their wet bodies glistened in the flickering light of the cave. Warlog said something to them, and they walked to the Spirit Fire.

"No!" Sotif screamed. He tried to run to stop them, but three warriors restrained him. The Spirit Fire screamed and shuttered and hissed as the water was poured on it. Sotif fought and finally slipped free from those holding him. He ran and threw himself into the fire pit. It was warm and slimy from wet ashes.

Warlog, Rayloc, and the warriors stood in a circle around the fire pit watching Sotif's agony. He sifted through the ashes. Some spots were still warm; others were already cool. Sotif found a hot coal on the side of the pit. It burned his hand as he held it. He blew on it, and it turned bright red. This was the last spark of the Spirit Fire that had symbolized the strength of the Alliance since the beginning. Sotif could not believe he was holding the final gasp of the life of that spirit. He did not notice the pain in his hand, but he could smell his flesh burning. It occurred to him that he would have to carry the mark of the Spirit Fire until he could figure out what symbol the Great Spirit would prepare for his people. The burning coal was in his left hand. Almost without thinking, he pushed it high on his left cheek in front of his left ear. The pain was excruciating. For a blinding instant, a light seemed to flash in his head, and he saw a vision of a group of ancient Earth People dressed in loose animal skins standing around a fire. One built a new fire over a living baby girl, and the fire took her spirit and became the Spirit Fire of the People. Sun People came to destroy the Spirit Fire, but a flood stopped them. The Spirit Fire moved behind the flood to the Heart of the Bison. A strong Spirit Man of the Sun People followed to destroy the Earth People, but Kectu defeated him.

The old stories had never been so clear to him. Sotif would not let these warriors be the ones to put the Spirit Fire out. There was a puddle of water near the center of the fire pit. Sotif crawled to the puddle. "Mother Earth, I return the Spirit Fire to you in honor. I will carry the mark of the Spirit Fire to your people until you give a new symbol." As he said the final words, he immersed the live coal of the Spirit Fire into the puddle of water. It hissed and then turned cold in his hand.

Sotif turned to Rayloc. "I am the History Man of my people. I put the Spirit Fire out. You had no power to do it."

CHAPTER 5

Soft Cloud—The Lover

Summer 3286 BCE

Warlog conquered the Heart of the Bison in the morning. Warriors were celebrating all through the village. Soft Cloud had heard many stories from the camp whores of how the warriors hurt the women when they were excited by a victory. She watched the young warrior walk from the camp alone. He was one of the warriors who guarded the Earth People, but he treated the people of the Alliance with respect, unlike the other warriors. Broken Stick liked the warrior. He said the warrior tried hard to learn the language of the Sun People and understand the Earth People.

No one was watching her, so she followed the young warrior. He sat on a stone at the edge of the camp. One of the guards posted around the camp leered at her as she approached the warrior.

"I am Soft Cloud." The warrior jumped as she spoke. He seemed to be in thought, and her voice startled him.

"Seen you, have I. Tincolad, am I."

"Your warriors have won a war today. All the warriors celebrate."

"Fight did not I. Guard, am I."

"My village is called the Winter Rest."

"This village, know I. People of you should not fight Warlog. From fighting comes much killing. People of you this killing do not know. Should not fight, people of you."

"Warlog takes everything from us. We have to fight."

119

"Many people, kills Warlog. Everything, takes he. Better to not fight. Many lives, people of you can save."

"I ran from my home. Warlog's warriors caught us. They killed all my family. They made me a camp whore. I must work for warriors and do everything they want. Camp whores must meet all their needs. Do you understand?"

"Yes." Tincolad seemed embarrassed.

"For my people, it's a bad thing for a woman to mate with a man before they do the mating ceremony. After the ceremony, they mate and have children. I did not mate with a man until the warriors forced me. It was a bad thing for me. The other camp whores say after a war, warriors are excited. Sometimes many warriors mate with one whore. Many whores are hurt. I have never seen warriors after they win a war. The other whores have told me it's a hard thing."

"Strong are warriors." Tincolad seemed uneasy with the implications of Soft Cloud's words.

"I am afraid, Tincolad. Broken Stick has told me you are not like other warriors. I have watched you, and I think you care more about people than the warriors do. Can you help me?"

"Not different from warriors, am I. Strong, am I." Tincolad seemed defensive.

"After winning a war, the warriors hurt the whores. I'm afraid."

"Strong, is warrior. To have woman, hard fight warrior. In camp, are no women. In camp, warriors must have whores."

"A whore is not a woman? What is a whore then?"

"For village, woman is. For camp, whore is."

"Oh. A woman in a village has respect?"

"Yes. For making children, is woman in village. For pleasure, is whore in camp."

"I am a woman from a village. Warlog's warriors took me from my village to be a camp whore. I did not choose this. Warriors force me. Can you help me?"

"In this war, fight did not I. Influence, do not have I."

There was finality to his words, even though what he said did not make sense to Soft Cloud. The guard was watching her. "Why must the women be hurt to please warriors?" Soft Cloud could tell by Tincolad's eyes that he understood the question. He had no answer for her. Another warrior came to relieve the guard who had been watching her. The guard walked toward her. "Tincolad, help me," she pleaded.

Tincolad stood and faced the guard. They spoke in their strange language. After a few sentences, the guard's voice became angry. He pushed Tincolad roughly aside and grabbed Soft Cloud by the upper arm. As he roughly pulled her with him, she shouted, "Please, Tincolad. Please help me!" He turned from her, and the warrior gave her arm a forceful jerk.

****

Tincolad could not get the girl from his mind all night. She was not pretty. Her nose was large, and her eyes were too close together. He liked her dark skin. He had not seen a woman with such clear skin. The women from his world had white skin that turned rough and leathery before they were old. Her almond-shaped eyes were pretty even though they were too close.

Tincolad had been so consumed with Warlog and his army since the day his mother died that he had given little thought to women. Now, this girl's face haunted his night. He knew she was just a camp whore. He could use her and the others to relieve his needs until the campaign was over. But there was something about this girl. It was her voice, her face, and her body. She wore a loose-fitting leather dress that covered her body when she was still but showed all the curves of a young woman when she moved. She was different from his people, and Warlog had beaten her village. He wondered if these things made it right to use her as the warriors did.

He tried to help Soft Cloud by telling the guard Fediclad he wanted her. Fediclad quickly put him in his place. Warriors who fought in a battle always had first choice of the camp whores on the night of a victory. Tincolad started to argue, but Fediclad became angry. As Tincolad thought about that confrontation, he realized how foolish he had been. He hoped Fediclad would not spread the story of his stupidity though the camp or say anything to Rencolad. Why had that foolish girl come to embarrass him?

Tincolad was frustrated that he had not been allowed to fight and prove himself. He hated the sight of the droglits. He would not have to return to their camp until after the midday meal, so he decided he would find Soft Cloud and demand his right as a warrior.

Tincolad walked to the area where the camp whores were kept. At the Fish River village and the Winter Rest village, he had seen many of the camp whores with bruises and other injuries, but he had not given it much thought. Now, the aftermath of the victory celebrations drew his attention in a different way.

It did not take long to find the one called Soft Cloud. He did not recognize the girl lying on her back. Her lip was broken in two places and was swollen. One of her eyes was swollen closed. Her clothes were torn and bloody. Her right arm was tied to her side.

As Tincolad stood looking at her, she turned her head to him. There were pain and embarrassment in her face. As soon as she saw him, she turned quickly away and hid her face. "Go away, please go away."

Tincolad was embarrassed to be in this place of broken women. As he rushed away, he was confused at the pity and embarrassment he felt for the girl he had not helped. Why had she picked him to help her?

Two days after taking the Heart of the Bison, Warlog and his army left to pursue Tall Tree. He left several warriors with Rayloc in charge. The male Earth People were camped at the entrance to the Heart of the Bison, where they worked day after day filling the entrance tunnel with boulders. The rest of the Earth People were kept near the warrior's camp.

The day after Warlog left, Tincolad ran into Soft Cloud when she was getting water. "Sorry am I that hurt you, warriors did," he stammered.

"Your warriors are cruel, Tincolad. Why do they kill?"

"Bring to people of you peace and prosperity."

"Peace? You're just learning our language. I think I do not understand what you mean by peace."

"Sorry that could not help you, I."

"Are you sorry your warriors killed all my family?"

Tincolad wished he could explain things better. "A hard thing, is war. The world saved, must be. People of you do not understand. When people of you understand better, then peace will see they. Then peace will understand they."

"What does Warlog save the world from?"

"From deep in earth, droglits come. To take sun, droglits come. To destroy people, droglits come."

"What are the droglits?"

"Big story, this is."

Soft Cloud sat down by the river. "Tell me about the droglits."

Tincolad tried to explain the story of Zendolot, Dracolot, and Afrodiluk. When he told her Zendolot was angry because Dracolot raped Afrodiluk, Soft Cloud stopped him.

"Zendolot was angry when Dracolot forced Afrodiluk to mate when she didn't want to?"

"Zendolot, he to praise, very angry was."

"Why? Because Dracolot made her a camp whore? I think these droglits have come from the dark caverns to become warriors for Warlog." Soft Cloud's tone was hard and sarcastic. Tincolad understood her words and her tone.

"What does this have to do with droglits?" Soft Cloud asked.

Tincolad explained that Zendolot changed Dracolot's name to Dracolut and banned him to darkness. He told her how the moon and stars were placed to keep Dracolut trapped in the dark caverns. Then he told her Dracolut's slaves were called droglits. "Evil, droglits are. To make dark the world, come the droglits."

"Where will Warlog find these droglits?"

"There!" Tincolad pointed to the Earth People.

"The Earth People? That's a laugh! Who do you think fixed my arm?"

"Laugh? What this is?"

"Ha, ha. See what I see, Tincolad. Your warriors broke my arm, and the Earth People fixed it. Who comes to destroy?" Soft Cloud laughed cynically.

"Droglits, magic have. With magic, droglits trick people of you."

"The warriors who broke my arm and made me mate with them did not use magic. They used strong arms. This I understand. Tricky magic I do not understand." Soft Cloud turned on her heel and started up the riverbank.

"Wait!" Tincolad shouted. Soft Cloud turned back. "Sorry, am I. Teach I about these droglits, you could?"

Standing on the bank looking down at him, Soft Cloud seemed fearless. She started to turn but then turned back. "I know *nothing* about droglits. Maybe I will teach you about Earth People. Not now. Come to see me in the mornings."

Tincolad began visiting Soft Cloud every morning. At first, they were both timid. Soon, Tincolad was spending most of his free time with Soft Cloud. He talked to her about the droglits and the magic they used to trick her people. She insisted the Earth People were not evil and insisted he stop calling them droglits. She explained the many ways they helped the Sun People and how the Sun People helped them.

When Soklo, the droglit medicine man, came to check Soft Cloud's arm, she helped Tincolad understand the things he said. Tincolad learned fast, and soon he could understand simple conversations with the Earth People about weather, food, and care for wounds.

Eight days later, Tincolad was just getting ready to go see Soft Cloud when Rencolad stopped him. "Are you going to see that camp whore again?"

"Yes." Tincolad had been expecting this conversation, though he had hoped he could avoid it.

"You spend a lot of time with her."

"She's teaching me to understand the droglits. I can learn much faster with her help than trying to figure things out from conversations between these people and droglits. Besides, she teaches me a lot about the magic of the droglits. The sooner I learn these things, the sooner I can fight with the warriors."

"Some warriors say you object to them mating with her."

"Her arm is still injured."

"They don't want her arm. I think you're becoming attached."

"The warriors hurt her pretty bad. She's afraid."

"So what? She belongs to Warlog's army now. She must learn her place just like everyone else."

"I know, but she trusts me because I protect her. She teaches me her language and her beliefs. She helps me understand the droglits. She's very useful to me."

A look of doubt crossed Rencolad's face. "I sponsored you to be a warrior. I trained you to be a warrior. Your blood is in me, and my blood is in you."

"I know this. I have always wanted to fight beside you and the other warriors … you know that. I want to fight and kill Warlog's enemies. You told me it's more important to Warlog for me to learn the ways and the language of the droglits. The woman helps me do this. So does the droglit that cares for her."

"The *woman*? There is talk in the camp that you are getting too close to this *whore*, maybe even too close to the droglits."

"I'm trying to learn as much as possible, as fast as possible. What difference does it make how I learn what I need to know?"

"You're a warrior." Rencolad pushed his finger into Tincolad's chest. "You have a responsibility to yourself as a warrior. The camp whores are here to provide for the physical needs of the warriors. We use them how we want, and when they are no longer useful, we cast them aside. We never get attached to them. When this war is over, you will return to our lands with glory. There you will find a woman to give you children. One of our *women*, not a camp *whore* from these strange, dark-skinned people. You will find a woman suitable to be the mother of your children, one they will be proud of.

"Soft Cloud is dirt, just like all her people. Look at her brown skin and dark hair. Zendolot, praise to him, has marked her and her people. We use her until she is no longer useful, and then we cast her off like the dirt she is. You must learn what you have to learn without getting close to these people and the monsters they seek to protect."

Tincolad knew Rencolad was right about the camp whores, but he could not see Soft Cloud in that way.

"You will not see Soft Cloud today. Tonight, I will use her for my needs. When I'm done, I will give her to the other warriors to use. Tomorrow, she will work with the other whores. If her arm cannot work, she will be cast aside. You will thank me for this when we return and you do not have attachments in this land.

"Runners have come. Warlog is returning. He will be here before midday. Tall Tree has escaped from him. He believes the Spirit Man, Sotif, knows how to find Tall Tree's army. It's getting late in the season, and Warlog wants to cross the Snow Mountains before winter comes. He does not want to leave Tall Tree and his army behind him. If you know something to make Sotif talk, it will reassure Warlog of the value of the work you do."

"All I know is Sotif puts a lot of value on the people of the Alliance, including the droglits. He would rather die than reveal anything to help Warlog harm the droglits. I don't think he will give us any good information."

"Maybe this is information Warlog can use. I will tell him what you have said. The cave is almost closed off. There are too many droglits to care for. I don't think Warlog will keep them from Rayloc. When they are gone, we will join the army as fighting warriors. You and your knowledge will be needed there." Rencolad slapped Tincolad playfully on the shoulder. "Soon you will be in the fighting. Then you can show what kind of warrior you really are. That's what you've been looking for. Think about that and prepare yourself for glory. Don't waste your time or energy worrying about camp whores and the droglits that have fooled them."

As Rencolad walked away, Tincolad was left in thought. His moment was coming. There were many strong droglit males working at the cave. He might get his chance for glory today. If they killed the droglits today, there would be a celebration tonight. Tincolad would have to kill many droglits so he would be entitled to choose a camp whore to celebrate with him. If he killed many droglits, Rencolad would not complain about him choosing Soft Cloud. It was the only way to protect her. But what would Soft Cloud think of him after he killed the droglits?

Warlog returned, but not with his army. Rencolad met with him. Tincolad watched Warlog go to Sotif's tent. He came out shortly in a bad mood. He pointed to an old droglit. "Kill that one," he ordered. The closest warrior killed him. Warlog pointed to an old female. "Kill that one."

Sotif screamed, "Stop! Stop it!"

But Warlog pointed to another old female. "Kill that one, and that one, and that one, and that one." The warriors nearest Warlog killed the ones he pointed out, including a droglit cub. It happened so fast Tincolad could hardly believe what he saw. He had no desire to kill the females and their children.

****

As Sotif sat in his tent, there was a commotion outside. Sotif stepped out to see, but his guards sent him back inside. Before going back, he got a glimpse of Warlog.

Warlog came to Sotif's tent with Rayloc. "Sotif, I have followed the trail of Tall Tree for many days. We should have caught him by now. Tall Tree runs too fast to be traveling with women and children. Tell me what he's doing."

"I don't know the mind of Tall Tree."

"I think you know what's going on. Where are the women and children?"

Sotif decided to give Warlog some information to convince him he was trying to cooperate. "The people of the village left in several groups. Those who travel slowest left first. There was much to do to harvest food and make preparations to abandon the village. The strongest stayed to leave last."

"Where did they go?"

"This was kept secret among the leaders of the groups. No one was told."

"Liar," Rayloc said.

"I think Rayloc is right, Sotif. I think you lie." Warlog stood up. He shouted something to the guards in his language and walked out of the tent. He walked to where the Earth People were kept under guard. The guards grabbed Sotif by his arms and took him after Warlog.

Warlog said to one of the warriors, *"Selack otey,"* pointing to an old male of the Earth People. The warrior thrust his spear into the old man's heart so fast Sotif was taken by surprise. *"Selack otey."* Warlog pointed to an old woman.

"Stop!" Sotif's word had no effect. The warrior killed the old lady. The rest of the Earth People began to shout and crowd away from Warlog. "Stop it!"

Warlog again said, *"Otey selack,"* pointing to another old woman. *"Dan selack, dan selack, dan selack."* Warlog walked through the Earth People pointing to an old man, a woman, and a child. All were killed in a heartbeat. Sotif struggled to break free of the guards that held him, and near panic ensued among the Earth People. The warriors circled tight around the Earth People, using their spears to threaten them. Two more were killed as the guards fought to regain control.

Warlog walked to Sotif. "The tunnel to the cave is nearly blocked. If these animals are to continue to live, you must tell me where Tall Tree is."

"I don't know."

Warlog turned his back to Sotif. *"Otey selack, dan selack, dan selack, dan selack."* The killing started again as Warlog picked those who would die.

"Stop it!" Sotif screamed.

Warlog continued walking around the Earth People. *"Dan selack, dan selack, dan selack, dan selack."* The old men, women, and children fell as fast as he could talk. Pandemonium broke out among the prisoners. Warlog was silent.

"I let these useless things live so the stronger ones will work. I don't care if they live or die, but Broken Stick says they should live to keep the males working. They are a burden to me. You keep telling me you don't know, and they all will die."

"What will you do when the tunnel is blocked?" Sotif asked.

"Otey selack." Another man was killed. "I will always need animals to do heavy work. For this many fighting men, the work is never done. That was one question, and one more useless animal stops eating my food. The next question will free up food from two more animals. Does Sotif have any other questions?"

Sotif was in shock. He had plenty of questions, but he could see Warlog enjoyed this game. Sotif stared at Warlog.

"Where have the Earth People gone?"

Sotif tried to think of a good answer. *"Otey selack, dan selack, dan selack, dan selack, dan selack."* The killing was beyond anything Sotif could have imagined. Warlog was slaughtering the weak and helpless, and he was enjoying it.

"Stop it! I'll … I will tell you everything! Stop it," Sotif screamed. The Earth People began to scatter. They ran in all directions screaming in fear, but the warriors rounded them up. Almost half were already dead.

****

Broken Stick and his friend Bent Spear were assigned to the cave where seventeen of the strongest male Earth People worked to block the entrance to the Heart of the Bison. Lotend was the leader of the Earth People men. They were guarded by six of Warlog's warriors. Broken Stick and Bent Spear helped the guards communicate with the Earth People. Broken Stick made things as easy as possible for the Earth People. He argued for reduced work hours and more food.

The summer was coming to a close. Broken Stick knew he needed to do something to free the Earth People in time to cross the Snow Mountains before winter. The work at the Heart of the Bison was almost complete. He could tell from the little he understood of the talk between warriors that Warlog would not keep the Earth People alive after the cave was sealed. Warlog and his army were gone, and there were not enough men to guard all the Earth People. In the past few days, Broken Stick had begun to think about ways of overpowering the guards and escaping. The Earth People could cover their trail so no one could follow them once they got away. The only thing preventing them was the fact that the women, children, and old members of the clan were being held in the valley below.

Warlog left enough warriors to kill all the Earth People in the village if the men at the cave did not do as they were told. If anything went wrong at the cave, a smoke signal from the cave would alert the guards in the village. Broken Stick knew Rayloc was determined to seal the entrance to the Heart of the Bison, and he needed the Earth People do it. But Broken Stick knew Rayloc would not hesitate to order all the Earth People killed at the slightest excuse.

The only thing Broken Stick could think of was a desperate plan. After the evening meal, he would approach the warrior who watched the signal fire. He would kill the guard before a signal could be sent. The rest of the men would kill the warriors who guarded them. They could then sneak in the dark to where the women and children were held and free them. Even though Broken Stick helped the warriors guard the Earth People, Lotend and his men trusted him. But the plan was dangerous. The signal fire and guard were above the entrance to the cave. The guard kept green sticks and grass nearby so at any sign of trouble he could throw the green plants on the fire, causing it to flare up and smoke. Even in the dark, the signal would be seen in the village below. Though Broken Stick worked with the warriors, they did not trust him. Each time he went to the signal fire, another warrior accompanied him. Broken Stick would have to kill two warriors before either one could send the signal.

The men had started back to work after the midday meal. Several workers began screaming in the language of the Earth People. Broken Stick, Lotend, and three guards ran to those who were screaming. Warlog's warriors did not understand what the Earth People were screaming. One of the guards who could speak Sun People language asked Broken Stick, "What happens?"

"The droglits say something is happening in the village."

"Everybody, quiet be," the guard said.

"Be no speak," Lotend said in Earth People language. "Lotend must see what is happening. Lotend must say what to do. All the Earth People must be no speak."

"What did say he?" the leader of the warriors demanded.

"He told them to be quiet," Bent Spear answered in Sun People language.

"What is happening?" Lotend asked in Earth People language.

Suloc, one of the Earth People, answered, "The Warlog people were killing the Earth People." He pointed to a group of people at the south end of Warlog's camp. "The Warlog people have stopped now."

"Is Suloc sure?" Lotend asked.

"Suloc is sure."

Lotend told Bent Spear. Bent Spear translated to the guards, "These people say the warriors were killing the Earth People in the village."

Broken Stick quietly walked away as Bent Spear translated. He realized things were going to get out of control, so he began to work his way to the signal fire. In the confusion, none of the warriors accompanied him. The warrior at the fire was on his feet near the green brush. It was one of the warriors who did not speak Sun People language. Broken Stick began to point to the upset. He motioned for the warrior to come to him. The warrior took a few steps and then seemed to be unsure. Broken Stick motioned again and started to walk away. The warrior came a few more steps.

"Warlog's people are killing again!" Suloc shouted so loud Broken Stick could hear him. The warrior turned back. He said something Broken Stick did not understand, but he was going for the green brush. Broken Stick rushed to him as fast as he could. The warrior bent to pick up the green material. Broken Stick ran into him and knocked him down. He stabbed him in the side with his dagger. The warrior continued to struggle, and Broken Stick stabbed him several more times.

When the warrior stopped struggling, Broken Stick looked back. Lotend and his men were fighting with the warriors. Broken Stick ran to help, but the warriors were all down when he got there.

Lotend began issuing orders in the Earth People language. "Run to the camp!" he yelled. "Stay low. Stay in the ravine. The men must get close before the warriors see."

There was cover in a small ravine filled with scrub oak. Near the bottom, the view of Warlog's camp was obscured by a small rise. Broken Stick realized that behind the rise they could get close enough to charge.

Broken Stick gathered the men while they were still out of sight. "When we go over the hill, stay low and go fast. We must get as close as possible to the camp before we are seen. The closer we get, the more lives we can save."

When he peeked over the rise, Broken Stick could tell most of the warriors had their backs to him. Lotend told him Sotif was facing up hill talking to Warlog, who also had his back to Broken Stick.

They started moving carefully down the hill. They had gone about fifty paces when everyone in the camp below turned. "We run now!" Broken Stick screamed.

Before they could start, Lotend shouted, "Not! Sotif holds his hands up. The warriors are not killing the people."

Broken Stick began to walk. "Walk fast. Watch the warriors. If they move toward the Earth People, we run."

"Sotif comes with five warriors," Lotend said.

When they got closer, Lotend said to Broken Stick, "Sotif shouts. Sotif comes to pretend to talk with Lotend. Warlog has killed many Earth People. Broken Stick must prepare to attack. Broken Stick must catch Warlog. Broken Stick must kill Warlog."

They were about thirty paces apart. "Warlog leaves with six warriors. The other warriors surround the Earth People," Lotend said.

"Warlog's men must try to kill all the Earth People if Lotend attacks now," Sotif shouted in Earth People language. "Warlog must kill all Earth People when the cave is blocked. Sotif thinks now must be the time to attack. Sotif thinks now some could be saved."

"Lotend will pretend to talk to these men." They were about twenty paces away. "When these men are relaxed, Lotend's men will kill them. Then Lotend will run to the camp."

When they were about ten paces apart, Sotif stopped. "Lotend is the leader of the Earth People," he said to the warriors. "He does not want any Earth People killed. You must tell him what you want."

"He to drop weapons of he. Must he to cave, go back," Kandilad, head of the warriors, said. His accent was thick, and he spoke the Sun People language poorly.

Broken Stick and his men advanced at a walk, pretending they wanted to talk. "Warriors of Warlog, where they are?" Kandilad asked.

"We tied them up," Broken Stick lied.

"Come you down, why?"

"Some thought you were killing the droglits." Broken Stick and his men continued walking toward Kandilad.

"Weapons of you, now drop. Back to cave, go you, or all droglits, kill we."

"Now!" Broken Stick shouted. Before Kandilad could react, Broken Stick killed him. Lotend's men killed the rest of the warriors. At the same instant, the warriors in the camp began to kill the Earth People. This time, the Earth People fought back. Lotend and his men ran to the camp as fast as they could.

****

Tincolad saw the droglits attack Kandilad and his men. They were killed before they could fight. There was confusion. Some of the warriors ran to kill all the droglits in the camp while others ran to meet the droglits charging from the cave. All around, the warriors started to kill droglits. This was the moment Tincolad had waited for, but they were killing the old and weak. There was no glory in this kind of killing.

Tincolad pulled back. He saw several of the eastern people try to defend the droglits. He knew he should help the warriors, but he hesitated. This was not the kind of fight he wanted. Then the strong male droglits reached the camps. They used clubs and rocks. They even picked up some warriors to throw them at others. Tincolad had never seen such strength. Maybe this was the magic of the droglits. Tincolad raced to where the Earth People men were fighting. Finally, he would fight a droglit and prove he was a warrior. He only had a dagger. A droglit knocked him to the ground. He rolled away just as another droglit threw a boulder that hit the spot where his head had been. When he stood up, he was face to face with a droglit swinging a club at him. Tincolad jumped back and tried to charge past the club, but the droglit was too quick. Tincolad couldn't get close enough to fight with his dagger. He turned away looking for a club or a spear.

Tincolad saw Soft Cloud swinging a club at the warriors with her good arm. He ran to her to save her from the fight. A warrior ran toward her with his dagger drawn back. Tincolad caught him from behind and threw him to the ground. "Run!" he shouted.

Soft Cloud looked at him defiantly. As he walked toward her, she opened her mouth to say something. Then he saw a burst of bright, white lights and felt a sharp blow to the back of his head. He fell, and as he hit the ground, there was another burst of lights, and then all was black.

****

The warriors turned to face Broken Stick and his men as they charged in. The fighting was vicious, but Broken Stick's men outnumbered the warriors, and soon the Earth People had defeated them.

Broken Stick looked across the field. There were a number of wounded from both sides stirring in the dust of the battle. A couple of Earth People men were going among the wounded and dead. They were carrying the dead Earth People to one side and helping the wounded Earth People from the field.

One of the Sun People found a wounded warrior. He used a club to smash his head. "No!" Sotif screamed. "The Alliance does not kill those who are helpless. If one of these warriors tires to fight, the warrior must be killed. If a warrior tries to follow the people, the warrior must be stopped. We will leave some food for the rest."

"If we don't kill them, when they recover, they will come to kill us," Broken Stick argued.

"We must take our wounded with us," Sotif said. "This will slow travel. We will leave the wounded of Warlog's army to slow him."

"They will not slow Warlog at all. He will just leave some men to take care of them until they are well," Broken Stick said.

"Then Warlog's army will be weaker because of those he will leave to care for the wounded."

"He may just leave them to die."

"Then they will be just as dead as if we kill them. And it will not be good for the warriors to see Warlog leave his wounded without care."

Broken Stick saw Sotif's logic. "You are right. We will leave them some food. Maybe some of them will not want to kill us if we help them now."

Broken Stick walked among the dead and wounded, helping to separate the bodies of the people of the Alliance. Sotif wanted them laid out near the path to the Heart of the Bison. He took a finger from the bodies of each of the Earth People to burn in a ceremony fire north of the Snow Mountains.

As Broken Stick looked for Earth People, he saw Soft Cloud kneel beside Tincolad at the edge of where the fighting had been most furious. He was lying motionless on his back. A large pool of blood soaked the dirt around his head. Broken Stick felt sad for this young warrior. He was smart and had a real interest in learning about the Alliance. He had come so far from his home to die in a strange land. He had come to be a warrior, but Broken Stick was certain he had never killed anyone.

As Broken Stick turned from Tincolad, Soft Cloud stood up. "He was the only good warrior," Broken Stick said.

"You knew him. Is there some ceremony or something that should be done?" Tears ran down Soft Cloud's cheeks.

"He never talked about such a thing." Broken Stick left her to grieve her warrior. There was much to do to clean up the battlefield. War was such a waste.

Broken Stick could see most of the Earth People women, children, and old ones had been killed. "What happened here?" he asked Sotif.

Sotif explained all that Warlog had done.

"What should we do now?"

"Is the Heart of the Bison closed?"

"Almost. Only the distance of one pace remains to completely fill the entrance."

"The people can't go back into the cave. We must run through the Snow Mountains."

Lotend came to Sotif. "There are only eleven strong men left. There are four women, six children, and three old ones. The strongest clan of the Alliance has been destroyed."

"Do not forget many Earth People left with Tall Tree," Sotif said.

"The Winding River clan was more than two hundred before Warlog came."

"We must prepare to leave," Sotif said to Broken Stick. "Warlog will send warriors to finish the killing. We must leave before night. The Earth People must hide the trail."

"Some of the people cannot travel," Lotend said.

"There's no choice. Warlog will kill all he can find," Broken Stick said. "It will be hard, but we must leave now. The strong will have to help the weak."

"The clan must gather all the food the clan can carry. The clan must leave before Earth's Fireball falls," Lotend said.

Soft Cloud approached the men. "The one called Tincolad still breathes. We must take him with us."

"It will be too hard for our people to escape. We cannot bring one of Warlog's warriors," Sotif said.

"He's not like the other warriors. He's young and compassionate. He will become hard like the other warriors if he stays with them."

"He is a warrior. He's trained to be a killer," Sotif argued.

"He is a warrior," Broken Stick said. "He's proud he's a warrior, but Soft Cloud is right. He's not a killer. I have seen his interest in the people of the Alliance. He tries to understand how the people of the Alliance live. He has learned much of the language of the Sun People. He has also learned to understand some of the language of the Earth People."

"We cannot take more wounded. It will be hard with just our own people," Sotif said.

"He knows much about how Warlog's armies fight. He knows how warriors are trained to kill. No one in all the Alliance knows what he knows."

"Why would he give such important information to the Alliance?"

"Maybe he wouldn't. I have associated with many warriors. There's something about Tincolad that's different from all the others. He has never killed anyone. If he can't be persuaded to help, we have lost very little. If we don't try, we may lose something that could make a difference next summer."

"I will help," Soft Cloud added. "I'm sure he likes me. He will listen to what I say. He can be convinced to help. I'm sure of it."

"I do not think he will help," Sotif said. "And if he will not, then what? We would have to kill him."

Broken Stick could see the problem. "Sotif is right. We will have to leave him. He's one of them."

"As you have said, he knows too much about the Alliance," Soft Cloud said. "You can't leave him alive to help Warlog. Would you kill him when he's helpless? Will you become like the warriors of Warlog?"

Broken Stick liked the warrior, but they faced a hard truth. "We must do hard things because of this war Warlog brought to us."

"Here," Soft Cloud said to Sotif.

"What is this?"

"It's a bag I found in Tincolad's shirt. It's Earth People. It must mean something."

Sotif opened the bag. "It has ashes in it. Did he say what this is and why he carries it?'

"No, I just now found it."

Sotif looked from Broken Stick to Soft Cloud. "We cannot kill him like this, and we cannot leave him to help Warlog. We will take the young man. I will talk to him of these ashes."

****

Soft Cloud was exhausted by the time they reached a place to camp. Two Earth People men carried Tincolad on a stretcher. It had been a hard run, but they were finally far enough away to rest. Soft Cloud noticed Tincolad stirring. "Tincolad, how do you feel?"

"Head of I, sore is," Tincolad answered weakly.

"I was so worried. Soklo is brewing some herbs that are very good for headaches."

"Not understand this, I."

Soft Cloud put a cool, damp leather wrap on his head. He looked confused, but his eyes did not show the sign of the sickness that sometimes came from a hard hit on the head. "The warrior you pushed away from me hit you in the head with a club."

"Not understand this, I. Where are warriors?"

"It was a bad fight, Tincolad. Warlog's warriors were killing everyone. We had to fight them. Many of them were killed … some were wounded."

"Defeat the warriors, people of you?" Tincolad's voice betrayed surprise.

"Yes. My people fought hard."

"Killed the wounded, people of you?"

Soft Cloud had spent much time trying to get Tincolad to speak correctly, but he just did not seem to get it. She had come to understand his way of talking pretty well. "No, we did not kill anyone after the fighting stopped. We left the wounded some food. We tried to tell them we will kill anyone who tries to fight us or follow us. Some seemed to understand."

"Better will get, they. Then fight you again, must they."

"This war you bring is hard. We don't like it. Maybe we don't do it right. Where did you get the bag of ashes you carried?"

"Where is bag?" Tincolad asked.

"Sotif has it. Ashes of the Earth People are very important to us. Do you know if these ashes were of the Earth People?"

"Ashes to Sotif, give I. Earth People ashes, were these."

"Why did you save the Earth People ashes?"

"Not know this, I." Tincolad told Soft Cloud the story of the Earth People woman and the ashes. "Go we, where?"

"We have to run from Warlog. He will kill all of us."

"Go we, where?"

Soft Cloud could see Tincolad was confused. "We have to go to another one of our villages." Soft Cloud did not want to let him know they were going to cross the Snow Mountains in case he recovered and escaped. She wanted to trust him, but it was too soon.

"Why take I, people of you?"

"You have not treated us like the other warriors. We need someone to teach us about Warlog."

"Back, must go I."

"Why? So you can kill my people and the Earth People?" Soft Cloud could feel the heat in her face.

"Warrior, am I."

"You are weak and hurt. You must rest." Soft Cloud did not want to argue. "I will get you some food."

Soft Cloud brought Tincolad something to eat. She wanted to talk about Warlog and what he might do, but Tincolad fell asleep after he ate. He seemed different now. Not friendly. She wondered if it had been a mistake to bring him.

Winter 3286/3285 BCE

The trip through the Snow Mountains was difficult for Sotif. It was comforting to realize how difficult it would be for Warlog's army to cross the mountains. Sotif did not like traveling. More than once along the path, he thought of Senlo's words that he would be a traveling History Man.

Many days after they started down the mountain, Sotif saw smoke rising in the distance. When the sun was reaching its highest point, Sotif walked over a ridge, and he could see the Mountain Pass colony nestled in the bend of a small stream. The fields of einkorn were golden, ready for harvest. The leaves were turning in the fruit orchards. The Mountain Pass colony was much smaller than the Winding River colony. It was late in the day when Sotif and his group dragged themselves into the camp.

The leader of the tribe came out to greet them. "I am Fast Bird. Welcome to the Mountain Pass village."

"I am Sotif, History Man of the Alliance."

Fast Bird stepped back a half step, and his jaw dropped. "I am happy to meet the History Man of the Alliance. Three groups of people from the Winding River village have come to the Mountain Pass village. Another group from the Flat Ridge village has also come. We have sent most of these people to other villages. I have also sent messengers to all the colonies north of the Snow Mountains. We hear terrible stories of killers who come from the West. We were told Sotif and many fighters had stayed to guard the Heart of the Bison."

"I come with the worst news. The Heart of the Bison is lost. The Spirit Fire is lost." Sotif explained about the war and how the History Room and the Heart of the Bison were sealed off. He described how he and his group had escaped to cross the Snow Mountains.

Twelve days after Sotif arrived, Tall Tree and his group walked into the village. The first winter snow caught them near the top of the pass as Tall Tree planned. Sotif was relieved to hear Warlog was caught on the other side of the Snow Mountains.

Representatives from the closest colonies had come in answer to Fast Bird's messengers. Even though many colonies had not arrived, Tall Tree called the first meeting of the leaders of the Alliance the day following his arrival. At the beginning of the meeting, Sotif described the arrival of Warlog and the defeat of the Fish River and the Winter Rest colonies.

"There is one among us who has information about Warlog and his intentions," Tall Tree said. "He has done much to help the Earth People. He came with Sotif's group. I have asked him to tell this council all he knows about Warlog."

Broken Stick's voice resonated with deep tones. Sotif could see he had changed much in a short time. He explained how he had joined Warlog's army at the Fish River village. He explained how the army was organized and trained to kill their opponents. He told them of Warlog's promise to the Fish River men that they could train to be warriors when they learned the language and accepted Zendolot as their Great Spirit. "For Warlog's people, it is the greatest honor to be a warrior."

He told them of Rayloc and his belief that Earth People were droglits and his desire to kill and burn all Earth People to ashes. He described what happened at the Earth People cave of the Fish River colony. "When the warriors returned from the cave, Rayloc gathered all the Earth People still in the village together so the warriors could kill them. I convinced Warlog they are strong and could be used to help his armies. I pretended to support Warlog."

Broken Stick described what happened at the Heart of the Bison. Broken Stick concluded, "Warlog will not stop at the Snow Mountains. Those of our people who have sworn allegiance to Warlog have told him much about the Alliance. His armies will try to destroy all the Earth People and all the Sun People who do not accept Warlog as their leader. The only hope for the Alliance is to keep Warlog from getting through the Snow Mountains." Broken Stick sat down.

Tall Tree stood. "When I sent Red Deer and his tribe through the Snow Mountains this summer, my plan was to organize an army to return to the Winding River and drive Warlog back across the Great Prairie west of the Fish River. I see that is impossible. Our best hope is to guard the passes through the Snow Mountains and keep Warlog and his armies south of the mountains."

Sotif couldn't believe what he heard. "What of the Heart of the Bison and the History Room?"

"These are things that have lasted through the generations," Tall Tree said. "The Spirit Fire has been extinguished, and the History Room has been sealed. Warlog's armies are strong, and they grow as they force our people into his army. The land south of the Snow Mountains cannot be recovered. There are only three passes where Warlog can bring his army through the Snow Mountains. From the high ground of those passes, a strong army can stop a much larger army."

"The Heart of the Bison and the History Wall symbolize the Alliance. They have been the foundation of the Alliance since the beginning," Sotif argued. "You talk of fighting Warlog with just our young men. You forget the strength of the Great Spirit and Mother Earth."

Putlo, shomot of the Ancients, rose to speak. "The Spirit Fire is the soul of the Earth People. The Spirit Fire takes the ashes of the Earth People. The Spirit Fire joins the Earth People. The Spirit Fire is no more. Warlog leaves the bodies of the Earth People to the winds and animals. Putlo does not know the meaning of this."

"Rayloc's fear of the Earth People drives him to burn all the bodies of the Earth People," Broken Stick said. "Sun People have secretly gathered ashes from many of these fires."

"You see the power of Mother Earth," Sotif said. "Even though Warlog has defeated our people for this short time, Mother Earth has planted a fear in Rayloc that keeps the power of the ashes. I took ashes from the Spirit Fire in the Heart of the Bison. Others have also collected ashes. Even the warrior, Tincolad, collected ashes. Mother Earth must have some plan to reunite the ashes we carry. Even in this disaster, the old Traditions are preserved."

Lotend spoke. "Lotend sees how the army of Warlog is. Tall Tree speaks the truth. Tall Tree says the Alliance cannot defeat Warlog. The Alliance must make new Traditions north of the Snow Mountains."

"What will the Alliance do without the Heart of the Bison?" Sotif asked.

"I'm ready to die to recover the Heart of the Bison," Tall Tree said. "But what good would it do if we all die to take back what we cannot win? And even if we could win it all back, what would be the reason if new armies can come across the Great Prairie at any time? We must remain north of the Snow Mountains. The Great Spirit has provided the Snow Mountains to protect the Alliance."

"Does Tall Tree say we must forget the Heart of the Bison and the History Room forever?" Sotif asked.

"Not forever. The Spirit Fire is dead, and the History Room and the Heart of the Bison are sealed. We must choose a new center of the Alliance. After many generations, our descendants will be stronger than the descendants of Warlog's people. Someday, we will go back. Until then, the Heart of the Bison is safe."

"How can a new Spirit Fire be made for the Earth People?" Putlo asked.

"I have given this much thought," Sotif said. "We cannot make a new Spirit Fire. I think we can make a Clan Fire. Each clan must contribute ashes to the Clan Fire. I have saved ashes from the Spirit Fire. With these ashes, the new Clan Fire will have the strength of all the ashes from the beginning of the Alliance. In this way, we will keep the Tradition of the Spirit Fire. If Kectu sends a new Spirit Fire, we will have the ashes of the Earth People in the Clan Fire."

Putlo stood. "Sotif speaks wisdom. A home for the new Clan Fire must be found. The clans must collect ashes from the clan fires."

Tall Tree spoke. "When the snows melt, Warlog's armies will come through the Snow Mountains. The Earth People have not learned to hunt with Sun People weapons, but Lotend and his men have shown Earth People can fight. All men must learn the weapons of war to defeat Warlog.

"We must send men down through the passes to warn us which pass Warlog comes through. Those who watch will warn us by setting fires with green wood in the pass Warlog chooses. We will send our strongest, bravest men to stop Warlog.

"After Warlog is driven from the Snow Mountains, we will create new Traditions for new times. We must always have an army to guard the passes through the Snow Mountains. A new time has come to the lands of Mother Earth," Tall Tree concluded.

****

Soft Cloud and Pale Water sat in front of the evening fire. Soft Cloud busied herself by mending a dress. It had been a great deal of work to get the new camp set up before winter. Dwellings had to be constructed, and food supplies had to be gathered and preserved.

"Many of the women think you are becoming too close to Tincolad," Pale Water said.

Soft Cloud knew how evil the warriors were. When she and her family had run from the Winter Rest village, she had seen the wonton slaughter of the Earth People, including mothers and their children. The warriors murdered her family when they caught them and only spared her to make her a camp whore. She hated warriors as much as anyone. "Tincolad is not like the warriors."

"The warriors are all the same. He's young, and some say he hasn't killed yet, but he's trained and hardened."

"I have not seen that, but I spend time with him for Tall Tree. Tincolad is trained to be a warrior; that's true. He knows much about how Warlog fights and how warriors are trained. He has knowledge to help Tall Tree fight Warlog. I befriend Tincolad to encourage him to help."

"He could help, but he doesn't. He's a warrior. He looks to find out about the Alliance to help destroy it. This is why he learns our language and our ways ... to help Warlog. Many of the women think you try to get him to join the Alliance so you can be his mate."

"Warriors taught me about mating. They taught me pain and shame. I used to dream of mating with a man and having strong children ... boys and girls. All my dreams of mating are turned to nightmares. I wake cold ... shivering in sweat. No, I don't think of mating with Tincolad. I will never mate with a man. I have no more desires for a man or children from a man. I will help other women with the children. That is enough for me."

"Yet you spend too much time with Tincolad."

"He's my friend. There's something about him; even Sotif thinks so. He had a chance to kill Earth People but did not. He saved ashes of the Earth People. I would be sad if he left or Tall Tree killed him. I would be happy and proud if he decides to help Tall Tree defeat Warlog. I would be happy for this, but I would not want him in my sleep robes. It's a thing I can't think about."

"I think he will not help, and Tall Tree must kill him soon."

"Why must this be so?"

"There is talk. Women hear things. He knows too much. If he doesn't decide to help soon, Tall Tree must kill him. It's a big risk that he might escape ... too big."

"Tall Tree could tie him and make him stay."

"It's a risk to keep him ... even tied up; he could get loose and escape."

Soft Cloud felt a strong emotion that was new to her. She knew, no matter the cost, she could not let Tincolad be killed, though she had no feelings to mate with him.

The air was warming. According to the people of the Mountain Pass village, this had been a mild winter. Soft Cloud had heard some of the men talking. There was a great fear the snow in the mountain passes would melt early and allow Warlog's army to pass through before the Alliance could get ready.

Soft Cloud spent every available minute with Tincolad, trying to persuade him to help. He was clear about his duties as a warrior, but there were signs he wanted to help.

As she spent more time with him, she began to understand him. He was carrying a secret that created indecision—something to do with Warlog. He wouldn't tell her what it was, but she was sure it involved his mother, and his father could help. Unfortunately, his father was with Warlog's army, and that was one of the reasons he wanted to go back to the army.

The times she spent with him were the best times of her dreary days. Today, she walked with him to check traps he had set to catch rabbits that burrowed under the snow to find grass that lay smashed under the snow drifts. He used a long stick to probe the snow fields until a tunnel was located. He carefully dug through the snow to set a trap in the tunnel. It was a kind of hunting he had learned as a boy growing up in his land.

They stopped to rest near a trunk of a large tree where the swirling wind had blown the snow off, leaving the frozen ground exposed. Tincolad laid a thick blanket on the ground and helped Soft Cloud remove the wide snow shoes he made for her.

The tree was old. Branches stretched in all directions, but each one was part of the whole. The Alliance was like that, but it had been declining since the big flood had split it. It seemed the Alliance was stuck in a decline that would end with only a stump. Warlog was bringing a fire that would hasten the decline into a blaze of destruction no one could prevent.

They sat side by side against the old tree truck eating the seasoned, dried meat Tincolad brought.

"The people say the snow in one moon will be gone," Tincolad said.

"That will bring a time of much war and killing. Will you help my people defeat Warlog's army then?"

"This is a hard thing. I must think. I don't like to talk about it now."

A cold breeze whipped around the trunk, and Soft Cloud leaned closer to Tincolad. He put his arm around her shoulder, and she put her head on his chest. He gently brushed the hair back from her face with his right hand and kissed her on her forehead.

Soft Cloud tensed. The mental images of the way the warriors had used her rose, thoughts filling her body. She knew she couldn't go through anything like that again.

"Afraid you are?"

"I'm not afraid, Tincolad. I don't want to be used. I'm not a camp whore."

Tincolad removed his arm. "No, you are not. I know this. Friends we are ... I feel ..."

"What do you feel, Tincolad?"

"We go back now." Tincolad stood up.

"No. Wait. Sit down, Tincolad. Tell me what you feel."

"I don't know words of you." Tincolad sat down. "More than friend you are. Part of me ... I don't want to lose."

Soft Cloud felt the warmth of his breath on her face. In his eyes, she saw truth. "I feel the same about you. Please put your arm around me ... the wind is cold."

Tincolad sat beside her, and she put her head on his shoulder. "Hold me." He put his arm around her shoulder. Soft Cloud relaxed into his arms. This time, the bad feeling didn't come. This time, a deeper feeling of surrender rose. She turned her face up and kissed Tincolad. A short exploratory kiss was followed by a powerfully passionate kiss that lasted until her body was tingling with desire for this man from a strange country.

They moved together, hands and emotions exploring new borders and new hungers. And after the boundaries were broken, Soft Cloud felt a sense of well-being she thought would never come to her life. Through it all, Tincolad was gentle, patient, loving.

They walked back to the village without a rabbit. Soft Cloud saw life clearer. Everything was beautiful. The sun sparkled on the snow. The tents and huts around the village seemed to glow in the warmth of the people. The people were beautiful and valuable. She sensed the love of the Great Spirit and Mother Earth, and she knew she was part of it. And Tincolad was part of it, even if he didn't know it yet.

****

Through all the history of the Alliance, there had been no words about war. Something new had begun—something that would never go away. Men would have to be taught to kill other men. Something special about people would be changed forever. Only something as powerful as the Spirit Fire could bring peace back to the earth again.

As Sotif thought, Lotend came into his tent. "What does Sotif think?"

"A new tradition comes to the Alliance. Warlog forces the Alliance to kill. Sotif sees something worse. Sotif sees young men excited about war. Sotif is afraid of this new thinking. A man must show courage to fight men. Glory must be found for this war thing. Many young men must die for this glory. All people must morn this loss. People must work much to get food for this glory. People must work much to get clothing for this glory. People must work much to get weapons for this glory. This is not a good thing."

"Tall Tree asks the men of the Earth People to become warriors. Earth People do not kill people."

"Earth People had to kill. At the Heart of the Bison, the killing began. Warlog comes to kill all Earth People. Earth People must choose to kill Warlog's warriors."

"Mother Earth must stop Warlog," Lotend insisted.

"Warlog must try to come through the Snow Mountains. Mother Earth must stop Warlog there. Rocks could fall on Warlog's army. Snow could fall on Warlog's army. Killing must come if Mother Earth does not stop Warlog. Then, the Alliance must choose this war thing."

"The Alliance must see if Mother Earth stops Warlog. If Mother Earth does not stop Warlog, the Earth People must run and hide from Warlog. Earth People hide from Sun People that are not part of the Alliance. Earth People did this from the beginning."

"The Sun People of the Alliance help the Earth People hide. The Sun People that are not of the Alliance do not look for the Earth People. If Warlog destroys the Alliance, the Sun People of the Alliance must help Warlog. Sotif has seen that the Sun People of the Alliance told Warlog about the Heart of the Bison. With no Alliance, Earth People cannot hide. Then must come the end of Earth People."

"Lotend does not know what to do. Earth People do not have the Heart of the Bison. Earth People do not have the Spirit Fire. Lotend thinks each clan must run to the mountains to find new caves. Lotend thinks the Alliance must be no more."

"Mother Earth cannot wish this. If the clans do not meet for the ceremonies, Earth People must be no more. It must be as it was before. Only the Alliance can save Earth People."

"Always, the Spirit Fire gave strength to Earth People. Lotend does not know what to do now."

"Earth People must create the Clan Fire. All the ashes of the Earth People must be mixed by fire in the Clan Fire." Sotif knew this was not a strong idea, but he could think of nothing else.

"The Spirit Fire came from Kectu. The Spirit Fire was blessed by Mother Earth. The Spirit Fire had the power of Kectu."

Sotif recognized the resignation in Lotend's voice. It was the same resignation he fought. Sotif lightly rubbed the scar on his left cheek. He thought of the blinding vision he had when he put the last spark of the Spirit Fire to his cheek. "The Traditions say in the beginning of the Spirit Fire, Sun People tried to destroy the Spirit Fire. The Traditions say Mother Earth caused a flood to protect the Spirit Fire. The Spirit Fire went from the flood to the Heart of the Bison. Mother Earth protected the Spirit Fire with water. This time Mother Earth did not protect the Spirit Fire. Mother Earth must be unhappy with Earth People. Earth People do not keep the Traditions."

"Mother Earth must let the Earth People be no more. Mother Earth must make a new people to keep the Traditions."

"Sotif does not believe this is what Mother Earth wants."

"Why did Mother Earth allow the Spirit Fire to be no more? Why did Mother Earth allow Warlog to close the Heart of the Bison?"

"Something comes to the mind of Sotif." Sotif walked away from Lotend in thought. After three slow steps, he turned quickly and walked back. "This comes to Sotif. The Traditions say Mother Earth protected the Spirit Fire with a flood. The Spirit Fire is protected by a flood. Sotif says … Mother Earth has protected the Spirit Fire with a flood again."

"How can that be? Sotif saw the Spirit Fire die. Sotif drowned the last living spark of the Spirit Fire."

"Sotif said the Spirit Fire is dead." Sotif began to pace as he talked. His words tumbled out excitedly. "The Spirit Fire was in two places. The Spirit Fire was in the Heart of the Bison. The Spirit Fire was in the Mammoth cave. The floods came. Mother Earth closed the path to the Mammoth cave with water. All people thought the eastern colonies were no more. Sotif thinks the eastern colonies are on the other side of the flood. Sotif says … Mother Earth has protected the Spirit Fire with a flood. Earth People must go east. Earth People must find the Spirit Fire. Mother Earth protected the Spirit Fire with water as in the beginning."

"How must Earth People find the Spirit Fire? How must the Earth People go across the water? How must the Earth People find the path to the Spirit Fire?"

"Far to the edge of the Alliance is the Finger Lake colony. Sotif has heard the people there make things to travel on the water of Finger Lake. Sotif has heard the people call these things boats. An Earth People boy lives in the Finger Lake colony. The boy is called Rodlu. This Rodlu has strong Memories of the eastern colonies. This Rodlu has strong Memories of the trade paths. Sotif must go to the Finger Lake colony. Sotif must talk with Rodlu. Sotif must take people who can make boats. Sotif must find the Alliance in the East. Sotif must find the Spirit Fire in the East."

"The Traditions say it must take two summers to travel east," Lotend said. "The Traditions say it must take two summers to return. Warlog comes now. Sotif must talk of this plan with Tall Tree. This plan will give hope to the people of the Alliance. The People of the Alliance must fight harder when the people know the Spirit Fire must return."

Sotif arranged to meet with Tall Tree, Broken Stick, Lewtud, Lotend, and Putlo that afternoon. Finally, he had something to hope for. After Sotif explained his plan, Tall Tree responded, "The flood came hundreds of generations ago. The Traditions say the water was great. I think the Traditions are right when they say the eastern colonies are no more. If the eastern colonies are still alive, why haven't they crossed the water? I say it's because they are no more, or the water is too great to cross."

"No one has been to the waters in the East for many generations. The eastern colonies do not cross the water because they think the western colonies are no more, or maybe they don't have boats. Boats can cross the water."

"I'm not sure. This plan would take many men and many summers. We need to fight now. We need all the strength of the Alliance, and we need Sotif here to help inspire the people of the Alliance."

"Tall Tree speaks wisely," Broken Stick said. "Sotif also speaks wisely. I ask to go to the East. I do not think a large group must go. I think a small group of strong men could travel east and return in less time than the travelers of the Traditions. I believe the people of the Finger Lake colonies can build good boats to cross the waters."

"This is a trip that goes for nothing," Tall Tree argued. "The eastern colonies are no more. We need all the strong men to fight the army of Warlog."

"Sotif speaks a true thing," Lewtud said. "Lewtud says ... Sotif must search for the Spirit Fire. Lewtud says ... this search must give hope to the people."

"And what will it do to the people when he comes back with no Spirit Fire?" Tall Tree argued.

"If Sotif comes back with no Spirit Fire, the people must be as the people are now," Sotif said. "Tall Tree speaks another true thing. Warlog comes now. The people of the Alliance need hope now."

"I have seen the despair and fear in the eyes of the people. This hunt for the Spirit Fire will lift their spirits. We will send a small group to explore, but Sotif must stay to lead ceremonies and speak to the people. He will do much good here and no good on a useless trip."

"You are agreeing to send a small group of men with no authority to bring back a Spirit Fire if they find it," Broken Stick argued. "What good is such a small group with no authority if they do find the Spirit Fire?"

"I don't believe there is a Spirit Fire. I don't want to waste any resource we have to fight Warlog. I only agree to such a trip because I realize we need the hope it would give to the people."

"This hope is important for the people," Sotif said. "But, I believe the Spirit Fire lives, and I must go to find it. If you send a weak group with no authority to bring the Spirit Fire back, the people will know there is no hope in the search."

Tall Tree walked to the entrance of the tent. He paused and then turned back. He looked at Sotif. "You leave as soon as possible for the Finger Lake colony." Then Tall Tree turned to Broken Stick. "You have fought hard for the Earth People. You will go to lead the Sun People on this voyage.

"The man, Tincolad, does not belong with my army. He has refused to help us. He will run back to Warlog and tell him about our army and how to get through the Snow Mountains. He's your friend, but he's a danger to us. Get him to go with you, or he must die."

"I think I know how to make him come with me," Broken Stick answered.

****

Love. Tincolad liked the sound of the new word Soft Cloud taught him. She was running back to her dwelling, and as she ran, he wondered if he would ever see her again.

Two days ago, Broken Stick had pressured him to teach Tall Tree and his men how to fight Warlog's warriors. Tincolad had tried to explain the warriors were his brothers in blood. It would be impossible for him to help the Alliance kill them. Broken Stick did not understand what Tincolad tried to tell him.

Tonight, Soft Cloud had come to talk to him after the evening meal. It was the time they often spent together while she taught him her language. Everything in her language was said backward. Though he knew many words, he was still having a hard time saying them backward.

Soft Cloud wanted to talk. She explained why the Spirit Fire was so important to her people. It was given to them by their Mother Earth. Soft Cloud told him it was as old as the mountains and had burned continuously from the beginning of the Alliance. It was hard for Tincolad to understand how a fire could burn so long, but it was gone now. Warlog had doused it in the Heart of the Bison on the day his army overran the cave.

Tincolad told her he would have liked to see such a fire. The excitement on her face when he said that was still fresh in his mind. She explained there was another Spirit Fire far to the east. Sotif and Broken Stick were leaving in two days to look for the Spirit Fire. Soft Cloud was going with them. "You can come with us. Sotif and Broken Stick want you to come."

He tried to explain to her that he needed to return to Warlog's army. She said she was sad and angry that he would choose to join the other warriors to kill her people and make her a camp whore again. He told her he would not help the warriors hurt her. He tried to explain the blood ties of a warrior and the honor required by the Warrior Ceremony. Soft Cloud did not understand and insisted he follow her to find this strange fire.

He refused, and she answered, "I must teach you a new word, Tincolad. The word is love. In my language, this means to care for someone more than life. Tincolad, I love you. If you go back, we can never see each other again as we do now. You or your warriors will kill me or try to make me a camp whore again. I die either way. Come with me."

They were sitting on a log. Tincolad stood up. He paced, trying to think of the words to answer her. He could think of no answer, so he said, "Warrior I am. I am promised to Zendolot, he to praise." Then he turned away.

Soft Cloud shouted, "Wait! Because I love you, I must tell you something very important. Tall Tree does not trust you. If you do not go with me, Tall Tree will have you killed. If you are not going with me, you must run away in the night. There, I have disgraced myself and betrayed my people for you. Do not give me an answer. I could not bear to hear you say you will leave. If you must go, I will know in the morning when you are not here." Soft Cloud ran from him.

Love. Soft Cloud had betrayed her people because of that word. Tincolad knew he would die to save her. He would not let the warriors make her a camp whore. That must be love. A woman could betray her family for the man she loved. Could a man dishonor himself for the woman he loved? Tincolad did not think so. He could die for her, but if he dishonored himself, what kind of man would he be? How could he be worthy of any woman's love? It only he had the words to explain this to Soft Cloud. But what would it matter? She was going east, and he had to go south.

Tincolad could not sleep. He thought about Soft Cloud. Her face and her eyes filled his mind. But Rencolad's words played in his ear. Soft Cloud was a camp whore. She was not the type of woman a warrior would take as a mate to have children. His people all thought she was brown, dirty, and stained. He knew he could not take her back to his people. He thought of what she had said. She would kill herself rather than be a camp whore again. Rencolad was wrong about her.

Tincolad stared at the scar on his left arm. He was a warrior. Warrior blood ran through his body. His blood ran with the army. It was in Rencolad and Rayloc. He could not have Soft Cloud and still be a warrior. It was hard, but he knew what his duty was.

Soft Cloud had warned him of his danger. He would sneak off before morning. His primary duty was to help Warlog and Rayloc kill all the droglits. He packed the few belongings he would need to travel and prepared to leave.

As he sat in silence with his bags, a new sense of confusion came to him. He had joined with Warlog to fight a glorious war. He had renounced his promise to his mother. He had renounced his father, and now he would abandon Soft Cloud, all because he believed Warlog was sent by Zendolot to rid the world of droglits. Everything depended on droglits!

As he thought of the Earth People, the eyes of the female in the cave came to him. She could have killed him. She should have killed him. But she had spared him, only to be killed herself—she and her baby. Was that something a droglit would do? Did droglits have families?

The whole question of what he should do with his life revolved around the Earth People. Were these ugly things really droglits or just another kind of people? Tincolad did not know the answer. How could he help Warlog destroy the Alliance and kill all the Earth People until he did?

Tincolad made his decision. He felt a sense of relief as soon as he knew what to do. He also felt a sense of joy because he would spend more time with Soft Cloud. He would stay with her and her people until he knew all there was to know about the Alliance and these strange Earth People. If he found they were droglits, he would have much information to give Warlog's army. If they were not droglits … he would think about that later.

CHAPTER 6

The Search

Late Summer 3285 BCE

The trip from the Mountain Pass colony had been difficult for Sotif. Though the land was flat, Broken Stick had pushed the travelers hard across the desert. Many nights, Sotif longed for the comfort of the Heart of the Bison. After crossing the desert, the past twelve days of struggling up the mountain to the Finger Lake colony had been brutal.

Finally, they stood on a hill overlooking the Finger Lake village and the huge lake it was named for. The village was about sixty paces up a slope from the shores of the lake. All around the village was a forest of tall pine trees except for a wide strip along the shore where grain fields and gardens flourished. Strange, long, narrow things sat half in the water and half on the shore. Ropes led to large rocks nearby. These must be the boats Sotif had heard about.

Though it was late in the day when they arrived, Sotif asked Chief Red Star to call a meeting the following morning. He specifically asked him to invite Rodlu.

Sotif was anxious to see the boats, but he was too tired after the evening meal. He slept soundly and woke early for the meeting.

After Chief Red Star called the group together, Sotif began speaking to Rodlu in the language of the Earth People. "Many seasons ago, Rodlu came to the Heart of the Bison. Many seasons ago, Rodlu said Rodlu has Memories of the eastern colonies. A time comes when men must find the eastern colonies. Do Rodlu's Memories show the way?"

"Rodlu has seen the paths. Rodlu has seen the Spirit Fire in the Mammoth cave," Rodlu answered.

"Can you find the Mammoth cave?" Red Star asked in Sun People language.

"Rodlu is not sure."

"Sotif says … the Spirit Fire is in the Mammoth cave. Sotif says … the people of the Alliance must go to the Mammoth cave fast. The people of the Alliance must bring back the Spirit Fire. Rodlu must lead the people of the Alliance to the Mammoth cave."

"Rodlu has Memories of three paths east. The shortest path goes from the Finger Lake through many mountains. Another path goes from the Mountain Path colony. The Longest path first goes west from the Finger Lake colony to the beginning of a large river. The large river goes north to a big water. The big water goes to the land of the East."

"Rodlu saw a path that follows water to the East," Sotif said. "Sotif asks if the boat things can travel on this water."

"Rodlu has Memories of the river. Rodlu has Memories of the big water. Rodlu says … the boats can travel on the river. Rodlu says … the boats can travel on the big water."

"Sotif has heard boats go faster than people walk."

"Our boats can go faster than a man can run," Round Rock said. Round Rock was the Sun People man who was in charge of the boats.

"Sotif says … the people of the Alliance must send people to the East. Sotif says … the people of the Alliance must take boats to the large river. The people of the Alliance must take the boats to the Mammoth cave."

"Rodlu says … the large river is too far to take boats. Rodlu says … it is better to take boat builders to the large river. Rodlu says … the people of the Alliance can travel to the large river before this time of snow. The boat builders can build boats during the time of snow. The people of the Alliance can follow the large river in the time of plants."

"I agree." Sotif changed to Sun People language. "I ask Red Star to send boat builders and those who know how to make the boats go fast."

"I will send all that is needed. Sotif will travel as fast as the eagle to bring the Spirit Fire back to the Alliance."

After the meeting was over, Sotif went to see the boats. The big ones were about eight paces long and two paces wide. The boats would carry many men with supplies. They were framed with large, hewn pine branches and covered with animal hides that were treated to prevent water from leaking. Sotif was anxious to see the men make them go.

The seekers of the Spirit Fire would have to cross the Finger Lake before traveling to the river that would start them on their water journey. Sotif watched much of the day as Round Rock supervised the bundling of supplies along the shore. They would be loaded in the boats the morning they left. Sotif looked at the mountains across the lake. It would take several days to walk that far. He asked Round Rock what they would do on the boats at night. Round Rock told Sotif it would only take half a day to cross the lake. It was hard for Sotif to imagine traveling so fast.

****

Tincolad had traveled many summers since leaving his father's tribe. He had never imagined the world could be so big. Tomorrow, Sotif would leave in search of the Spirit Fire. It would take three or four summers to make the trip and return. Sotif would surely reach the end of the world. But it would be too late to save the Alliance by the time he returned. Tincolad envied those who would make this trip to the end of the world. What a sight that would be!

Tincolad had learned all he could about the Alliance. He knew the Earth People were not droglits. He believed the stories of droglits were only old legends. If he could convince Warlog the Earth People were not droglits, there would be peace without killing the Earth People. Though he wanted to go with Sotif, he knew his duty was to find Warlog and change his mind before the Alliance was destroyed and all the Earth People and their magic were gone.

"Broken Stick just told me you're not going with him to find the Spirit Fire." It was Soft Cloud's voice.

Tincolad stood, and they kissed. "I have talked to Sotif. He says this might take four summers. This is much travel to me."

"This is the most important journey people have ever taken."

"You do not go on this important trip?"

"I would if they were taking women."

"Four summers is a long time to not see you."

"I know, Tincolad. That's the worst part. I will be right here when you return."

"In four summers, Warlog destroys everything."

"Do you think he will?"

"I see the Alliance. I know Warlog and the army. He will destroy everything in two summers."

"Not if you teach Tall Tree how to fight him. If you don't go on this trip, you must help Tall Tree fight. With your help, Tall Tree could hold Warlog for four summers."

"I cannot teach Tall Tree to kill warriors."

"Why not? You don't think Rayloc should kill all the Earth People, do you?"

"No, the Earth People are not droglits. I believe the Earth People must live. There must be peace with Warlog."

"Why won't you help Tall Tree?"

"The warriors are brothers of me. The warriors share blood of me. If I teach Tall Tree warrior fighting, then must die many warriors."

"But they came to kill my people. My people do not want this war. Warlog and his warriors came to kill *us*. Now we *have* to fight. If we don't kill the warriors, they will kill us. Someone must be killed. You have to decide who. If you do not help us, the warriors will kill us. If you help us, the warriors must die. But they are the ones who brought this killing. *You* have to choose."

"The warriors come not to kill. The warriors come to follow Warlog. Warlog says to kill droglits. I will teach Warlog that Earth People are not droglits. Then go home, will he."

"I don't think Warlog is going to listen to you. If he doesn't, you will never get away from him to help us."

"I cannot turn against brother warriors. When they die, a part of me dies. I cannot say more on this."

"Then I have nothing to say." Soft Cloud ran from Tincolad. Tincolad stood alone watching her leave.

As Tincolad walked back to the village, Broken Stick met him. "Tomorrow we leave to find the Alliance in the East."

"Soft Cloud told this. She wants I to go with you."

"You know I want you to come."

"I know this, but I must find Warlog and tell him about Earth People."

"Would you like to ride on the boats?"

"I have been on small boats in my home, but I want to ride on these big boats."

"Many men from this village will ride with us tomorrow to help unload the boats and make a camp on the other side of the lake. They will come back the next day. Do you want to come and help us make camp?"

"Yes, I will go to ride on these big boats."

When he got back to the village, Tincolad walked down to the lake shore to look at the boats. He tried to figure out how they were built. They had strong frames with animal hides stretched over them. He wondered how these light boats could carry men on the water.

He walked to Soft Cloud's dwelling to tell her he would be gone for two days. She would not speak to him. She had taught him the meaning of the word love. He wondered if there was a word for this new feeling.

It was just before dawn when the five loaded boats shoved off the bank near the Finger Lake village. The early morning mist hung over the water in patches. The sun had not risen, but the sky had turned gray. Tincolad was amazed at all the food, skins, and tools packed into the five boats.

Three men with paddles sat on each side of the boat Tincolad rode in. Broken Stick, Rodlu, and two other Earth People were the passengers in this boat. Sotif rode in one of the other boats. Tincolad had learned much of the language of the Sun People, and he understood the language of the Earth People.

The men with paddles quickly got into a rhythm. They took a deep breath as they swung their paddles forward. They dipped the paddle into the water and blew the air from their lungs as they pulled the paddle deep into the water and back. As the paddle came out of the water, they took another deep breath and swung the paddle forward to repeat the motion. The paddles slipped in and out of the water almost without sound. The rhythm of the breathing accented the motion of the boats. As they surged into the lake, a breeze blew off the water. Tincolad pulled his fur coat close to keep warm. The men working the paddles soon removed their furs. Even though it was cold for Tincolad, the bodies of the men working the paddles glistened with sweat.

When the sun finally came over the horizon, Tincolad enjoyed its warmth on his back. He sat near the front of the boat where he could hear the quiet sound of water breaking away from the front of the boat. Tincolad could see a faint outline of mountains across the water. The people of this village said it would take less than half a day to cross the Finger Lake. Tincolad could not imagine such speed—they must be wrong.

As Tincolad watched the far horizon, he noticed something floating in the water in front of the boat. The thing seemed to be growing. Soon he could see it was just a branch from a tree. It came upon them at a speed Tincolad had never imagined. It passed by about two paces to the side, and it was going faster than he could run. He realized the branch was not creating a wake in the water. It was not moving at all. It passed by so fast because that was how fast the boat was going! The breeze he felt was created by the speed they were traveling through the still air.

It was exhilarating to be traveling so fast the air blew through his hair. *This must be what an eagle feels as he swoops down for his prey,* he thought.

The sun was not far past the highest point in the sky when the five boats arrived at the other side of Finger Lake. While those who had paddled the boats rested, Tincolad helped those who had been passengers unload the boats and set up a camp. All the supplies had to be unloaded and organized into packs to be carried through the mountains to the winter camp.

When the camp was set up, Tincolad sat on a rock looking out over the water. In his travels from colony to colony on the way to Finger Lake, he had come to know many of the Earth People. They had magic, but they always used it to help the people of the Alliance.

"What are you thinking?" It was Broken Stick.

"I have thought of this great speed of boats. My people use boats; they do not travel so fast."

"I have never known such speed. Tomorrow you will speed back to spend the winter with those of the Finger Lake colony."

"I must go to find Warlog when comes the summer. With Warlog is father of me."

"Why do you need to find him?"

"I have been confused. These Earth People are not the things Rayloc says. I had a great fight with Father before I left. I must speak to Father."

"Why?"

Tincolad told Broken Stick about his mother's death and how Warlog had killed her family. His mother had barely escaped, and Warlog hunted her to destroy all the lineage of her family. "Mother hated Warlog. I promised to her I will kill Warlog. Father and I joined army of Warlog to kill him. I became confused. I told father Warlog is important. I would kill father first."

"Why did you join Warlog?"

"To destroy droglits. Earth People are not droglits, why is Warlog important? This is the confusion. I must talk with Father to know the secret of Mother. Maybe this will explain confusion."

"She did not tell you her secret?"

"I was not old enough to know. Mother said Father would tell me when it is time to know."

"How did you and your father get into Warlog's army?"

Tincolad told Sotif how he and his father joined with Warlog. He told him about the importance the Warrior Ceremony, though he didn't tell him any of the details. He talked about his training and explained how warriors were bound together by blood.

"If you find Warlog's army, what will you do?"

"I will find father, and I will find truth. Then maybe I must kill Warlog."

"Those in Warlog's army know you were with me when the Earth People escaped and killed his warriors. They will guess you helped. You will not be welcomed."

"I will tell them I was prisoner."

"They might believe you, but I think not. Even if there's a small doubt, Warlog will have you killed. I have heard how he does things. If they kill you, what will they do to your father?"

"I did not think of that."

"You're young. You have the hot blood of a young man."

"When I joined Warlog's army, I saw glory and organization. I forget the words of Mother. When Warlog ordered to kill women and children at Heart of the Bison, I grow more confused. I try to find truth. Father has truth to clear knowing."

"But if you return, it could mean his death and yours."

"I am a warrior. My place is with warriors."

"You are not a killer. I saw you at the first cave. You found Sed's baby and put it with her in the fire. This was pity. You did not kill."

"But I wanted to kill. I wanted to be a warrior and fight with warriors."

"At the Heart of the Bison, there was much killing of Earth People. I found you wounded on the ground. Your dagger and your spear were not wet with blood. You did not kill. You are not a warrior."

Tincolad held up his left arm showing the scar. "Warrior I am."

"There is still much you do not know about the Earth People and the Sun People. The history of the Alliance is older than the mountains. I go with Sotif to find our brothers in the East. Come with me."

"Why do you run now, when the Alliance needs all people to fight Warlog?"

"Warlog's army is strong. His army fights in ways we do not understand. When the eastern Alliance is found and is reunited with the Alliance, we will be stronger than any army. What we do is the most important thing that can be done. We will bring back a strong army of the Alliance."

"I hear stories saying the eastern colonies of the Alliance are lost in a giant flood."

"Some believe that, but Sotif believes the eastern Alliance still exists on the other side of the big water. Sotif is a very powerful Spirit Man. I believe him."

"I think the strong days of the Alliance are gone. I do not see warriors in colonies. I see hunters and farmers. They do not have spirit to fight the war Warlog brings. Warlog always wins."

"The people of the Alliance are sad because the Spirit Fire was lost."

"Why? It's easy to start a new fire."

"The Spirit Fire was started by Mother Earth. It was given to the people when the Alliance was first formed. The Spirit Fire has burned since Mother Earth gave it to the people. The Spirit Fire shows the people that Mother Earth is with the Alliance. The Spirit Fire is gone; the people feel Mother Earth has abandoned the Alliance. Without Mother Earth, the Alliance will be broken and destroyed by Warlog's armies. It's hard to be strong to fight when the people believe Mother Earth has abandoned them."

"Soft Cloud says the same thing about the Spirit Fire. Warlog destroyed the Spirit Fire of you. He will destroy the Alliance of you. This trip is a waste. People of you are weak because they do not have this Spirit Fire. The same is with the army of Warlog when he is dead. The most important is kill Warlog and Rayloc. When Warlog is dead, warriors will return to families."

"You are wise for a young man. I hope your father or someone else is successful. But I think it will be very hard to get to Warlog. It will not help your father for you to return to Warlog's army. Warlog will kill you both. This you already know.

"We have been wrong to think our brothers in the East no longer exist. Sotif believes Mother Earth allowed Warlog to destroy the Spirit Fire to force the Alliance to find the Alliance in the East.

"If we find the Spirit Fire and bring the sparks of the fire back to the Alliance, all the people will rise to defeat Warlog. This will show the people that Mother Earth still protects the Alliance. Then Warlog will see the power of Mother Earth in the army of the Alliance. He will be driven from our lands, and we will return to the Heart of the Bison. The eastern colonies of the Alliance will rejoin the western colonies, and the Alliance will be strong enough to live in peace forever."

"Do you believe this Spirit Fire still burns?"

"I believe it burns. I believe what this group does will change the whole world. You do more to bring an end to Warlog by coming with this group than anything else you could do. If you help return the Spirit Fire and reunite the Alliance to defeat Warlog, your mother will be proud of you. Come with me."

"I not know if Warlog must be killed. I must talk to father of me. I must find the secret Mother did not tell I."

"If you return to Warlog's army, you and your father will be killed. If you die knowing the secret, what good is that? Perhaps your father has already tried to kill Warlog and has been killed himself. Come with me. Find the Spirit Fire, and you will find a greater truth, a greater secret."

Tincolad could see Broken Stick was right. It would be almost impossible to kill Warlog by himself, and Rayloc would never believe the Earth People were not droglits. "I will go with you. I will see this Spirit Fire and the magic it holds."

"Do not tell anyone you will go with us until I have talked to Sotif. I will tell him you are coming to our winter camp to help carry supplies and help the boat builders."

"Why?"

"Sotif has already picked those who will go. I will have to convince him to let you go."

Summer 3284 BCE

It had not been a long winter. It was Sotif's second winter outside the Heart of the Bison cave. He thought of that first day when he arrived at the Fish Lake colony at the end of last summer. He remembered how amazed he had been to see the boats near the shore of Finger Lake. Looking north and south from the middle of the lake, the water went to the sky. He had never imagined such big water.

The ride across the lake in the boats had been easy. From there to this winter camp was the most difficult traveling Sotif had done. The forest was thick with trees and undergrowth. There were no paths or hunting trails. The Sun People of the Finger Lake village had carried heavy loads of supplies to the headwaters of the river Rodlu said they were to follow. They had traveled down the small stream as it grew to a river. In many places, it crashed over cliffs, creating beautiful waterfalls. When they had finally stopped to set up the winter camp, Sotif did not tell anyone how relieved he was. He would not have been able to travel this hard all the way to the eastern Alliance. Without the boats, the trip would have been impossible.

Although the dwellings the Sun People of the Finger Lake colony built for the winter camp were cozy, it was not like living in the Heart of the Bison. The dwellings were small, and it was necessary to leave them often. High in the mountains, the air seemed weak. Even small walks caused Sotif to be out of breath. Fortunately, with the warm air, it seemed to get strong. At first, Sotif had doubted he would be able to travel even in boats with such weak air. He was pleased the air was getting stronger. The weak air did not affect the people of the Finger Lake colony. They worked hard and strong even during those first days when the air was weakest.

The boat builders of Finger Lake spent the winter preparing materials and tools to build boats for the trip down the river. As the weather began to warm, they started building the boats.

As soon as the ice in the river began to melt and the water began to flow, everyone in the party made final preparations to continue the journey. The boats were finished before the ice in the river had completely melted. There were three large boats that could be paddled by six men each. One small boat was provided to run ahead of the main group. Two men occupied this boat. Their job was to check currents and look for dangerous snags in the river. Most important, they warned the larger boats of dangerous rapids and waterfalls. At such places, it was necessary to carry the boats and supplies on land to where the water was safer. The river was still young and violent.

Sotif looked at the packed boats.

"Today we begin a new adventure," Broken Stick said. "The Finger Lake colony has used these boats on the lake for many generations. This is the first time they will be used on a river."

"Warlog's army will not stop. With these boats, we might find the Spirit Fire this summer and bring it back next summer."

"The people of the Alliance know all the land north of the Snow Mountains. It will not be easy for Warlog to defeat them, even if he gets through the Snow Mountains."

"That is our hope, but we must not delay our return with the Spirit Fire."

Broken Stick paused. "I came to ask that Tincolad come with us."

"We go on a very important search. We must send him back to the Finger Lake village with the boat builders for Gray Sky to decide what to do with him. If he continues to refuse to help, he has a dark future."

"The boy has a good spirit."

"He still refuses to help the Alliance defeat Warlog. He is still loyal to Warlog. It's dangerous to take such a person with us."

"Loyalty is a good thing. He has participated in some ceremony that makes him loyal to Warlog's warriors. He's reluctant to forget that ceremony. He has reasons to hate Warlog. He would be happy to see Warlog lose. He wishes to help find the Spirit Fire. He will be loyal to the search. That is his nature."

"The trip has been planned for thirty-three men. I go with authority to manage the Spirit Fire sparks. Rodlu goes to show us the path. Twenty Sun People come to care for the boats. Ten Earth People come to provide strength to set up camps and carry heavy loads when the boats must be taken from the water. You come as a hunter to lead the men on hunts when we need food. We are supplied for these men. They meet all our needs."

"Each of the large boats can carry eleven men, and the small boat carries two. When the boats are loaded, two of the large boats carry only ten men. We have room to carry two more. Tincolad is an excellent shot with a bow. He would be valuable to me on the hunt. He will provide more than he eats."

"This boy is not of the Alliance."

Broken Stick dropped his head. It seemed he had no answer for this.

Sotif took advantage of Broken Stick's apparent confusion. "This group of searchers is made of the Sun People and the Earth People. We go to restore the blessing of Mother Earth to the Alliance."

"Is the Spirit Fire only for the Alliance? The Alliance will never be what it was before the war. After Warlog is defeated, all people will know about the Earth People. It will not be possible to hide them again."

Sotif thought of all the men who had told him things must change. Change had come in spite of anything Sotif could do to stop it. "I wonder if it's Mother Earth's desire to welcome the other people into the Alliance, after they are defeated."

"Can those people who have never known Earth People accept them?"

"This war with Warlog will show the value of Earth People. It will be strange for some people to accept them at first, but they will learn of the Earth People magic, and they will see the heart of the Earth People."

"I see another problem. Many of the Alliance do not trust the people who are not of the Alliance. This war only strengthens their fears, and yet, there can be no peace unless all people know and respect each other."

Sotif and Broken Stick sat in silence. "I have thought of these things all winter," Sotif continued. "After Warlog is defeated, the Alliance will become strong again. It will once again spread all across the world. Many will argue to return to the old ways. I see this can never be."

"The Earth People will reject the people who are not of the Alliance. Warlog has proven they are right to fear the other people."

"It is as you say. The Earth People are right to fear those people from the West. They were right to argue against expanded trade. They were right then, but things have changed. The people who are not of the Alliance know of the Earth People. We will return with the Spirit Fire and an army from the East to defeat Warlog. Then the Alliance will be strong again.

"After the wars are over, the Alliance will have to open its councils to all people so that no other Warlog can build an army to defeat the Alliance. The return of the Spirit Fire will begin the defeat of Warlog and start the beginning of a new alliance. Tincolad's participation in the return of the Spirit Fire will show the Earth People that the others have a right to the promises of the Sprit Fire and Mother Earth. We will take Tincolad. His help will heal some of the wounds of war."

The day finally came to put the boats in the river. This was a great day in the history of the Alliance. Sotif knew he would have to make a painting for the History Room to include boats.

As the boats started down the river, the water was turbulent. Even the experienced boatmen of the Finger Lake colony found it difficult to avoid rocks and snags in the river, but they learned quickly.

Travel was slowed many times while they carried boats and supplies around dangerous rapids and waterfalls. More than once, Sotif was tempted to leave the boats. He was sure they could travel faster without them. The first days of summer were spent battling the river out of the mountains.

Once the land leveled out and the river grew wider and less turbulent, the advantage of using boats was obvious. The boatmen paddled from early morning until the sun was high. They rested until the sun passed the high point. They took up the paddles again and worked until dusk. But even when they rested during the day, the boats continued to drift downstream. The Earth People learned to paddle, so they could paddle when the Sun People rested. The boats sped down the river from dawn to dusk. Every few days, they stopped part of the day to make repairs on the boats and allow Broken Stick and his men to resupply them with meat.

Sotif noticed the changing path of Earth's Fireball. The time of daylight was much longer than he had known before. This allowed the boats to travel longer each day. During those long days, Sotif had little to do except sit at the front of the boat and watch the scenery speed by. They had left the trees, and now they traveled through a flat land. The ground was green. The river was so wide it seemed like a small lake. The banks of the river were lined with shallow water, plants, and swarms of mosquitos. In this boring landscape, Sotif thought mostly of the Heart of the Bison, the Spirit Fire, and the History Room.

This trip to find the Spirit Fire would require one of the most important paintings of the History Room. The painting would have to show the story of Warlog, his armies, and the loss of the western Spirit Fire. It would have to show how the History Room and the Heart of the Bison were sealed. The use of boats in the search for the eastern Spirit Fire would have to be shown. It would have to show how Warlog was defeated when the Spirit Fire was returned. It would have to show the return to the Heart of the Bison with the Spirit Fire. It would have to show the new alliance embracing all peoples. This story would be the most complicated of all stories. Sotif tried for days to imagine a painting that could tell such a story.

One day as Sotif thought, Tincolad sat beside him. "Old man, what do you think of all these days?"

Sotif had come to like the irreverent young warrior. Tincolad worked hard to do his share. He spent his free time learning language, the Traditions, and beliefs of the Alliance. "I think of the history of the Alliance. Our people have many stories and Traditions."

"I like the stories of the Alliance and Kectu."

"These stories teach the people."

"I want to see this History Room all the people talk about. Someday, maybe I will see this … this Heart of the Bison."

"This cannot happen unless Warlog is defeated." Tincolad did not answer. Sotif broke the uncomfortable silence. "It seems like more than one lifetime since I last looked upon the wall of paintings. I think of the History Room much of the time. The paintings on the wall show the history of the Alliance."

"This history painting must be wonderful."

"Yes, and now the story of Warlog and our search for the Spirit Fire must be painted on the wall. This will be one of the greatest stories in the History Room. Tincolad is part of this history. Tincolad must be painted in the History Room."

"Tincolad will be on this great wall?"

"I don't know how to make a painting to tell such a large story, but when it's done, Tincolad must be part of it."

"How can a painting tell a story? Can a painting speak?"

"These paintings do not speak. Only those who know the stories can speak the stories the History Room tells. The paintings remind those who know the stories."

"If I went to this History Room alone, the paintings would not talk to me? I would not know the history of the Alliance unless someone explained the painting?"

"Always one of the Ancients must explain the meaning of the paintings."

"If the Ancients must explain, what use are paintings?"

"The magic in the paintings is only for those who know the stories. I see each of Warlog's warriors carries a tattoo on his left forearm. Even you carry this tattoo. It must have meaning. To me, the meaning is hidden. To the warriors, the tattoo tells a story."

"Yes. Each finger of a warrior's hand also tells its own story. What if all those who know the stories of the History Room die before the Alliance frees the Heart of the Bison? Then is this magic dead?"

"You ask many questions." The old man and the young man sat pondering in silence. Sotif thought of the many stories in the History Room. There would be much about the story of Warlog to remember.

"The paintings in the History Room can remind people of the stories. Could Sotif make better pictures? Could Sotif make pictures to tell stories to everyone?"

Sotif laughed. "That would be strong magic."

"Hey, Tincolad, how about taking a turn at the paddles," Broken Stick shouted from the other end of the boat.

Tincolad jumped up. "I like to hear these stories of the magic painting wall."

Sotif watched the young man carefully walk to Broken Stick. He looked at the faces of the boatmen from the Finger Lake village. Each one had an up-facing crescent tattooed on his forehead. This told everyone he was a boatman. Sotif thought of the hunters in the Winding River colony. They each had a tattoo of an arrow on the right arm above the elbow that told everyone he was a hunter. These were symbols that had meaning. Throughout the Alliance, each of the colonies had special tattoos to mark important men. The tattoos for hunters were similar, but different enough so that a stranger could tell what village the hunter was from. Sotif had his own tattoo marking him as the History Man.

Sotif recalled that the names of people in the first painting on the history wall were shown as symbols. For White Cloud, the symbol showed a horizon with a fluffy cloud above. For Sky Runner, there was a horizon with a stickman running in the sky.

As Sotif thought how tattoos and symbols were used as words, an idea began to grow in his mind. With enough symbols for important words, any story could be told. Anyone who knew the meaning of the symbols could understand any story painted on the wall using the symbols.

For several days, Sotif thought about his idea. Someone would have to think up the symbols, paint them, and teach them to others. It would be harder than tattoos because it would take many symbols to tell a story.

Sotif began creating symbols in his mind while the boats traveled down the river. He thought of symbols for important words, and then he imagined some stories, creating symbols in his mind to tell the story. Soon he began to use charcoal to draw the symbols on animal skins.

Tincolad and Rodlu were interested in Sotif's new symbols. All three men worked together creating symbols and memorizing them. Soon Sotif could draw out simple stories with his symbols, and Rodlu and Tincolad could tell the story from Sotif's symbols. Rodlu told the stories in the language of the Earth People, while Tincolad told the same stories in the language of the Sun People. It was a strange kind of magic because the same symbol story could be told in different languages. Working with Sotif on the picture stories helped Tincolad improve his ability to speak the eastern language.

As the days got longer, all the men took turns paddling and sleeping. Food became more difficult to find. Anytime animals were spotted, at least one boat would turn in to hunt. The men from the Fish Lake colony were expert fishermen, and even though fishing in the river was different from fishing in the lake, they were able to add a supply of fresh fish.

Soon, the night was just a long twilight that turned into a gray predawn without ever getting dark. It seemed to Sotif that Earth's Fireball was just slipping below the horizon before rising again.

A day came when Earth's Fireball just touched the horizon but did not disappear. It was like a flat rock that skipped on the surface of a calm pond. Finally, Earth's Fireball just circled above the horizon. By taking turns at the paddles, it was possible to keep the boats constantly going in the endless daylight. Sotif realized Mother Earth was keeping Earth's Fireball in the sky to make it possible to travel all the time. There were no stops for darkness. It was only necessary to stop to make repairs. The men were getting better at fishing, so stops for food were rarely necessary. The land had turned to an endless tundra with very little to hunt.

One day the river emptied into a large body of water. The water was salty. Sotif talked to Rodlu. "What shall we do now? The water is poisoned. Animals on the land are rare, and now we will have no fish."

Tincolad overheard Sotif's question. "In my land, there are much waters of salt like this one. People cannot drink such water. It is poison to drink, but in these salty waters are many fish that are good to eat. We will fish. You will see."

"I hope so," Sotif answered.

"It is the time to turn east," Rodlu said.

For three turns of Earth's Fireball in the sky, they paddled their boats. The men fished. They had some luck with their nets, and the fish they caught were good to eat, but they did not know how to catch fish very well in this water. Tincolad said he was not a fisherman, and he was little help in getting food. The men were all hungry.

On the third day, when Earth's Fireball was in the southern horizon and Rodlu and Sotif were working on the story symbols, Rodlu froze in his seat. "Look," he whispered.

Sotif looked in the direction Rodlu pointed. A strange dog was swimming in the water. Soon the men saw many of the dogs swimming around the boats. Sotif had eaten dogs before. He didn't like them, but they were better than starving. Tincolad unpacked his bow and arrows. He made a clean shot at one of the closest dogs. It flipped and splashed, and then the body floated near the boats. The other dogs all disappeared in the water. When they retrieved the dead dog, they discovered its ears were very small, and its legs were broad and flat with no paws. The dogs that had disappeared did not return. Sotif thought they may have been so scared they drowned. He told everyone to watch for their bodies to float, but they didn't see any more.

They butchered and cooked the dog. The meat was full of fat and tasted much better than other dogs.

The next day, the Earth People said they heard a sound like many dogs barking. Coming around a large rock peninsula, they saw something no one could have imagined. There were so many dogs on the shore ahead of them that the land seemed alive. The sound of the dogs barking was so loud it was hard for Sotif to talk to the men in the same boat with him.

The men were afraid to go on the land with so many dogs. Finally, Broken Stick and Tincolad took the small boat and landed on the beach. The dogs did not attack them. Broken Stick used a spear to kill one. There was excitement, and the dogs near them began to run clumsily to the water on their strange legs.

Broken Stick and Tincolad killed eight more of the dogs. By then, all the dogs near them had run away. Those that were farther away barked loudly, but they did not run. The boats came to the beach, and the men filled themselves on the water dogs.

In time, the men learned to catch several kinds of fish. They were also able to find and kill more of the water dogs. They found animals that lived in large shells in the shallow water along the beach. Food was plentiful, so they could travel without stopping to hunt. They did stop at every stream to get fresh water. The boats traveled east constantly as Earth's Fireball slowly circled around the horizon. No men had ever traveled so fast.

Gradually, the shoreline turned southeast. Earth's Fireball began to dip lower and lower in the sky. When it began to dip below the horizon again, the shoreline turned south.

Rodlu came to Sotif. "Rodlu's Memories say from this land the boats must turn east."

"How far must the people go into the water?"

"Rodlu does not know this. Rodlu thinks not too far. The boats travel fast."

"The people must stop here. The people must fill the boats with food and water to make this big trip."

Sotif called all the boats together. "Today, we must make preparations because tomorrow we must go east into the saltwater."

"I don't see the other side of this water," one of the Sun People said. "Do the Earth People see the other side?"

No one could see the other side.

"We cannot cross water that has only one side," another of the Sun People said.

"We have come to cross the flood and find the Spirit Fire," Sotif argued.

"We did not come this far to die," one of the Sun People men said.

"I agree. If we go on this water, and there is no other side, we will die. We cannot find good water in this salty water," another said.

Most of the men expressed concern and reluctance to paddle out in the water. They were in a strange land with strange animals. They were surrounded by water they could not drink, and even the sun behaved strangely.

Tincolad spoke. "I came from a land that is strange to you. I have seen many strange things, but this land is the strangest. Rodlu says the Spirit Fire is east. If we follow the shore south, who knows what strange lands we may see or how far we will have to go in order to finally go around to the other side of this great water? Maybe it will take many seasons. Warlog brings warriors who do not fear strange things. Should we be afraid because we cannot see every part of our path? Don't the people of the Finger Lake tribe cross the Finger Lake when it's foggy and they cannot see the other side?"

Several of the Sun People said it was because they already knew the Finger Lake. Broken Stick stood. "I say we should gather food and water. We should fill the boats with cooked water dogs and fresh water. We will paddle into the water until half of the food and water is gone. If we have not seen the other side by then, we will turn back."

"This is a good plan," Sotif said.

Some of the men were reluctant, but Sotif's insistence and Tincolad's bravery shamed them into agreeing to try Broken Stick's plan.

After a day's preparation, the boats started out into the sea. Before the end of the first day, the shore was out of sight. It was a frightening time for the Sun People. They became confused about the direction they should go. The Earth People had no confusion about the direction. In the middle of the second day, the Sun People began to panic. How could they turn back when the food was half gone if they did not know which way was back? Fortunately, they were having good luck fishing, and they found large chucks of ice, some much bigger than the boats. When they melted the ice, the water was pure and sweet.

The Earth People directed the boats into the fourth day, and then Earth People could see land far away. They reached the land early on the fifth day. From there they turned south along the shore. Rodlu directed their travels. After two more days, they came to the mouth of a large river. Rodlu told Sotif they were in the land of the eastern colonies, but he did not know where the Spirit Fire was. Sotif decided to turn up the river and look for a colony. For two days, they traveled up the river.

Winter 3284/3283 BCE

Rodlu stood up in the boat. "Wait!" he shouted.

"What?" Sotif asked.

"These mountains are in Rodlu's memory. These mountains are close to the Mammoth cave."

Sotif's spirit soared. He had thought and dreamed of this day since he realized the Spirit Fire might still live. No one had seen any signs of people since they crossed the saltwater. Even now, Sotif could not see signs of the Alliance.

Many times he had wondered what he would do if he couldn't find the Spirit Fire. He always pushed such doubts from his mind. Rodlu said this was the place of the Spirit Fire, but there were no signs of the Alliance.

"We start to drift down the river," Broken Stick said. "What do you want to do?"

"Which shore?" Sotif asked Rodlu.

"Rodlu thinks the Mammoth cave is on the south shore."

As they approached the shore, Rodlu exclaimed, "Look!"

"Where?" Sotif asked.

"Four people watch this boat. Four people are on that hill." Rodlu pointed.

Sotif could see the hill, and he thought he could make something out, but it was too far for him. "What kind of people?"

"Rodlu sees only Earth People. Rodlu sees no Sun People. The Earth People come down."

The people Rodlu had spotted descended into the trees. The boats glided smoothly to the shore. "What do we do now?" Broken Stick asked.

"Rodlu saw Earth People on the hill," Sotif responded. "If he saw them, they saw us. We will wait here. They will come."

"Maybe we should go find them," Tincolad suggested.

"That would be a wrong thing. We will make camp and wait here," Sotif said.

As they were setting up the camp, Rodlu said, "The Earth People call in a soft voice."

"What do they say?" Sotif asked.

"The Earth People speak strangely. Rodlu thinks they say these Earth People fear Sun People."

"Tell them the Sun People bring the people of the Alliance to the Spirit Fire."

Rodlu shouted, "These people come from the Alliance of Earth People and Sun People." Rodlu listened. Then he spoke to Sotif. "These Earth People have no alliance. These Earth People fear Sun People. These Earth People hide from Sun People."

"Tell them these people come to see the Spirit Fi—"

"Wait," Rodlu interrupted. "These Earth People say, 'Send Earth People into the trees.' These Earth People must talk to Earth People."

"Rodlu must go to meet with them. Rodlu must find out why they fear Sun People. Rodlu must find out where the Alliance is."

"Rodlu must do as Sotif says." Rodlu picked two other Earth People to go with him.

Sotif waited the rest of the day. What kind of Earth People were these who would not talk to Sun People? What would he do if Rodlu did not return? Finally, just after dark, Rodlu returned alone.

"What happened?" Sotif asked.

"Rodlu has much to tell." Rodlu sat by the fire. "The Spirit Fire is here. Rodlu has seen the Spirit Fire. The shomot of the Earth People is called Leco."

"Then all is well!"

"The Alliance of the East is no more."

"What does Rodlu mean?"

"The Memories and stories of these people say there was a great alliance. These people say Mother Earth divided the Alliance with a flood. These people say jealousy divided the Earth People and Sun People. Sun People learned to kill Earth People. Earth People learned to hide from Sun People. All Sun People have forgotten the old Traditions. Sun People have forgotten the Alliance. Sun People have forgotten Earth People. Sun People must never learn of Earth People."

Sotif was stunned. "All people are stronger when there is an alliance. Sun People and Earth People help each other in an alliance."

"These Earth People are much afraid of Sun People. These Earth People say Sun People must stay by the river. These Earth People say Sotif must not come to the cave of the Spirit Fire."

"How must Sotif speak to the Earth People?"

"Tomorrow, the Earth People will show Rodlu where to take Sotif. All Sun People must wait by the river. So says the shomot of the Earth People. So says Leco, so it shall be."

"So says Leco, so it shall be." After all this traveling, Sotif was discouraged to find the Alliance was dead and these people would not allow him to see the Spirit Fire. How would he convince them to let him take hot coals of the living fire back to the Heart of the Bison if they would not even let him see the Spirit Fire? How could he get an army if there was no alliance?

The rest of the day, everyone was busy building a camp and preparing for winter. Several Sun People went to hunt. They found some deer and a lot of elk. Ducks and swans were also plentiful near the river. There were no water dogs this far up the river, but otters and beaver were plentiful.

The rest of the people began building shelters for the winter. There were too many trees in the forest, but closer to the river was a large meadow that was suitable to making a winter camp. They started to build shelters by digging holes about eight paces long and four paces wide. When the holes were knee deep, they dug a deep trench in the bottom around the perimeter to stand logs, making a wall all around the hole. The wall was chest high above the ground on the outside of the shelter. For added strength, they would place large rocks against the logs around the inside of the hole, and they would pile the dirt from the hole against the logs around the outside of the shelter. They would lash smaller logs together using sinew and birch bark and use them to construct a pitched roof over the dwellings. A hole at the top would allow smoke from the fire pit to escape. Each dwelling would comfortably house twelve men.

The Sun People began construction of a smoke room to smoke and cure meat from the hunts.

The Earth People collected roots, berries, and fruits. They prepared them for storage by drying them and weaving baskets for them. They also went to the kill sites to prepare and cure the meat and help carry it back to the camp. Everyone was busy getting ready for the long winter.

The next morning, Rodlu led Sotif through the forest for most of the day. In late afternoon, they crossed a ridge, and in a valley below, Sotif saw a small dwelling.

When they approached the dwelling, two young Earth People men came out. One of the men said something to Sotif. Sotif recognized the Earth People language, but the accent was different, and Sotif could not understand the sounds he made. He looked questioningly at Rodlu.

"The man says Leco waits inside. Soon Sotif must get used to the words of these Earth People."

Sotif entered the dwelling. An old man sat to Sotif's left. He said something. Sotif understood "Leco, shomot, talk," and "sit." Sotif could speak the language of the Earth People, however, some sounds he could only approximate. He said, in Sun People language, "I am Sotif. I am the History Man of the Alliance of the West."

Rodlu translated for Sotif. Leco answered, and again Sotif only understood a few words, but already he was beginning to get the sense of what the old man said.

Rodlu translated. "Leco says it is Tradition of these Earth People that the Earth People of the West used to bring Spirit Fire ashes. Leco says all the clans of the Earth People have moved to a land far south of this place. Leco says the time of snow in this place is too long. Leco says Leco is happy the Earth People of the West have finally come."

"Tell Leco, Sotif has brought the Spirit Fire ashes. Sotif wants to make the Ceremony of the Ashes. Then all Earth People will be one people."

The old man stood up and paced as he responded to Rodlu's translation. Sotif understood most of what Leco said. After Rodlu finished translating the old man's words, Sotif understood the depth of his problem. Leco and his clan did not trust Sun People. For many generations, they had hid from the Sun People. They did not trust the Sun People who had brought Rodlu across the water. They agreed to this conference because Sotif was half Earth People.

Leco and his people were sure the Sun People in the East had all forgotten about the Alliance and the Earth People. The Earth People could hear, see, and smell Sun People well enough to avoid them when they were away from their caves. They used their skills to make sure they left no tracks the Sun People could see or follow. Their caves were located far from areas where Sun People lived, and the openings were disguised. They believed the Sun People were evil and must be avoided.

"Tell Leco the Sun People of the Alliance are as they were in ancient times when Shekek created the Alliance."

Sotif noticed that Leco sat up and became more alert when he heard the name Shekek. "Leco is wise not to trust Sun People who do not respect the Alliance," Rodlu explained to Leco. "In the West, there are Sun People who do not respect the Alliance. These Sun People are evil. These Sun People have strong magic. Earth People cannot fight the strong magic of Sun People. It is wise to hide from those Sun People.

"Sun People of the Alliance have strong magic to protect Earth People from the evil Sun People. The Sun People who brought Rodlu and Sotif are Sun People of the Alliance. Sun People of the Alliance are brothers to all Earth People since the days of Kectu. Sun People of the Alliance have strong magic to cross the big water."

"Sun People change. Sun People use Sun People magic to kill Earth People. The magic of the Sun People is evil." Sotif understood Leco's response.

"Tell Leco that Sotif comes across the world to unite the clans and bring Spirit Fire ashes for the Spirit Fire of the East."

"This Sotif has come from the Heart of the Bison," Rodlu explained. "This Sotif is sent by Mother Earth. Mother Earth put a Fireball that stayed in the sky many days so this Sotif could bring ashes to the eastern clans."

"Tell this Sotif that Leco must accept the ashes. Tell this Sotif that Leco must perform the Ceremony of the Ashes. Tell this Sotif that Leco must give Rodlu ashes to take to the Spirit Fire in the West."

Sotif understood Leco's words. "Tell Leco that Sotif must help in the Ceremony of the Ashes to represent all the generations of the Earth People."

Leco watched Sotif intently as he talked. When he was finished, Leco turned to Rodlu to hear the translation. "This Sotif is the History Man of the clans of the West. This Sotif is the History Man that Mother Earth sent with the ashes of the Spirit Fire. This Sotif must be part of the ceremony to please Mother Earth."

"This Sotif is only half Earth People. This Sotif has no right to the Spirit Fire of Kectu."

Sotif was becoming frustrated. Rodlu spoke again. "This Sotif is a powerful man to Mother Earth. This Sotif is a powerful man to the Spirit Fire. Hear a story of Sotif. Hear a story of the Spirit Fire."

Leco nodded assent.

"Evil Sun People came to destroy the Alliance. Evil Sun People came to kill all the Earth People." Leco nodded his head.

Rodlu explained how Warlog had taken the Heart of the Bison. He told Leco that Warlog had put the fire out, but Sotif had pushed the last hot coal of the Spirit Fire in his face. "Sotif took the ashes of the Spirit Fire to bring to the East. Mother Earth has sent Sotif with the power of the Spirit Fire burned into Sotif's face. Mother Earth has sent Sotif with the ashes of all the generations of the clans of the Earth People."

Leco looked at Sotif and his scar in a different manner. "Sotif understands the words of the Earth People?" Leco asked, still looking at Sotif.

"Sotif—" Leco held his hand up with his palm turned to Rodlu, but he kept his eyes on Sotif. Rodlu ceased speaking, and there was silence.

Sotif spoke slowly with his thick accent. "Sotif understands the words of the Earth People. Sotif speaks the words of the Earth People."

Leco looked puzzled, and Sotif knew he did not understand. He repeated his words, this time more slowly. Leco nodded.

"Sotif speaks the words of the Earth People. The words of Sotif sound different."

"Sotif speaks the words of the Earth People with the sounds of the Sun People," Sotif explained.

"What does Sotif want of the Earth People of the East?"

"Mother Earth allowed the evil Sun People to destroy the Spirit Fire." Sotif spoke slowly, watching Leco's eyes intently. He proceeded when he saw Leco understood him. He explained Mother Earth wanted all the clans to join together again to share the ashes of the Spirit Fire between two Spirit Fires as it was before the flood. "Mother Earth burned this vision into Sotif as Sotif held the last spark of the Spirit Fire to Sotif's face."

"How shall the Spirit Fire of the West accept the ashes of the eastern Earth People? Sotif has said the Spirit Fire of the West is no more."

"Powerful people roam through the lands of the West. Powerful people kill Earth People. Earth People of the West lose spirit. Earth People of the West need the Spirit Fire. Sotif comes to take burning coals of the Spirit Fire west. The Spirit Fire will give the Earth People new hope. Sotif has come to do as Mother Earth says."

After some thought, Leco said, "Leco does not know what to do. Leco must talk to the leaders of all the clans. Leco does not know how to decide this question."

"Where are the leaders of the clans?" Sotif asked.

"This land is not a good land for Earth People. The time of plants is too short. The time of snow is too long. Only Leco's clan lives here to care for the Spirit Fire. This cave has been the home of the Spirit Fire from the day the Spirit Fire was brought to this land. The ancient Traditions say the Spirit Fire must stay here until the Earth People of the West come.

"All the other clans have moved south. Each summer, the clans of the South send travelers bringing the ashes of their dead to mix in the Spirit Fire. The travelers must travel all the time of plants to come. The travelers bring their ashes to join the Spirit Fire.

"Leco must leave early in the time of plants to go south. Leco must travel all through the time of plants. Sotif must come. Sotif must meet with the leaders. If the leaders agree, Sotif must take sparks of the Spirit Fire west."

Sotif was stunned. It would take two summers to get permission to take sparks and another summer to make the trip back to the West. "Sotif has said the Earth People of the West are in great danger. Evil people kill the Earth People. The Earth People must have the Spirit Fire next time of plants. If the Earth People do not have the Spirit Fire next time of plants, many must die. If the Earth People do not have the Spirit Fire next time of plants, maybe all must die. Sotif cannot go south. Sotif must take sparks of the Spirit Fire next time of plants."

"Leco does not know what to do."

"Mother Earth has given a sign," Rodlu said.

"What sign?"

"Sotif came through a land far to the north. In this land, Mother Earth put Earth's Fireball in the sky many days so Sotif could travel without stopping. This is a strong sign from Mother Earth. Sotif must not wait to return."

"This is a strong sign to Sotif. This is not a strong sign to Leco. Always, in the time of plants, Earth's Fireball stays in the sky longer in this land. In the time of snow, Earth's Fireball stays only a short time."

"Leco can see the magic trees Mother Earth gave to Sotif to cross the water," Rodlu insisted.

"Leco must look for a sign to Leco during this time of snow. If Leco gets the sign from Mother Earth, Leco must give this Sotif sparks of the Spirit Fire. If Leco does not get a sign from Mother Earth, this Sotif must come south to meet with the leaders of the clan."

Sotif could see Leco was firm. Rather than arguing more, he decided to wait and see what sign Mother Earth would give. "Sotif must return to Sotif's winter camp. Sotif must wait for the sign from Mother Earth." The meeting was over. Sotif and Rodlu stayed the night in the dwelling. The next day, Sotif returned to the winter camp, and Rodlu went with Leco to the Spirit Fire cave.

The first storm of the winter came the day after Sotif returned to the winter camp. Sotif made a ceremony tent and performed a ceremony to Mother Earth. During the ceremony, he dreamed of grave danger in the West. He saw Tall Tree and the army of the Alliance running from Warlog. He knew he had to get the Spirit Fire back to the Alliance next summer or it would be too late. He had a chilling feeling it might be too late for the Alliance already.

After the snows of the first storm melted, Rodlu returned to the winter camp. "What took so long?" Sotif asked.

"These Earth People do not leave their caves when there is snow on the ground."

"Why not?"

"These Earth People are afraid of the Sun People. These Earth People do not leave tracks in the snow to show the Sun People where the Spirit Fire cave is."

"This fear is a hard thing."

"Rodlu has ancient Memories of the Earth People before the time of Kectu. These Earth People are like the ancient Earth People before the Alliance. These Earth People live without the magic of the Sun People. In the cave, there is little food. The food in the cave must be spoiled too soon. There must be no food in the Mammoth cave. The Earth People cannot hunt when snow is on the ground. The Earth People must do the famine ceremony often."

"The famine ceremony is from before the Alliance. It is hard to let people die so they can be eaten in the famine ceremony."

"Leco says the clans in the South are well. Leco says the clans of the South live on the north side of a giant river that flows into this great saltwater. There are giant trees in this land. This magic land does not have a time of snow. This magic land has a time of rain. There is much food. Only the Spirit Fire clan must live in the North. When there are not enough Earth People in the Spirit Fire clan, Earth People come from the South to join. It is a great sacrifice for all the clans of the Earth People to keep the Spirit Fire north. Many want to move the Spirit Fire south. All the leaders of the clans met last time of plants. The leaders of the clans decided if the Earth People of the West do not come this time of plants, the Earth People must move the Spirit Fire to a new Spirit Fire cave in the South."

Things became clear to Sotif. "Sotif knows Mother Earth let the Spirit Fire in the West die to make Sotif come this time of plants. Mother Earth put Earth's Fireball in the sky all this time of plants to make sure Sotif came before the Earth People of the East move the Spirit Fire where it cannot be found. Leco must understand the sparks of the Spirit Fire must be sent back to the people of the West."

"The things Sotif said to Leco have strong magic with Leco. The things Sotif said to Leco have strong magic with the others at the Mammoth cave. It is hard for the Earth People of the Mammoth cave to trust Sotif. Sotif has life force of the Sun People mixed with life force of the Earth People.

"Rodlu spoke much to the Earth People of the Mammoth cave. Rodlu told of Broken Stick. Rodlu told how Kectu spoke to Rodlu's spirit on the thinking stone at the Heart of the Bison. Rodlu told of Kectu's desire to bring all the ashes of the Earth People together."

"Did Leco agree to send sparks of the Spirit Fire?"

"Leco must think on this. This time of snow must be very difficult. Sotif must stay here until the time of plants comes. Leco must think on this until the time of plants. Sotif must prepare to take two Earth People of the East with Sotif. Two of the Earth People of the West must travel south with Leco and the Spirit Fire."

"Sotif knows Sotif must stay here this time of snow. The people have built a camp for the time of snow. The people are filling it with food for the time of snow."

"Leco is worried that the Earth People that came with Sotif are too thin to last through the time of snow. Leco does not understand the magic of storing food. Leco does not understand building shelters.

"This is a hard thing," Sotif said. "All the people of the Alliance must stay in this camp. But when the snow begins to melt, Sotif must leave. Sotif must convince Leco to give Sotif sparks to take back. Rodlu and Sotif must take stored food to the Mammoth cave. There must not be a famine ceremony. Tell Sotif about the Spirit Fire."

"When Rodlu entered the Mammoth cave, Rodlu felt the power of the Spirit Fire. The Spirit Fire does not move around the hearth as the Spirit Fire in the Heart of the Bison. The Spirit Fire has two hearths. In the time of plants, the Spirit Fire is in one hearth. In the time of snow, the Spirit Fire is moved to the other hearth. While the Spirit Fire is in one hearth, the cold ashes are collected from the other hearth."

"Sotif would like to see this Spirit Fire."

"Leco said Sotif must bring the ashes to the Spirit Fire. Leco said Sotif must help with the Ceremony of the Ashes."

Sotif was speechless with gratitude to Mother Earth. He nodded his head and sat back against the wall of the dwelling. The scars on his hand and face burned.

Sotif did not sleep all night. He sat on his sleep robes thinking of the Spirit Fire in the Heart of the Bison. He thought of the terrible war and the need to return the Spirit Fire next summer. He wished he knew Leco better. He would have to think of an argument to convince him. When the gray light of dawn came into the dwelling, Sotif realized there was nothing he could do to get the Spirit Fire. Leco had asked for a sign. Sotif would trust Mother Earth to make a sure sign for Leco.

Sotif was ready to go before the morning meal. He had four Earth People loaded with dried meat and berries. The air was cold, although the sky was clear. As Sotif walked through the forest, his body heated up. This forest was thicker than the forests around Fish Lake. It was strange to Sotif that he had to travel so much, when all he wanted to do was live in the light of the Spirit Fire in the Heart of the Bison.

Rodlu led the way to the Mammoth cave. The sun was still not high in the sky when Rodlu pointed up the north side of a deep ravine. "The Mammoth cave is there."

They had been following a small stream up the deep ravine. Most of the north slope was covered in pine trees and birch trees. The south slope was barren and rocky. Except for a few patches, the snow was all melted away. There was no path up. There were several large groups of trees and bushes at various places. They looked natural, but Sotif suspected they were planted and cared for by the Earth People of the Mammoth cave. He was sure the Mammoth cave was behind one of the groups, but he could not tell which one.

Rodlu pointed to one of the groups of trees to the left, about halfway up. "The Mammoth cave is there. Rodlu, Sotif, and the rest must take different paths. There must be no tracks to the cave."

Sotif nodded and started making his way up the slope. The climb was steep and difficult. He was breathing heavily when he reached the trees.

Rodlu looked across the valley to see if they were being watched. After a careful look, he stepped into the trees. The rest followed. Rodlu carefully pushed some shrubs to the side and beckoned for Sotif to go past him. Sotif stepped into the entrance of a cave. He was surprised at how large the opening was. It was a little taller than him and about five paces wide. The Earth People had been very clever in the way they had arranged the planting to hide the large opening. They walked a short distance down a tunnel into the cave.

As Sotif blinked his eyes to get accustomed to the dim light of the cave, Leco came to him. "Leco welcomes Sotif, History Man of the Alliance, to the Mammoth cave."

Near the entrance was a special kiln-like hearth. Sotif recognized it as a hearth where the Earth People could create a fire hot enough to completely consume the bodies, including the bones, of their dead so only ashes would be left for the Spirit Fire.

"Sotif is honored Leco has invited Sotif to the Mammoth cave," Sotif said in his best Earth People language.

"Leco is happy Sotif has brought the Spirit Fire ashes to join with the Spirit Fire. Leco says Mother Earth must be happy. Leco says Kectu must be happy."

As his eyes fell upon the Spirit Fire, Sotif's heart jumped. There was something about the Spirit Fire that was different from any other fire in all the earth. It wasn't something he could see or smell. It was the feeling of the spirit of the fire. In the Heart of the Bison, the feeling was so familiar he had become accustomed to it.

"Sotif sees the wisdom in Mother Earth. Sotif sees the loss of the Spirit Fire forced Sotif to find the way to the Earth People of the East. The Spirit Fire must build new strength in the Alliance. The Spirit Fire must build new strength in Sotif."

"Everything is ready," Leco said. "The travelers from the South have come. The ashes from the clans of the South have been added to the Spirit Fire. Sotif and Leco will do the Ceremony of the Ashes with the ashes from the clans of the West."

Sotif was humbled by the prospect of what was to happen. For the first time in hundreds of generations, the ashes of the western clans and the eastern clans would be joined together in the Spirit Fire. This would be the strongest power in the earth. Not even Warlog, with all his armies, could stand against such power.

"Today the ashes of the Earth People of the West must join the ashes of the Earth People of the East," Leco began. "From this day, the clans of the West must open a path to the clans of the East. From this day, the ashes of the East and the ashes of the West must live together in the Spirit Fire."

Even though there were some minor differences in the way the eastern clans performed the Ceremony of the Ashes, Sotif was inspired by the power of what was happening. Here, in this unknown cave, in an unknown world, the power to defeat Warlog was being restored. All across the lands of the Alliance, the people were engaged in their daily activities. Even now, Tall Tree and Warlog might be fighting. This was such a powerful force, Sotif wondered if some of the spirit men of the Alliance could sense it.

The ceremony ended. The traditional feast was meager. The food supplies were not properly stored, and supplies were dwindling. Rodlu presented the food they brought and showed the Earth People how to store and use it. They used it sparingly in the feast.

"Sotif comes at a hard time," Leco said. "At the end of the next time of plants, the Spirit Fire must be moved to the southern clans. At the end of the next time of plants, Sotif must see a big feast."

"Leco is kind to invite Sotif to the Ceremony of the Ashes. Sotif must return to the Alliance. There is great danger to the Alliance. Sotif must take part of the Spirit Fire as soon as the hard snows of this time of snow have passed."

"Not! Sotif must not take fire from the Spirit Fire. Sotif must speak of this to all the shomots of the eastern clans. The shomots of the eastern clans must decide this."

"Not." Sotif took a chance that he could intimidate Leco. "Sotif must decide these things of the Alliance."

"Not." Leco was calm but firm. "In the East, there is no alliance. In the East, there is no History Man. Leco tells Sotif the Sun People cannot be trusted. Leco says … Sotif has seen this already. Leco says … the Spirit Fire must never be taken to the Sun People. Mother Earth allowed the Spirit Fire to be destroyed to teach the Earth People not to trust the Sun People. There must be no Spirit Fire in the West until the Alliance is no more. So says Leco, so shall it be."

Those of Leco's clan repeated, "So says Leco, so it shall be."

Sotif could think of no answer.

"The Ceremony of the Ashes is over," Leco said. "Sotif must return to Sotif's camp. A big storm comes. Sotif must leave before snow comes to the ground to show Sotif's tracks."

"Sotif has explained the signs of Mother Earth that say there must be a Spirit Fire in the West."

"Not." Leco remained calm. "The signs of Mother Earth say there must be no Spirit Fire in the West until the Alliance is no more."

Sotif decided it would only make Leco become more firm to argue. "Sotif must leave now. Sotif thanks his friend Leco. Sotif says there must be another sign to make all the signs clear. Sotif will wait for this new sign."

"Leco must also look for a sign. Leco thanks Sotif for the food Sotif brought."

"Sotif must send more food to the Mammoth cave. The Earth People with Sotif have prepared much food for the time of snow. The Earth People must bring food to the Mammoth cave. There must be no more famine ceremonies."

"Leco thanks the Earth People and the Sun People for this food. Earth People must bring food. Sun People must not come to the Mammoth cave. So says Leco, so it shall be."

"So says Leco, so it shall be," Sotif and Rodlu said in unison.

Winter was almost over. Sotif sat near the campfire working on the symbols for his painting stories. Rodlu and Tincolad had worked with Sotif from the beginning of the painting stories. The three had created and learned more than four hundred symbols. As they began to make messages with the symbols, others began to show interest in this new kind of symbol painting. The nights were long during the time of snow. It was as if Mother Earth were allowing Earth's Fireball to rest from the last time of plants. During the long darkness, Rodlu spent much of his time by the fire using the symbols to make a record of the trip to the Mammoth cave.

Rodlu and some of the Earth People took preserved food to the Mammoth cave each time the snow to the cave melted. There was no need for a famine ceremony.

As the time of snow dwindled, the days got longer. Sotif knew he must leave soon. There was no word from Leco about taking fire coals of the Spirit Fire. Sotif sent Rodlu and Renko to see if Leco had seen a sign from Mother Earth.

Sotif was working on a story about hunting when Rodlu came running into camp. "Sotif! Sotif! The Spirit Fire is dead! The Earth People of the East are dead!"

"How can this be?"

Rodlu took a deep breath. "Renko and Rodlu found all the Earth People killed. The Sun People found the Mammoth cave. The signs say Sun People killed the Earth People. Sun People killed the Spirit Fire. Rodlu found the Spirit Fire hearth full of water. Now, Sotif has come on this long journey for nothing."

"Rodlu must have gone to the wrong cave."

"Not." Rodlu's voice sounded dejected and weak.

"Come, Rodlu must take Sotif to see this."

Sotif asked Broken Stick, Tincolad, and five strong Sun People to go in case the killers were still near the cave. When they got to the cave, it was as Rodlu had said. Sotif checked the Spirit Fire hearth. It was still warm in some spots. He stumbled from the cave in a daze and sat on a rock. His mind was blank. He could not think what this could mean or what he should do. Perhaps Mother Earth was no more. Perhaps Kectu was no more.

Broken Stick sat beside Sotif. "We have checked everything closely. Nine Sun People came from on top of the hill to the Spirit Fire cave. When the Sun People left, they took one Earth People man with them. Leco's body is not among the dead. The tracks are fresh, and the ashes of the Spirit Fire are warm."

Broken Stick paused. When Sotif said nothing, Broken Stick continued. "They must have left this morning. We can catch up with Leco and those who have him. I will leave two Sun People men to take you back to the camp. I will take the rest of the Sun People and Rodlu to find Leco."

"Why?" Sotif asked, not thinking about what he said or expecting an answer.

"The Earth People say a big storm comes in three days. If we don't hurry to catch Leco, the tracks will be covered in snow, and we will never find him."

Sotif's head began to clear. "We have failed. Leco is no help to us now. We must go back to the Alliance and tell them there is no Spirit Fire. Warlog will win, and the Alliance will be no more."

"We will return to the Alliance. Then we will bring those who want to save the Alliance back to this land. Warlog cannot follow a trail in water."

"There is no Alliance here. What is the Alliance without the Spirit Fire?"

"I don't know. Will you allow Warlog to kill everyone?" Rodlu asked.

"What reason do the Earth People have to live if there is no Mother Earth?"

"Earth's Fireball still flies into the sky every morning. This is a strong sign. It is stronger than the Spirit Fire. The Spirit Fire only lives if people feed and care for it, but what man can make a fireball and send it into the sky? This only Mother Earth can do. This is a sure sign. I will find Leco. Then we will decide the future for the Alliance."

"I have seen the beginning of the Spirit Fire in my dreams. Kectu put the spirit of her sister into the Spirit Fire. She gave the Spirit Fire to the Earth People. The people in the West and the people in the East have let Sun People destroy the spirit of Kectu's sister. From the beginning, Earth People have lived with the promise. I have seen the end of the promise. The time of the Earth People is over. Mother Earth has left them to struggle alone. Soon, they will be no more. This is a sad thing. Our trip is a failure."

Broken Stick put his hands on Sotif's shoulders. "This trip is not a failure. We have the ashes of the eastern clans. We will take the ashes to the Alliance. We will make clan fires to bring the strength of all the ages of Earth People to the Alliance."

Sotif sat on a fallen tree trunk. In his first meeting with Rodlu and Leco, Rodlu told Leco that Sotif burned the power of the Spirit Fire into his body with the last spark of the Spirit Fire. That was it! The Spirit Fire began when

Kectu's sister gave her spirit to the Spirit Fire. Sotif had burned her spirit into his body. He carried the spirit of the Spirit Fire! He thought of Senlo's words that someday Sotif would have to choose to give his life for the Spirit Fire. He understood.

"You are right," Sotif said. "This trip is not a failure. Sotif knows the secret of the Spirit Fire."

"What secret?" Broken Stick asked.

"The spirit of the Spirit Fire is burned into Sotif's body. I took the spirit of Kectu's sister when I pressed the last hot coal of the Spirit Fire at the Heart of the Bison into my face."

"What can we do to put the spirit back into the Spirit Fire?"

"We must hurry back to Tall Tree. We must tell the people of the Alliance that the Spirit Fire lives in me. Then Tall Tree's army must drive Warlog from the land. I will hold the spirit of Kectu's sister in my body until the Alliance regains the Heart of the Bison. We must do a Spirit Fire Ceremony. This time, in order to put Kectu's sister into the fire, Sotif must be burned in the fire."

"You must be burned alive in the fire?"

"It's the only way. Kectu's sister was put in the fire alive so her spirit would go into the fire. The last fire coal of the Spirit Fire burned Kectu's sister's spirit into me. I must give this spirit back to the fire from my living body. When I die in the fire, the spirit of Kectu's sister will go into the fire, and it will become the Spirit Fire. That way the line of the spirit will be unbroken. We must hurry back."

"But we have no army to lead back."

"I carry the promises of Kectu and Mother Earth. Mother Earth will not let the Earth People be destroyed."

"This is a hard thing for Sotif to die in a fire."

"This is a blessing to Sotif," Sotif said in Earth People language. "Sotif must always be remembered as the living bridge for the promises of the Spirit Fire. Come, Sotif must prepare to go back."

Tincolad caught up with the two men. "The men are ready. The tracks are fresh. If we start now, we will catch the killers and Leco before the next storm."

Sotif stopped. "No! We cannot send men after Leco." Sotif spoke in the Sun People language.

"Why?" Tincolad asked.

"Sotif is right," Broken Stick answered. "We must take the ashes back to Tall Tree and start a new fire. Sotif will make a new Spirit Fire."

"We must also send men south to find the clans of the East," Sotif said. "We must tell them of the Spirit Fire and the Alliance. The men who took Leco are killers. They are nine. We are only an old man, seven Sun People, and one Earth People. If we catch them, many will be killed. Perhaps they will kill Leco when the fighting starts. If our men are killed trying to save Leco, we will not have enough men to do what must be done. It's a risk we must not take."

The party started down the path to the winter camp. Sotif and Broken Stick were walking together when Tincolad caught up with them again. "We must save Leco," he said.

"I have said the risk is too great," Sotif answered.

Tincolad threw his spear to the ground. "No! I have traveled from the west end of the earth to the east end, always trying to know what my duty is. I am a warrior. I trained to become a warrior. I thought I came to your land to kill droglits. When I got to your land, I went with the warriors to the Earth People cave to kill droglits. Broken Stick watched me come from the cave and unite the body of a mother to the body of a child. Do you know what happened before that?" Tincolad shouted the question at Broken Stick. Sotif was stunned by the force of Tincolad's words.

Tincolad told the story of the woman in the cave and how he put her baby in the fire with her. "The ashes I gave to Sotif come from the fire where she and her baby were burned.

"I killed no Earth People. Many times, I have thought of the woman. She told me something with her eyes, but I couldn't tell what it was. She gave me life, but I could not give her life. I could not give her baby life.

"I couldn't understand what her eyes told me because I thought she was a droglit. I know Earth People are not droglits. I have learned their language and their customs. I understand what the woman wanted to tell me."

Sotif's eyes were focused on the young man. "What did she tell you?"

"The eyes say, 'Save my people.' I know what I must do."

"What is that?" Broken Stick asked.

"I must lead you to save Leco. Then I must teach Tall Tree how to fight Warlog. It's late now, but maybe not too late."

"Sotif says we must send men to look for the Earth People clans of the East," Broken Stick said. "We do not have men to spare to fight these eastern Sun People. Some will be killed, and then we will not have enough men to travel rapidly. You must return quickly to teach Tall Tree. That's the most important way to save the Earth People."

"The Earth People say a storm is coming. We cannot leave until after the storm. That's enough time to save Leco."

"When these people see us coming, they will kill Leco. They know more about killing than we do. They will kill many of our men. We will not have enough men to get back in time to help Tall Tree," Broken Stick argued.

"The eyes of the woman tell me to save the Earth People. I do not see 'wait' in these eyes, but I have waited too long already. I will not wait. I will do as the eyes say."

"Every man is needed to get back to help Tall Tree," Broken Stick challenged.

"I have seen the tracks of these Sun People and their camp on the hill. I have seen the tracks of how they travel. These people understand killing, but they do not understand war. With the Sun People we have and Rodlu to help track, we can save Leco. I will show you how to save Leco without losing one man. I will show you war! I will show you how war is done!

"The bodies scattered in the Spirit Fire cave are the peace lovers. They are dead—killed by warriors of this land. They take Leco. I know how to stop them. No one knows war better than I do. Not even Warlog! We will save Leco, and then I *will* kill Warlog, and then there will be no war.

"Broken Stick, come with me. Give me trust, and I will show you how to fight these killers. Not one of your people will be hurt. We will bring Leco back. I will teach you how to fight Warlog. I have watched Warlog. I know his weakness. We go now!"

Tincolad wrapped his coat around his waist and picked up his spear. "Now!" he shouted.

"We don't have food to travel."

"This is your answer? Do you want to eat … or do you want to save Leco?" Tincolad walked back up the path.

Broken Stick looked at the other men. "Two of you must take Sotif to the camp." He picked up his spear, and without another word, he shrugged his shoulders and followed Tincolad.

It was late afternoon when Tincolad started after the Sun People. Broken Stick followed. Behind him, three other Sun People and Rodlu followed. As Sotif watched the six men follow the Mammoth cave killers, he thought of Tincolad's words. Tincolad was young. Sotif hoped his words were true.

****

The tracks told Broken Stick that Leco and the Sun People were not traveling fast. Three had split from the main group. Broken Stick guessed they spread out to hunt. The main group moved slowly, probably to allow the hunters to circle back at night, bringing anything they managed to kill.

Night came quickly. Broken Stick stopped near the top of a hill on the west side of a wide valley. Rodlu sat on a rock overlooking the valley while the others prepared the camp and built a small fire.

Rodlu jumped from the rock he was sitting on. "Look!" he said to Broken Stick in Earth People language. "There is a fire across the valley."

Broken Stick looked but could not see a fire. He could not see as well as Earth People.

"Move the campfire behind that boulder," Tincolad ordered the men. "Keep the fire low ... just enough to cook. We will wrap up in our blankets to keep warm. The people we seek are across this valley. We will not warn them by letting them see our fire."

Broken Stick had thought about the fight at the Heart of the Bison a great deal since that day. There was something exhilarating about fighting in a battle where the prize was life or death. As he contemplated the battle that lay before him, the sense of anxiety and anticipation confused him. The men who had killed the Earth People in the cave were close. Broken Stick knew he would catch them tomorrow. The thought of a life or death struggle sent a shiver of excitement up his spine. Tomorrow, he would fight again. If he won, the killers would die at his hands. The deaths in the cave would be avenged, and Leco would be saved. If he lost, he would die. His confusion disappeared when he realized it was not just to right the wrong of the cave that drove him. It was the contest to conquer an opponent even at the risk of death. *I am a warrior*, he thought. He looked forward to returning to fight Warlog.

The next morning, Broken Stick and his men woke early. "When will Tincolad show us how to fight these men?" Flat Valley asked.

"I will show you how to kill them all," Tincolad answered.

"It is well for you to say such a thing," Cool Rain said. "You come from where this kind of killing is normal. We of the Finger Lake tribe have never seen this kind of killing."

"These Sun People of the East are like the warriors of Warlog's army," Broken Stick said. "They are used to killing. The tracks show nine men came to the Spirit Fire cave. Fourteen strong Earth People were killed, and the tracks show nine Sun People walked away. This was not a fight. The Earth

People were killed so fast they did not have a chance to fight. You must kill as Tincolad will teach. Our men must not die."

Cool Rain responded, "All our men are needed; we should turn back now. Leco is one man, and he is old. We should not lose any men to save a man who is useless."

Broken Stick put his hand up. Everyone in the group stopped to listen. "Leco is not useless. The people of the East and the West must be joined together to strengthen the Alliance. Leco is needed to show the way to the clans of the East and introduce our people to his people."

"Without the Spirit Fire, there is no alliance," Flat Valley said.

"Since the day the Heart of the Bison was lost, I have heard Sun People say that. Sotif has found a way to make a new Spirit Fire. I fight to save the Alliance and to chase Warlog from the Winding River valley and the Heart of the Bison."

"Without the Spirit Fire, the Heart of the Bison has no meaning," Flat Valley argued.

"We must return now," Cool Rain said.

"No one said you had to come. If fear fills your heart, return to Sotif," Broken Stick said.

"I do not know of History Rooms or Alliances or Spirit Fires," Tincolad said. "I know the Sun People we follow killed Earth People. Leco is the last of the people of the Mammoth cave. He is the last of the people who can show the way to the rest of the clans of Earth People in the East. We must get Leco. I will show you how to defeat these Sun People without losing our own people."

"You carry the mark of Warlog on your arm," Flat Valley said. "You have said you will not teach the Alliance how to fight Warlog. Why should we trust you?"

"I have traveled with Broken Stick for two summers. I have seen the Alliance. I have seen the killing. I see the killing comes from Warlog, not Earth People."

"We will listen to Tincolad's plan," Broken Stick said. "Then we will decide."

"We must do what Warlog's armies call an ambush. We do not catch up with them and ask them to give Leco back. They would fight, and we would fight, and many from each side would be killed and wounded. In the fighting, one of them will kill Leco. Warlog's warriors never take chances like this."

"What is this ambush you talk of?" Flat Valley asked cynically.

"We take a path beside their path. We travel fast and get in front of them before they know we chase them. We find a place where we can hide. When they come in range of our arrows, we all shoot at one signal. We kill them before they know what is happening. Each man is assigned a man to kill. Someone gets the first in line. Someone else gets the second and so on. Most of their men will go down with the first shots. Everyone shoots at any man still alive. In their confusion, they will not be able to make a shot back. These ambushes work."

"You're saying we should kill all these men without even a warning?" Standing Bear asked.

"Warlog invented war. Warlog is the best at war because he understands the simplicity of it. War means to kill your enemy. War is not about talking. If Warlog talks, he lies to make it easier to kill. The choice he gives is to join him or be killed. Tall Tree will only hold Warlog back and delay him until the people of the Alliance learn to kill first. If the Alliance does not learn this, Warlog will win. Warlog's enemies have not learned this. They've all been defeated.

"These people killed all the Earth People in the Spirit Fire cave except Leco. The signs show none of these people were hurt. This tells me they know how to kill. They will fight hard if you give them a chance. I say if you give them a chance to fight, they will win. You may kill some of them, but at the end, all of you will be killed. This is the price of warning them with talk. This is the price of not understanding the only object of war is to kill the enemy until he can fight no more."

"Tincolad speaks with the wisdom of war," Broken Stick said. "In time of war, we must listen to the wisdom of war. There is a time of different wisdom when there is not war. The men who have taken Leco have made war. We will follow Tincolad to fight this war and rescue Leco."

Broken Stick and the rest followed Tincolad to a good place for an ambush on the path he decided the killers would take. It was beside a small stream. Tincolad placed the Sun People in places around a small clearing. They were hidden on both sides of the stream where each had a clear view of the clearing where the men would be. They were placed so they couldn't accidentally shoot each other if they missed their targets. Tincolad found a place where he could see everything and where each of his men could see him.

Broken Stick sat behind a large rock. He felt cold. He had killed three Sun People during the fight at the Heart of the Bison. The man at the signal fire had seen Broken Stick pull his dagger. He had fought hard. The one on the slope did not expect the attack when Broken Stick stabbed him in the heart. The other one was near the village where the fighting had begun. Many were killed that day. This time, his men would kill the Sun People who did not know what was happening. They would have no chance to fight back.

Rodlu and Flat Valley followed the Sun People to make sure they stayed on the route Tincolad thought they would follow. They arrived and gave the signal that the Sun People were coming as Tincolad expected. Three of the Sun People had split off again this morning. Only six guarded Leco. Tincolad would shoot the first and second men. Broken Stick had the third, Flat Valley had the forth, Standing Bear had the fifth, and Cool Rain had the sixth.

Broken Stick would be able to see Tincolad when the signal was given. He took a breath and waited. The Sun People wore long coats of heavy fur. They carried large packs on their backs. Their bows and arrows were tied to the back of their packs. They would not be able to get their bows free in time to save themselves, just as Tincolad had said.

Broken Stick let the air out of his chest slowly through his nose the way Tincolad had shown him. He watched to make sure his breath did not rise in a cloud the enemy could see. He began to shake as the Sun People got closer. Leco was at the back. He began to move to the side, increasing his distance from the group. He must have smelled or seen rescuers.

All the Sun People were in clear view, and still there was no signal from Tincolad. Broken Sick had already put his first arrow in the bow. They walked through the snow in a line as Tincolad said they would. Broken Stick concentrated on the man he was to kill. He saw the man's breath coming from under the hood of his coat. Broken Stick tried to see the face of the man he would kill, but it was in the shadow of his hood. He was so close; Broken Stick could not miss, if he could stop shaking. The closer the man got, the more Broken Stick shook. He took a deep breath and held it. Tincolad was taking too long!

Finally, the signal was given. Broken Stick pulled the arrow taut on the string, and the shaking stopped. At the last second, the man he aimed at sensed something. Perhaps he had seen the signal, or he had seen Broken Stick or one of the other men move. His head popped up, and he started to turn.

Broken Stick's arrow seemed to fly as slowly as a circling hawk on a hot summer day, but it moved faster than its target. Broken Stick watched the arc of the arrow flying to its mark. The man screamed and fell.

Broken Stick could hardly keep up with what happened next. Three of the Sun People fell. The second in line began to try to reach his bow. The other two started to run. Broken Stick picked one and quickly shot his second arrow. He followed his arrow with his eyes. It hit the man just below the hip. At the same instant, two other arrows hit him, and he fell. The second man in the line fell at the same time.

Broken Stick saw the last man stumbling in the snow. As he loaded his third arrow, he saw two other arrows fly, and the last man fell dead.

It happened so fast Broken Stick stood with the third arrow still in his bow. All the Sun People were down before Broken Stick could shoot three arrows! Two of the Sun People were still writhing on the ground. Cool Rain and Standing Bear used their daggers to kill them.

In only a few moments, the group of Sun People had turned into dark, silent lumps lying in the snow, surrounded by pools of red that were unrealistically bright on the white snow. Broken Stick saw another side of war now. An ecstatic feeling flooded through his body. His people had won! He had won! There had been much confusion in that first battle at the Heart of the Bison. He remembered he was excited, but he was afraid of Warlog's army. He had to worry about making his escape. This time, it was a complete victory. The worry as he had waited in ambush, the emotional build up as he watched for the signal, the doubt, then the release of the attack all built up in him, and now it was over, and they had won! No one from his people had been hurt. Leco was saved. Broken Stick surged with excitement and emotion like nothing he had ever known before. He wanted to laugh and shout, but he remained quiet. This was the side of war he had not known. This was why Warlog created his army and made war. Broken Stick knew the secret of war. Now he knew there would always be war.

Leco was talking rapidly to Rodlu. Broken Stick could not hear them, and he found it very difficult to understand the old man of the eastern Earth People anyway. The rest of the Sun People were dragging the bodies in a row.

Rodlu left the old man and came to Broken Stick. "Leco says these Sun People came to the Mammoth cave to get fire. Leco says each of these Sun People carries the coals of the Spirit Fire. The men must take the Spirit Fire coals back to the Spirit Fire cave."

"Then our journey to the eastern clans has not been for nothing. We will return the Spirit Fire to the Heart of the Bison." Not only had Broken Stick's men won, but they had won the greatest prize possible. Sotif would not have to sacrifice himself in the Spirit Fire.

The victors took the clothes and weapons of those who had fallen. They found each man carried a fire basket with live fire coals.

Tincolad and Flat Valley went ahead to scout the trail, and Cool Rain and Standing Water stayed back to watch the trail behind them. That night, Tincolad and the Sun People took turns guarding the camp.

Broken Stick was sure the three men who had been hunting when the attack was made would not try to follow him, but he did not want to take chances. He and his men were warriors now.

Everyone enjoyed the warmth of the Spirit Fire as they sat around it to talk of the day's adventure. Tincolad was the hero.

****

Three days ago, when Broken Stick had left to rescue Leco, Sotif was sure he carried the spirit of the Spirit Fire in his body. It seemed simple then, but now doubts entered his heart. When should he be burned in the fire? Should he wait until the Heart of the Bison was recaptured, or should he do it now in the East? If he did it now, the new Spirit Fire could be divided so there would be a Spirit Fire in the East and the West. But if he did it now, how would he teach the meaning of the new Spirit Fire to the people in the West?

Sotif had spent all day yesterday in a dream tent asking the Great Spirit and Mother Earth what he should do. He slept fitfully last night. Could he really carry the spirit of Kectu's sister to a new Spirit Fire? He needed a sign.

In most of his dreams, the Earth People hid in their caves, and the Sun People forgot they existed. This was Leco's way. This would be the end of the Alliance. Perhaps this was the meaning of the loss of the Spirit Fire. But if that was the meaning of the loss of the Spirit Fire, why did the Earth People who hid in the caves have the Spirit Fire in all of Sotif's dreams? It must mean Sotif did carry the spirit of Kectu's sister. Leco was a respected shomot of the eastern clans. He hoped Broken Stick could rescue Leco so he could help Sotif understand the meaning of his dreams.

"Sotif must come with Rodlu." Rodlu's voice was soft, but it seemed more mature than it was three days ago.

Sotif started. "Broken Stick has returned already?"

"Broken Stick and the Sun People have taken Leco to the Mammoth cave. It was as Tincolad said; not one of our people was hurt. Leco asks Sotif to come to the Mammoth cave. Leco has much to say to Sotif."

"It is late. Soon it must be dark."

"A storm comes. Leco says Sotif must spend the night in the Mammoth cave. Sotif must carry an important message to the clans of the West. Leco says a new time for all Earth People has begun."

All the way to the cave, Sotif thought about the future. It was good Leco had been saved. Leco's clans had survived many generations without the Alliance, but they had the Spirit Fire. Sotif felt the warmth coming from the cave as he approached the entrance. *Leco has built a new fire. It must be big and close to the entrance*, Sotif thought.

Sotif stopped short. Could it be? He saw the fire raging in the Spirit Fire hearth. Logs were piled high, and the flames danced almost to the ceiling, but it was more than the sight of the raging fire. Something deep inside told him this was the Spirit Fire!

"Welcome, Leco's friend." It was Leco's voice that brought Sotif back. His mind was racing back to the Heart of the Bison, back to happy times he had spent in front of the Spirit Fire.

"Sotif is thinking of a day long ago. Sotif is thinking of living in the Heart of the Bison. Sotif is thinking of living in the warmth of the Spirit Fire."

"Leco understands the pain of losing the Spirit Fire. Leco knows the joy of finding the Spirit Fire."

"How was the Spirit Fire saved? Sotif sifted through all the ashes looking for life. The Spirit Fire was cold."

Leco explained that Sun People had camped on the hilltop above the Mammoth cave. There were numerous small cracks in the rocks that let the hot air of the Spirit Fire escape. When Leco realized the men would be camping there, he sent one of the Earth People to sneak up and see what they were doing. They had no fire. They were huddled around the places where warm air came from the cave. The next morning, they began searching the mountainside. Leco believed they did not have fire and they were searching to find where the warm air was coming from. "The Sun People who came to kill took live coals from the Spirit Fire. The Sun People who came to kill took Leco. Leco was saved by Sun People. The Spirit Fire was saved by Sun People. Mother Earth has given Leco a sign. The Spirit Fire is for all people. The Spirit Fire must go to the Alliance of the West."

All the questions Sotif had brought to the cave were answered in a way he had not expected. Senlo had said he would have to be willing to give his life for the Spirit Fire. He had not said Sotif would actually give his life.

Sotif discovered the Spirit Fire was more important than any man, and he was willing to sacrifice himself to prove it. Mother Earth smiled on him.

The Spirit Fire was restored, and Sotif would live to help join the Earth People of the East with the Earth People of the West. He would take the Spirit Fire back to the Alliance! "Sotif thanks Leco for all the western clans."

"Leco knows Mother Earth has sent Sotif. Leco and Sotif must do the Ceremony of Ashes. Sotif must take ashes and Spirit Fire west. Leco must take ashes and Spirit Fire south. All Earth People must be stronger from the ashes of this fire. Tonight the last storm of the time of snow comes. Tomorrow's tomorrow, Sotif and Leco must leave this place. Leco must never see Sotif again. Sotif must never see Leco again. Always Leco must remember Sotif. Always Sotif must remember Leco."

"Sotif sees this is so," Sotif said. "Travelers must carry ashes between the two fires. All the Earth People must be joined again in the Spirit Fire. All the Earth People must be stronger for this."

"Sotif speaks a truth. Rodlu must go south with Leco. Rodlu must show a path of water between east and west. Then, the ashes of all the clans of the Earth People must be joined in two arms of the Spirit Fire of Mother Earth. Then, Kectu must be pleased with the Earth People."

CHAPTER 7

The War

Summer 3283 BCE

Sotif enjoyed his last day with Leco in the Mammoth cave. They exchanged a great deal of knowledge. Leco was excited by the word symbols Sotif had made. Rodlu would stay with Leco to learn where the southern clans were. He would teach them the meanings of the symbols so that travelers carrying ashes between the two branches of the Spirit Fire could carry messages between the East and the West. It was a hard good-bye, but Sotif was anxious to get started on the important trip back.

There was still some ice in the river when they started, but the Earth People assured Sotif there would be no more winter storms. They moved quickly down the river into the big saltwater. There was much more ice floating in the water.

After they crossed the saltwater, the men spent several days killing water dogs and smoking the meat. When the boats were full, they started following the shoreline to the great river.

Once again, Mother Earth kept Earth's Fireball in the sky so there was no night. The men took turns paddling the boats and sleeping. They paddled harder than ever before.

Sotif worked on his word symbols. Tincolad still worked with him when he had time, but Sotif missed Rodlu.

When they turned up the river, traveling got difficult, and progress slowed as they worked against the current. There was more water in the river, and the current was stronger. The boatmen had to be constantly on visual because of logs and other debris that were in the water.

After they had traveled many days on the river, the short nights gradually got longer. It was too dangerous to paddle upstream in the dark, so they tied the boats each night. The hunters hunted and fished in the dark. Others worked on repairs to the boats, their clothing, and weapons. All the members of the group took turns sleeping, but there were always at least a few awake doing something to help the group move as rapidly as possible.

They came to a point where the boats could not move upstream fast enough. Conditions would only get worse with waterfalls and rapids. The boats had to be abandoned.

Summer was nearing its end when they reached the camp where they had built the boats. Broken Stick wanted to stop and set up a winter camp, but Sotif convinced them to push on the Finger Lake. They were slowed by two winter storms before they reached the Finger Lake.

There was no one on the west side of the lake. They set up a camp and built a large fire from the Spirit Fire coals. On the trip back, they had used live coals from the Spirit Fire to start their campfires. Each morning, they removed coals from the campfire to use for the next night's fire. Ten men carried coals each day in case one or more coals died or were lost during the day.

Sotif watched a fire blinking far away on the other side of the lake. The Finger Lake colony had seen their fire. The Earth People said the winter would start hard, but it would be short. Sotif would be able to make it out of the mountains early next summer. Tall Tree and his army would have the Spirit Fire and Tincolad's help to lead them against Warlog and drive him from the land. Perhaps by the end of next summer, he would once again sit in the History Room and watch the Spirit Fire mark the seasons as it circled the hearth in the Heart of the Bison. He dropped into a deep sleep thinking of the return to the good days and the added blessing of reconnecting with eastern clans. The Spirit Fire would bring all the Earth People together for the first time in hundreds of generations. It was a good time to live. It was a good time to be the History Man. The People of the Alliance would look back with pride at these times for hundreds of generations to come. Sotif dreamed he would paint the story on the history wall with the language of symbols he had created on this trip. All Spirit Men would learn this language, and the stories of the people would be preserved forever. Then he dreamed of Earth People hiding from Sun People in their caves.

Boats from the Finger Lake colony arrived before midday. Although the men were excited to hear the story of the recovery of the Spirit Fire, they seemed grim. The men of Sotif's group volunteered to paddle the boats back the same day. On the way back, the men from the Finger Lake colony told Sotif about the war. Tall Tree's army turned Warlog back in the Snow Mountains. Then, Warlog feinted at one pass with his army and got through another pass before Tall Tree could stop him. Tall Tree's army was large. He met Warlog near the pass, and after a hard day of fighting, Warlog and his army ran away.

There was a big celebration, and many of Tall Tree's warriors turned for home. Tall Tree sent men to follow Warlog until his armies returned through the Snow Mountains. The scouts came back to report Warlog had not turned back but was moving east along the foothills of the Snow Mountains. By then, Tall Tree's army was not big enough to chase Warlog.

Tall Tree had men follow Warlog. They reported Warlog set up a camp and sent his men throughout the eastern land. Tall Tree guessed Warlog was scouting the land and the colonies so he could attack the weakest colony. All winter, Tall Tree scrambled to bring his men back and prepare them to protect any village Warlog attacked. This was the winter Sotif was preparing boats to start his travel east.

The next summer, Warlog began attacking villages that did not belong to the Alliance. With each village, his army grew. Tall Tree had made no preparations to defend them.

Tall Tree sent his wisest men to warn the other villages. It was difficult because they did not speak the same language.

By midsummer, Warlog's army had grown large enough to begin attacking the colonies of the Alliance. By the time winter came, Warlog had defeated six of the eighteen colonies and many villages that were not part of the colonies. His army had grown large enough to defeat Tall Tree.

Sotif thought of the summer he was racing down the river to the big saltwater to find the Spirit Fire. While he was eating water dogs, Warlog had destroyed six colonies and killed all the Earth People in them.

During the winter, Tall Tree learned to speak some of the language of the other Sun People villages. Word spread that Warlog was a threat to everyone. By summer, Tall Tree had joined with several other villages, and his army was growing, but language and cultural differences made coordination difficult. Many of the men from the other colonies did not want to follow Tall Tree.

When last summer came, Warlog burst from his winter camp and overran every village in his path, those of the Alliance and all others. Tall Tree spent the time trying to put his new army together while avoiding a direct conflict with Warlog.

As the summer wound down, Tall Tree and his army were backed up to the Finger Lake Mountains near the Trade Pass colony. Every other colony except the Trade Pass colony and the Finger Lake colony had been defeated. There, the two armies clashed for three days. Tall Tree's army was decimated. On the third night, the remnants of the army sneaked into the Finger Lake Mountains and just managed to get out of Warlog's reach before the first big snow storm. That would have been the first storm that hit Sotif on his way to the Finger Lake.

When the boats docked, Tall Tree was waiting at the edge of the village. "So it's my old friend Sotif," he said, embracing Sotif.

"I have returned with good news," Sotif said. He handed Tall Tree a basket that was lined with moss and bark shavings. Sotif lifted a birch bark cover, and three coals glowed bright red as the fresh air blew across them.

"Tall Tree holds the endless fire that has blessed the Alliance from the beginning. This is the fire of Kectu and the promise of Mother Earth. This is the Spirit Fire."

"The Alliance of the East still lives?" Tall Tree asked with excitement.

"Many things have changed in the East. The Earth People of the East hide from the Sun People. The Alliance there is no more, but the clans of the Earth People have preserved the Spirit Fire."

"There's no alliance?" Tall Tree's voice was filled with disappointment.

"Earth People hide from Sun People. They are weak. They do not trust Sun People. We will have to teach them of the Alliance. It will take time, but they will learn, and then the Alliance will be strong over the whole earth again. No one will dare challenge the Spirit Fire and the Alliance."

Tall Tree dropped his head. "Then all is lost. Come, my friend. The Finger Lake colony has given me a tent. We will sit and talk of old times and the final days of the Alliance."

Sotif could hardly believe Tall Tree's sudden change of attitude as he followed him to the tent.

"Sit," Tall Tree said when he and Sotif got in his tent. "I will have food brought, and we will eat."

"I was hungry on the boat, but now I could not eat. I have brought the Spirit Fire. I am told Warlog's army is at the Trade Pass colony. Now, with

Spirit Fire, we will be able to defeat Warlog and take back the Heart of the Bison."

Tall Tree sat on his robes. "Here, sit, Sotif." Tall Tree pointed to robes near him. Sotif sat expectantly. "This war is a terrible thing," Tall Tree began. "I could not have dreamed of such killing. We do not understand war. Warlog was always ahead of us. He has defeated the Alliance. There is no more army to fight. We were overpowered at the Trade Pass colony. There were so few of us left we were able to sneak away during the night. We have run from Warlog to the end of the world. All the land of the Alliance belongs to Warlog, except this village.

"Most of the men left in our army are from the tribes who are not part of the Alliance. We have great difficulty understanding them. They think we should gather all the Earth People and take them to Warlog. Many of my Sun People men agree with the others. Rather than die or run, they talk of joining with Warlog so they can return to their villages and see their families. They say it's better to live under Warlog's rule than to die for no purpose. When the snow melts, Warlog and Rayloc will bring their army to Finger Lake to finish the destruction of the Alliance. When he comes, the Sun People will make a gift to Warlog … a gift of the last of the Earth People."

"I have returned with the Spirit Fire, and the army will fight. This is a sign from Mother Earth to the Alliance."

"Mother Earth and the Spirit Fire are things of the Earth People. In all the land, there are only enough Earth People to make one clan. The Sun People men of the Alliance are nearly all dead. Those who remain are tired of war. The only strength in the land comes from the Sun People who are not part of the Alliance. They fight with us because they hoped to defeat Warlog. They know nothing of Spirit Fires or the Alliance. They would help Warlog find and destroy the Earth People. I have heard them talk. Even though their language is new and strange to me, I understand more than they think. Even if Warlog left, they would destroy the Earth People. They blame the Earth People for all their troubles."

Sotif left Tall Tree's tent in despair. He had struggled so hard to find the Spirit Fire, but all he had done was possibly open the road of destruction to the eastern colonies. Every time he thought he finally understood the meaning of war, a new disaster fell on the Alliance.

****

All during the trip across Finger Lake, Tincolad could think only of Soft Cloud. He helped save the Spirit Fire. He knew she would be happy to hear all about it. When the boats pulled into the shore, Tincolad observed there were many tents around the village, and people were everywhere. He got out of the boat and began to stretch his cramped muscles. He was used to sitting in the boats for longer periods of time, but it always felt good to stand and stretch on firm ground.

Many people ran down from the village to greet family and friends they had not seen for two summers. Tincolad did not see the face he looked for. Perhaps it had been too long for a young woman to wait. Watching the celebration, he realized these people were not his people. Without Soft Cloud, he was alone here. He wandered away and leaned against a tree outside the happy confusion. He thought about the people of his tribe and his mother. He wondered what had become of his father.

As Tincolad was in thought, a dog broke through the mass of people and ran to him. He recognized the bark first. The dog jumped on Tincolad and began licking his face.

"Razid!" Tincolad exclaimed.

Tincolad was desperate to find who had brought Razid. Everyone was so busy renewing friendships and talking to family members, they had no patience with a stranger. Tincolad found an old woman who was watching the people with a smile on her face.

"Old woman," Tincolad said in greeting. His accent was nearly gone now. "Whose dog is this?"

"People are saying Sotif found the Spirit Fire ... could this be true?"

"Yes, old woman. Sotif found the Earth People and the Spirit Fire. He has returned with the Spirit Fire."

"Oh ... so much I had hoped for success. I will see the Spirit Fire before I die."

"The dog?"

"This dog came with the army of Tall Tree."

"Do you know where the army of Tall Tree got this dog?"

"Oh no. This dog does not belong to Tall Tree's army. He is not a dog of the Alliance. He is very different. Anyone can see that."

"But you said tha—"

"Tall Tree brought six men who came with Warlog. The dog belongs to one of those men. I have been told they helped Tall Tree and his army."

"Where are these men?"

"There." The woman pointed to a new tent at the edge of the village. Tincolad could clearly see the familiar shape and workmanship. He walked to the dwelling with his heart in his throat. He pushed the elk skin flap to the side and stepped in with Razid at his side.

"Tincolad?" Tincolad's eyes were not accustomed to the dark, but he recognized the voice.

"Father!"

A dark figure jumped up from the fire. "I thought you were dead."

It had been so long since Tincolad had heard his own language, for a second, he didn't understand what his father said. "I was afraid I would never see you again." Tincolad hugged his father.

"I heard in this village that a young man of Warlog's warriors had gone with Sotif. These people do not pronounce our words well, but the name of the young man sounded like Tincolad. When I heard the boats with Sotif's men had returned, I stayed here and sent Razid to find you because I was afraid the young man was not you. Where have you been so long?"

Tincolad explained what happened at the battle at the Heart of the Bison, how he woke up in the mountains, and how Broken Stick became his friend.

"I pretended to join with the Alliance, but I was only waiting for a chance to escape and return to Warlog. By the time we reached this village, I realized Warlog and Rayloc were wrong about the Earth People.

"When I heard Broken Stick would go with Sotif to find this Spirit Fire, I decided to go with him. I knew the Earth People were not droglits, but I did not know what I should do. I was a warrior, and the warriors were my brothers. I hoped to find a way to help the Earth People without helping the Alliance kill my brother warriors."

Tincolad told of the trip east and how he had helped save the Spirit Fire. "I finally realized I needed to help these people fight the warriors. Then I remembered my promise to my mother."

"Tincolad, this is a double new birth. I thought I lost your spirit when you became a warrior. Then I thought you had died."

Tincolad put his arm around Lenoclad's shoulder. "I feel proud of what I'm doing for the first time since I joined Warlog's army."

Lendoclad stood and walked a couple of steps from Tincolad. "I have something to tell you. Your mother made me promise I would not tell you until you had become a man. I see you are a man. When we found your mother running from Warlog, she had a small child. She was nearly dead. I knew when we found her, she was a special woman. It took a great deal of strength for her to live in the wilderness, running from Warlog and caring for a child. A woman was with her, but she died shortly after we found them."

"What became of the child?"

"We took the woman and child into our tribe. We heard Warlog was looking for a woman and a child. We heard he wanted to kill them, so we hid them from him. After two summers, I took the woman as my mate. I raised the child as my son."

"Are you saying you are not my father?" Tincolad looked deeply into Lendoclad's eyes. He saw it was true.

"Your mother's name was not Testolik. We changed her name to help hide her from Warlog. Her real name was Conchelik. She was heritage mate to Sincolad, who was heritage son to the great chief Seccolog. You are the only heritage son of Sincolad. You are the only rightful chief of Seccolog's village. This is why Warlog searched so long for you. Warlog is a son of one of Seccolog's pleasure mates. Warlog killed all of Seccolog's family so he could be chief. Your mother escaped with you before he could kill you."

"Then Warlog is my uncle." Tincolad thought of his last argument with Lendoclad.

"Warlog is no one's uncle. Warlog is a murderer. He killed all his brothers, sisters, nieces, nephews, and his father. Only you escaped him. Throughout the land, Warlog killed anyone who had any claim to leadership."

"I was a fool to believe in him. Warlog must be defeated before he destroys the people of the Alliance."

"It's too late now. Warlog's army has destroyed Tall Tree's army."

"Why did you leave Warlog's army?"

"Of those who survived the battle at the Heart of the Bison, none saw you fight. Some said you were wounded, but you were not left behind like the other wounded warriors. Rayloc suspected you went with Broken Stick to help Tall Tree's army. Razid did not go with you. That was the only thing that created doubt in Warlog's mind. He thought if you had gone willingly, you would have taken Razid. I knew if Warlog decided you had helped the Alliance, he would kill me. I ran from Warlog as soon as his armies crossed the Snow Mountains. I have lived with Tall Tree's army two summers. I taught him as much as I know about the army. Tall Tree's army fought bravely, but Warlog's army is too powerful. What you see in the village is all is left of the Alliance. Tall Tree only escaped because we got into the mountains just ahead of the winter snow.

"Warlog's army is at the foot of the mountains waiting for warm weather to open his way to destroy the last of the Alliance and the Earth People. Some talk of trying to find a path east to find Sotif. Many talk of surrendering to Warlog and giving all the Earth People to Rayloc. After this winter, there will be no more Alliance. It's the end of the world for these people. I planned to fight and die with them. But now Sotif has returned. There is new hope we can escape. Sotif can show them the path to safety."

Tincolad shook his head. "These people do not know Rayloc. You do. He will not rest as long as one of the Earth People is left alive. It may take many summers, but he will find the path east. Even if Warlog goes back, Rayloc and the army will not leave until there are no more Earth People. We must fight Warlog, and I must kill him. I promised Conchelik with my life that I would kill him. My life is not my own until I succeed. Warlog must be defeated before he destroys the people of the Alliance."

"It's too late, Tincolad."

Tincolad stood up and paced back and forth in the tent. His mother's face came to his mind. He thought of the Earth People and the destruction Lendoclad had talked of. He turned to his father. "I will kill Warlog."

"Perhaps you will, but first there's someone else you want to see." Lendoclad was smiling.

"What do you mean?"

"When I came here, I heard the story of the young warrior from Warlog's army who had gone to search for the Spirit Fire of the Alliance. I asked about this young warrior, and the people told me the girl, Soft Cloud, knew the young warrior."

"You know Soft Cloud? How is she? Where is she?"

"When we got here, I spoke only a little of the Sun People language. Soft Cloud has been my friend. She has taught me her language ... as she taught you. When we heard Sotif had sent the signal across the lake, she knew you would be coming back. No one expected Sotif to return so soon. Many thought something bad had happened. Soft Cloud was sure her young warrior would bring good news. She was sure her young warrior was my son even though it was too much for me to hope. Soft Cloud said it was most important that I talk to her warrior as soon as the boat landed. She did not want to distract you. She is waiting in a friend's dwelling for you."

"Where? Which friend?"

"Are you so soon through with me?"

"Uh ... well ... I mean ... we can talk much more tomorrow."

Lendoclad laughed. "Delonclad will take you to her. Yes, we will talk more tomorrow. Right now there is someone who wants to see you as much as I did. Go."

The last time Tincolad had talked to Soft Cloud, she had walked away in anger. He knocked on the entry post. An old woman came to the entrance. "I am Tincolad. I have been told Soft Cloud is here. I come to see her."

The woman grunted. Tincolad could hear giggling from the dwelling. The woman dropped the leather flap that served as a door. There were shuffling sounds and more giggling. Then the flap opened, and a beautiful young woman stood in the opening. He had not thought she was beautiful before. It took a moment for him to recognize her. "Soft Cloud?" he asked.

"Tincolad, you have changed. I mean you look older and ... and ... stronger ... more manly."

Tincolad could see she was nervous—maybe more nervous than he. "You have also changed."

"It has been two summers since you left."

"I know. You were angry with me." There was more giggling behind Soft Cloud.

"Come, let's talk." Soft Cloud walked out of the dwelling. He wanted to take her in his arms and kiss her, but her voice seemed cool. She had a female aroma of cooking and working with leather. He had not smelled such an aroma since he had crossed Finger Lake two summers ago. Until right now, he had not realized how much he had missed that smell—how much he had missed Soft Cloud.

Soft Cloud asked him, "Do you know where we are?"

Tincolad's mind had been in such deep thought he had not noticed where they had walked. "No."

"This is where we last talked."

Tincolad thought he saw a twinkle in her eye, but it was too dark to be sure. "I'm sorry we fought."

"I was so happy and so sad when they told me you had gone with Sotif. I was happy because I knew if you went with him, you would help bring the Spirit Fire back. I was sad because I didn't think I would see you for four summers. I was miserable when I thought of that. There was something I wanted to tell you before you left."

"What?"

Soft Cloud hesitated. "I wanted to tell you how proud I was that you had made the decision to go."

"And so ... you have missed me?" Tincolad voice was much weaker than he planned.

Soft Cloud shook her head slowly. Then she stepped to Tincolad, put her arms around him, and kissed him. He felt her body shudder in his arms. "You're crying."

"Miss you? I have nearly died missing you. I was so foolish to treat you as I did. So many times I was in despair. What if something happened to you? What if I did not get a chance to tell you I'm sorry? I *am* sorry. Let's never fight again." She kissed him again before he could think of an answer.

"I've changed," Tincolad said when their lips parted.

"How?" Soft Cloud's voice was barely a whisper.

"You wanted me to teach Tall Tree's army how to fight Warlog's warriors. I was confused then. I thought I had a special calling from Zendolot to be a warrior. I thought all warriors were my brothers, but now I realize anyone who kills people, women and children, just because they don't know or understand them cannot be my brother. I have already shown Broken Stick how to fight Warlog. I will show Tall Tree all I know. We will drive Warlog's army out of the land of the Alliance."

"It's too late for that, Tincolad." Soft Cloud was resolute. "Tall Tree's army has been destroyed. The hope you bring is to show the survivors the way east."

"My father ... I mean Lendoclad, already told me this. I don't believe it's too late. I will think about this. I do not look to run. I promised my mother I would kill Warlog. I will do what I promised."

"How will you do this when he is protected by his army?"

"I must think about this. I know many things about Warlog and his army. I think I will not sleep tonight."

"Will you think better if I leave you?" Soft Cloud asked the question, but the tone in her voice told Tincolad she knew the answer.

"What I most needed from you was to know you love me. That is enough for now. After Warlog is dealt with, we will talk of our life and our plans."

"What I most need from you is to know you love me. Forget about Warlog. The Alliance is lost. It will do no good to kill Warlog now. Help lead us to safety in the East."

"I must kill Warlog."

"But why now when it will do no good?"

Tincolad held Soft Cloud's shoulders and looked into her eyes. "There's no place for Sun People in the East. There's no escape in the East."

Soft Cloud turned to walk away. "Come with me."

Tincolad followed her back to the dwelling. "Wait here," Soft Cloud said. A few moments later, she reappeared carrying a small boy on her hip. Tincolad was speechless. "This is your son. I was with child when you left. This is what I wanted to tell you before you left. I have talked a great deal with Lendoclad. Your son's name is Sincolad, after your true father. Is killing Warlog more important than I am? More important than we are?" Tears spilled from Soft Cloud's eyes.

Tincolad struggled with his answer. He had a son. He had his own family now. But he still had the responsibilities of a man. "I can't be the kind of man who lives with honor if I don't do what I was born to do. Warlog killed my father and all my family. From that murder came war. I am a man of no honor if I do not restore peace."

"But who is *my* family? Warlog also killed my family, and now *you* are my family. Would you go to be killed? Sincolad and I are your family. The time for killing is over."

"Not yet."

"All right, I'm not running away this time. I'm walking. But you must think about your responsibility to your dead family and your responsibility to me and Sincolad … your living family."

Again Tincolad was left to think about his future.

****

Broken Stick wandered aimlessly through Tall Tree's army talking to warriors about the war. The stories he heard were disheartening. The Spirit Fire searchers had returned too late. The war was over, and the only thing to decide was whether to surrender to Warlog and join his army or run to the strange land in the East. The Earth People could run east, but there was nothing for him or the Sun People there. The Alliance was dead. His thoughts of winning glory in a successful war against Warlog were forever lost.

Warlog would return to his homeland. He would leave his government and part of his army to rule the land. Broken Stick and his people would become accustomed to Warlog's rule.

As Broken Stick contemplated his future, he noticed a woman speaking to a group Broken Stick had been talking to. One of the men pointed to Broken Stick. The woman left the men and slowly approached him. There was something familiar in the way she walked. When he could see her face clearly, he recognized the beautiful young woman.

"Bright Moon?"

"You do remember."

"I lost all hope I would see you again."

Bright Moon cautiously approached. "Life has not gone as we planned." She stopped about four paces from him.

"I went to your dwelling in the Winding River village when Warlog's army came. It was all ashes."

"I heard you had joined Warlog's army and saved many Earth People. Then I heard you went in search of the Spirit Fire."

"I heard nothing of you."

"My family and I crossed the Snow Mountains ahead of Warlog."

"How is your family?"

"My brother fought with Tall Tree's army. He was killed when Warlog's army first came over the Snow Mountains. My father could not get over his death. In less than a season, he died. My mother died right after. They lost their desire to live."

"I'm so sorry to hear such bad news. Who has cared for you? Have you found a mate?"

"After my mother died, I joined Tall Tree's army. I helped care for the wounded. I heard you brought Sotif across the Snow Mountains. I was so proud of you. One day, Tall Tree told me you had gone to look for a new Spirit Fire. He said you would be gone many summers.

"I stayed with Tall Tree's army to do everything I could to defeat Warlog. I saw too much blood and suffering. After one of the battles, there were some of Warlog's warriors among the wounded. They were men of the Fish River village who had joined Warlog's army. I asked if they knew Broken Stick. One of them did."

"Who was he?"

"I don't remember his name. I only remember one thing."

"What?"

"He said when the survivors of the rebellion at the Heart of the Bison told Warlog you helped the Earth People escape, he was angry. He ordered his warriors to return to the village and kill your family."

Broken Stick sat down on a fallen tree. He groaned. "I was stupid not to consider what Warlog would do to my family. I killed them with my own stupidity."

"What could you have done to save them?"

Broken Stick tried to answer. Had he fought Warlog at that first Earth People cave, he and his family would be dead. Had he joined Warlog's army to fight for him, his family would have died of shame. "I don't know."

"Of course you don't know. That's because Warlog brought this killing. Everyone in the Alliance has lost friends and family. The man from Fish River village said your family was proud of what you did. They died with that pride."

"The Alliance is dead. There's no way to escape Warlog. What will you do? Do you have a mate?"

"After a summer and a half with the army, I had seen too much blood and death. I left Tall Tree's army and came to this village to wait for you. There is no man for me except Broken Stick. I do not know what I will do. You must tell me that."

Broken Stick stood, and Bright Moon ran to his arms. In the depths of his sadness, Broken Stick sensed a warm pool of happiness he had never expected to feel. "Tomorrow morning, I will meet with Sotif, Tall Tree, and the other leaders. We will decide what to do."

"Many people talk of giving the Earth People to Rayloc to make peace."

"I can't make a decision like that. It will be for the council to decide. If they decide to give the Earth People to Warlog, I will fight Tall Tree as I would fight Warlog."

"I have nothing left except you. If you fight, I will pick up a spear and fight beside you."

"Tomorrow, we will decide how this war will end. I have been lucky to find you. It's hard to think of dying now that there is something to live for."

"You must speak for the Earth People."

****

Sotif was hungry, but he could not eat. He was tired, but he could not sleep. All night he thought about the Spirit Fire and the Alliance. He was the History Man, but the History Man of what?

Someone knocked on the entrance post on his tent. He noticed the gray light of predawn. Had he slept at all? There was a second knock. His body was stiff. He could feel the impact of age.

"Who is it?"

"Lewtud comes to talk with the History Man. Lewtud brings Tall Tree, Broken Stick, and Tincolad."

Sotif pushed the tent flap aside. The four men stood in front of the tent. In the cold morning, their breath mingled into a single cloud that hovered opaquely in the air above them. "Enter," Sotif said.

"Lewtud has lived too long. Lewtud has seen what Lewtud cannot bear." Lewtud sat on an animal skin rug.

"It's true then ... the Alliance is no more," Sotif said.

"The Earth People clans are no more," Lewtud said. "The Sun People now talk of the death of all Earth People. Only Tall Tree and a few Sun People speak for the Earth People. Mother Earth has abandoned the Earth People. The time of the Earth People has ended."

Sotif looked questioningly at Tincolad. "I understand the language of the Earth People well enough to know what Lewtud says," Tincolad responded to the unasked question.

"Now is the end of Earth People, Spirit Fires, the History Room, and the History Man," Sotif said.

"This has not been a night of sleeping," Broken Stick said. "I have spoken with the leaders of this army. When the snow melts, they will take the last of the Earth People down the mountain to Warlog. Rayloc will destroy the Earth People, and Warlog will make peace with the Sun People. Warlog will return to his home."

"How do you know Warlog will kill all the Earth People? Perhaps if the army surrenders, that will satisfy him," Sotif asked.

"They believe Earth People are droglits," Broken Stick answered. "Droglits come to enslave all people and drive the sun from the sky. Rayloc will not feel safe until all the Earth People are no more."

"Will no one fight for the Earth People? Do all the Sun People want the Earth People to be no more?"

"Some Sun People of the Alliance look for a way to save the Earth People, but they are few. Most of the men in my army come from villages that are not of the Alliance," Tall Tree said.

"The Earth People must escape and travel east," Sotif said.

"These Sun People men will not let the Earth People go. Only those who can hide in the winter snow will survive," Tall Tree said.

"We must make sure Warlog does not hear of the Earth People in the East," Sotif said.

"The Sun People who are not of the Alliance have heard the stories of the Sotif and the search for the Spirit Fire," Tall Tree said. "They have seen the return of Sotif and have heard the stories of the Earth People of the East. There is no hiding in the East."

"Warlog's warriors killed all my family," Broken Stick said. "When the snows melt, I will meet Warlog's army in the mountain passes. I will attack him from ambush. I will attack and run, attack and run, and kill his warriors until they catch me. I will kill many before they catch me."

"What is this ambush?" Tall Tree asked.

Broken Stick looked to Tincolad. Gradually, everyone followed Broken Stick's eyes until everyone was looking expectantly at Tincolad.

Tincolad looked at Tall Tree. "Ambush is a kind of fighting. But there is a better way to defeat Warlog."

"What way?" Sotif asked.

"I have also spent much of the night talking and thinking. The other Sun People say Earth People are ugly, but they do not say they are droglits. They want to trade them to Warlog for peace because they fear Warlog."

"How does this help the Earth People?" Sotif asked.

"If the Earth People help destroy Warlog and Rayloc, then the Sun People would not need to trade them. Then the other Sun People would respect them."

"Warlog has destroyed all the Alliance except for these few men who have run to the mountains. Even with the help of the Earth People and the other Sun People, the Alliance has fallen," Sotif said.

"I've heard there was much fighting and killing last summer. I've listened carefully to what Lendoclad has told me of this fighting. I've thought much about it. Warlog's army is weak now. He won't be able to rebuild until summer."

"Warlog's army is more powerful than our army," Tall Tree said. "The next fight will be the end. We are trapped at the end of the world. His army will grow stronger while our army can only get weaker. All the men know this. They know they must give the Earth People to Warlog or die."

"What Tall Tree says is true. But we have the Spirit Fire, and we have something more."

"The Spirit Fire has abandoned the Earth People. They began to question the promise of the Spirit Fire even before Warlog," Sotif said.

"There was much destruction while we searched for the Spirit Fire," Broken Stick said. "Now that we have returned with the Spirit Fire, some of the Alliance Sun People think Mother Earth will rain fire on Warlog to drive him out of our lands. Others think Sotif will lead them to the Alliance in the East where they can escape."

"But you know there is no alliance in the East," Sotif said. "There are no stories of fire from the sky. Maybe Mother Earth might send another flood, but it is too late for that."

"I do not speak of any of those things," Tincolad said.

"You speak of Warlog's army. You speak of his weakness when he is much stronger than we are," Broken Stick said.

"I have said we have the Spirit Fire, not for magic or the power of Mother Earth. I speak of the Spirit Fire because it gives the people of the Alliance something to hope for … something to fight for that is more important to them than their lives. With this, they will dare much."

"How does this help when Warlog's army is still much stronger than Tall Tree's army?" Sotif asked. "Most of Tall Tree's army is of the others who do not believe in the Spirit Fire anyway."

"I know Warlog's army. I know how he keeps his army in winter. Warlog's strength is his organization. Everyone knows what is expected at all times. Everything goes smoothly. This is the only way a large army can operate."

"I see in these words more to cause worry," Tall Tree said. "I don't see how this helps our warriors or the Earth People."

"I have said Warlog's organization is his strength, but I also say it's his weakness."

"What do you mean?" Broken Stick asked.

"All Warlog's men know exactly how to set up a camp. Everyone has his place, and everyone knows what to do. I know where Warlog's tent will be in the camp. I know how Warlog places his guards. I know Warlog's pattern for eating and sleeping. I know his daily meetings."

"Why would you help the Alliance? You're a warrior in Warlog's army?" Tall Tree asked.

"Warlog is an evil man. He ruined my mother's life, and I promised her I would kill him. When my mother died, Lendoclad and I joined Warlog's army only so we could find a way to kill him. While I studied to be a warrior, I watched his camp and thought many times of how he could be killed. Lendoclad and I dedicated ourselves to finding a way to kill him. We studied every move he made and exactly how he was guarded.

"When I became a warrior, I was confused about droglits. I've seen there are no droglits in this land.

"Last night, Lendoclad, the man I always thought was my father, told me Warlog killed my true father before I was born.

"I have learned enough about Warlog to know a small army can invade his winter camp. Warlog knows how weak Tall Tree's army is. He will not expect Tall Tree to come through the snow and attack him in the winter. His army is relaxed. They're not thinking about an attack from Tall Tree. They're making their plans for next summer. In war, there is fighting, and there is planning how to fight. I have studied all the ways of his army. I did this to become a warrior, but I was better at planning than any of the other warriors.

"We have the advantage of the Earth People who know the weather. We also have the advantage of the Earth People who can sneak up on Sun People. With their ability to see, hear, and smell, the Earth People can tell much about Warlog's guards. I can show Tall Tree how to kill the camp guards. A small army could sneak into the camp in the dark. I can show Tall Tree every place to send his men to surprise the warriors. I can find Warlog's tent, defeat his guards, and kill him. I can teach Tall Tree's warriors how to fight Warlog's warriors. Warlog will not expect this.

"In the winter, Warlog sends large groups of warriors out to hunt. If we sneak in at night when most of his warriors are on a hunt, even a small army could destroy Warlog's army.

"Warlog leads his men by his personal power. When he speaks, he raises their spirits. He knows how to flatter and what to promise. He shares the wealth of conquest and takes care of the warriors' families by his promise and his organization. There is no one like Warlog.

"Rayloc holds great power with the army because of Warlog. If Warlog dies, Rayloc might be able to hold the army together. If Warlog and Rayloc both die, the army will fall apart. With the leadership and the promises of Warlog gone, the warriors will return to their villages and families. They are taught their power comes from Warlog and Rayloc. Their most important ceremony shows them they cannot stand without Warlog."

"This Tincolad is young," Lewtud said. "This Tincolad speaks of great plans with few men. Does this Tincolad know a whole army fought Warlog? Does this Tincolad know Warlog has killed a whole army?"

"I can say—" Broken Stick began.

"The big wind blows the tree, and if it's strong, it stands," Tincolad interrupted. "The small beaver chews the bottom, and the strong tree falls. Who can say what this small beaver can do if the Spirit Fire chooses to help?" Tincolad pointed his finger at his chest.

Broken Stick stood. "I have seen this boy grow to be a man on the trip to get the Spirit Fire. The Spirit Fire was taken by Sun People killers. Tincolad used his knowledge to defeat those killers. I followed him then, and we defeated them and saved the Spirit Fire. Not one of our men received even a small wound. I followed him then, and I will follow him now. He is young, but he is wise in the ways of war, and he is brave."

"I believe Broken Stick's words," Tall Tree said. "I will follow the plans of this small beaver."

Sotif stood. He put his right hand on Tincolad's shoulder. "I like this plan. I will support it to the Alliance. Tall Tree will send his army to defeat Warlog according to Tincolad's plans. Tincolad is a strange name. He will be remembered as Small Beaver if his plan works. If it doesn't work, nothing will be remembered, and the stories of the Alliance and the Earth People will disappear forever from all the land. So says Sotif, so it shall be."

"So says Sotif, so it shall be," Lewtud said.

Winter 3283/3282 BCE

The men showed their trust for Tincolad as he taught Tall Tree and his army how to fight Warlog. He trained them to use their weapons to fight against the warriors' weapons and kill them.

Tincolad showed Tall Tree how Warlog set up his camp and how to find where the warriors would be sleeping. He showed him how Warlog would place guards and how to sneak up and kill them.

Tall Tree picked his best men to be the first ones to silently kill the guards. He spent days and days with these men teaching them the few phrases Warlog's guards might say to an approaching warrior. He taught them the appropriate answer and drilled them over and over until they could repeat these few phrases without an accent. Only those who could pass Tincolad's most rigorous testing in language would be part of the first force.

Soft Cloud had learned some of Tincolad's language when she had taught him the language of the Alliance. She worked with Tincolad every day, and very soon, she was an invaluable assistant to him. She grilled the men in the phrases of Warlog's language while Tincolad worked on other phases of the plan. Tincolad spent as much time as he could with his son, Sincolad. He played games about hunting and fishing, but he didn't teach him about war.

With the help of some of the artisans of the Finger Lake tribe, Tincolad built a model of how Warlog would set up his camp. Again and again,

Tincolad rehearsed how the attack was to proceed. He taught the men the commands warriors give to their war dogs. He used Razid for the men to practice the proper tone and force for the commands to quiet the dogs and to direct their attacks. The men who would be fighting Warlog's warriors grew beards through the winter. In the spring, Tincolad taught Tall Tree's men how to cut their hair and beards to look like Warlog's warriors.

The day finally came when the Earth People said the weather would be right to sneak out of the mountains. There was still much snow, but no new storms would come for at least fifteen days. By using the wide snowshoes the Earth People made, they were able to travel over the deep snow between them and Warlog's camp. It was a difficult and dangerous trip, but all the men were anxious to get started.

Using their keen senses of smell, hearing, and sight, the Earth People scouts guided Tall Tree's army in position on the foothills above Warlog's winter camp.

Tincolad studied the camp. From his knowledge of the operation of Warlog's army, he was able to determine the weaknesses of the camp and make needed changes to his plans. After two days of planning and watching, Tincolad was relieved to see a large hunting party leave Warlog's camp. Tall Tree prepared his men to make the attack that night. Tincolad showed them how to draw fake tattoos on their arms with charcoal mixed with lard. He showed them the warrior greeting.

Tincolad tried to sleep the rest of the day, but it was impossible. He talked quietly with Lendoclad about his mother. Tonight, he would have the opportunity to fulfill his promise to her.

It got dark, and the camp was silent. The men huddled in animal skins trying to stay warm as they awaited Tall Tree's order. The longer Tincolad waited, the more upset his stomach became.

The night was clear, and the air got bitter cold after sunset. The hairs in Tincolad's nose turned stiff and prickly when he inhaled the frigid air and became soft and moist when he exhaled. It reminded him of the land where he grew up. He was homesick for that land now, and he wondered if he would ever see it again. Someone touched his shoulder. He turned to face Soft Cloud.

"What?"

"Before you go, I want to tell you I am proud of all you have done with Tall Tree's army. I think there's a good chance Tall Tree's army may win. But I'm so afraid for you."

"I will be careful."

"Must you fight Warlog? He's an experienced fighter. He has fought many men and killed them. How many men have you killed?"

"I have killed no one."

"How many men have you fought in battle?"

"None."

"Tincolad, you are a great warrior to plan war. I think you are better than Warlog. Your plan will defeat Warlog. I'm sure of that, but you're not a fighter. I'm so afraid of what will happen if you fight Warlog."

"Don't worry, Soft Cloud. Maybe I haven't fought, but I know about fighting. I'm younger and faster than Warlog."

"Knowing about fighting and fighting are not the same."

Tincolad stared into the night. Soft Cloud's words were true, but what scared Tincolad most was even though Tall Tree's warriors had studied the plan carefully, it would be something else when the fighting started. Tincolad wondered if these men would follow the plan when the confusion of the fight started. The moon was high in the sky. It was not much more than a smiling crescent, but the sky was full of stars. They gave enough light to see Warlog's camp in the distance. Several flickering fires were scattered through the camp. He took Soft Cloud in his arms and kissed her. "I will be careful. The sky is full of Zendolot's warriors. Tonight they will guide Tall Tree's army. It's a good sign." He ran his fingers through Soft Cloud's hair one more time and then turned to join the army.

Tincolad led the advance group of Earth People and Sun People. They found the camp guards and lookouts and silently killed them. When Tall Tree's main army sneaked into the camp, it was undefended. Tall Tree's men moved silently and efficiently into the first dwellings. The deadly work progressed in near silence. Tincolad heard muffled cries and scuffling, but no one sounded the alarm as he led his select group of men to the compound where Tincolad knew they would find Warlog and his guards.

This conflict would pit Tall Tree's best men against Warlog's choice guards. If Tincolad could lead his men to the right place before an alarm was sounded, he would have the advantage of surprise.

"Who goes there?" One of Warlog's guards confronted Tincolad. The guard was out of place and surprised him.

Tincolad quickly raised his left arm to give the Warrior Greeting and expose his warrior's tattoo. Tincolad spoke in Warlog's language. "I am Tincolad, warrior of Warlog, Zendolot's Great Eagle. I bring an important message." Tincolad, with Broken Stick behind him, closed the distance between them and the guard quickly. The guard was momentarily confused. In that moment, Broken Stick grabbed the man's hair with his left hand and sliced hard and deep with his dagger across the man's throat. There was a gulp with some gurgling as steam billowed up from the blood that gushed out.

"What's that?" another guard shouted. Tincolad's group attacked immediately, just as he had prepared them.

As Tall Tree's army sneaked into camp, the battle began slowly and then built. At first Tincolad heard a few cries here and there through the camp, but it quickly grew until everything seemed to be confusion and disorder. The disorder confirmed Tall Tree's army had entered the camp as planned. Tincolad realized Warlog's warriors were responding with practiced efficiency, racing to defensive positions. When they took their positions to defend against an enemy without, Tincolad knew they were being decimated by the enemy already within. Even their war dogs were confused and turned against them.

By the time the gray light of dawn crept down the mountainside, the fighting was over. Tincolad's men stood guard around Warlog's tent. Warlog had not come out. Then several of Tall Tree's men brought Rayloc to Warlog's tent.

Tall Tree arrived at the same time. "Tincolad, the war went as you planned it. Many of the warriors are dead. Most ran into the wilderness. What shall we do if they gather together and come back?"

"A wolf with no head cannot attack the sheep. We will cut the head from this army."

"What do we do with this fake shaman?" one of the men holding Rayloc asked.

"This is the man who calls the Earth People droglits. This is the man who would burn all Earth People. Give him to the Earth People," another man shouted.

Rayloc was handed over to the Earth People. Lewtud spoke. "This man burned most of the Earth People. This man must burn. So says Lewtud, so it shall be."

"So says Lewtud, so it shall be," the Earth People repeated.

"What did they say?" Rayloc asked. No one answered. The Earth People tied Rayloc's hands and legs. They put extra wood on the campfire and threw him into the fire. Rayloc screamed and rolled out of the fire.

"Warlog! Come out and save me," he shouted. The Earth People picked him up. "No! No!" he screamed, but they threw him back into the fire.

Rayloc rolled out again. Warlog stepped from his tent dressed in his ceremony robes. For a moment, there was silence. Rayloc managed to roll himself to his knees. He was burned severely in several places. The blackened skin of his left cheek hung from his jaw, and bright red blood glistened above it.

"Warlog, save me."

"You will have to save yourself. I would have left this cursed land except you wanted to kill droglits. I don't even think they are droglits." Warlog turned to Tall Tree. "I have waited in my tent for my warriors to report they had destroyed your army. Now the sun rises, and you come dragging my shaman with you. I was wrong to think he spoke for Zendolot. Zendolot, praise to him, has given him to you. Do as you please with him. Let me go, and I will take my army back to my land."

"You can't trade me for your freedom!" Rayloc shouted.

"You are the cause of this war. I listened to you too much. I see this mistake. I will take my army back to my country where my people are. I will never come back to this land."

"Your land! Your people! You think of changing your name to Warlot to be one of the gods. What a fool you are. When I studied under Nacoloc to become shaman, Rundolik came to him. She told him Seccolog was fat and ugly. She told Nacoloc she mated secretly with one of Seccolog's hunters. The hunter was the father of her child. You are no son of Seccolog, and you have no right to rule the People."

"Silence, liar!" Warlog commanded. Even the men of Tall Tree's army who didn't understand Warlog's language responded to the command. Warlog surveyed the silent scene.

Tall Tree stepped forward. "Your army has been defeated and is scattered."

"No," Warlog said. "Even now they prepare to attack."

"Who leads them?" Tall Tree asked.

Warlog was silent. He looked around at Tall Tree and his army. "Who is man enough to kill Warlog, Zendolot's Great Eagle?"

Tincolad stepped forward. "I come to kill Warlog ... as is my right."

"What right?" Warlog shouted.

"I am Tincolad. My mother was Conchelik. I am heritage son of Sincolad. It's my heritage right to rule Seccolog's village. You are no son of Seccolog. You're a fraud. You will die for what you did to my mother."

Warlog began to laugh hysterically. Then his face went cold. "Your father and grandfather died because of what they did to *my* mother. You are me. You come to avenge *your* mother as I avenged *my* mother. You follow my path, but you are weak. You *are* the son of Sincolad. The only man weaker than Sincolad was Seccolog, his father. They did not die as men. They died as animals. Slaughtered like goats that cannot fight. I am no goat. I am glad no blood of Seccolog runs in my body. I have no fear of a son of Sincolad. You carry the weakness of Sincolad and his father, Seccolog." There was great disdain in Warlog's voice. He threw his robes from his shoulders. The muscles in his arms and chest glistened in the early morning light. A jagged scar ran down his left shoulder. His chest rose and fell, staring all the while into Tincolad's eyes.

Warlog picked the stone that hung from a leather thong around his neck. "This is the point of Sincolad's dagger. It broke off in my shoulder when he tried to kill me. I killed him as he pleaded for his life ... like a child."

As Tincolad looked at the mighty Warlog, his heart raced, and his body began to shake. Then his mother's face filled his mind, and he became calm. "You say I am weak because I am son of Sincolad, heritage son of a mighty chief. You are a bastard son of a no-name hunter." Tincolad's voice was steady.

"Fool!" Warlog boomed. "I am son of Rundolik. Rundolik gives me my strength."

Tincolad was not cowed. "Double fool!" he shouted back. "Rundolik let Seccolog make her a camp whore. I am son of Conchelik. Conchelik, who escaped your evil hands to live an *honorable* life."

"Aurgh!" Warlog screamed. He grabbed a spear and charged Tincolad in a rage. Tincolad remained cool. Warlog rushed, thrusting his spear. Tincolad reacted with the strength and agility of a young man. He pushed the shaft of Warlog's spear aside with his left hand and leaned into Warlog, ramming his dagger into the left side of Warlog's chest. Warlog stumbled and lay gasping for air on the ground.

"Know this, Warlog. I will return to my village. I am heritage grandson of the great Seccolog. I will destroy the empire you built. I will take my place as chief of *my* tribe. Then, there will be no empire. Things will be as they were before Warlog. Warlog will be forgotten, but the names of Seccolog and Sincolad will remain forever in the stories of the People."

"You will kill me," Warlog gasped, "but even if you succeed in all your plans, you will have no peace. I have taught war to the People. Take away the leaders, and the People will find new ones. Take away their weapons, and they will make new ones. Break up the empire, and the People will create new empires. Scatter my army, and the People will create new armies. The

People have learned the power of war. Long after no one speaks of Seccolog or Tincolad, there will be those who love war."

"Someday peace will win. It's over for you and your army." Tincolad dropped his dagger and turned to Tall Tree. "Warlog is yours. Do as you please with him."

Someone yelled. Tincolad turned to see Warlog almost upon him. "Meet my dagger," Warlog said as he charged Tincolad, but then he stopped, and his eyes became wide. He staggered back and dropped his dagger. He slowly raised his left hand and made the sign of Warlog, Zendolot's Great Eagle. He looked in the sky as though he saw something. "Podeclad, my friend, my brother, forgive me. I should not have—" His eyes and mouth opened wide. "No!" he screamed at the sky, and then he fell forward at Tincolad's feet—dead. An arrow stuck up from his back. Broken Stick stood with an empty bow in his hand.

"So ends Warlog, Zendolot's Great Eagle," Tall Tree said.

"When the warriors know Warlog is no more, they will return to their homes," Tincolad said. "You must cut his head off and put it on a tall post at the edge of his camp. You must cut his left hand off and then cut the first two fingers from his hand. Tie the hand to the post below the head with the knuckles out. Release all the prisoners and send all them out of the camp so they see Warlog's head. They will disperse and pass the word to all the warriors on the plains. Move your army from this camp and leave it abandoned. Any warriors who return will see the defeat of Warlog. They will have no more taste for war against Tall Tree."

"Do as Tincolad says and throw the shaman, Rayloc, into the fire," Tall Tree ordered.

Broken Stick pulled the dagger point from the string on Warlog's neck. "This is from your father's dagger," he said as he handed it to Tincolad.

As the men grabbed Rayloc, he shouted, "Throw me in the fire, but you will not be able to live in peace."

Rayloc rolled out of the fire three more times before the power of the flames consumed him.

****

Sotif entered the camp. Many of the tents of Warlog's camp had been set on fire. In the early morning light, the glow of the fires could be seen across the prairie, announcing the defeat of Warlog's army. Sotif had watched the battle from Tall Tree's camp in the foothills.

The sun was shining on a new day as Sotif followed Broken Stick through the smoldering remains of the army that had come to destroy the Alliance and kill all the Earth People. It was a time for rejoicing, but for Sotif, there was great emptiness. So much fighting and so much killing, and the world was only worse.

It was hard to think back on those days at the Heart of the Bison when Senlo had told him he would be a traveling History Man. As Sotif walked through the final destruction of Warlog's army on a plain far from the Heart of the Bison, he wondered if Senlo had seen just how far he would travel.

"This was Warlog's tent," Broken Stick said. "Tall Tree is inside."

Sotif entered the tent. Tall Tree was talking with Tincolad. He looked up. "Sotif, my old friend. The victory is finally ours."

"What of Warlog and Rayloc?"

"Warlog's head is stuck on a pole at the south edge of the camp. Rayloc's body burns to ashes in the campfire."

"Tall Tree has released all of Warlog's people who were captured," Tincolad said. "They carry a message that Warlog and Rayloc are both dead. Tall Tree has promised if they return to their villages all will be forgotten, but if they choose to fight, Tall Tree and his army will kill everyone who fights.

"Warlog was the one who held the army together. All warriors are pledged to Warlog. The sign they make by holding up their second finger as they go into battle is a reminder of their pledge to Warlog. The warriors believe in their Warrior Ceremony. In this ceremony, the warriors are taught a warrior cannot stand without Warlog. As soon as they know Warlog is dead, they will leave."

"I hope you are right," Sotif said. "We have won this battle, but our army is weak. It could not stand against those who have escaped if they band together to attack again."

"I believe what Tincolad says. Without Warlog, there is nothing to fight for," Broken Stick said.

"Then the war is truly over," Tall Tree said.

Tincolad broke the silence. "Summer has come. Soon, I will start the long journey back to my mother's village. Only Pothialik and Pothelad are left to hold the Empire Warlog started. I must complete the destruction of Warlog's evil by ridding the world his Empire. Broken Stick has asked to return with me. He is a strong warrior. I will need him to finish what has been started here. If we succeed, we will never see such a large army marching across the land to conquer and destroy."

"I wish you luck," Tall Tree said. "But I'm afraid the thing Warlog said is true."

"What thing?" Sotif asked.

"Now that war has come to the land, it will always be here. We have defeated Warlog, but Tincolad must return to his land and make a war on Pothelad to prevent war. I will return to the Winding River village. If I find it ruled by Warlog's warriors, I will also make a war to drive them out. When it's necessary to make war to stop war, I worry for the future."

"Why go back then?" Sotif asked. The four men sat in silence.

Once again, Tincolad was the first to speak. "Warlog's army came from the unity of Warlog's Empire. Pothialik and Pothelad will hold the Empire together. They will rebuild the army, and Pothelad will make himself Warlog."

Again all was silent. Tall Tree spoke. "If Warlog's warriors still rule in the Winding River village, my family and friends cannot return to their homes. Perhaps when the warriors hear of Warlog's defeat, they will leave. If they refuse, I must drive them out."

"Before there was war, there was no need for war," Sotif said, "but now there will always be a need for it."

"What will you do now?" Tall Tree asked Sotif.

"I am a man of the Sun People and the Earth People. The Alliance is dead. The Earth People in the East broke from the Alliance many generations ago. There they hide in caves, and the Sun People have forgotten the Alliance and the Earth People.

"The Earth People in the West have been destroyed by the Sun People. The few who remain fear the Sun People. The Sun People who were of the Alliance have joined the Sun People who are not of the Alliance to fight Warlog. As it is in the East, so it must be in the West. The Earth People must go deep into the mountains. There they must hide from the Sun People.

"The strong bond of the Memories and Traditions will fade from the Sun People. The stories of the storytellers will change. The Alliance and the Earth People will fade from the stories of the Sun People. When the Sun People no longer remember the Earth People, it will be a good thing.

"Tall Tree and Small Beaver must no longer tell stories of the Alliance and the Earth People. These things must be forgotten."

"If the Sun People and the Earth People separate, what will Sotif do?" Tall Tree asked.

"I have thought of this all the time you prepared your army to attack. I will go with the Earth People."

"Come with me, Sotif. We will open the Heart of the Bison. We will open the History Room. You will paint the final painting of the Alliance. Bring the Spirit Fire. Once again you will be History Man for the Heart of the Bison."

"The Heart of the Bison and the History Room are things of the Alliance. These things preserve the memory of the Alliance. The Spirit Fire is a symbol to the Earth People. It belongs with the Earth People. The Spirit Fire cannot dwell in the Heart of the Bison now.

"You must *not* open the Heart of the Bison. You must forget those things of the Alliance. Sometime in a future generation, when Sun People find a way to live in peace and trust, a new alliance will be formed. Then our children's children will open the Heart of the Bison and find the richness of the culture we had before Warlog."

"If we are to forget the stories of the Alliance, how will anyone ever find the Heart of the Bison?" Tall Tree asked.

"I am the History Man of the Alliance. After me, there will be no more History Man. I have made a way to tell the stories of the Alliance and the Heart of the Bison with symbols like small tattoos. I have taught this to Rodlu. Rodlu has used this to tell the story of the Spirit Fire search. I will teach the symbols to others. I will use these symbols to tell the stories of the Alliance and the Heart of the Bison. These stories will remain unchanged with the Earth People until a time of peace comes. I will start new clans of Earth People in the West. When the time is right, they will restore the Heart of the Bison, and the Spirit Fire will once again live in the Heart of the Bison."

"Why don't you teach the symbols to the Sun People?" Tall Tree asked.

"It is better to leave the stories with the Earth People. Sun People learn new things and new ways fast. Sun People change fast. Earth People are slow to learn but slow to change. The stories will be safe with them for all time. The Earth People will be safer if the Sun People do not remember them. It has been only three summers since Warlog came, and already the Sun People have learned war. You must go back to the Winding River village prepared to make war. Small Beaver must go back to his village with war in his mind. This must be so with the Sun People. The Earth People have not learned war. The Earth People cannot understand you must make war to stop war. I must go with Earth People and teach them to hide from Sun People."

"Here, take this." Tincolad handed Sotif the tip of his father's dagger.

"What is this?"

"This is the point of my father's dagger. It broke off in Warlog's shoulder when my father fought for his life. Take this as a gift from Small Beaver to remind the Earth People there are Sun People who would fight for them."

"I will take this symbol, and I will teach the Earth People of the good Sun People and of Small Beaver, the greatest warrior. I will preserve the history of the Alliance and the time before war came. It is a great sadness to me to know I will never again sit at the Spirit Fire hearth in the Heart of the Bison, but my calling takes me away from the Heart of the Bison."

****

As soon as the meeting with Sotif was over, Tincolad rushed to the camp in the foothills. Soft Cloud would be waiting anxiously for word. When he started up the hill, he met her coming down. "Did you do it? Did you kill Warlog?" she asked as soon as she saw him.

"I didn't kill him, but I wounded him."

"And his army? And Rayloc? What about them?"

"Rayloc is dead. Warlog is dead. His army is scattered. We have won the war, and now there will be peace in this land."

"Warlog is dead? Are you sure? You said you just wounded him."

"Broken Stick killed him. His head is on a post outside his camp. Rayloc was burned to ashes. Warlog's army will not fight without them. The warriors have scattered."

"Can this be so? In just one day Warlog's whole army is defeated? How can this be?"

"Warlog was smart, but he had his weakness."

"Now what?"

"Warlog has a son in the village where I come from."

"I know. You already told me about him."

"He will become Warlog when news of his father's death gets back to my land. I must go back and make sure he doesn't organize another army. I must go back and become chief of my village and make things like they were before Warlog."

"But … you never said anything to me about returning. What am I to do?"

"All your family is dead. Everything in this land will change now. There will be no Alliance. Sotif is taking the last of the Earth People to hide in the mountains. The Sun People of the Alliance will learn the language and the ways of the other Sun People. Nothing in this land will ever be as it was. Broken Stick and Bright Moon will come with me. Come with us, Soft Cloud. You will be heritage mate of the chief, and when I die, Sincolad will take his proper place as chief."

Tears flowed down Soft Cloud's cheeks. "This is my land, Tincolad. But it is as you say. It is my land, and yet it's all different. I will go with you. You will be my family. Your language will be my language. I will learn your ways. I will do this, but it's hard to know everything I grew up with is gone."

Tincolad hugged Soft Cloud and kissed her. "You will not be sorry. We will go to the West and make a new life of peace and friendship among all people. We will end war and remove Warlog from the memory of the people."

Summer 3282 BCE

Sotif sent word for all Earth People to gather at the Fish Lake village. Tall Tree maintained his camp near the Trade Pass village until it was confirmed that Warlog's army had broken up. In the early summer, Tall Tree, Tincolad, and Broken Stick started their journeys with the hope that they could use war to stop war. Sotif was saddened to say good-bye to his friends for the last time.

Sotif sent his strongest men into the mountains to find a new home for the Earth People where they could hide from the Sun People and live in peace. The men returned with news that they had found a place. Sotif prepared to lead the Earth People into the mountains and away from Sun People. There was still enough time to move and prepare for the first winter without the Alliance. Sotif would miss the deep blue water of Finger Lake as he missed the Heart of the Bison.

"A long time ago, the History Man, Senlo, told me I would be a traveling History Man," Sotif said to Luko. "Now, I must travel one more time." He spoke in Sun People language.

"We will leave guides at Finger Lake to lead the Earth People that gather to our new home. Next summer, I will send men to the Mammoth cave to watch for Rodlu. He will lead him to the Spirit Fire in the West, and they will bring him back to the new Spirit Fire cave in the East. Once again travelers will carry ceremony ashes between the two Spirit Fires, and all the Earth People will be joined by the magic of the Spirit Fire.

"We will find a shorter path to join the peoples in the East with the peoples in the West. We will hide from the Sun People until a time of peace returns and the power of war no longer fills the hearts of the Sun People.

"I will put all the Traditions of the people on animal skins with the symbols I have made. I will make a new law for all the people, and I will put the law on animal skins. The Traditions and the law will last forever, unchanged.

"I speak now in the language of the Sun People for the last time. You and I have heard the sound of their language for the last time. From this day, a new time begins. From this day, there is no Alliance, and the Earth People will be hidden from the Sun People."

"Sotif speaks the truth for the Earth People," Luko said.

"Sotif is ready to travel one last time," Sotif said in Earth People language. "Sotif is sad for those who have died because of Warlog. Sotif is happy for each one of the Earth People that lives now. The clans of the Earth People and the Spirit Fire will grow strong together."

Sotif stood and turned his back to Fish Lake for the last time. The clan waited, ready to follow him to their new home far from the threat of the Sun People.

"From this small clan, a new family of Earth People must rise. So says Sotif, so it shall be."

"So says Sotif, so it shall be," Luko and the others repeated.

Summer 3269 BCE

Sotif sat on his robes in front of the Spirit Fire. "The travelers have been spotted," Kenlu reported. The writing skin from last time of plants said Rodlu would come this time of plants. Rodlu was old. If he had truly come, this would be his last trip.

As Sotif thought of what to say to Rodlu, an old man came to him. "Sotif?"

"This is Sotif."

"Sotif has changed much. Rodlu does not know this Sotif."

"Rodlu, my old friend." Sotif struggled to his feet and hugged Rodlu. "How are the clans of the East?"

"The clans of the East become stronger each year. Sotif's new Republic brings the clans closer."

"Sotif's days are near the end. Sotif has seen the world change," Sotif said.

"Sotif's writing has brought all Earth People together. Rodlu teaches this writing to all shomots. With this writing, the Earth People speak across the distance."

"The writing skins are strong magic to speak across a great distance. Writing skins are strong magic to speak across the generations."

Rodlu looked confused.

"For many seasons, Sotif has put all the Traditions on writing skins. Each new generation will learn the meaning of the writing symbols. Then each generation will find all the Traditions on the writing skins. These writing skins will be called history skins. These history skins will be the new History Man of the Earth People.

"Sotif has made two history skins for each of the Traditions. Sotif has added the history Rodlu made of the Spirit Fire search. Sotif has made a history of Small Beaver. Sotif has made a history of the defeat of Warlog." Sotif pointed to two large bundles of animal skins. "One history skin will be kept with each Spirit Fire. The shomot of the Spirit Fire cave must care for the history skins. In this way, the Traditions will be safe with the Spirit Fire. These history skins will become the History Room. Earth People will add new history to the history skins as paintings were added in the History Room."

"Sotif has been wise to make the history skins. The history skins must show the Earth People the beginning of the Spirit Fire."

"Sotif has made other writing skins. Sotif has made writing skins to show the Earth People how to grow stronger. Sotif has made writing skins to show the Earth People how to prepare for a new alliance many generations from now. Sotif has made writing skins to make Earth People magic as strong as Sun People magic.

"The western clans understand these writing skins. Rodlu must take these skins to the eastern clans. The eastern clans must accept these writing skins. When they do, there must be one law for all Earth People. Earth People must make good magic as strong as the Sun People."

"How can Earth People learn to make magic like Sun People?"

"Earth People must become like Sun People."

The puzzled look on Rodlu's face asked the question for him.

"The Sun People have shown us how to do this." The puzzled look deepened. Sotif laughed. "Rodlu wonders at Sotif's words. The Sun People call this magic *breeding*."

"Sun People breeding is for dogs and goats."

"The Sun People watch their goats. When a goat gives more milk, they breed it. When a goat gives little milk, they do not breed it. When a goat grows large with much meat, the Sun People breed it. When a goat is small, the Sun People do not breed it. In this way, goats get better with each generation.

"The parent animals pass the good things to the next generation in their life force. From the generations, the good things get stronger. From the generations, the bad things disappear. The Traditions say there were no dogs. The Traditions say the Sun People used the magic of breeding to make dogs from wolves. Now there are dwelling dogs that are small and live in the dwellings with the Sun People. Now there are herding dogs that live with the goats. Many kinds of dogs come from one kind of wolf. This is the magic of breeding. The Earth People must use the magic of breeding to make new kinds of Earth People."

"This breeding is for animals."

"The world has changed. There must be breeders to look for the magic to make new kinds of Earth People."

"This is a thing for animals. This is not a thing for Earth People."

"Rodlu makes a wrong to think this. The Earth People have already used breeding for many generations. Breeding is not a new thing for the Earth People."

"What breeding?"

"The Ancients must be children of the Ancients. This is true because the children carry the strength of the parents. This is breeding. Always the History Man was the child of Earth People and Sun People. This is also breeding.

"The Earth People of the western clan accept the magic of breeding. It is not hard. Rodlu must carry these ideas to the eastern clans."

"What kind of new Earth People must this breeding make?"

"The Earth People need men who go outside the cave to get all things for the clan. These new people must be Gatherers. The Gatherers must hear, see, and smell better than Earth People do now. The Gatherers must be made to go outside the cave without leaving any signs for the Sun People to follow.

"Some people must be made to look like the Sun People. These people must be the Watchers. The Watchers must be made so they can speak the language of the Sun People. The Watchers must live with the Sun People. The Watchers must learn all the magic of the Sun People. The Watchers must tell the clans when Sun People come.

"Some people must be made to hold the Memories. These are the Ancients. The Ancients must strengthen the Memories.

"Some People must be made to think in new ways. These must be the Thinkers. The Thinkers must be made to think up magic that is better than the Sun People magic.

"Sotif has put all this on writing skins. Sotif has called these the wisdom skins. There is much in the wisdom skins about the magic of breeding. There is much in the wisdom skins about the laws of Earth People. These laws are made to help Earth People stay hidden from Sun People. These laws are made to help Earth People become stronger.

"Sotif, last History Man of the Alliance, gives the Earth People the history skins to teach the people the Traditions. Sotif, last History Man of the Alliance, gives the Earth People the wisdom skins to teach the people how to protect the clans. The history skins and the wisdom skins show the Earth People how to become stronger than the Sun People."

"How long must the Earth People hide from the Sun People?"

"Sotif has dreamed a dream. In this dream, Sotif has seen the time when Warlog killed Small Beaver's father. Warlog broke the point of the dagger that Small Beaver's father carried. From this broken dagger, Warlog began the thing called war. Warlog carried the point of this dagger as a symbol of war. Small Beaver defeated Warlog. Then Small Beaver gave the point of the dagger to Sotif as a symbol of peace. In Sotif's dream, the point of the dagger must find the dagger of Small Beaver's father. When the dagger and the point are brought together, the first steps to stop war will begin.

"After the point finds the dagger, the Earth People must return to the Heart of the Bison. Then a girl child must be born. This child must be taught from a young age in the Heart of the Bison. This child must be daughter of shorec. This child must become shorec. This child must be taught in the place where Kectu is buried. This child must learn of the Alliance in the History Room. This child must be daughter of Kectu.

"This daughter of Kectu must find powerful Sun People to break the trap of war. From the Heart of the Bison, the daughter of Kectu and the Sun People must begin a powerful work to break the trap of war.

"The daughter of Kectu must lead Earth People to defeat the Great Aurochs."

"There are no aurochs. The aurochs are only shown in the History Room. The same is true of the mammoth."

"The Great Aurochs is a symbol of those who do not respect Mother Earth. The Great Aurochs is a symbol of people who would follow the trap of war. The Great Aurochs does not walk on the earth. The Great Aurochs lives in the hearts of people who follow the ideals of the Great Aurochs. The ideals of the Great Aurochs must be defeated."

"Rodlu would like to see the day of a new Alliance."

"Sotif has seen this day in dreams. Perhaps Rodlu must see this day in dreams. So says Sotif, last of the History Men, so shall it be."

"So says Sotif, so it shall be," Rodlu repeated.

October—2001 CE

Beads of sweat trickled down Solero's back, probably because the meeting in his conference room was getting tense. The floor, walls, and ceiling were made of dy-emeralite, a pale emerald-green material used for most of the structures in Solero's world. The dy-emeralite was impregnated with bionic LED material, which caused it to give off a soft light when excited by small electrical impulses. There was no other light source and no shadows in the office, but everyone could see clearly. The room was fourteen feet long and twelve feet wide with no pictures on the walls. At each end of the room there was a door, and along each side there were three faux windows. Through the windows, there was a realistic hologram. On one side, the hologram was of a densely forested mountain scene in Oregon. On the other side, the hologram looked out on desert scene near Bryce Canyon in Utah.

Rajel's jaw tightened. He was in charge of coordination and execution of *Operation Reclaim*. He was of the Earth People race called Gatherers. He was seven feet, four inches tall. Except for his face, the bottoms of his feet, and the palms of his hands, his body was covered with straight, reddish hair. His black eyes were intent as he stared at Solero. "It was all al-Qaeda. No other group was involved." After ten minutes of being grilled, Rajel's exasperation was beginning to show.

"I need to be completely clear on this point, so reassure me again. Was *Operation Reclaim* connected with the attack at *any* level?" Solero asked again.

Rajel expelled a blast of air through his mouth before answering. "I do not know how to *make* it clearer. I have spent the past six weeks reviewing all our activities and interviewing our moles. Our people were not involved, and the attack was not connected in any way to *Operation Reclaim*."

"I cannot over emphasize how important it is that *Operation Reclaim* stay uninvolved in any terrorist activities until time to initiate the final phase," Solero stressed. Solero was the Minority Leader of the Earth People Supreme Council. He was also the leader of the secret program titled *Operation Reclaim*. "I have been assured we have moles planted in *all* the major terrorist groups, so you can see why I am surprised an attack of that magnitude could have happened without our knowledge." Solero was of the Earth People race called Watchers. Watchers were bred and taught to look and act like the Sun People, those who lived on the surface of earth.

"We have not infiltrated the decision-making levels of al-Qaeda yet."

"So you say. But we do have four moles in al-Qaeda."

"You are supposed to maintain deniability on the operation. How did you get those details?" Rajel was obviously surprised.

"When President Bush announced it was an al-Qaeda attack, I needed more information. The question stands. How come we did not know about the attack?"

"This was a high-level al-Qaeda operation. Our moles are still in the lower levels of the organization."

"Pulgo says … without al-Qaeda, *Operation Reclaim* cannot succeed." Pulgo spoke in the ancient language of the Earth People. He understood the English spoken by the others, and they understood what he said. He was of the Earth People race called Ancients. His four-foot, nine-inch body was muscular and wide with shoulder-length blond hair that was clean but uncombed. He had almost no chin or forehead. His big blue eyes looked out openly from beneath a large brow ridge covered with bushy hair. His nose was large and wide. His large mouth, filled with oversized, crooked teeth, was framed with full lips.

"Pulgo is right," Solero said. "The next referendum is in two years. At that time, I expect to be elected Majority Party Leader. But whether I am elected or not, we have to initiate *Operation Reclaim* no later than right after the referendum."

"Why the rush?" Rajel asked.

"Have you heard of EarthScope?" Rajel looked puzzled. "I thought not," Solero continued before Rajel could answer. "What about interferometers?"

"What do those things have to do with our timing?"

"EarthScope is a Sun People project to map all slippage areas on the tectonic plates in North America. Some of their seismic studies involve mapping deep geologic structures."

"That is not the first time Sun People have gathered information about below-ground geology. We have always avoided detection."

"This is much more intense than their oil explorations. Our Thinkers are working to counter the effect of EarthScope, but we have not resolved all issues yet. However, interferometers are a different story."

"Interferometers? Sounds like a high school science project."

"Do not let the funny name fool you. They are based on very advanced physics using Bose-Einstein condensates. With them, Sun People will be able to get very accurate surveys of deep geologic features. They work similar to the cavern-finder technology we are using to look for the Heart of the Bison. Our Thinkers believe the Sun People will be able to fly over an area in an airplane equipped with an interferometer and pick out oil fields on a computer screen. Our concern is that all caves, tunnels, and other voids will also show up."

Rajel appeared to be suitably surprised. "When will this happen?"

"They are near completion of a prototype. Our information indicates it will work, but it will be too heavy to use in the field. It will take more time to do the miniaturization, but it will be ready in a few years. Naturally, our Thinkers are working furiously to counter these technologies. Perhaps they will succeed, but it is just a matter of time before we are discovered. I want things in shape before the referendum, just in case there is an earlier threat of discovery. Do not give me details, but generally, how is the plan going?"

Rajel twisted in his seat, obviously uncomfortable with the direction the conversation was taking. "We have infiltrated all the targeted terrorist organizations. In all of them, except al-Qaeda, we are in positions of influence. Other agents have acquired covert control over enough existing stockpiles of nuclear, bio, and chemical weapons in many countries, including some in the United States and Russia, to accomplish the goals set out in the computer simulations. The weapons can be delivered to the appropriate organizations in a two-week period. Iraq is planning to move all its weapons of mass destruction out before President Bush forces his hand. Negotiations are underway to move them to Syria. If that happens, we have people in place to get control of them. Even without those added weapons, the *Operation Reclaim* signal is set, and our plans to send it are finalized. But after the signal is given, it will take about four weeks to coordinate the groups and get the commitments. We will not give the signal until we have a final go ahead."

"Why so long?" Solero asked.

"After the signal is sent, we have to put sensitive information out to the various terrorist leaders. Do you want that information out before we make the decision to move? Because there is a real risk some parts of the plan could be compromised."

"Streamline the plan. I need a quicker response."

"I am already working on it."

"It does not matter how fast you can implement it, the plan is useless if we do not achieve complete destruction of infrastructure and technology," Tofraprin said. Tofraprin, who was in charge of security and intelligence for *Operation Reclaim*, sat to Solero's left. Like Solero, Tofraprin was a Watcher. "There must not be more than one billion survivors on the entire planet—preferably around a half billion. We cannot gain control over enough weapons to create that much destruction. The success of the plan depends on retaliation from countries like the United States, Russia, and England. The civil governments must be destroyed so low-level military leaders will be left in charge. None of our computer simulations achieve anything near that goal without the targets assigned to al-Qaeda."

"What about assigning them to the organizations we can control?" Solero asked.

"None of those organizations is capable." Tofraprin spoke in a tone that left no doubt he knew what he was talking about. "We could directly train a couple of them and bring them up to that level in six to eight months."

"No. We are on shaky ground as it is. That level of involvement would put us in too deep ... at least for now. Once we achieve Majority Party status, we could do that, but I want to be ready before then. What is the problem with our al-Qaeda moles?"

Rajel put the palms of his hands on the pale green dy-emeralite conference table and leaned forward. "Our people have spent a lot of time building trust, but as things stand, the positions of influence are held by the early organizers from the Afghan war with Russia."

"Pulgo has heard al-Qaeda will not accept new leaders. The Minority Party Leaders must not follow this plan. This plan cannot work without al-Qaeda. Pulgo says ... this plan makes a big wrong."

"I understand the concern the al-Qaeda problem creates," Rajel said. "But recent developments work to our advantage."

"How so?" Solero asked.

Rajel leaned back in his chair and spoke with confidence. "The 9/11 attack will change everything. There is no doubt the United States will attack Afghanistan ... probably before the end of the year. They will not approach this the way the Russians did. People in my office believe they will disrupt the Taliban organization in less than a year."

Solero looked at Tofraprin. "What do you say?"

"It will be only a few months."

"And so?" Solero said, looking at Rajel.

"The US will disrupt al-Qaeda. They will capture or kill many of its leaders. That will put stress on the organization and create openings our moles are prepared to take advantage of."

Solero looked questioningly at Tofraprin. "The US will not destroy al-Qaeda, but Rajel is right," Tofraprin said, "they will do serious damage. Also, President Bush's plan to attack al-Qaeda on financial fronts will open opportunities for us."

"We cannot offer or provide any direct financial assistance to any terrorist group," Solero said.

"That is not necessary," Rajel said. "Our moles are prepared to respond to stresses on al-Qaeda in ways that will put them in favorable positions with the leadership. It is a matter of the US damaging al-Qaeda but not destroying the organization."

"Al-Qaeda will survive any attack in Afghanistan," Tofraprin assured Solero.

"Okay then, things look good on the original timetable. However, something else has come up."

"What something, Pulgo asks?"

"You are all aware of the Iceman discovery in the Alps and the fact that the dagger found with it matches the Small Beaver artifact. Many think that proves the Sotif story of the Warmonger is true. Even though that does not add credibility to the Points of the Wisdom Skins, we can expect to lose some votes because of it. That, by itself, is not a problem, but something else has come up. Tofraprin?" Solero nodded to Tofraprin.

Tofraprin pulled several reports bound in blue covers from his briefcase. "The Supreme Council has come in possession of an unpublished report of some work done in the Middle East by a university professor from Arizona State. The man's name is Marc Metcalf. It appears he found some troubling fossils this past summer." Tofraprin passed copies to everyone at the table.

"What exactly are you talking about?" Rajel asked.

"You can read the report for yourself, but basically it contains two astounding discoveries. Metcalf found the remains of a Neandertal child in a cave in the Middle East. The child had four smooth black stones—one in each hand and one near each foot. The skull has puncture wounds consistent with the bite of a large cat of some sort."

Rajel gasped. Pulgo remained stoic. Everyone else leaned forward.

"Not far from the cave where they found the child, they found a grave. They did not have time to recover the skeletons in the grave, but they took pictures before burying their find for later recovery. The report says the grave contained the remains of a Cro-Magnon man embracing a female. Alriel has examined the photos."

"I have examined the report and photos." Alriel was in charge of science and technology for *Operation Reclaim*. He was of the Earth People race called Thinkers. He was five foot, seven inches tall and weighed 106 pounds. His body was completely hairless, not even eyelashes or eyebrows. In the green light of the dy-emeralite room, his pale white skin seemed to have a green tint. His face was compressed into the bottom of a triangle formed by a large, wide forehead and a small, pointed chin. His mouth was small with narrow lips. His nose consisted of two small openings above his thin upper lip. His eyes, however, were about twice as big as those of the Watchers. His thin arms and legs were disproportionately long. He spoke clearly, but his voice had a watery tone to it. "I have no doubt the female is half Earth People and half Sun People. The skeletons were not fully excavated, but from what I could see of the female's hips, I am 70 percent certain she had given birth."

"Tuka," Pulgo muttered in awe.

"Tuka and Sky Man, parents of Shekek!" Rajel exclaimed. "Then it is as Sotif wrote."

"This is all preliminary," Solero stated. "It is conjecture to assume these are Tuka and Sky Man. And if they are, it does not prove there is a Heart of the Bison cave."

"What if it is true?" Rajel asked. "What if the Heart of the Bison really existed?"

Solero pounded his fist on the table. He stood up and looked around the table at the other members of the *Operation Reclaim* leadership. "That is completely irrelevant," he stated in a controlled, quiet voice contrasting sharply with his actions. He walked deliberately to Rajel's seat at the large dy-emeralite conference table. "It does not matter what those *ancient* people thought. The world has changed. Sotif could never have seen the world we live in. Nothing in any of his writings relates to *this* world.

"Footnote number six of the report says the grave was discovered through a dream one of Metcalf's students had ... a woman by the name of Sandi Hartwell. I don't know exactly how or when, but I expect to interview her about her dreams.

"When the Sun People discover us, we will not be able to resist them if we do not prepare. Their history is clear—they will kill or enslave us all if we let them! We *must* take control of this planet before that can happen. We could develop the technology to destroy them first. The earth was ours before they came. It is only the old tales and superstitions of the wisdom skins that prevent us from taking it back. So now, we have to trick them into killing themselves.

"Opinion is swinging our way. By the next referendum, we will become the Majority Party. Then we can initiate *Operation Reclaim* in the open. In addition, we will be able to participate directly to depopulate the planet without the damage of nuclear weapons. But it is still two years before the next referendum. I am convinced we must prepare to act sooner! It is becoming more difficult to maintain all our security systems. In my opinion, there are too many possible ways for the system to fail."

Solero walked to one of the faux windows and looked out on the hologram of the Southwest United States. He paused at the window for effect. Then turning, he continued. "Fortunately, the Metcalf Report does not reveal the location of the cave where the skeletons were found. It is in or near Afghanistan or Pakistan. Because of the potential for war in the area, Ronaldo will not be able to put people there right away. However, he is already working on plans to find out where the cave is and get our people in."

"How will he do that?" Rajel asked.

"Ronaldo is working with influential Watchers in the Middle East. They should be able to bypass roadblocks. The Metcalf Report is supposed to be secret, but a Watcher, Garret Chandler, managed to get a copy, which he sent to Ronaldo. Ronaldo is putting a team together to be led by Garret. Garret will trick Metcalf into revealing the location of the cave, and then the team will go in to begin the search for the Heart of the Bison."

"The Heart of the Bison may be irrelevant to us and *Operation Reclaim*," Alriel said, "but if there is a Heart of the Bison, and Ronaldo finds it, you will not be able to convince the people to support you or *Operation Reclaim*. You will never be Majority Party Leader if the Heart of the Bison is found."

"That is exactly why we have to make sure Ronaldo does not find anything he can claim to be the Heart of the Bison," Solero said. "Tofraprin is following developments along those lines."

"Ronaldo has begun to form a team," Tofraprin said. "So far, we have one operative on the team, and I think we can get at least one more. We will know everything that is going on. Depending on what they are doing, we can disrupt and delay them."

Solero paced behind Rajel, who turned uncomfortably in his chair to watch him. "Alriel is right. Unfortunately, our people are still caught up in this old religion of magic. We have to make sure they do not find anything they can call the Heart of the Bison. And there is another problem."

"What?" Pulgo asked.

"President Bush has declared war on all terror. It is hard to tell, at this point, how much success he will have, but anything he does to weaken terrorist organizations ultimately weakens *Operation Reclaim*. The people in *Operation Reclaim* are all of one mind. We know that, whatever the cost, the Sun People on this planet must be conquered and ruled by Earth People. Any other road is a road to our destruction."

"Pulgo wonders what Solero can do. This *Operation Reclaim* cannot be strong without al-Qaeda."

"We have challenges." Solero was convincing and charismatic. "Time works against us on many fronts. If the Heart of the Bison is found, we will lose the election. Then we will have to set *Operation Reclaim* in motion without sanction from the Council. That is politically dangerous. And if President Bush manages to render too many of our terrorist friends ineffective, the destruction will not reach the critical mass required in the simulations. Finally, if Ronaldo somehow discovers our plans prematurely, they will be countermanded."

Solero turned to Rajel. "It will be up to you to solidify our plan by accomplishing the al-Qaeda infiltration and working out operational problems. You cannot be too familiar with the computer simulation and all foreseeable ramifications. It is critical that you be ready to implement *Operation Reclaim* quickly if an emergency comes up.

"This is a critical time for you too, Tofraprin. You have to make sure your operatives are close to all three situations. If it appears any one of those things … discovery of the Heart of the Bison, weakening of the terrorist groups, or leaks to Ronaldo … you have to keep me … I have to know those details, so if a decision has to be made, I can do it. We cannot let this get away from us. If *Operation Reclaim* fails, we will not be able to recover in time to save our world. You must keep yourself and me informed."

The meeting ended, and the men filed out of the office. The sobering realization of the danger of their situation weighed upon each of the *Operation Reclaim* leaders.

Follow the breathtaking story of *Operation Reclaim* in the exciting conclusion of the Neandertal Trilogy. Read *Search for the Heart of the Bison*, Neandertals Book Three.

CPSIA information can be obtained
at www.ICGtesting.com
Printed in the USA
BVOW09s0851221217
503027BV00001B/143/P